PRAISE FOR PAUL CLEAVE

WINNER of the Thriller & Suspense Gold Foreword Indie Award
SHORTLISTED for the Ngaio Marsh Award
BEST INDIE NOVEL: Crime Fiction Lover Awards

'Expect the unexpected is all I can really say. Prepare to be revulsed, amused, surprised and stunned, but most of all prepare to be entertained. I love the tension, the pace and the occasional madness of *His Favourite Graves*' Jen Med's Book Reviews

'A totally must-read novel. *His Favourite Graves* had me at page one and never let go. It is full of twists and turns and plenty of "what the hell?" moments ... A completely different take on a crime story but very enjoyable. Highly recommended' Sally Boocock

'Had me by the eyeballs. Spectacular ending!' Coffee & Books

'You may think you know where it's going, but you couldn't be more wrong. A true page-turner filled with dread, rage, doubt and more twists than the Remutaka Pass' Linwood Barclay

'Paul Cleave is an automatic must-read for me' Lee Child

'Riveting from start to finish. Smart and twisty, this book will get under your skin' Liz Nugent

'Shocking and chilling. A literary ice plunge. I absolutely loved it' Helen Fields

'Almost three books in one! Multiple murders, dedicated detectives – past and present. Complex, detailed and oh, so clever' Sam Holland

'An absolute BELTER of a book ... I'd forgotten how good Paul Cleave is!' Sarah Pinborough

'Another blisteringly good read from Paul Cleave ... Gripping from the first page and full of deliciously dark twists and turns. You can't be a true fan of crime fiction if you're not reading Cleave's books' Tom Wood

'Cleave conjures a wrenching tale that moves swiftly and hits hard ... the crackle in his sentences and a dark seam of humour prevent things from getting too bleak. A superb novel from a champion storyteller' Craig Sisterson

'The sense of dread builds unstoppably ... an intense, chilling read' Gilly Macmillan

'What starts out as a slow burn quickly ratchets up the tension and the twists, sending you spiralling down a hill of depravity and desperation' Kirsten McKenzie

'I don't think I breathed from about halfway through to the end. A masterpiece from a crime genius' Susi Holliday

'Cleave writes the kind of dark, intense thrillers that I never want to end. Do yourself a favour and check him out' Simon Kernick

'Tense, thrilling, touching. Paul Cleave is very good indeed' John Connolly

'Relentlessly gripping, deliciously twisted and shot through with a vein of humour that's as dark as hell' Mark Billingham

'An intense adrenaline rush from start to finish' S.J. Watson

'A riveting and all-too realistic thriller' Tess Gerritsen

'A gripping thriller ... I couldn't put it down' Meg Gardiner

'This very clever novel did my head in time and again' Michael Robotham

'A true page-turner, with an intriguing premise, a rollercoaster plot and a cast of believably flawed characters' *Guardian*

'Nerve-shredding' *Crime Monthly*

'The complicated, pacey plot is full of ideas and intelligence, as well as characters that work' *Literary Review*

To the cast and crew of *Dark City – The Cleaner* ...
thanks for making miracles happen.

ABOUT THE AUTHOR

Paul is an award-winning author who often divides his time between his home city of Christchurch, New Zealand, where most of his novels are set, and Europe. He's won the New Zealand Ngaio Marsh Award three times, the Saint-Maur book festival's crime novel of the year award in France, and has been shortlisted for the Edgar and the Barry in the US and the Ned Kelly in Australia. His books have been translated into more than twenty languages. He's thrown his Frisbee in more than fifty countries, plays tennis badly, golf even worse, and has two cats – which is often two too many. The critically acclaimed *The Quiet People* was published in 2021 and was followed in 2022 by *The Pain Tourist*.

Follow Paul on Twitter @PaulCleave, facebook.com/PaulCleave, Instagram @paul.cleave and his website: paulcleave.com.

Also by Paul Cleave and available from Orenda Books
The Quiet People
The Pain Tourist

His Favourite Graves

PAUL CLEAVE

ORENDA
BOOKS

Orenda Books
16 Carson Road
West Dulwich
London SE21 8HU
www.orendabooks.co.uk

First published in the United Kingdom by Orenda Books 2023
Copyright © Paul Cleave 2023

A catalogue record for this book is available from the British Library.

ISBN 978-1-914585-88-3
eISBN 978-1-914585-89-0

Typeset in Garamond by Elaine Sharples

Printed and bound by CPI Group (UK) Ltd, Croydon CR0 4YY

For sales and distribution, please contact *info@orendabooks.co.uk* or visit
www.orendabooks.co.uk.

Day One

Chapter One

The coffin has a set of vents low in the front, angled down, giving Lucas a narrow view of the floor. When he presses his hands against the metal walls, they flex fractionally outwards before bouncing back, seemingly closer after each attempt as though the walls are shrinking around him. When he tries to turn his body, elbows and knees hit walls, and when he attempts to straighten the cramp out of his back, his head hits the ceiling. He's a five-foot-eight, thin and flexible sixteen-year-old teenager in an upright coffin that's six feet tall, but with a shelf three-quarters of the way up that can't be moved, forcing him to hunch. If he hadn't been so thin the others probably couldn't have stuffed him in here in the first place, but they did, and they laughed while doing it, while other students walked by, ignoring his pleas for help. Why would they care? It's not like he's the first kid in the history of kids and schools to be stuffed into a locker. He's going to wet himself, pass out and then die, and tomorrow morning they'll find his body ankle-deep in piss. He focuses on the air vents. It's a chicken-and-egg scenario. Did bullies see the vents and figure they could stuff kids into lockers without them running out of air, or did the manufacturers figure kids would get stuffed inside and didn't want them suffocating?

The way he sees it, he's on his own. His cellphone is in his bag, which might be on top of the lockers, or in a dumpster behind the school, or stuffed into a toilet. It's been half an hour since he heard anybody, and soon one of two things is going to happen. His dad is either going to notice Lucas isn't there, and do something about it, or he isn't going to notice, and do nothing. It's going to come down to whether his dad started his drinking today before three, or after, which is something his dad has gotten particularly good at since his mom up and announced she was leaving them two years back.

In the distance, a slight whirring that, over the following few minutes, grows louder as it gets closer. All the teachers are gone. Mondays are like that, teachers wanting to place the day in their rear-view mirrors so they can rush home and uncork the wine. What he's hearing is the janitor pushing a floor polisher. It has to be. He holds off banging on the door because there is no way the guy will hear him over the noise, not yet anyway. So he waits, and he tries not to wet his pants, and the air gets thicker and the idea he could be in here till tomorrow solidifies. Would he survive? He imagines his gravestone:

Lucas Connor, sixteen years old, gone too soon, but who really cares?

Certainly not his mom, who left, and not his dad, who would drink himself into a state where he wouldn't even recognise he was now living alone.

He focuses on the whirring, picturing the janitor as he pushes the floor polisher closer, and when he thinks it's as close as it's going to get, he bangs on the door.

The floor polisher doesn't slow down. Of course it doesn't, because the janitor will be wearing ear muffs, and there could be a hundred kids banging from a hundred lockers, and this guy wouldn't have the slightest idea.

He keeps hammering at the door. The floor polisher is now on its way in the other direction. He gives it everything he has because if he doesn't he's going to die in here, and if he doesn't die, he'll at least go mad, and maybe, just maybe, if the janitor can't hear him he will at least see the door rattling.

Which might be what happens, because the floor polisher stops moving, and the motor slows, and dies, and then there are footsteps. Through the vent he can see heavy brown shoes come to a stop in front of him.

Lucas gives the door one last whack, and says, 'Please. Please help me.'

The feet come closer, and the janitor asks, 'What is this? You pulling some kind of prank on me?' His voice is low, and slow, and confused-sounding. Lucas has never spoken to the guy before, but he's heard other students calling him Simple Simon.

'No prank. I got locked in here. Please, you have to help me.'

'Damn kids,' the janitor says, and he taps on the door. 'This one?'

'Yes.'

'What's the combination?'

'I don't know it.'

'How can you not know?'

'It's not my locker.'

'What kind of boy gets himself thrown into somebody else's locker?'

One who can't stand up for himself, Lucas thinks. One who is smaller than the boys putting him in here. One who doesn't have any friends to help him. One who's shy and tries to keep himself to himself. One whose parents don't even like spending time with him. Instead of any of those, he says, 'Can you just get help?'

'There's nobody to get,' the janitor says. He taps his knuckles against the door, and Lucas imagines him looking at it like it's some kind of puzzle to solve. 'Let me get something I can pry it with. Wait here.'

Lucas isn't sure if that last part is a joke, and figures it isn't since the guy sounds genuinely put out by it all. The footsteps fade. He counts them until they disappear, then he counts off two long minutes where he becomes convinced the janitor isn't going to return, but then he does, Lucas counting the footsteps as they get louder.

'Okay. This might be loud,' the janitor says, and before Lucas can get his fingers into his ears, the crowbar bangs heavily into the locker. Metal squeaks against metal, and slivers of light appear around one side of the door as it twists. Those slivers turn into cracks. The tip of a crowbar comes into view, then disappears and comes back, able to take a bigger bite now. More squeaking as the door twists, then it folds around the lock and pops open. The need to get out is so urgent he panics when he can't. He can't because he's been stuck in this position for so long his back and legs have locked. He looks up at the janitor.

'Help me.'

The janitor is a guy around thirty, a little over six foot, but skinny like Lucas, with hollowed-in cheeks framed by a short beard, and long fingers topped off with dirty nails. A nametag sewn into his overalls tells the world his name is Simon, meaning the kids calling him Simple Simon are at least half right. He stares unblinking at Lucas for a few moments, then offers a hand with the third and fourth fingers missing – rumour being he bit them off when growing up in an insane asylum. Of course, there's no truth to the rumour. At least he seriously hopes there isn't as he reaches out and takes hold of Simon's hand.

He gets one leg out, then can't control himself as he collapses under his own weight, too quickly for Simon to keep him upright. The best Lucas can do before hitting the floor is to stop his nose breaking against it by cushioning his face with his hands. He tries to get right back up, but his legs are wracked with pins and needles, and he can't manage it. His bladder is tight and full and aware he now has access to a bathroom. He can see his school bag up on the shelf. His phone is in there – or, if not in there, in a dumpster, or in a toilet, or in pieces out on the field. He needs to call his dad and let him know what's happening.

He looks up at the janitor, who is studying him with that unblinking stare, as if, of all the people he's pulled out of lockers today, Lucas is the most curious.

'I'm sorry,' Simon says, and Lucas doesn't know what he's sorry for, and doesn't get the chance to figure it out before a rag is pressed hard against his nose and mouth. He fights against the janitor, but the fumes are strong and he's already breathing them in, breathing in that dirty rag, the fumes dimming the world around him.

He feels the front of his pants go warm.

Then he can't feel anything.

Chapter Two

The office is low-key, somewhat worn out, which is a good match for my close-to-retirement lawyer, Devon Murdoch, who looks like he slept in his clothes and used his tie as a napkin at breakfast. He's not the cheapest lawyer in town, but he's the next best thing, and he's sure as hell the best I can afford. He has framed diplomas hanging behind him, and in one of them I can see my reflection – a tired-looking guy who needs a haircut and a shave, and a good night's sleep, and who a year ago had mostly black hair, which this year is mostly grey. I have to be the oldest-looking forty-year-old guy in town.

'It's here somewhere,' Murdoch says, hunting through a pile of papers on his desk. His hand finally lands on what he's looking for, and he seems pleased with himself when he says, 'Here we go.'

He hands the bill to me, and it makes him one step closer to becoming a cheap lawyer out of my price range.

'Jesus.'

'Sorry, Sheriff, it was never going to be cheap.'

'I know, but...'

'And there will be more.'

'I know that too.'

'I'm managing to keep the wolves at bay, but it's not easy.'

'They want blood.'

'Of course they do.'

I look at the bill again. It's a little over eight thousand dollars. As was the one last month. Two months ago it was ten thousand.

'Look, James, I know things are tight, so I'm giving you an extra month on it, but ... well, things are tight for everybody.'

'We all have bills to pay, I get it.'

'How did things go with the bank?'

'Not great,' I say. It's been three months since I paid my mortgage. 'Last week they sent a letter to say if I miss another payment, then it's the end of the road. You know the irony?'

'Tell me.'

'If I refuse to leave, then, as sheriff, it will be my job to force my own eviction. Hell, maybe I should do just that – throw my own arse in jail just so I have somewhere to stay.'

'I'm sorry, James. It's a shitty situation, and one of the worst I've seen. And selling?'

'I got a real-estate agent coming by later this week. It's an option, but not a good one. Anything I come out of the house with will get thrown into more fees, plus I'd still have to pay rent somewhere. And that's even if I could sell it, in time. Plus my dad still needs care, and that's not cheap. I'll see what they say.'

'It sounds exhausting.'

'You got no idea,' I say, and the truth is I've barely slept more than a few hours a night since this all started.

'And Cassandra?'

'She'd help, I guess, but it's not like we can move in with her. She did leave for a reason.'

Murdoch looks at me, seeming to search for something to say that can make this easier. I'm losing my family and my house. We're throwing Band-Aids at gaping wounds, and I don't know what to do. I really don't. A month from now I'll probably be homeless.

'I still don't know how I got here,' I say. 'It wasn't his fault.'

'I completely agree with you, as would most, but somebody died, James.'

'I know somebody died.'

'It's a tragic loss, it really is. But your father lit the fire that burned down the entire care home, and it's a miracle there weren't more casualties. And that family is hurting. This is emotional for them – and they're on a crusade.'

I say what I've told him a hundred times already. 'The care home should have been keeping a better eye on him.'

'I know, and you know I agree with you, and it's why the care home have settled, but—'

'But the family is hurting, and they want us to hurt too.'

'That's what it comes down to. I have another meeting with their lawyer next week, but unless there's a sudden change of mind, then you need to prepare yourself for the storm that's coming.'

I fold up the bill and tuck it into my pocket, knowing everything he has just told me will make up part of the next bill. I need to get out of here before we tick over into the next half-hour. 'Thanks,' I say, standing up.

He stands up too. 'I'll keep you updated.'

I head out to the street. My police cruiser is parked outside a bar. The cruiser is a white SUV with a strip of lights on the roof and a bull bar on the front, *Acacia Sheriff's Department* in blocky blue letters running down the side. I'm unlocking it when I look up at the bar. I could go in there and find a dark corner to drown my sorrows. The problem is I'd probably fall asleep. That's the problem when you're a borderline insomniac – it's hard to sleep at nights but easy to nod off when you're not meant to. My lawyer summed things up well when he said it's a shitty situation. My dad spent his entire working life as a chef, and from the age of forty even owned his own restaurant. He got worried a few years ago when he started to forget the simplest of things, and remember things that never happened. There was paranoia and mood swings, and then he started saying some very cruel things to my mother, which she would have taken offence to if it wasn't for the fact she died ten years ago. What followed was a diagnosis – my dad had Alzheimer's. Things spiralled fast for him, and last year he moved into a care home. The problem is he had fifty years' worth of muscle memory driving him to cook, which is exactly what he tried to do at three in the morning at the start of this year. He ended up burning down the entire care home, and now he lives with me and, every second week, me and my son,

Nathan. Cassandra moved out two months after my dad moved in. It was hard for her to stay, with my dad calling her the worst of names every day.

I don't give into the temptation of the bar, but I do pop a couple of pills to perk me up. My doctor prescribed me Adderall a few months back. I went from trying to not rely on it, to needing it every day, to having to up the dosage. I'm not proud of it, but it helps.

I drive home, picturing the cold beers in the fridge. The moment I pull up in the driveway, the front door opens and Deborah, my dad's nurse-slash-caretaker, comes hurrying out. Deborah is in her mid-sixties, warm, compassionate, and went through with her own parents what I'm going through with Dad.

'Everything okay?' I ask.

'Everything is fine, I'm just running late is all,' she says. 'I have a date,' she adds, grinning at me.

'Who's the lucky guy?'

'Somebody I met online. I still can't believe that's how it's done these days. Can you imagine the action I would have been getting forty years ago if this had been a thing?'

'I'd rather not.'

She laughs. 'Your dad had a good day,' she says.

'Thanks, Deborah. Have fun.'

'I intend to.'

She drives away and I head inside. My dad is standing in front of the TV, watching a guy with veins sticking out of his arms pitching a piece of gym equipment that will get your own veins sticking out too if you're willing to give it three minutes a day.

'Hey, Dad, how was your day?'

Dad doesn't answer.

'Can I get you something? A drink maybe?'

Still no answer. I move him to the couch and sit him down, and I'm not sure he knows I'm here. I can hear gunfire and explosions coming from Nathan's bedroom as he plays whatever the hell it is he plays on his computer. I knock on Nathan's door and open it. There's an annoyed-sounding 'what?', and then I step in.

'Just letting you know I'm home.'

'Whatever.'

Nathan is a big kid with angular features that ought to make him good-looking, but are betrayed by a meanness that crept in around the time his mom moved out. He has dark hair swept to the side that overhangs his right eye. His other eye is fixed on a computer monitor as his hands fly across the keyboard.

'Any requests for dinner?'

'You could leave me alone for starters.'

I don't have the energy to answer him, so I head into the kitchen and grab a beer. I'm just about to open it when my phone goes. It's the station.

I hit answer. 'What is it, Sharon?' I ask, sounding grumpier than I intended.

Before I can apologise, she says, 'Sheriff, Peter Connor is on the line for you. Says it's urgent.'

I've known Peter since I was a kid. He was a year ahead of me in school and was always the cool guy because he was the guitarist in a school rock band. He gave up on the music, and went on to become a novelist with a range of successes. But the last few years haven't been kind to him. He never bounced back after the critics turned on him after his last book, one saying it was aimed at people who liked to tear out the pages and set fire to them, before going on to call it Z-grade trash. Not long after that his wife walked out on him, having discovered the same thing that Deborah discovered – online dating. The only relationship Peter has formed since being single is with the bottle.

'Put him through,' I say, wondering if he's gotten behind the wheel of his car and ended up in a ditch somewhere.

He comes on the line. His words are rapid-fire, and I can't pick where one ends and the other begins.

'Whoa, whoa, slow down, Peter. Slow down and try again.'

Another flow of syllables.

'Take a deep breath,' I say.

Peter takes a deep breath. I hear it happen, like a vacuum cleaner flicked on for a brief moment. I picture him pacing the room, his knuckles white as he holds the phone tightly. 'My boy,' he says, slower now, not by much, but enough for me to understand him. 'My boy didn't come home from school.'

Something twitches in my stomach, and I picture his son Lucas.

Peter fires off short sentences. 'He always comes home. From school. He has a curfew. Five o'clock. He knows if he's not home by then he gets in trouble. So he's always home by then. Always. Usually by four. Always by four. Never fails. Except for today. I need you to find him. It's … You … you have to find him.'

It's a little after five now. Summer is close and the days are getting longer. There are three more hours of daylight left, and this time next month it won't be getting dark till well after nine. We're fast approaching the time of the year we spend the rest of the year waiting for. It's also the season for kids being notoriously late. They're off swimming in quarries or smoking in the woods or hitting baseballs. They're breaking curfews and not giving a damn.

'Kids always have a way of showing up,' I say, and immediately regret my choice of words. I am, after all, on the phone to a crime writer. There's only one thing a crime writer is going to say to a statement like that.

Peter goes ahead and says it. 'And sometimes they show up dead. They show up in shallow graves stabbed or strangled, or tossed into dumpsters. And as you well know, Sheriff, the world is full of kids who go missing and never show up at all.'

He's right. But still … 'Maybe he's got a flat tire. Or he's gone to a friend's house. You've called his friends?'

'He doesn't have any.'

'Have you called the school?'

'Nobody was answering, which is why I've come here.'

'You're at the school?'

'And he doesn't have a flat tire because his bike is here and it's perfectly fine. Something has stopped him from biking home, and from calling me.'

The twitch in my stomach twitches again.

This can't be like last time, can it?

Chapter Three

It's all happening fast – too fast. Of course it is … there was never any plan. Has he made mistakes? It's a stupid question – of course he has. But in that moment he didn't care. It was like a biological impulse took over, and he stopped being Simon Grove and became something else – something different, a something that he has been other times during his life. He doesn't like that something, but he can't control it. Nobody can control biology. There are pills, and medications, and therapies to try and get you to think one way when all you can think is another … but that can't forever repress a fundamental need. And right now his need has him speeding away from town with a boy in the trunk of his car, and, Jesus, it's not like he hasn't been in this situation before.

They're on the highway. There's not a lot of traffic and there's no reason that he stands out, just one car among many, but he wonders if other drivers can tell how nervous he is. He sure as hell didn't wake up today knowing he'd end it by burning bridges, which is a very real possibility right now. He can't turn back – in part because he has no real excuse for why he stuffed the kid into the trunk, and in part because he doesn't want to. He also can't keep driving, because he's bursting with the same need that got him into this mess. But at some point soon somebody is going to notice the kid isn't where he's meant to be. Could be it's happened already, or it could be the kid has shitty parents who haven't even noticed – though Simon seriously doubts the parents could be like the ones he had growing up. He pictures phone calls being made to friends before a call is placed to the police, then the police going to the school, finding the busted-open locker with the crowbar out front.

Jesus. He didn't even take the time to clean up after himself. He couldn't, because the need was both sudden and strong, and it had been a while, and when you're driven by biology ... well, you think about the consequences later. This need has been building for a while, as it always does, and the irony is he had put in for vacation next week anyway. He was going to head away and scratch the itch with some random kid in some random city, where he could walk away without any consequences, dining on the memory until the need became too strong again to ignore. Why the hell couldn't he have just waited till then?

Biology. That's why. Fucking biology.

However, there might just be a way he can have his cake and eat it too – something his final mother used to say, which was just one more reason to have killed her. Recently he bought a camera to film these occasions, but perhaps it can have a second purpose.

Up ahead is the turnoff for the old sawmill. He learned the history of this place when he moved here a while back. The town of Acacia Pines came into existence a hundred and fifty years ago, with a sawmill as the heart and the churches built around it as the soul. Soon the stores and the houses were expanding outwards, eating up the land at a slow but steady rate, then sixty years ago they'd eaten up enough of it that there were more folks who didn't like the trucks barrelling past their houses and shaking the china in their cupboards than there were those who did. So the sawmill was torn down and rebuilt out of town, on a bigger site with more room for expansion, but, like towns and cities are apt to do, long-term forecasts of how big places are going to be and how busy the roads are going to get don't tend to look as far into the future as they ought to be looking. After all, something in fifty years' time is somebody else's problem.

Ten years ago, Acacia started being featured on travel shows. The forests were popular spots for hikers. Motels had to be built. More restaurants. More industry. The town has been expanding constantly over the last ten years as people come to visit and don't want to leave. A few years back there was a spike in the service sector on account of some hikers at the end of that summer claiming they spotted Bigfoot out in the mountains (complete with out-of-focus photograph), though he suspects the rumour was started by an owner of one of the new motels – motels which were booked up solidly as people from across the country came looking for proof. The sawmill needed to expand too. But instead of expanding it, a new one got built a few miles closer to town than the old one, the old one left abandoned for nature to reclaim.

He takes the turnoff.

The road to the mill is curved and rutted with dips and troughs and made up of gravel pushed so hard into the ground by thousands of trucks that it doesn't make much noise driving over it. Soon the old mill comes into view, large cinderblock walls stained with exhaust, windows high up, some of them broken, a flat roof, some of it rusted, and large roll-up doors along the front, some of them dented, all surrounded by a sea of concrete which, in turn, is surrounded by an ocean of trees. He pulls up to the main door. He leaves the car running and gets out. He unlocks a small side door and steps through, then uses the chains to roll up the large ones. The rattling chains remind him of that Charles Dickens novel where Christmas ghosts preach doom and gloom to a man destined to die alone. Not that he read the book, but he has seen various versions of the movie.

He gets the door all the way open, and goes back to the car. A minute later he's parked inside and those chains are rattling again as the door closes. They're all alone. All alone in the middle of nowhere where nobody can hear a thing.

His nerves turn to excitement.

Chapter Four

I go back into Nathan's room.

'I gotta go out for a bit. I need you to keep an eye on your grandfather.'

'I'm busy.'

'Hopefully it won't be for long.'

He doesn't say anything. Instead he keeps playing the game.

'Nathan?'

'What?'

'I said I...

'For fuck's sake,' he says, and he stands up and switches off the computer.

'Goddamn it, Nathan, I'm just asking for—'

'I said I'll do it, okay? Didn't you just say you have somewhere to be?'

I stare at him for a few moments, not knowing the best response. This is classic Nathan these days, and every way I've tried to deal with it has only ever been the wrong way. I could ground him, or take his computer away, but in the past things like that have only made him worse. And right now I don't have the time to deal with it.

'I'll call you soon to check in,' I say.

I radio Sharon on my way to the school. I update her, ask her to have Deputy Hutchison meet me at the school, and to get Principal Chambers on the line. She says she'll get right on it. I drive through town. Stores are closing and restaurants are opening as people go from buying books and clothes and camping equipment to thinking about food and wine and dessert. Sharon calls my cellphone, saying she has Chambers on the line. She transfers the call. I tell Chambers what's going on. He sounds concerned. Of course he does. We went through this two months ago. He tells me he'll be at the school in ten minutes.

I buzz the sirens at intersections and cars pull aside. People on sidewalks turn to look. It's a rare sight. I pass storefronts where the sun reflects off the windows, blinding drivers. I pass a swimming pool, a movie theatre, a bowling alley, a strip mall, more stores and offices and motels, then there's the school. A long driveway edged with trees sweeps from the road to a drop-off area, but also branches into a parking lot. There's a low wall out front with *Acacia High School* lettered across it, along with painted-over graffiti. Beyond it the main building is made up of three wings forming a squared-off C, each wing long, and plain, and identical, as if churned out by kitset manufacturers and shipped here ready to assemble, complete with flags to hang every thirty yards for colour. Peter Connor is pacing the ground, and only stops once I'm out of my car and in front of him.

Peter is a few inches taller than me, topping out at six foot. He's always been solid, but it doesn't look as good on him as it did back in high school, when he was on stage in tight clothes impressing all the girls with his music and his muscles. Now all that mass has been redistributed, mostly to the centre, where it stretches at his faded T-shirt that says *Cats Against Being Eaten,* which was the name of his band back then. His eyes are sunken, and his greying hair a mess, like a man who gave into middle age without a fight. We don't shake hands. He's panicked. Jittery.

'Show me the bike,' I say.

We walk to the bike stands. They're in the same place they used to be, and where they will remain long after the ice caps have melted. Coming to my old school makes me question how twenty years have gone by so fast, all while making me sadly aware the next twenty will go the same. The school has expanded over that time, with more buildings added beyond the three main wings, a brand-new gym too, and a bigger assembly hall. That's what Acacia Pines is, a town that expands – from the grocery stores to the schools to the motels and farms and graveyards. Ten years ago we had twenty thousand people, now we have thirty.

The bike stands are exposed to the elements. There are enough for five hundred bikes, but right now there's only one in there, a lonely blue mountain bike a couple of years old at best. There's a lock around it.

'This is definitely Lucas's bike?'

'Yes.'

'And the lock?'

He looks at me, confused. 'What?'

'Is that his lock?'

'Why wouldn't it be?'

'Because somebody might have played a practical joke on him by locking the bike with a lock that isn't his.'

He still looks confused. 'Then he would have gone and gotten a teacher, or he would have called me.'

It's what I figured, but I still had to ask. A cruiser identical to mine approaches. Deputy Hutchison. And, behind her, a white sedan. Principal Chambers.

'Maybe,' I say. 'But is it Lucas's lock or not?'

'I don't know. Probably.'

We walk to the main entrance. Chambers and Hutch stop talking when we reach them. Deputy Lisa Hutchison is thirty, tall, good-looking, serious. She grew up wanting to be a cop because her dad was a cop. Her dark hair is pulled into a ponytail and her thumbs are hitched over the top of her holster. Chambers is tall, balding, with wisps of grey hair combed flat along the sides. His glasses are too big and his mouth too small, his ears wide and his nose long, like he was put together at the Mr Potato Head factory by Mr Potato himself. He was one of my teachers back when I came here. The guy taught history, and now he's become it.

None of us shake hands. 'I want to see Lucas's locker,' I say.

If Lucas's bike is here, then there's every reason to think he's here too. Kids got jammed into lockers back when I came here, and I doubt the practice has ended, along with lunch money being stolen and hallway wedgies.

'Then follow me,' Chambers says, and he leads the way.

Chapter Five

The coffin is metal, and narrow, and after spending thirty minutes on the road, has finally come to a stop. Lucas may be a shitty judge of janitors, but he's an excellent judge of time. You can't drive in Acacia Pines for thirty minutes unless you're driving in circles, meaning they've left the confines of town and headed south, because south is the only direction you can go. Since they left town he's been wondering what they're heading for out here. It's all farms and forestry, and he figures there are dozens of ways to be disappeared in either.

As for the coffin, he is folded and jammed into it, and something hard digs into his back, all angles, all solid, something he can't get away from. Mostly the ride has been in darkness, except for when the trunk glows red from the brake lights, but it's back to being dark, and the only sound he can hear is the engine pinging and tinging. A moment ago it was all rattling chains and heavy doors. His wet jeans are tighter now, and cold, and they smell, and the denim chafes against his thighs. His chest is tight, and the duct tape across his mouth is preventing him from sucking in deep breaths, and his hands being taped behind him puts pressure on his shoulders. The only parts of his body not threatening cramp are the parts humming with pins and needles. He has never in his life ever come as close to being as scared as he is right now. And to make things even worse, whatever the janitor used to knock him out has given him a headache. He feels sick too. Not just terrified sick, but nauseous sick. He tries to roll over, to shift his weight off his right shoulder onto his left, but can't manage it. Aside from urine, he can smell gas, and cleaning products, and can still smell the chemical the janitor used to knock him out. The air tastes combustible. But, no matter what, he's come to the decision that he's not going to cry. He's not going to beg for mercy either – in part because he doesn't think a guy who throws children into the trunks of cars will be merciful, and in part because he thinks Simple Simon will get off on it.

How would his dad write somebody out of this situation? That's a question he's been asking over and over on the drive out here, but his mind has only been able to find examples where those characters didn't make it. Some must have survived, surely, but when he tries to think of them he draws a blank. At some stage he's going to go from praying he can survive this to praying that the end comes quickly. He doesn't watch a lot of movies, but he has seen enough to know that once the duct tape appears, a shallow grave being pawed open by wildlife isn't far behind. Soon the question won't just be will they ever find him, but in how many pieces?

He's pulled from his thoughts by footsteps getting closer. The car door opens, then there's a click, and the trunk pops up an inch. A moment later it's opened the rest of the way, and a moment after that Lucas is blinking against the light of a dimly lit building that's far brighter than the inside of the trunk. The janitor reaches in and hauls Lucas up and over the edge of the trunk before letting momentum and gravity take him to the floor, the impact hard enough to make his teeth rattle and have him taste blood. He fights to keep the tears back.

The janitor looks down at him. He's different from before. Same overalls, same hair, same beard, but all of it dark and rotten. The rumours are true – this guy did bite off two of his own fingers, and was probably in the insane asylum for biting off other people's fingers too. He imagines the janitor's darkness as a physical entity, a parasite that has taken over and is now controlling him like a puppet, that parasite a tapeworm looping and slithering around inside the janitor and pulling all the levers.

Simple Simon cuts the tape between Lucas's feet, then gets him standing. They're in an emptied-out factory, a few shelves with cardboard boxes left behind, some pieces of wire and steel cut-offs and sawdust littering the floor, along with glass from the windows where rocks have been thrown through them. He can smell wood.

And glue. And grease. There's an old mountain bike leaning against the wall and an empty drum, heavily dented, lying on its side. He looks at the drum and wonders if the janitor has stuffed some other unlucky soul into it in the past. There are cinderblock walls and steel beams and high ceilings. The metal door is big enough for trucks to roll in and roll back out. There's a set of offices and rooms at the back at floor level, and another set above.

It's the old sawmill. He's never been here before, but it can't be anything else.

Simple Simon shoves him toward the offices at the back. The pins and needles in his legs have him stumbling, and the janitor grabs at him to keep him balanced. His body has been forced into uncomfortable shapes over the last few hours, and now his mind races with images of further shapes to come. They reach the office closest to the stairs, one with a window looking out into the forest. There's a wooden desk to his right and an old filing cabinet on its side with a camera on top of it to his left. There's a broken pot in the corner containing a dead plant, and stacked next to it a pile of phonebooks almost as tall as him. There's a diseased-looking mattress on the floor, and it's to the mattress that Lucas is shoved. He falls onto it, dust puffing out of it, along with enough bacteria to start a pandemic. Still, he fights the tears, even though he knows what the mattress is for, just as he knows why the camera with the glowing red light on the filing cabinet is pointing at him.

There is no help coming.

No hope.

Lucas starts to cry.

Chapter Six

The main entrance to the school is a large set of double doors with the type of wired-glass panels that, as a kid, I used to imagine could turn a person into cubes if they were pushed through it. Chambers pulls out a fist-sized set of keys from a pocket that must be reinforced to stop them falling through. There have to be thirty of them, a memory test he passes because he gets the right one on the first try. I feel alert, and I don't know if it's from the Adderall or the situation, and figure it's a combination of both.

We step into a corridor that's eighty yards long, cinderblock painted grey, with the top quarter light blue, the lockers dark blue, the floor tiled in dark grey. Our footfalls echo as we walk. Some things have changed over the years, and many things haven't. New computers, same classrooms; new whiteboards, same lockers; new posters, same paint, same smell, same feel. Through the windows I can see the football field and the gym beyond, glimpses into the world of high-school students, glimpses into my past. I've been here a few times over the years since my days as a student. I've come to parent-teacher interviews, I've spoken as a police officer to kids about the dangers of drugs, of drinking and driving, I've come here to bust kids for vandalism, and once I had to come here to tell Chambers that one of his students had been killed in a car accident that morning. I was here two months ago when Taylor Reed climbed onto the roof and, in view of everybody, jumped to his death the final day of the school term. Sometimes I see him when I'm trying to get to sleep, broken and bloody on the pavement. I can still see his parents as the reality of what they were being told took hold.

The last time I came here was the first day of the term. I had come here to learn what I could about Freddy Holt, a sixteen-year-old boy who climbed out of his bedroom window during the break and into a rabbit hole that closed behind him. Two boys – one dead, one missing.

And now Lucas Connor.

I tap the lockers with my knuckle as I pass, each one echoing out.

'What are you doing?' Peter asks.

'He's checking if Lucas is in one of them,' Hutch says.

'Wait ... you don't think ... shit,' Peter says, realising how possible that is. 'Shit,' he says again, then goes about banging on the lockers on the other side of the corridor, calling out for his son at the same time – calls that go unanswered.

The administration area takes up the final twenty yards of the corridor, and goes around the corner. It's made up of out-of-date offices filled with out-of-date equipment. We go into Chambers' office and he sits at a computer with an old bulky screen and taps in his ID and password. Lucas's file appears. 'Locker two-oh-six,' he says. 'It's around the corner.'

We take that corner. The administration area turns back into classrooms. This corridor is a good third longer than the previous one, but looks the same: lockers, posters, classrooms, only more of them. In the middle of the corridor is a floor polisher and a puddle of water.

'That's odd,' Chambers says. 'The janitor always puts everything away.' The floor polisher is in front of a set of lockers, but more specifically, it's in front of one with a twisted front door that's been prised open, and the bar that did that prying is on the floor. It's not Lucas's locker, but the one next to it. I pull on a pair of latex gloves and take down the school bag that's on the top shelf.

'That's Lucas's,' Peter says.

I put it on the floor and open it. There are books inside. Gym clothes. A cellphone. I touch the home button on the phone. The display lights up. There's a picture of a dog, a German Shepherd, and a message box saying there are nine missed calls from 'Dad'.

'I told you something was wrong,' Peter says.

I think about how it could have played out. Some kids jammed Lucas in there. They figured he'd make his way out, or somebody would let him out, but that doesn't happen. Lucas ends up being in there longer than they anticipated. Nobody finds him, the school clears out, then the janitor comes along. Lucas bangs on the door. He's been in there a couple of hours. The janitor wrenches the door open.

Then what?

Why wouldn't Lucas grab his phone? Why not bike home?

Hutch is playing out the same scenario and coming up with the same questions. 'I'll call the hospital and doctors' surgeries and find out if Lucas was taken to any of them,' she says. 'Could be Lucas passed out once he was freed.'

'Only...'

'Only the police would have been called,' she says. 'But of course it's possible there's some crossover. Could be they left here a minute before we arrived, in which case they haven't called yet.'

She moves a few feet away and pulls out her phone. I interviewed the janitor a few months back. I can't remember his name, but I can remember a little of what he looked like, and that he was a very low-key guy. The most memorable thing about him was he was down two fingers. I questioned him the same way we questioned everybody in connection to Taylor Reed, and then Freddy Holt. We knew Taylor Reed had jumped, and that he had been bullied mercilessly online in the months leading up to it. We found messages on his social-media accounts from somebody who had set up an account under the name *Everybody At School*. *Everybody At School* sent direct messages across different platforms abusing Taylor, telling him that everybody hated him, telling him he ought to kill himself. Whoever it was had used a burner phone to set up the account – but we were never able to find the phone, or the whoever. The janitor didn't raise any red flags. But then Freddy Holt disappeared, and the timing made us wonder if the two things were related. Holt may have been responsible, and split. We spoke to plenty of students who said Freddy would shove them into doorways, call them losers, some he would bail up for lunch money, so bullying Taylor Reed was certainly in his wheelhouse.

'The janitor,' I say, turning to Chambers. 'What's his name?'

'You think the janitor took Lucas?' Peter asks, and I wish he'd go wait out in the car so I could think.

'Simon Grove,' Chambers says.

Simon Grove. I remember now. 'What time does Grove finish here?'

'Around seven. He's the only one here after the teachers have gone. He locks up when he leaves.'

I look at my watch. It's almost six o'clock now.

'Wouldn't teachers have walked past this locker?'

'Not necessarily,' Chambers says. 'There are other exits.'

'Does Simon Grove park where the teachers park?'

'We should go to his house,' Peter says.

I put my hand on his shoulder and he doesn't shrug it off. His face is tight with panic. He's sweating. 'I need you to stay calm and let us do our job,' I say.

'We should—'

'We'll go to his house, but first I want to see if his car is here.'

Peter seems about to argue, then nods. 'Good idea,' he says.

I turn back to Chambers and he tells me Grove parks in the faculty parking lot.

'Let's go.'

Hutch stays by the lockers on her phone, and I head with Peter Connor and Chambers out through a different exit to the parking lot. It's empty. Chambers points out where Grove would have parked.

'Get me his number,' I say. 'And his address.'

Chambers disappears back inside. I walk down to the parking space, Peter following. 'You really think this guy took him to the hospital?' Peter asks.

'Day like this, it would have been warm in that locker. Your son might be suffering from exhaustion, or heatstroke. Maybe he fainted the moment Grove set him free. It'd explain why he didn't try to call you. Could be the janitor doesn't even know who Lucas is. Same might go for the hospital. They might have him in there and can't identify him.'

'Wouldn't he have called an ambulance?'

'That's what you would have done, or what I would have done, but that doesn't make it something anybody else would do. People are different. They respond different. He could have weighed it all up and figured it was best to rush Lucas to the hospital.'

Against the kerb where Grove parks is a dirty white rag the size of a handkerchief that's been wadded up into a ball. I hook it with my pen and carefully take a sniff. It has a strong chemical smell. But the guy is, after all, a janitor, and janitors deal with strong chemical smells. Even so, I'm no longer imagining Grove panicking at finding Lucas in the locker, but rubbing his hands with glee.

'I told you,' Peter says, when I shake an evidence bag out of my pocket and put the rag in there. 'I fucking told you.'

I head back the way we came. He follows. He keeps asking questions I can't answer. We meet Hutch at the lockers.

'I've called the hospital, and I've got Sharon calling around the doctors,' she says. 'Nothing so far. Maybe our guy gave Lucas a ride home.' She stares at me hard, trying to tell me something. I know what that something is, because I want the same something – which is Peter gone. I nod, and she turns to Peter and carries on. 'You should head back home. It's the first place Lucas would return to. Or he might call you there.'

Before he can argue, I get in first. 'We have things at the school covered, and there's no reason for you to be here. It'd be a great help if you went home and kept us updated.'

'Doesn't explain the rag,' Peter says.

'Rag?' Hutch asks.

'Rag soaked with chloroform,' Peter says.

'We don't know that,' I say.

'If Lucas has been taken to hospital, or taken home, he would have called me.'

'Please, Peter,' Hutch says. 'You're more help to Lucas if you go home and make some calls.'

'Let us do our jobs, Peter,' I say.

Peter doesn't say anything, just turns and walks away. He punches the last locker on the end before going around the corner. I crouch down closer to the puddle of water.

'It's not water,' Hutch says.

'No, it's not,' I say, the smell of urine stronger at floor level. Whatever happened here scared Lucas Connor into wetting himself.

Chapter Seven

'Don't fight back. It will only make it worse.'

The kid is a mess. There's tears and snot on his face, and his pants are wet, and he looks like he's about to have a heart attack. And it's not like he isn't sympathetic to the kid – he knows how it feels to be on the other end of a situation like this.

'You hear me?'

The kid nods. And sniffs. And wipes his tears on his knees.

'I'm going to remove the tape, but you're going to have to promise you won't scream. Nobody would hear you anyway, but I hate the sound of it. Okay?'

More nodding.

Simon pulls the duct tape from his mouth. The kid takes a deep breath, and though he looks like he has a million questions, he says nothing. He gets the sense the kid is going to try and be defiant, and good for him if that's the case. Good for Simon too, because a bit of a struggle can be fun.

'What's your name?'

'L—' he says, then he coughs, and gets his breath, and tries again. 'Lucas.'

'Okay, Lucas. Don't be embarrassed that you wet yourself. My dad, well, he'd have laughed at you for it, but not me. It's one of the reasons I hated him so much.'

Lucas tries bucking his body as Simon goes to put duct tape around his ankles.

'What did I just say?'

Lucas doesn't move. Simon gets the tape on, then lines up a pair of scissors with the bottom of Lucas's jeans. Lucas jerks his feet away, and goddamn it, doesn't this kid know he's being serious?

He puts the tip of the scissors under Lucas's chin. 'What the fuck did I just say?'

'I ... I'm sorry.'

'I get that this isn't easy for you, but I'm telling you, you fuck around and this will go so much worse. You hear me?'

'I'm sorry.'

'Good,' he says, and gets back cutting away at the bottom of the jeans before running the blade north. 'I reckon he figured out just how much I hated him while he burned.'

'What?'

'My dad. When I killed him.'

He gets the blade all the way up to the waist, then flips Lucas onto his front. He puts his knee heavily into the middle of his back and goes back to work with the scissors.

'Look, Simon,' Lucas says, and Simon wonders if the kid is using his first name deliberately. Maybe they teach that at school, that if you use your abductor's first name you can humanise yourself in their eyes. He's curious as to where this will go, but mostly it's all fuel for the fire that is burning inside him. He knows it's not right. He knows he's broken. But hey, it's not his fault – it's the need. It's the biology.

'I'm grateful you let me out of the locker,' Lucas says. 'You saved me, and now it's time to let me go home. Let me go home and I won't tell anybody. I promise.'

Jesus, did the school teach him that too? 'Okay.'

'Okay?'

'Yes, okay, but first you have to help me, like I helped you.' He turns his attention back to Lucas's jeans and continues the cut. He's almost done. The fire can't get much hotter.

'Help you how?'

'I share it with you, and it softens some, and I share it again, and it softens some more. You see, the pieces keep getting smaller.'

'I don't understand.'

No, they never do. 'You will, I promise. I'll teach you when all this is done.'

'That means you're going to let me go when ... when this is over?'

'Of course. That's why the camera is here.'

He finishes the cut and pulls the jeans away before climbing off, leaving Lucas in his T-shirt and underwear. Lucas rolls onto his back and shimmies to the furthest edge of the mattress, where it meets the wall, looking like he's trying to blend into it.

'The camera makes it different this time,' he says, and tosses the jeans aside, and then, because he can, he adds, 'I didn't have it for your friend. What was his name again?'

The way these words make Lucas look even more scared tells Simon Lucas knows exactly who he's talking about. Simon smiles and leans in, and goes to work on the T-shirt. It sure cuts easier than the jeans did. When Lucas doesn't answer, he adds, 'Wasn't it Freddy?'

Now the kid looks like he couldn't answer even if he wanted to.

'It was different for him,' Simon says, carrying on, 'but I have it for you. It's how we can trust each other,' he says, and the camera means maybe all those bridges aren't burned after all. 'See, you'll never say anything to anybody about what happens out here, because if you do, everything I record goes out over the Internet. You wouldn't want that, would you? But your friend – I didn't own a camera back then, so I wasn't able to give him that option. It's a pity really, but it is why I couldn't let him go.'

Chapter Eight

I call Cassandra while Chambers hunts down Simon Grove's address. We haven't spoken in a few days. When Cass moved out, it was amicable. We still loved each other, we just didn't love the situation we were in. She needed a safe space for both her and Nathan. My dad had gone from being the nicest guy in the world to the meanest. I'd never known anybody with Alzheimer's before my dad got it, but to me it has become the scariest disease in the world, and the cruellest. It strips away the person you used to be, and who it replaces you with is a complete lottery. But over the last few months there has been a growing distance between Cass and myself, and it doesn't help when there are no solutions on the horizon. For all we know my dad could live another thirty years. For all we know I'll be living on the street with him, or sleeping in the car.

'How are you?' she asks. 'You getting any sleep?'

'I'm okay.'

'How'd you get on with the lawyer?'

'I don't know. He's doing what he can.'

'Meaning?'

'Meaning he'll keep taking my money while I have it. Listen, it'll be on the news soon: a boy from school has gone missing, and all the signs are pointing to him being abducted.'

'Jesus.'

Chambers tears a piece of paper from his workday diary and writes down Simon Grove's number and address. The combination of shaking hands and sweat sees that page dropping to the floor when he tries to hand it to me, and he follows that up by banging his head against the desk when he tries to get it.

'Listen, I had to leave Nathan looking after Dad. Given the circumstances, I'm—'

'Of course, I'll go there right now.'

'It could be a late night.'

'I understand. I'll stay with them as long as you need.'

'Thanks, Cass.'

We hang up. Chambers hands me the page and rubs his forehead as I dial the number he wrote down. It goes through to an answering service. I don't leave a message.

'Lucas is okay, right?' Chambers asks, his voice full of worry.

If it is a crime, then it's a crime of opportunity. That much is obvious by the way everything has been left. It's obvious because Simon Grove couldn't have been expecting to find a kid trapped inside a locker. Might be the kind of guy to fantasise about it, but couldn't have predicted it.

'Sheriff?'

That's the first point. The second point is I can't imagine a scenario where some everyday, average guy helps a kid out of a locker only to abduct him. Which means Simon Grove is not an everyday, average guy. There is a history to him. We've already run his name for a record, and so far there's nothing. But there has to be something buried in this guy's past, dots of sickness along his timeline that have led to today.

Chambers looks like he's going to have a heart attack.

'I can't give you the answer you want,' I tell him.

'I feel sick.'

'Who owns the locker Lucas was stuffed into?'

'It belonged to Taylor Reed.'

The boy who jumped from the roof. I try not to take it as a bad omen.

I go back out to the locker, my footfalls echoing down the corridor. I hand the evidence bag with the rag inside it to Hutch and tell her to get it tested. Then I hand her a folder Chambers gave me in his office. She opens the cover and looks at the details on the first page. It has Grove's employment history in it. Before this he's worked as a picture framer, a farmhand, he's bussed dishes, painted houses, and mowed lawns. He used to work on a fishing boat before he moved to Acacia Pines ten years ago. I suspect that's where those dots of sickness will connect – somewhere back before he moved here. He's been a caretaker at this school for the last six years.

'Also, run this for prints,' I say. I pick up the crowbar and carefully drop it into an evidence bag so it doesn't punch a hole through the bottom. 'Maybe we'll get a hit somewhere.'

'Where are you going to be?' she asks, as we walk to the exit.

'Grove's house. Keep me updated.'

We get into our respective cars.

It's a seven-minute drive to Grove's house with my lights blaring and traffic getting out of the way. His street is lined with elm trees that need to be trimmed. The house is small and tidy, wooden trim freshly painted, the roof water-blasted clean of moss. The front door is bright red. The lawns are freshly mowed and the yard well cared for. There are birdhouses hanging in the trees. Maybe it's the wrong house. I was expecting warped weatherboards and lumps in the front yard covering things that have been buried. There's no car up the driveway, but there could be one in the garage. My phone vibrates as I get out of the car. It's Peter Connor ringing to tell me there's no sign of Lucas at home.

'What are we going to do?' he asks, as I open the mailbox. There's mail in here addressed to Simon Grove, so it's the right house.

'Let me call you back,' I say, as my phone beeps with a second call. It's Hutch. I put the mail back and keep my eyes on the house, looking for movement, maybe a curtain being pulled aside. Nothing.

Hutch tells me that Rick, the forensic technician who runs the small lab at the station, says the rag I found was soaked in chloroform. I rest my hand on the gun. I was promoted to sheriff only a year ago, but before that I was deputy for fifteen, and in that time I've never had to pull my gun from its holster in the line of duty. Today might be the day.

Hutch carries on. 'Rick says it's not like you see in the movies, that the rag would need to be held over Lucas's face for at least a couple of minutes – which I'm figuring may not have been hard to do if the kid was already exhausted and sore from being in the locker. Rick also says Lucas would have been weakened by the chloroform, he'd have gotten dizzy and passed out, but the effect wouldn't have lasted long. Maybe a few minutes.'

'Long enough to restrain him and put him into his car.'

'Easily. For all we know Grove has been wandering around with chloroform in his pocket for years waiting for an opportunity like this.'

'He probably had it in the supply room, and got it when he grabbed the crowbar. Let's get Grove's picture circulated. Go to the news station and get it on the air. Get Lucas's picture on the air too. We want all eyes on this. Chambers says Grove drives a dark-blue Toyota, maybe twenty years old. DMV will have the rest of the details. I'm at Grove's house and am about to take a look around. I'm going to leave the line open. You hear anything bad, you bring everybody down here.'

'You don't want to wait for backup?'

'There's no time.'

I tuck the phone into my pocket. I take the gun out of its holster and keep it pointed down as I approach the front of the house, keeping away from the windows, then peek through them when I'm up close. There are no signs of life. The bright-red door is locked.

I kick the door as hard as I can, landing my boot beneath the handle where the wood has been hollowed out for the lock mechanism. It's a heavy blow that leaves a mark behind but doesn't break the door. I give it a second kick, and this time wood splinters. A third kick gets the job done. I step inside and take an immediate left into the lounge. It's sparse. Cheap furniture, an old couch, a TV that's even older, but all of it well looked after, books all tidy in the shelves of a bookcase that's been lovingly restored. I move from room to room. Old beds, old drawers, out-of-date furnishing, all of it tidy, an office with an old computer. I check the garage. There's no car, and no room for one because it's full of old office furniture in the process of being restored.

I holster my gun, update Hutch and hang up.

I go back to the room where I saw the computer. It hums loudly when I switch it on. After it's warmed up it asks for a password. I don't try anything. I check out the kitchen. I go through the cupboards. Canned goods neatly stacked with the labels facing outward. The fridge is full of ready meals and beer, the meals have the day of the week written on them and the beer cans all have the fronts facing forward. I call Hutch.

'There's a computer here, but it's password-protected. Give your brother a call and get him down here.'

'Will do,' she says. Her brother, Mike, set up all the computers at the police station. He also owns a store in town that sells them. He knows more about them than any of us, including Rick. It will be quicker for him to come here than for me to take the computer into the station.

'And get hold of phone records for Grove's house. Maybe his Internet provider can give us something. Maybe this guy has got emails on a server somewhere we can access.'

'On it.'

'And our guy is a planner. Meticulously so.'

'Not meticulous enough. He left behind a crime scene with prints everywhere.'

'This was a crime of opportunity, but I also think he's been preparing for something like this and just wasn't expecting it to be today. It could mean he also had a location in mind. He's careful, but he's given in to his excitement.'

'Did we get it wrong with the other boys?' she asks.

I should have been expecting her question, because I've been asking myself the same thing. The other boys. Taylor Reed and Freddy Holt. 'I don't know. We can't assume Grove had anything to do with what happened to them, but it's possible. Talk to Grove's previous employers in town. Maybe they can shed some light on our guy. Maybe one of those places he used to work is abandoned. Check empty houses too – places that are for sale. Places where folks are on holiday too. Could be an empty house, or a cabin in the woods, or just a clearing in the woods, or maybe not even a clearing. There's a thousand miles of wilderness surrounding Acacia Pines – a hundred thousand hiding places. Could be an empty apartment, could be he's doing whatever he's doing in his car parked off the side of the road somewhere. Get hold of the fire department, get them to volunteer to go through empty houses, but tell them to be careful. Nobody goes in alone.'

'Copy that.'

'One more thing: there are no photographs in his house, nothing to suggest Simon Grove has any kind of family or any kind of past or any kind of ego, but it also suggests no connection to anybody – no traces of a wife, of a girlfriend, no traces he ever had any parents.'

'You think he's distanced himself from all that?'

'Could be a story there, yeah. Could be he came to Acacia to run from something.'

'There's still nothing on the criminal-record front.'

'Could be he was on the other side of it.'

'A victim?'

'It's possible.'

'I'll look into it.'

My phone beeps with another call. I tell Hutch to call me as soon as she knows something, then take the new call. It's Chambers.

'Simon Grove applied for and was given leave for a week from next Monday,' he says.

I throw that into the mix but can't find any meaning to it. Not yet anyway. 'You know where he's going?'

'No.'

'Does Grove have a second job? Does he clean anywhere else?'

'As far as I know just the school,' Chambers says.

'He ever mention anywhere he likes to go? A favourite camping spot? Somewhere he goes for peace and quiet?'

'The only conversation we ever make are hellos and goodbyes.'

'Does anybody on the faculty know him?'

'I can ring around and ask.'

'Do that. And find out where he was going next week.'

'I'm sorry,' Chambers says. 'I ... I should never have hired the guy.'

'Call me when you have something.'

I look at my watch. Darkness is two hours away. It feels like a deadline, that if we don't find Lucas before then we're going to be too late. Pessimistic, sure – but optimistic too. Optimistic because I'm hoping the things Grove is planning to do to Lucas Connor haven't already been done.

I have to believe Lucas still has a chance to survive this.

Chapter Nine

The janitor's words are still hanging in the air. *But your friend – I didn't own a camera back then, so I wasn't able to give him that option. It's a pity really, but it is why I couldn't let him go.* Lucas can feel everything he's eaten over the last day sloshing around in his stomach, getting ready to start a journey upward. He misses his mom, and wishes she hadn't left. He misses his dad, and wishes he hadn't left too – because that's essentially what he did. How different things would be if they were still a family. Perhaps one of them would have been picking him up today from school. He'd have been found earlier, and not by this madman.

'You killed Freddy Holt?' he asks, but his words aren't much more than a whisper.

'What?'

'You – you killed Freddy?'

'I had no choice.'

Lucas doesn't know what to say to that. Years ago him and Freddy used to be friends. They'd lie out in sleeping bags in the backyard, looking up at the stars while telling each other ghost stories, or talking about the girls at school they wanted to kiss. They once spent a summer making a tree house, or at least they were until Freddy fell and broke his arm, which soured the whole tree-house experience. Somehow it soured the friendship too, and they drifted apart.

'Whereas you do have one,' Simple Simon says. 'You go along

with it, which will make things easier for both of us, and nobody ever has to see what we do here.'

Lucas imagines the footage being uploaded and emailed – first through the school, then town, then the country, and then the world. There's no surviving that. He doesn't know how he'd end things, but he would. Maybe he'd do what Taylor Reed did.

Or he does what Simple Simon says, and that's to go along with things and hope he keeps his word.

'So? What's it to be?'

'You promise not to show the video?'

'That's up to you.'

'I ... I won't struggle.'

'And?'

'And I won't tell anybody.'

All Lucas has left now is his underwear, and that's only for a few more seconds because the janitor cuts that away too. Lucas tucks his knees back to his chest, which puts more pressure on his shoulders because of his hands taped behind him. He keeps pulling at the duct tape around his wrists as the janitor unzips his overalls and pulls out his arms, leaving the top half to hang over the bottom. There are cigarette burns over his arms. Fat ones, thin ones, some that look cratered into the skin as if the same spot was hit over and over. Lucas hasn't stopped wondering how his father would write a character's escape from this situation, and has come up with something he doesn't think his dad would have used, but hopefully it'll work. His stomach is gurgling. There's an acidic taste building in his mouth. His cheeks feel like they're being sucked inward. He has no intention of not struggling. No intention of not telling people.

The janitor pulls his T-shirt off. The cigarette burns aren't just contained to his arms, but cover his chest and stomach too. A constellation of scars.

'Please, you don't need to do this,' Lucas says.

'That's where you're wrong. This will soften the pain.'

'I still don't understand.'

'You will. After.' The janitor kicks one shoe off, then has to fiddle with the laces to loosen the other. He lowers his overalls, revealing a pair of white briefs covered in yellow stains.

It's just what Lucas needs to see.

His stomach turns, and drops, then rises quickly. It comes then, bile and vomit and digested and half-digested food, all rushing upward, burning his throat on its way out. He directs it over his chest and stomach and into his lap and over his thighs. It's hot, and it stinks, and he's never been so happy to be so sick.

It has the effect he wanted, because the janitor jumps back. 'I can't...' he says, and he looks disgusted. 'Wait here,' he says, and he pulls his overalls up and tugs his shoes back on and picks up the scissors and walks out of the office, leaving Lucas covered in his own sick.

But, more importantly, leaving Lucas alone.

Chapter Ten

The screaming sirens and squealing tires from my arrival earlier have put the neighbourhood on alert, which means there aren't any delays when I knock on doors. A small town like this, people are keen to talk. The only problem is they don't have a lot to say, at least nothing useful, which is on full show when the woman next door to Grove tells me he keeps himself to himself, before suggesting I talk to somebody at the school because she's sure he mows the lawns there. I've been learning the same thing all the way up the block, and then all the way back down, folks lining up to get involved. During that learning Mike has shown up, accompanied by Deputy Charlie Wade, and I wrap up with the neighbour I'm questioning to go and meet them. They're already in Grove's house, with Mike hunched over the computer, by the time I get there, Wade half hovering over him while keeping an eye on the door. Wade is a big guy, over six foot and two hundred and thirty pounds, his mop of thick hair a couple of pounds of that. He's been on the force for over ten years. He's calm, and experienced, but even he looks panicked by all of this. Mike is tall, and skinny, like a pole vaulter, or perhaps more like the pole a pole vaulter would use. He has the goatee of a ventriloquist and the comb-over of somebody who believes in miracles. He's talking to the computer as he taps away at the keyboard, as if he can convince it to let go of its secrets.

'How are you getting on?'

'I was able to access recovery mode and reset the password,' he says. 'First thing I did after booting it up was check the guy's address book. It's empty. I've checked his emails, but the only emails this guy has are from an auction website, where he's been selling old office furniture and tools.'

That must be all the used furniture in Grove's garage.

'Browser history?'

'He doesn't have one. Either the guy has never been online, or he deletes it.'

'So maybe he has a hidden folder somewhere he tucks things away in.'

'I've been looking for it.'

'Grove's photo went out on the air ten minutes ago,' Wade says, 'along with a description of his car. So far there have been no calls. If we'd added a reward, the phones would have lit up like Christmas trees.'

He's right. Big cities and small towns have that in common: people care more when there's something in it for them.

Mike rolls the chair back from the computer. He looks pale. His hands are shaking.

'You found the hidden folder?'

'I did,' he says, before sucking in some deep breaths. But then he must figure he doesn't want the air from a house like this getting deep into his lungs, because he heads for the door.

'Go with him,' I tell Wade.

I sit down in front of the computer. I'm expecting to see a folder full of photographs of children, but instead there are videos. There are enough thumbnails to fill the screen, and more, if I scroll down. An information bar at the bottom tells me there are forty of them. Each thumbnail has a frame from within the footage, so even without opening one I know what I'm looking at. I glance from image to image, a few are dark, where the video hasn't captured much yet, or it's grainy, but in most there's a young teenager, always naked, and in others there's a man with him, and he's naked too. I want to go out and join Mike. I use a slider on the bottom of the screen to make the thumbnails larger. It's the same boy in each of the videos, and the boy has the third and fourth fingers missing from his left hand.

Why would Simon Grove hang on to videos of his own abuse?

Chapter Eleven

Throwing up has hollowed Lucas out, as though both organs and bone have been scooped away and discarded, turning him into one of those octopuses that can squeeze through a hole the size of a quarter. He thinks about his dad and how he's going to take the news. He thinks about the boys who stuffed him into the locker. Will they be shocked? Will they laugh and talk shit about him?

Will they be punished?

He doesn't know. He thinks about Freddy Holt. Freddy dead and buried with dirt in his mouth, and his eyes open, and a look on his face that says *how did this happen?*

He pictures himself looking the same way ... Feeling returns to his arms and legs.

He pictures the video of him and the janitor spreading like wildfire across the Internet ... Feeling returns to his chest, and stomach, to his core.

He has to hurry.

He rolls onto his side. He tries to bring his hands under his feet and out front, but can't stretch his arms that far. He can get to his feet, but how far could he expect to hop before falling over and getting caught? If only the janitor hadn't taken the scissors with him.

The office doesn't have much to offer beyond the desk and the filing cabinet, but there is the window, and breaking it could get him a shard of glass he can use to cut the tape. Only problem is the janitor will hear it and come running back. This is where the luck part comes into his plan.

The concrete floor is unforgiving on his naked body as he rolls under the desk. Desk drawers contain all sorts of things that cut. Usually. And this desk has three of them. Each drawer has a metal knob for a handle. He gets his mouth around the first one and pulls back and the drawer opens easily enough. It's empty. Strike one. He closes it, puts his mouth around the second handle. It wiggles in his mouth as he pulls the drawer open. It's also empty. Strike two.

The third drawer is locked and won't open.

Strike three.

If he had a paperclip, maybe he could...

Could what? Pick it? Not in a million years – even if he could use his hands.

He turns his attention back to the second drawer. He opens it back up, then turns around to get his fingers onto the loose handle. He pulls against it while turning it, and a moment later it drops into his hand. He pushes the tip of the screw protruding through the hole and fetches it out the other side. It's an inch and a half long, with a wide, twisting thread turning to a sharp point. He keeps the handle in one hand, and with the other puts the screw tip against the tape and slices at it.

Footsteps approaching.

He rolls back onto the mattress. He keeps scratching the screw at the tape. He's going to have to stall the janitor. And when he gets through the tape? Then what?

The *then what* can wait. Right now he needs to focus on getting his hands free.

The janitor enters the room carrying a pair of plastic buckets. One he puts down, and the other he swings toward Lucas, sloshing the contents over him. The water is icy cold. It hits his face hard and washes most of the vomit down his body, but it also makes him drop the screw and handle.

He has to get the janitor talking.

'My dad will have called the police when I didn't come home,' he says, and he leans back and pats the mattress. Where the hell is the screw? 'They'll have gone to the school to look for me. They're going to find the locker you broke open. How long until they figure out I was in there, and that you were the one who found me?'

The janitor says nothing, but Lucas can see him thinking about it. He keeps patting at the mattress – how the hell has the screw disapp—

Yes! He finds the handle. He keeps looking.

'Or did you clean up after you took me? Did you put a new door on the locker? Make it look like I found my own way out? Did you hide the fact it was prised open from the outside?'

'All that matters is what I tell you to tell them. Or have you forgotten about the camera?'

He hasn't forgotten about the camera. 'It won't matter,' Lucas says. 'I have a curfew, and—'

The janitor picks up the second bucket of water and pours it over Lucas, washing away the remaining vomit, which then pools in the creases of the mattress. It has the added bonus of pushing the screw into his buttock. He shifts forward and gets it between his fingers.

'I don't want to hear any more,' the janitor says, kicking off his shoes. He takes the scissors out of his pocket and puts them on the desk.

'Tell me more about Freddy,' Lucas says, desperate now for a few more seconds as he carries on cutting away at the tape.

The janitor lowers his overalls.

'What about—?'

The janitor reaches down and slaps Lucas with an open hand, cutting off his question. The sound echoes out into the building. Lucas almost drops the screw again, but manages to hold on. His fingers feel like they're going to cramp.

The janitor pulls one foot out of the overalls then the other, leaving him in stained underwear he's almost bulging out of.

'I said I don't want to hear any more. Shut up and make this easy, or talk and make it hard. Decide.'

Lucas's face stings. He can feel it going red. Can feel the tears in his eyes. Can feel the hole in the tape getting bigger.

'Get on your knees for me and bend over,' the janitor says.

When Lucas doesn't move, the janitor grabs him by the shoulder and tries to tip him, but his hands slip off his wet skin. Lucas keeps sawing. He's close now.

'Then let's make it difficult,' the janitor says, and he lowers his underwear and steps out of them. 'This is on you,' he adds, as he picks up the scissors.

Chapter Twelve

It wasn't until after the last boy that he realised he needed to start filming things, the same way his last dad used to film him. There are times when those days with his dad were a hundred years ago, and then there are times he still wakes up screaming, still able to smell his dad's sweat. He found all that footage before he left home. Back then he took it to use as evidence, but what was the point? What was done was done, and his parents would have gone to jail for five years, or ten, or maybe twenty, but that was too good for them.

The boy smells like vomit, but it could be worse. He lowers his knees onto the mattress and the boy slinks further back. He doesn't want to have to use the scissors on him – that makes things messy, and it means he really will be burning that bridge. But it might happen – something like this, biology takes over, and one minute he's looking down at some kid and the next they're both covered in blood, and sometimes he barely remembers the bits in between. He glances at the camera to make sure it's recording – it is – and it will do the remembering for him.

'Let's...' he says, turning back to Lucas, just in time to see a fist swinging ... 'Fuck!'

He screams and falls back, oh Jesus, his eye, his fucking eye, he's been stabbed in the eye, and it's like a bomb going off in his head! He puts his hand over it, almost stabbing himself with the scissors in the other eye in the process, but whatever he got stabbed with is still in there! He doesn't hesitate, just grabs it and pulls, and maybe it's the worst thing he could do but he does it anyway, does it because he doesn't want to think about it. Thank God it doesn't tug his whole damn eye out, and whatever it is lands on the floor with a small metallic thud, and he looks down to see a drawer handle with a screw jammed into the back of it, the flat bit having been poked into his eye.

He kicks at the floor and uses his free hand to push himself away. He gets to his feet, staggers, bangs into the filing cabinet, which sends the camera onto the floor. He regains balance and gets himself into the corner of the room, his hand tight on his ruined eye. He hunches over, naked, blood running down his face, the scissors held out ahead of him. If the kid comes toward him or tries to get out the door, he will bury those scissors in his throat. His chest. His stomach. He'll use them to cut out his fucking eyes!

The kid picks up the camera and hurls it at the window. What the fuck? It bounces back off, leaving nothing but a small spiderweb of cracks in the centre. The little shit is trying to smash the glass! He throws it a second time and the spiderweb doubles in size, then triples. It spreads to the edges, and a triangle of glass tips out from the top and lands outside, followed by another, then another, then most of them. If he tries to get out that way he's going to shred himself to pieces.

Simon pulls his hand away from his wound – he has an urge to see the blood on his palm, but the lack of pressure against the wound gets him screaming. He's going to make the kid pay for this. He ought to drag him back and forth through the smashed window, over and over the jagged pieces of glass. One of those pieces has fallen inside. The kid snatches it up, only to drop it just as quickly as it cuts his palm. He grabs his underwear and wraps them around the glass as a handle. A moment later he's slicing through the tape binding his feet.

The kid gets to his feet and looks at the window. There's no way he can get through it without being sliced into ribbons. He's going to have to go for the door. Which is exactly what he does, sprinting right at it. Simon slashes the scissors at him, but either the kid is too fast or Simon's perspective is out of whack with his eye all covered over, because he completely misses, and the next thing he knows the kid is running free through the sawmill.

He follows, running but not really running, more like throwing himself in that direction, limping, hunched over, the pain in his eye bad but going to get worse once he's killed the kid and the adrenaline has worn off. He can hear his own and the kid's bare feet slapping across the factory floor. He likes the high-pitched squeal the boy is making, until he realises that he's the one making it.

Lucas heads for the door Simon walked through earlier – except he locked it earlier, something the kid quickly learns when he tries to push it open. He heads for the chains, but there's no way he'll get the door open enough before Simon reaches him. The distance is closing. The kid looks around – sees the car – goes for it. It's a lifeboat in a sea of concrete, and Simon left the damn keys in the ignition. No reason not to. Can the kid crash the damn thing through the roller door? Simon figures they're both going to find out, because the kid gets into the car and locks the doors.

'You fucker!' Simon screams, banging on the windows.

The kid fumbles with the keys and gets it started.

Then stalls it.

Ha! The little fucker doesn't know how to drive.

He gets it started a second time, and it bunny-hops forward a couple of feet before stalling again.

That's when Simon notices the trunk is still open.

He goes to it as the engine turns over. He grabs the tire iron that will easily get through the windscreen, but then something else in the trunk catches his attention.

He puts the tire iron back down.

This is going to be even better.

Chapter Thirteen

Mike is sitting on the front doorstep when I head outside, and Wade is talking to one of the neighbours. All that's going on, all that I just saw, has had the effect of dulling the edge of the Adderall, and when I sit down next to Mike, I can feel every one of my recent sleepless nights.

'I'm sorry you had to see that,' I tell him.

'Me too.'

'Can you tell when Grove last looked at the videos?'

'I don't want to go back in there.'

'Please, Mike. I wouldn't ask if it weren't important.'

'I can't.'

'You know what we're up against here.'

'Screw you, James,' he says, but even so, he gets up and goes inside.

I follow him in. He clicks on the videos and begins opening windows and typing commands while I take another pill, dry swallowing it. Like everything else going on in my life, I don't see that being something that gets better anytime soon. Or at all.

Mike checks the videos off one by one; this one was watched over the weekend, so was this one, and that one, and as it turns out, all of them. The videos range in length from five minutes to twenty minutes.

'They all have the same created date on them,' Mike says.

'Meaning?'

'Meaning it's likely they were converted from another format, or edited, all at the same time – that time being twelve years ago.'

'Can you tell when he watched them before this weekend?'

'If there's a way to do that, I don't know what it is,' Mike says. 'I need a drink.'

'Go and get one. A strong one.'

He goes back outside. I think about Grove watching the videos. Does he watch them every weekend, or just this weekend, so he can work himself up to a level to hurt a child? He was, after all, getting ready to take time off from work. He was in the zone, counting down the days, primed and ready to go. Then he finds Lucas in the locker, and the frenzy he has been working himself into means he takes the opportunity, the consequences be damned.

I head back outside. Mike hasn't gotten far. He's leaning against my car. I lean next to him and we stare silently at Grove's house. I imagine the windows as eyes, the door as a mouth, the entire thing watching me. I imagine it growing legs and chasing me, the house a monster, the man who lives here a monster too. There's something in that house I've overlooked – or perhaps that's wishful thinking. But I don't think so. Something Mike said is turning in the back of my mind. I close my eyes and take myself back through the house. The lounge, all the books, the kitchen, the fridge, everything lined up neatly and labelled, the garage with the cheap furniture being restored, the bedrooms, the computer, the...

I turn to Mike. 'His auctions. Was he buying or selling?'

'Huh?'

I'm almost frantic when I ask him again. 'The auctions, was he buying or selling?'

'Best I can tell he was just selling, but I'd need to...'

I don't hear the rest because I'm already racing back into the house and to the garage. If Grove wasn't buying, then where did the furniture in the garage come from? From a business closing down, the furniture not worth the time to dump? I paw through it, my shirt wet with sweat, dust coming off everything and making my nose itch. I open desk drawers and filing cabinets, hoping to find files or documents, but they're all empty. The drawers of the filing cabinet are stuffed full of cables and plugs but nothing else. I slam them closed. There's an old computer with no monitor, an old TV, some in/out trays, bits of shelving. I toss things aside looking for anything that can help, then come across an old answering machine with cables wrapped around it.

Bingo.

I unwind them and plug the machine into the wall and press play.

'Welcome to Acacia Sawmill. You're calling outside of office hours, but if you'd like to leave a...'

I rush back outside. The old sawmill. Closed down when a bigger one was built, abandoned, empty, isolated.

I should have thought of it sooner.

Chapter Fourteen

The car lurches forward again. Why couldn't it have been an automatic? Lucas knows the basics of a manual, even if he's never driven one before – clutch, brake, accelerator – but there's an art to it.

Simple Simon comes around to the side of the car – with the gas container that was in the trunk with him earlier. He takes the lid off and pours the contents over the roof. Gasoline rolls down the windscreen in waves and across the hood. If Lucas stays in the car, he's going to burn to death. If he gets out, he's going to get stabbed.

He turns the key and the car lurches again, and that's when he remembers the gear stick needs to be in neutral. He gets it there, tries the car, and when it starts it doesn't hop forward. He gets his foot on the clutch, pushes the stick up into first, only to hear a graunch of gears.

He looks out to Simple Simon. He's holding up a road flare. 'Shit.'

Simple Simon pops the flare and tosses it onto the car.

The effect is immediate, with a giant *whoomph* as flames turn the car into a metal and glass coffin. He's going to be cremated in it. The flames will eat through the windscreen, and melting glass will rain into the car. Metal is going to twist. Plastic is going to peel. Flesh is going to cook. Will he die first from poisonous smoke, or will he burn?

He gets the gear stick into first, and slowly applies pressure on the accelerator as the rubber on the window wipers peels upward. The temperature is rising quickly. He can't see the janitor. Can't see anything but fire and smoke. The car rolls forward. He adds more pressure on the accelerator. His wipes tears from his eyes and more appear. He can't hold his breath any longer. The smoke expands in his nose and mouth and throat. It fills his lungs. He coughs it out. The car gains speed. Is the janitor jogging alongside? Or is he rooted to the spot, or—

The car crashes into the wall, throwing Lucas into the steering wheel. The driver's side is where Simple Simon concentrated the gasoline, so he scoots across the seat and opens the passenger door. Smoke is sucked past his body as he climbs out. His vision is blurred, but he can make out the office he was in earlier. He runs into it, coughing up a dirty wad of phlegm and spitting it onto the floor on the way. His chest is tight, and he can't recall ever being in so much pain. The janitor is loping toward him, one hand over his eye, giving him a lopsided gait. He's still carrying the scissors.

Lucas doesn't hesitate. He picks up the mattress and holds it ahead as he launches himself at the broken window, riding the mattress like a surfboard. It snaps at the remaining triangles of glass, slides for a bit, snags, then comes to a fast halt. He continues forward, tumbling off the other end onto the ground outside.

He gets to his feet. It doesn't feel like he's stepped on any glass from the broken window. The trees are to his left, the building to his right, and straight ahead what has to be the edge of the parking lot and, hopefully, not much further, the highway. If he can get there he can flag somebody down.

He runs, but he can't come close to the speed from before. His chest is too tight, he's lightheaded from coughing, and his bare feet are in pain. He reaches the corner of the building and sure enough, it is the parking lot, and on the other side the road to the highway. He had forgotten that road was gravel, and not only that, he doesn't know how long it is. There's no possible way he can run it without shoes. He's going to have to cut through the forest. If he's lucky he can find a rock or a branch to defend himself, or perhaps he can loop around to the—

The car runs into him. At least that's his first thought as a massive weight drives him into the ground, banging his elbows and knees heavily into it. It's not until he's rolled onto his back that he sees it's the janitor. He grabs Lucas's hair and pulls his head upward before driving it heavily into the ground. It kicks off an immediate high-pitched whistling sound while blurring the edges of his vision.

'This is your fault,' the janitor screams as he straddles him, his naked body against Lucas, the janitor's skin almost as hot to the touch as the car was when Lucas abandoned it. Lucas stares into the damaged eye, swollen closed and shiny with gore.

The janitor slaps him, hard. Lucas gets his hand up to try and block the next one that comes, and shudders as blood rolls off the janitor's face directly into his sliced-open palm. It's no good anyway, because Simple Simon moves the hand out of the way and hits him again, not a slap this time, but a punch. The world goes even darker, but even so, there's no mistaking the scissors when the janitor holds them up.

'It didn't have to be like this,' Simple Simon says.

There's nothing left to do. He can't move. Can't fight. Can't do anything but lie here, naked beneath a naked man.

He thinks about his mom.

He thinks about his dad.

The best he can hope for is that dying isn't going to be as painful as living has been.

Chapter Fifteen

Traffic pulls aside as I speed over the only bridge in and out of town. Ahead, the highway is mostly straight with subtle curves, farms on either side for the first half of the journey, forest for the second half.

I radio the station.

'I'm heading out to the old sawmill,' I tell Sharon. 'I think there's a good chance that's where Grove took Lucas.'

'I'll send backup.'

'Just send a couple of cars, and keep everybody else doing what they're doing in case I'm wrong.'

'I'll get Hutch and Wade out there.'

'Thanks.'

'Listen, Sheriff, there's...'

She peters out, and doesn't carry on.

'Sharon?'

'It's nothing.'

'What is it?'

'Well, this isn't the best time to tell you, but let me start out by saying everybody is okay, and nobody was hurt.'

'Jesus, Sharon, what is it?'

'The fire department are at your house.'

Even though she said everybody is okay, my heart still freezes for a moment as I picture my house looking like the care home, only this time nobody made it out.

'Cassandra got there to find a fire in the kitchen. She was able to put it out, and the fire department only showed up as a precaution, but I wanted to let you know that it's all under control in case you hear it anyway.'

'What happened?'

'I don't know,' she says, but I do. My dad happened. Nathan didn't keep an eye on him at all, and my dad tried to cook something. 'Nobody was hurt, and that's all that matters. But I do know there's a fair amount of damage. There's an engineer on his way to make sure the roof isn't going to collapse.'

'Jesus.'

'This is why we have insurance.'

She's right – or would be, if I had insurance. I stopped paying those bills a couple of months ago. Maybe when the bank takes my house away, they'll charge me for the repairs. I make a mental note to cancel the realtor who was coming around this week. Nobody is going to want to take a look at my house until I fix up the damage, something I'm going to have to take care of myself after I've googled how. And how the hell am I going to pay for an engineer? And can I even sleep there tonight?

'Okay, thanks Sharon, I appreciate it.'

We disconnect. I try not to think about what would have happened if I hadn't called Cassandra earlier, which is easy to do because I have Lucas and Grove to think about instead. Sharon radios back to say Hutch is five minutes behind me.

It takes fifteen minutes to reach the turnoff to the sawmill. I slow down and roll forward quietly, then pull over before the mill comes into view. I figure it's best to go on foot rather than risk being heard. It's a short jog along the tree line to the mill. When I get there, the smoke pouring from it is so eye-catching it takes a few moments to realise I'm overlooking what's happening in the parking lot – a naked Simon Grove is beating on a naked Lucas Connor. At least I think that's what I'm looking at – both are covered in dirt and smeared in blood.

I pull my gun and run toward them, drawing a bead on Grove and yelling for him to stop. He's holding a pair of scissors with the blade pointing at Lucas. From this range I could shoot him easily if I wanted to – and I do want to – only he is already getting to his feet, and if I miss I could hit Lucas. He drops the scissors and turns and runs, long strides and an awkward gait that makes him look like he might fall over. Thirty yards become forty. A more difficult shot, but still makeable. If I pull the trigger.

Which I don't.

Because you can't shoot an unarmed man in the back who's running away, even a guy who hurts children, and I doubt taking somebody's life is going to help with the insomnia. Right now my priority is to protect Lucas. Grove will disappear into the forest, but we'll find him. I holster my gun when I reach Lucas. He's trying to prop himself up onto his elbow.

'You okay?'

He doesn't answer. I can't tell if he even knows I'm here. His eyes aren't focusing. I put my hand on his shoulder. He jumps and pulls away. 'Lucas, it's Sheriff Cohen. You're okay now. I got you.'

He tries to get up, and falls into a coughing fit instead. I can feel Grove getting further away, physically feel it, an elastic band between us that is getting tighter. There is blood coming from Lucas's hand and from his head, but thankfully not from anywhere else. He stops coughing. He looks up at me and finally sees me. He blinks hard a few times and clears his vision, and he says, 'I need water.'

I need Hutch to get here. Need her to look after Lucas so I can chase Grove down before it gets dark. Yes, we'll find him, but the sooner the better. The smoke is getting thicker. I take off my shirt and drape it over Lucas, leaving me in a T-shirt.

'Can you walk?'

'Yes.'

But it's a no, because when I help him to his feet he stumbles and would fall if it weren't for me holding on to him. I end up taking most of his weight as we stumble back to my car. I get him in the passenger seat, radio Sharon and update her, and ask her to call the fire department. She says an ambulance is already on the way. I radio Hutch. She's two minutes out. I pop the tailgate and rummage around in the back for a couple of bottles of water and a blanket. I put my shirt back on while Lucas pulls the blanket over himself like a cape. I hand him the bottles. He gulps half of one down, then winces when he pours the rest over a large slice on his hand. It's hard to know if he's wincing from the pain of it or the sight. Then he leans out of the car and tries to throw up, but very little comes out. He rinses his mouth and spits it out, then leans back in the car.

'I want to go home,' he says.

'You will, and soon,' I tell him, though he might not make it home today because his next stop is the hospital. I drive us into the parking lot where I can keep an eye on the building and the tree line in case Grove shows back up. I fight the urge to call Cassandra to check in, and know she'll have fought the same urge to let me know, not wanting me to be distracted. Perhaps Sharon shouldn't have told me. Lucas opens the second bottle and drinks this one at a more measured rate.

'You're going to be okay,' I tell him, but I don't know if that's true. I don't know what's happened to him. I do know he's put up one hell of a fight. Maybe he'll come through this okay. Maybe things have happened he won't want to tell us about.

'Shit,' I say.

'What?'

I really must be slipping, because Grove isn't on foot at all, because he drove out here. 'Where's his car?'

Lucas points toward the building. 'He was going to kill me. The janitor. He ... drove us in there. His car ... is in there. The smoke, that's the car. It's on fire.'

'His car is on fire?'

'Yes.'

'That was the only car out here? The janitor is on foot now?'

Lucas nods. My mistake hasn't cost us anything.

'Why is his car on fire?'

Lucas touches his forehead with his fingertips then studies them. They're clean. He does the same with the back of his head, and when he pulls them away there's blood on them. And dirt, and grease, and sawdust.

'Because I poked him in the eye with a screw, and locked myself in his car,' Lucas says. He takes another sip of water.

The elastic band stretches further as Grove keeps running. Soon it's going to snap, and when that happens Grove will be gone. Where is Hutch? Is Grove circling his way out to the road to flag down a passer-by? I should have driven out there to watch the highway, not the mill.

Lucas carries on: 'He set fire to it to get me out.'

'He what?'

'I locked myself in there. He poured gasoline all over it, and lit it with a road flare.'

'Jesus.'

'But I managed to get out.'

I'm eager to hear more, but suddenly I realise there's another pressing question that I haven't asked. What the hell is wrong with me? 'Does he have a gun?'

'Not that I saw.'

'You're sure?'

'He would have used it on me if he had.'

Hutch arrives, lights flashing and sirens blaring, tires skidding as she pulls up next to us. She jumps out of the car, leaving the door open, and looks at Lucas wrapped in the blanket and then at me and then at the factory, and she does that looking without any emotion on her face and with her hand resting on her gun. I get out of the car and stand next to her.

'He okay?' she asks.

'He's alive. As for if he's okay...' I don't finish the sentence.

'And Grove?'

'Gone.' I take my gun out of the holster. 'I'm going after him. Stick with Lucas until the ambulance has taken him out of here. You see Grove in any position other than his hands in the air surrendering, you shoot him.'

I head toward the forest. Years of searching for missing hikers out there has given me enough skills to be able to track somebody running through it.

She reaches out and puts a hand on my arm. 'Wait,' she says.

'Prints came back. Grove is wanted in connection with two other cases, one in which a child was murdered, and another where one disappeared.'

'Jesus.'

'Both are out of state – one ten years ago, the other four, and for all we know there are others too. There's a reward for him too. Sixty thousand dollars. Grove is a real bad apple, Sheriff. I don't think you should be going after him alone.'

I spend a moment to take it all in. Two boys: one dead, the other likely dead too, and others left in Grove's wake. However many there are, he is on a roll, and if he makes it to the highway that number might get bigger, and if it gets bigger it's on me for not squeezing the trigger when I had the chance.

'Sheriff?'

'How far out is backup?'

'Ten minutes.'

I do the math. Foot speed and car speed and angles and distances. I weigh it all up, figuring what can be done and what can't. 'If he makes it to the road and flags somebody down, we could end up with multiple victims. I'm heading after him. Take Lucas and meet the ambulance on the way in from town, then patrol the highway. Get Wade to set up roadblocks.'

'I can't leave you out there alone.'

'You can, and you will. When enough backup is on the highway looking for Grove, come back here with search and rescue. Fire department is on the way too, and I want somebody standing guard with them. But until then you protect that highway.'

'You sure about this?'

'No, but do it anyway.'

Chapter Sixteen

His eye hurts like nothing he's ever experienced. It's a hundred cigarette burns all rolled into one, and punched into the very core of his nervous system. He's going to lose his eye – that he's sure of – but what will happen before then? He knows he could step back out into the parking lot and surrender. They'd call an ambulance for him, they'd take him to hospital, they'd operate on him, and then they'd throw his arse in jail. He'd rather die than let that happen.

Safe money is to circle back to the road and flag down a car. But who the hell is going to stop for a naked man covered in blood? He could head into the trees and run in the opposite direction, but a few steps in and he'll quickly lose where opposite even is. Forests swallow people up. The idea of walking from A to B doesn't work because you're already at C and don't know it, then you're walking in circles.

No, safe money is on getting his hands on the sheriff before any other backup gets here, get his car, and drive as fast as he can away from this dumpster fire. Deal with the pain, get into another state, and get medical attention. He's sure he can make up a story about getting mugged.

Goddamn it, biology has fucked him. Not cleaning up at the school has led the police to him, but how they figured to come here is a mystery.

The blaze inside the building has taken hold, but there's not a hell of a lot in there to burn. Hell, the fire would probably just put itself out if left long enough, assuming it didn't somehow reach the forest. Then you'd have an inferno big enough to be seen from space, and you could say goodbye to Acacia Pines. Which isn't such a bad thing, really.

He watches from the trees as the woman cop helps the kid into the police car, then she's pulling away as Sheriff Cohen heads toward the building. He's spoken to Cohen a couple of times, first after that kid at school pitched himself from the roof, then after Freddy Holt disappeared. He'd stayed calm during those interviews and gave no reason for Cohen to suspect anything. He didn't like the guy, nor did he dislike him, but he might have to kill him. It's a risk. Kill a kid or two, and you might be facing life in prison. But kill a cop, and the rest of them will gun you down before taking you into custody. He tightens his grip on the piece of rebar he found earlier running back past the building – a nice two-foot-long piece of steel that, if aimed right, there's no coming back from it. Maybe he ought to just beat the shit out of Cohen, leave him be, and hightail it out of here.

Cohen reaches the corner of the mill. He has his gun gripped in both hands, pointing ahead. Simon holds his breath and doesn't move from the tree line. Cohen rounds the corner and approaches the broken window the kid leapt from earlier and smoke billows out of now. The building stretches sixty or seventy yards along, with lots of doors that are all locked. All but one. Rather than launch himself out through that broken window earlier, and having to walk over all that broken glass, Simon had moved down to the next door, which was a fire exit, and unlocked it from the inside.

Cohen is hesitant as he approaches the smoke. He pauses at the mattress as if trying to make sense of it, then carries on, through the smoke and out the other side.

He spots the open door. He remains hesitant as he approaches it. 'Come on, you can do it, come on,' Simon says, keeping his voice low. Cohen goes inside.

Simon steps out of the trees and follows.

Chapter Seventeen

Lucas's feet feel like the bottom layer has been stripped away, nerves and muscles and tendons exposed. His lungs are still burning, his head hurts, but the worst thing is the itch in his wounded hand. He winds down the window, puts his hand out and rinses it with water. He wants to go home. He wants to close the curtains, climb into bed, and wake up tomorrow in a world where none of this happened. And since that can't happen, he'll settle for Sheriff Cohen coming over the radio and saying he has the janitor in custody.

Really? Is that what you want?

Yes. Really.

Really?

No. Of course not. What he wants is for Sheriff Cohen to radio in and say the janitor is down, that he's lying on the ground with all those dark thoughts of his leaking from a bullet hole in the front of his skull. He can visualise it. Can hear the gunshots, can see Sheriff Cohen walking around the corner of the building, holstering his weapon gunslinger style, patting his hands clean with a job-well-done smile on his face. Wouldn't the world be better off if that happened? He thinks it would.

'How are you feeling?' the deputy asks, pulling him from his thoughts. She has a name badge, but the name badge is too blurry to read.

'I ... I don't really know.'

'You're in shock,' she says. 'You want to tell me what happened?'

He wants to, but when he goes to he finds he can't. Now that he's no longer being chased, a switch has been flicked inside his body to *off*. He has nothing left. He's a car that's run out of gas. A phone with a dead battery. He closes his eyes tight, and when he opens them nothing will focus. 'I don't feel well.'

'You'll be at the hospital soon. Was there anybody else inside the sawmill?'

He looks up. Stares out at the highway. Can't see any buildings. Can see sunlight flicking through trees, strobing, making him dizzy. They're driving slowly.

'Lucas?'

'Huh?'

'The sawmill. Was there anybody else in it?'

'Like who?'

'Anybody. Maybe other children you might have seen.'

He shakes his head, and regrets it immediately. He squeezes his eyes shut and focuses all his energy on not throwing up. This time he keeps them closed.

'Lucas?'

'Nobody.'

'Are you sure? Are you absolutely sure?'

'Yes,' he says, but then he thinks about it. Could be the janitor brought others out here too. There could be others buried under the floorboards – but then he remembers the floor was concrete, not wooden, so maybe those others are buried out in the woods. Or perhaps the offices have been converted into cages, and they're full of people who can't escape. Then he remembers what the janitor said about Freddy.

'Freddy might be there.'

'Excuse me?'

'Freddy Holt. He said he killed him, so maybe he's out there too.'

'He said that?'

'He did.'

'Are you sure?'

Suddenly he isn't. Did Simple Simon say that? Yes. Or no. He was sure of it until the deputy asked him if he was sure. 'I ... I don't know anymore.'

She says nothing for a few moments, and then when she asks him something else he doesn't hear her. He takes a look at the cut on his hand. It's deeper than he thought, and longer. He wonders how many stitches he's going to need and if they're going to hurt. He's never had them before.

'I killed them,' he says.

'Excuse me?'

'If there are others out there in cages, then they're burning because of me.' He turns to look at the deputy. 'I didn't know that was going to happen. I'm sorry.'

'I don't think there are others out there,' she says, only now she's the one who doesn't sound so sure. 'And anyway, whatever happens, none of it is your fault.'

He's not so sure that's true.

Chapter Eighteen

The sawmill is a world of possibilities, and many of them come to mind as I make my way inside. Grove might have come back in here to grab his clothes before disappearing into the woods. Roughing it out there naked, let alone barefoot, would be impossible. Or perhaps he's come through the mill and exited out the other side, back into the parking lot, with the goal of reaching the road. Acacia Pines is the kind of place where somebody would pull over and offer to help. Problem is Simon Grove is the kind of person to kill you for doing so. Of course he could be hiding in here, watching me this very moment, or he could have found a space where he'll hole up until the fire department have been and gone. He also might have taken the decision to hightail it through the forest. If it's that last one, then there's every chance he's already gotten himself lost. Maybe a hiker in five years will find his remains and claim the sixty thousand dollars.

The factory floor is as big as a football field with beams reaching up to the ceiling and empty shelves lining the walls. Grove's car is a ball of fire jammed between a metal staircase and a wall, that same fire having now spread to the adjoining offices, one of which has the mattress hanging out the window. I suspect the mattress might have been Lucas's escape path, and I'm eager to hear how that played out.

The fire sounds like a hurricane. Smoke is pooling beneath the ceiling, but at my level it's still pretty clear. The metal beams and roof both make pinging sounds as the heat makes them expand. There are nooks and crannies and shadows and a hundred places to hide. I make my way further in. If this had been an active mill, the entire place would have burned down by now, and taken half the forest with it. I keep a safe distance and arc my way toward the centre of the mill. There doesn't seem to be any danger of collapsing walls, not yet anyway. I jump and almost squeeze a shot off when the heat breaks one of the windows from one of the offices. Another breaks a few moments later. This place is too big to search alone. Which leaves the forest, which is even bigger.

I watch the flames for a few more moments, aware that my house just came close to looking the same way. I shake the image and head back toward the door.

I'm one foot out when Grove steps into view. One of his eyes is swollen shut, and looks like raw meat. His face is red, and his teeth are gritted. He's carrying a piece of rebar, which is already swinging at me. It gets me in the chest, and I double over and hit the ground, the gun falling out of my grip.

'This is your fault,' he says.

'Wait,' I say, trying to get my arm up to ward off the next blow. He doesn't wait.

Chapter Nineteen

Lucas is spaced out, like time is slipping away in chunks. Evidence of that is the fact that he's being helped into the back of an ambulance the patrol car has met on the way back into town, but he doesn't remember pulling over. One moment he's climbing into it, the next he's sitting on the edge of a gurney with a paramedic crouching in front of him, talking to him, looking at his wounds. His vision is a little better, not great, but good enough to see the serious look on the paramedic's face. She reminds him of his gym teacher, Mrs Randolph with the hairy legs and permanent frown and big arms. He looks past the paramedic at a long highway with trees on either side. The patrol car he was in is parked a few yards away, the woman who drove him leaning against it.

'Where are we?'

'We're still out near the sawmill,' the paramedic says, before launching into a series of general-knowledge questions that should be easy to answer but aren't. What is the date today, what is five times six, what's his middle name, why do people keep abandoning him? He doesn't think that last question is real, but it ought to be. As for the others, the answers are there, he just can't get to them. The doors of the ambulance have closed and he didn't see it happen. They're moving – which also comes as news. And when did he lie down? His hand is bandaged and doesn't hurt so much. He figures there can't be anything too wrong with him otherwise the ambulance would be speeding, and if it were speeding he'd hear sirens, and he doesn't hear sirens.

'You have a concussion,' the paramedic says. 'We're going to get you to the hospital, where we can take a better look at you.'

'I want to go home.'

'And you will, but not yet. Your dad is going to meet you at the hospital.'

He hopes his dad is sober. It's embarrassing the way people look at him sometimes as he fumbles his way through conversations, or stumbles through a grocery store, or the way he often smells like he bathed in his last drink. When it comes to his dad, you never know what you're going to get. He's come home from school to find him working away at a keyboard, writing up a new idea, and other times he's come home to find him passed out on the couch.

He realises that the paramedic is asking more questions. She wants him to keep talking. So he answers what he can, and keeps answering all the way to the hospital, which makes him even more tired. When the doors open, his dad is standing there waiting, looking soberer than he's seen him in weeks. Maybe Lucas ought to get himself abducted every day.

'Lucas,' his dad says, and he steps into the ambulance and wraps his arms around him, and he doesn't smell like beer. 'I thought I had lost you.'

'I'm here,' Lucas says, and he doesn't have the strength to hug his dad back. His dad is crying. He hasn't seen his dad cry since the day Mom packed her bags.

'I want to go home,' he says.

'Let's get you checked out first,' his dad says.

The paramedic fetches a wheelchair for him, and a moment later he's being wheeled into the hospital.

'Did he find him?' Lucas asks.

'What's that?' his dad asks.

'Did Sheriff Cowhand find the janitor?' he asks, and something he said doesn't make sense. He can't believe how tired he is. Sheriff Cowhand? Is that right? Or is it Calhone? He decides to try it out. 'Did Sheriff Calhone find the bad man?' No. That isn't right either.

'They're still looking for him.'

'What if they dons fwind him and he comes hospital?'

'If he comes here then I'll kill him myself,' his dad says, which is such a dad thing for him to say, and Lucas smiles, or at least he thinks he does, he can't feel it.

Chapter Twenty

'I don't want to hear it.'

Hutch is back. Others are patrolling the highway, and the fire department has arrived. The blaze has a hold of the northwest corner of the building. Firefighters have ripped off the side door and are battling the flames, while Wade keeps his hand on his gun, watching in case Grove comes out of the tree line. I'm more afraid of Wade accidentally shooting somebody than I am of Grove.

'Seriously,' I say to Hutch. 'I don't want to hear I told you so.'

Hutch is running the gamut from being concerned to being

disappointed, before settling on annoyed. But she doesn't give me the I told you so. She keeps her hand on her gun as, like Wade, she scans our surroundings. My hand isn't on my gun, because my gun is with Grove, so instead I have it on my shirt, which I have balled up against the side of my head. It has a good dose of blood on it, as does the side of my face. The wound is still leaking, but mostly it's okay. I'm embarrassed too. Embarrassed I let Grove fool me so easily. My ribs are aching from the blow they took, and I wouldn't be surprised if at least one is cracked. There's a ringing in my ears, and sitting on the hood of my car feels like I'm sitting on top of a tub of jelly, every small movement I make exaggerated.

The sun is on its final arc into the trees, meaning in twenty minutes it's going to start getting dark. I take another look at my shirt and find a clean patch to put back against my head. Grove's attack with the rebar was a glancing blow that's torn skin, and left a hell of a lump, and stunned me, but all things considered, that's a good result. Other patrol cars show up. Armed officers join Wade and others patrol the perimeter. Search and rescue, and dogs, are fifteen minutes away. Probably the media too. Roadblocks have been set up on the highway.

'What happened?' Hutch asks.

I tell her what happened. The unlocked door. Going inside. Coming back out and right into Grove, who was waiting for me. My words are heavy and slow and I have the urge to curl up somewhere and fall asleep. Some more Adderall might help with that, but I can't exactly pop a couple in front of Hutch.

'You're lucky he didn't kill you.'

'He tried.'

'I mean, after he struck you down. You're lucky he didn't shoot you when he took your gun, or beat you to death with the rebar.'

Her words open a Pandora's box that, since the attack, I've managed to keep closed. Now all I can see is myself lying on the ground, broken arms from shielding the blows, a broken skull from when those arms gave way. How many times does he pound it into my skull? Enough that I'm flat enough to slide into a letterbox? Then Cassandra gets the knock on the door she's always feared, and she collapses in a heap before Hutch even says a word. I see her at my funeral with Nathan. They're holding hands and she's crying, and maybe Nathan is too. Maybe he hates me a little less now that I'm dead, or maybe it's just one more thing for him to be pissed off about. The only positive is my life insurance will dig my family out of a hole, just as I'm being lowered into one.

Hutch puts a hand on my arm. 'You look like you're about to be sick.'

I feel it. I hold my breath and close my eyes and get myself under control. I take a drink and try to purge those thoughts. I could have died. Right now Hutch could be looking over my body. In another timeline she is doing just that. 'I'll be okay.'

'Any idea which direction he took?'

'Best guess is he's staying parallel with the highway until he can find transport, if he hasn't done so already. We need to warn people. He's wounded too. Something about his eye. Lucas stabbed him with something. He's got blood all over his face, which might work in his favour because people won't recognise him and will be eager to help,' I say. 'The only thing we know for an absolute fact is Grove is armed, wounded, and probably with a nothing-to-lose mindset.'

Search and rescue arrive. People file out into the parking lot. One of the search-and-rescue guys spreads a map out over the hood of a patrol car and draws lines on it as others watch. Dogs are five minutes out.

'There's something else,' she says, and the way she says it, I already know it's bad. 'When I had Lucas in the car earlier, he said that Grove killed Freddy Holt.'

I don't know what I was expecting, but not that. Jesus. 'He's sure?'

'He has a concussion that's messing with him. He said it, but then didn't seem so sure. But if he's right, it could also mean Grove was the one bullying Taylor Reed.'

Since the rebar hit my head, I've had a throbbing headache, but now it feels like there's a bull in there, stomping around looking for an exit.

'Jesus.'

'I know what you're thinking,' Hutch says.

'Do you?'

'None of us saw it,' she says. 'You're not the only one who spoke to Grove two months ago. We looked into him like we looked into everybody, but there was no reason to suspect him. You know as well as I do the timing suggested Freddy ran after Taylor Reed killed himself because he had something to do with it.'

Her words don't make me feel any better. Identifying a serial killer should be one of the fundamental tenets of the job. How can I still be a police officer when I can't recognise a cold-blooded killer right in front of me?

'I let those kids down,' I say.

'This isn't on you, Sheriff.'

'Isn't it?'

'You need to get checked out at the hospital.'

She's right, and I was a moment away from suggesting it. I slide off the hood and onto my feet. The parking lot sways, as does the cruiser, and the tree line, and the sky. I head to the driver's door as though I'm on a ship at sea. 'I'll talk to Lucas while I'm there too, see if he remembers anything more.'

'You don't seriously think you're going to drive yourself there.'

'I'm fine,' I say, opening the car door. 'It's worse than it looks.'

'That's because you're in shock. If Grove walked out of the trees right now I think you'd open fire on him.'

She's right. I would. If I had my gun.

'We can't afford to lose any manpower,' I say.

'Sheriff...'

'I appreciate your concern,' I say, getting into the cruiser. 'I really do, but I'm fine, and I need you out here running things. We need everybody out here.' I get the cruiser started. I wind the window down and close the door. Hutch stares at me with her hands on her hips. 'I'll get checked out and be back here as soon as I can.'

Chapter Twenty-One

The hospital hallways smell like science class during chemistry and look like science class during biology. Posters tell people what to look out for – warning signs of headaches, of back pain, of what having a heart attack looks like. Another poster displays the human body as if a skilled chef has filleted away the top layers. The floor is streaked with black marks from wheelchairs that have turned too quickly and burned rubber. There are other patients floating around, some walking with IV stands on wheels, others sitting on chairs in the corridor, many with bored looks on their faces. They reach a private room and a doctor helps Lucas sit up on the bed. The doctor is pale, as if something has just frightened her, that same fright streaking her hair grey. She asks how he's feeling. He's tired. Distracted. He wants to go home. Can the fire reach the hospital? Can the janitor? People say bad things come in threes. Lucas got stuffed into a locker, then abducted by Simple Simon. What's the third thing? Is the doctor going to have to amputate his hand?

The doctor asks questions similar to those he was asked on the ride here, only now he can answer them better. He knows his name, his address, what today's date is, who his teachers are. The doctor asks if he can detail how he got his concussion. So he does – at least the bits he can remember. He was slapped, he was punched, his head was pounded into a pavement. The doctor is happy with his answers, but not happy he was slapped, punched, and pounded. Nor is his dad, who paces the room listening to the answers, constantly gripping the back of his neck and shaking his head. The doctor asks if he's experiencing any dizziness – he isn't – then she uses a small flashlight to study his eyes. She tells him he's lucky he didn't get any burns, and that a nurse will be in soon to take a closer look at his hand and the bump on his head.

'You're going to need to stay in overnight so we can keep an eye on you,' she adds.

He doesn't want to be here now, let alone overnight. How do sick people kill time in hospitals, other than lie in bed being sick? 'Do I have to?'

'We want to make sure you're okay.'

'It will be for the best,' his dad adds, as if anything his dad does these days is with Lucas's best intentions in mind.

Lucas knows they're right, but it doesn't make it any easier. The doctor is replaced by a nurse who is tall and tanned, with muscles in her forearms that Lucas watches as she moves his hand around, taking a closer look.

'It's going to need stitches,' she says. 'Have you had them before?'

'No.'

'He has,' his dad says, which comes as a surprise to Lucas. He stares at his dad, who carries on: 'He was bitten by a dog when he was younger.'

No he wasn't.

'You don't remember that?' the nurse asks, sounding concerned.

Lucas doesn't, but he looks at his arm and sees there are scars, so perhaps...

'Wolfy,' he says, his dog coming back to him now. Wolfy bit him, he can remember that, but when he tries to picture Wolfy, he can't. The doctor is right to say he needs to stay in hospital overnight.

'It just slipped my mind,' he says, 'but I remember now.'

Well, almost remembers.

He's sure the nurse is going to pass this on to the doctor, who will probably insist Lucas stays a few nights now. He hopes not. She flushes the wound and swabs iodine over it. She loads up a needle with a clear fluid, and warns him it might sting a little, and it does, but soon his entire hand is numb. Watching her go to work is like watching a medical documentary, and a memory suddenly comes rushing back at him: that time he was eight and some kids at school were watching one where a surgeon was removing, via a man's mouth, a six-foot-long tapeworm that had grown through the man's colon and intestine. The narrator said worms can feed and grow inside people for years without them knowing, that they can change your personality the way brain tumours or strokes can. They can give you epilepsy, or take your sight, or make you lose your mind. You can waste away as worms create cysts in your brain. They can make good people turn bad. He couldn't sleep for a long time after that – how could anybody, really, with the knowledge monsters could be growing inside of you? He couldn't eat either. What if the food was tainted, or the person who made it hadn't cleaned their hands properly? Worms came from eggs so small you could barely see them. Who's to say they weren't in your hamburger, or your drink, or on your pillow?

He was prescribed pills that helped him sleep, but sleep only brought nightmares of worms growing inside of him, so many his body burst from the pressure. He was given pills for anxiety, and pills to kill any worms growing inside him, though he questioned if the latter was a placebo. Eventually he was diagnosed with Ekbom Syndrome, a psychiatric disorder where patients believe parasites are living inside them, a belief so strong if they push on their skin, they can feel the crunch of worms squirming beneath the surface. He was prescribed different medication, and soon the dreams faded, and he allowed himself to believe – and rightly so – that the worming tablets were indeed worming tablets, and would kill anything growing inside him.

'You're doing okay?' the nurse asks.

'Just thinking.'

'No dizziness?'

'None.'

'Okay. Let me know if this starts to hurt.'

His dad steps over to the window, where the night presses against the glass, and where he doesn't have to see Lucas's hand getting stitched.

'You'll need to keep it dry,' the nurse says when she's tied off the final stitch. 'And you'll need to have it checked and redressed every day for the next week.'

She cleans the lump on his head, puts some ointment on it, and tells him to keep that dry too. The final thing she does is to give Lucas a tetanus shot.

'You're going to be okay,' she says as she leaves.

'Thank you,' he says.

Then he stares at his hand. Already the cut is itching beneath the bandage, making him think it's only a matter of time before he tears both that and his stitches open.

Chapter Twenty-Two

I pour water onto my shirt, and use it to wipe blood from my face as I drive. It's a struggle to focus on the road as the headache rages on, and Hutch probably wasn't wrong when she said I shouldn't be driving. The roadblock covers both lanes, with a dozen cars waiting to be cleared. I skip the queue and acknowledge the deputies on the way past at the same time the dogs are being brought through. It's getting dark quickly now. Without any street lighting out here, the highway will soon be pitch-black. I pop the glove compartment and rummage around for a box of painkillers. They expired years ago, but what's the worst that can happen? Maybe I'll get superpowers. I swallow a couple with the hope it won't be long before the headache loses its bite. I look at the wound in the rear-view mirror. It's a hell of a lump, but it won't need stitches. In a few days the lump will be down, and in a week it'll be like it never happened.

I pass the turnoff to the new sawmill. Its proximity to the old sawmill means it will be searched. I pass the turnoff to the hiking tracks, the parking lot out of sight from the highway, but this time of the year there'll be a handful of cars in there, folks scattered across the trails, hiking and camping and fishing and being warned by search and rescue about Grove. Every year some of those folks get lost. They stray from the track and can't stray back. Mostly we find them, but sometimes we don't, some of them having fallen into a river, or a lake, or a ravine, or off a cliff. The forest can absorb hikers the same way a black hole absorbs light.

I reach the closed-up gas station, its boarded windows, the pumps removed, neglect spilling out over every surface, an old payphone out front cracked and faded by the sun, beer cans scattered across the pavement from teenagers who like to come here and drink. I carry on. Miles of highway, lined by farms now, fields rolling into the horizon, all of it becoming a blur. The exhaustion is catching up. Suddenly I feel so tired that the idea of crashing into a ditch or a tree seems pretty good to me if it comes with some coma time. I pull over at the old Kelly farm, heading up the driveway rather than risk staying parked on the side of a pitch-black highway. This place has been on the market for almost fifteen years, the previous owners having died. I'm not sure who owns it these days, and I'm not sure who'd want it. Only thing that grows out here is dirt. The farmhouse is behind a ring of pine trees with roots so large they've sucked the moisture out of the surrounding ground.

I grab the Adderall and stare at the container, knowing it's a mistake to take one, but I don't see myself making it back into town if I don't. So I take two. I lean my head back and close my eyes and ride the waves of pain, hoping the painkillers and the Adderall will kick in soon. I'm still riding those waves a few minutes later when my phone goes. It's Cassandra.

'I saw in the news you found the boy,' Cassandra says.

'We did,' I reply, leaning my head back and closing my eyes again.

'Is he going to be okay?'

'Physically I think so. As for the rest, I don't know.'

'What a nightmare for him and his family. I can't imagine. And you? You sound tired.'

'I'm okay,' I say, as the waves keep coming.

'You sure?'

'Grove got away.'

'You'll get him.'

'I know.'

'I'm worried about you, James.'

'I know that too.' I straighten up and look out at the farmhouse. Some folks think the place is haunted. If it is, the ghosts don't have a lot of taste. The farmhouse burned down last summer, and the walls that didn't collapse look like blackened toast. Pieces of furniture are still on display, some still in okay condition, some badly charred, some turned to ash. Right now my house could have been looking the same way. 'I heard about the kitchen fire.'

'I asked Sharon not to tell you.'

'Is everybody okay?'

'We're all fine. Your father was trying to cook some steak, but he put it directly onto the stove without a pan.'

I shake my head at the image, which makes the waves bigger.

'Then he added some wine to flavour it.'

'Jesus. If I hadn't called you...'

'But you did, and I got there in time.'

'How is he now?'

'He's okay. He's in the lounge watching TV. I got us all some takeout, and he seems happy. I'm not even sure he knows what happened.'

'And Nathan?'

'He knows what happened, but doesn't seem to care much.'

I stare through the windscreen as the final light bleeds out of the sky. The farmhouse is a good place to hide. 'He was meant to keep an eye on him.'

'I know,' she says. 'Next time ... I mean, you know, if something like this happens again, just call me sooner, okay?'

'Okay. And the kitchen?'

'It's not great, but structurally it's safe. It'll need the ceiling replaced, and the benchtop, some dry wall, and a new stove too. It won't be cheap.'

Of course it won't be.

'I'm heading home in a bit to change and freshen up, but then I gotta head back out. Are you okay to keep an eye on them?'

'Of course. I'm here for you if you need anything, James.'

I rub the side of my head where Grove got me with the rebar. 'Thanks.'

We hang up.

I radio Sharon. 'Has anybody checked the old Kelly farm?'

'Not yet.'

'Okay. I'm there now. How far away is the closest backup?'

'Everybody is still out at the sawmill, or close to it. I can get somebody to meet you there.'

'It's fine. I'm going to take a look around.'

'By yourself?'

'If you don't hear from me in five minutes, let Hutch know.'

With my headache still raging, but with the Adderall kicking in, I grab a flashlight and head out of the car. The Kelly farmhouse should have been bulldozed after the fire, but nobody could figure out whose job that ought to be – the same way nobody could figure out who'd care one way or the other. Every direction I point the flashlight shows poisoned earth. The fire that took this place was never reported at the time, and it burned itself out. I do a perimeter, shining the flashlight into what remains of the house. I shine it into the trees and the fields – there's nobody here. I remember that when I came here after the fire, I went down into a basement, where the wooden steps had survived the blaze. Taking them felt like descending into a coal mine. I pick my way through the damage and find them again now, and when I take them that feeling doesn't change. I light the basement up. Four cinderblock walls, a wooden ceiling, some of it damaged, some of it okay, shelving with all kinds of junk, Christmas lights spilling out of a box covered in dust and ash, the bulbs having popped in the heat.

There's a chest freezer against the wall and an old TV with a busted tube on the floor.

There's nobody out here.

I head back outside.

Chapter Twenty-Three

On the TV in his hospital room, a live report is coming from the sawmill. Both Lucas and his dad are watching it, but for Lucas, the events of the afternoon are taking their toll. There is a heaviness to his body, one so strong it's trying to pull him through the bed and into the floor. He feels like he is watching the TV from the bottom of a well. He could sleep for a week – or would, if it wasn't for his hand. Was the itch this bad when he had stitches last time? He can't remember. The more he tries to ignore it, the worse it gets. He has serious doubts he'll make it through the night without tearing into the bandaging and scratching at the cut.

He doesn't recognise the reporter on the TV because he doesn't watch the news, so he doesn't know if it's somebody local, or from out of town. The story will have gone national on account of what the reporter is saying about other boys in other parts of the country who the janitor hurt. Two of them, it seems, but there are no names or ages. The sawmill looks like an aircraft hangar. The entire scene is lit up with floodlights that burn away the colour and destroy the shadows. There are fire trucks and firefighters, police and police cars, search and rescue, and dogs, and people wearing bright orange vests all moving back and forth. How can the janitor still be on the loose when half of the town is out there looking for him?

He turns to the window, and for the briefest of moments he's expecting the janitor's face to be pressed against the glass, but given they're on the second storey of a three-storey building, it's not going to happen, unless Grove can fly. His dad is watching the TV intently, his hands shaking. They shake like this on the days when he is doing his best to be sober. Which isn't often. Mostly his dad sits in front of his computer, panicking about the fact he hasn't produced a novel in the last few years, complaining how the great ideas have all been taken. There's no doubt in Lucas's mind that the first thing his dad is going to do when he gets home tonight is have a drink, and the second thing will be to repeat the first. In fact, it's a miracle he's still here.

Freddy Holt's photograph comes up on the TV. Lucas shivers – looking at the picture he sees what could have been his future. Instead of being in hospital right now, he could have been—

'You okay?' his dad asks.

How to even begin answering that question? 'I would have been the next missing boy.'

'But you're not. That's all you need to think about.'

But what he's thinking about is what Freddy went through. What it must have been like. The fear, the confusion, the pain, the blood. For Freddy there was nobody to show up at the last moment to save him.

He comes back to his dad's original question, one he'll be asked a lot as the days march on. Is he okay? Well he survived, and he survived well. Compared to a hundred other alternatives, then yes, he's okay, and will continue to be.

Two more photographs come up. They are now naming Grove's previous victims. Harry Waltz, who went missing, and Eric Delany, whose body was found. Two more alternate timelines unable to be broken by the kind of luck Lucas had earlier. In each case there's a thirty-thousand-dollar reward for information leading to an arrest. Then it's back to the sawmill and aerial footage shot from a drone. It's believed Grove fled on foot into the forest, and that Freddy Holt is out there somewhere, in the ground. A photograph of Taylor Reed comes up, taken long before thoughts of jumping to his death would consume him. Are they connecting the janitor to that too? Most people, Lucas included, thought Freddy Holt was responsible for that, but maybe most people were wrong.

'He's got nowhere to hide,' his dad says.

'Except for miles and miles of forest,' Lucas says.

'Getting in there is one thing,' Sheriff Cohen says, stepping into the room. He's holding a bloody shirt up to his head, and there's blood over his T-shirt too. He leans slowly against the door, grimacing as he does so. 'Getting out is another. He'll probably get lost in there and die of thirst.'

'What happened to you?' Lucas asks, shocked to see him looking so rough. There was nothing in the news about that.

'Grove clocked me pretty good out there,' Sheriff Cohen says. 'The son of a bitch ambushed me with a piece of rebar before turning tail.'

'You were lucky,' his dad says.

Sheriff Cohen pulls the shirt away from his head to look at the blood on it, and Lucas can see the side of his head where he took the blow. The skin is badly torn, and there's a large, dark lump. Sheriff Cohen puts the shirt back on it, then says, 'Could have been worse, you're right about that. So, Lucas, how you feeling?'

'I'm also feeling lucky. If you hadn't shown up when you did—'

'You looked like you were doing a pretty good job of handling yourself,' Sheriff Cohen says. 'Grove is the one who was lucky I showed up.'

Lucas knows that's not true, but the sentiment makes him feel like a hero.

'You really think Grove might die of thirst out there?' his dad asks.

'It's doubtful, but the forest can be pretty unforgiving, so who knows. My guess is we'll find him soon.'

'You never did say how you found me,' Lucas says. 'Dad told me about how you found the locker, but what after that?'

Cohen fills in the blanks. Grove's house, furniture, an auction website. Lucas gets the sense there are things he's not telling him, but he's too tired to care. Then Cohen gives a brief outline of his escape – twisting a screw into a drawer handle, stabbing the janitor in the eye with it, smashing the window, the burning car, the leap with the mattress. Some of this he thinks he told the sheriff earlier out at the mill, or maybe he told the deputy in the car, or maybe he didn't mention any of it at all. He can remember every little detail up until his head was bashed in the parking lot.

'I'm heading back out there once I get this taken care of,' Cohen says, pointing to his wound, 'but I'm going to come see you tomorrow morning, okay? To go over everything that happened to you, if you're all right with that.'

'At school?'

'At your home. Doctor told me you'll be off for at least a few days, but I'm sure nobody would object if you took the entire week off.'

Lucas hadn't thought about that. He could sleep for that entire week. 'Almost makes everything I went through worth it.'

Sheriff Cohen laughs. Then he grimaces – something must hurt – and he nods slowly, and he says, 'Listen, Lucas, there's one more thing I need to ask you. Deputy Hutchison said that you told her Grove killed Freddy Holt.'

He doesn't remember telling her that, but he does remember Grove confessing to it. 'He did.'

'He say where?'

'He didn't tell me much about it, but he said I would end up like him if I … you know … if I struggled.'

'Okay. We'll talk more about this tomorrow too. For now I'll leave you be.' He turns to leave, pauses, then turns back. 'Actually, there is something else. Who put you into the locker?'

Lucas looks at his hand and fiddles with the edge of the bandage. His dad asked him this earlier too, and he told his dad he couldn't remember, that the blow to his head had fuzzed up the details. And the truth is some of those details *are* fuzzy. But he knows who put him into the locker. 'I'm not sure.'

'You're not sure? Or you're not sure you want to tell me?'

'It's all fuzzy. I'm sorry.'

'Try to think,' his dad says.

'Even if I could remember,' Lucas says, 'would it change you finding the janitor?'

'It won't change that,' Sheriff Cohen says, 'but this is serious, Lucas. The student or students who did this need to be reprimanded.'

Reprimanded. What does that even mean? He's seen students complain to teachers about bullying, and their tormentors are taken aside and warned, only to double down the next day. Teachers ought to be honest. They ought to hang up signs at the school telling you to keep your mouth shut because things will only get worse.

'Lucas?'

'Will they go to jail?'

'So it was more than one person?'

'I don't know. It could have been. Would they be expelled?'

Sheriff Cohen sighs heavily. 'If you're worried they're going to hurt you some more, I can promise you they won't.'

If Sheriff Cohen honestly believes that, then it means everything else he says and believes can't be trusted. And in this case it's even worse, because the boy who shoved him into that locker is Nathan Cohen, Sheriff Cohen's son. Nathan, who on other occasions has tipped rubbish bins over him, or held his head in a toilet bowl, or pushed him off his bike or let the tires down. Nathan, who has laughed at him, shoved him, tripped him, slapped him, threatened him...

'Lucas?'

Mocked him, spat on him, pissed on his school bag, Nathan who has called him loser, bitch, dick wad, shit stain, paedophile, pussy – an endless selection, sometimes the same thing, sometimes something new, but always something. What's the best-case scenario from telling Sheriff Cohen any of this? That he arrests his own son? That's never going to happen. There is no best-case scenario. There may not be any more lockers in Lucas's future, but Nathan will be sure to make Lucas's life a day-to-day misery.

'I'll tell you if I can remember.'

'That's the best I can ask for. Oh, and I almost forgot,' Sheriff Cohen says, and he reaches into his pocket and pulls out a phone. Lucas's cellphone. He hands it to him, and Lucas taps the screen. It lights up with missed calls and messages. 'Get some rest and I'll come and see you in the morning.'

Chapter Twenty-Four

A nurse leads me into a room and sits me on the edge of the bed. I ask her how Lucas was when he first came in. She tells me he had a concussion, that they stitched up his hand and tidied up the wound on the back of his head. She confirms they are keeping him overnight, but all in all, he's in good shape. Then she goes about washing my face and wound with cotton swabs and disinfectant. The bump on the side of my forehead turns to fire when she swabs it.

'You should see the other guy,' I tell her.

'You didn't drive here by yourself, did you?'

'Are you going to stop treating me if I tell you I did?'

She frowns at me and tells me driving here was stupid. I tell her I'm impatient to be on my way. Which I am. I don't tell her about my ribs because I can't afford the time. I want to get back out to the sawmill. I glance at my watch. Then glance at it again a minute later. I'm tempted to ask the nurse to put a Band-Aid on my head and let me go – which, as it turns out, is pretty much what she does. Except for the letting me go bit. She tells me I don't need stitches, but I will need to stay in here for a few more hours to be monitored for a concussion.

'I need to get back out there.'

'What you need is to rest.'

'What I need is to find this guy before he hurts anybody else.'

'I know you want to get out there, but...'

She tapers off when Peter Connor comes into the room.

'Sorry, but do you have a few more minutes?' he asks.

'I'll leave you two alone,' the nurse says, 'but I'll be back. Our conversation isn't over.'

She walks out, leaving me alone with Peter. This is where he will thank me for finding his son, before berating me for not taking him seriously enough, fast enough.

'Listen, Peter, if you're here—'

'Lucas remembered something that might be helpful.'

'Let's go.'

I follow Peter back into Lucas's room. The corridor seems to have steadied since I last walked it. My system is swimming in enough Adderall to get me through the rest of the night.

Lucas looks nervous. 'Do people know I was naked when you found me?' he asks.

I'm not sure where he's going with this. 'Only Deputy Hutchison,' I say, then think on it for another moment. 'The paramedics too, and the doctors who helped you, but that's it. It won't be made public.'

'So nobody will find out?'

'There is no reason for them to.'

Lucas chews on that for a few moments. I'm eager to prompt him so I can make my exit, but I wait him out. The way he's looking, I get the sense this is going to be important.

'If it gets into the news, people will ... well, you know what people are like,' Lucas says.

'I do. Is that why you wanted to see me again?'

'No. Well, yes and no. I mean, if people found out at school what happened, I could never show my face there again. But ... there was a camera.'

'What?'

'The caretaker was filming us.' Lucas can't look at either of us as he says this, choosing instead to focus on his bandaged hand. He's turning red too. This is a lot for anybody to handle, let alone a teenager. 'He was going to, you know. I mean … you know what he was going to do, and he was going to film it.'

I think of the videos I saw on Grove's computer earlier. I feel sick. The other boys he's killed, did he film them too? Is Freddy Holt's murder on tape?

Lucas carries on. 'He said he was going to let me go after, and that if I ever told, he would put it online.'

Peter is pacing the room. He looks like he needs a drink. 'Jesus.'

'He said it was different for Freddy, because he didn't own a camera back then.'

Meaning he just bought it. 'Where was it?'

'It was in the office with the mattress. It's what I threw at the window to break it.'

'Did it go through or bounce back in?'

'It came back in. Everything he said about Freddy will be on it, if it didn't get burned.'

I break out in a cold chill thinking about it. 'If it survived, I'll find it.'

'Maybe they've found it already,' Peter says.

'Nobody will be going into the mill until it's been signed off by the fire department, which will be later tonight, but I'll find it. I'm sorry you had to go through that, Lucas, I really am. We'll get this guy, I promise, but for now I need you to keep what he said about Freddy to yourself, okay?'

'Okay.'

'I mean it, Lucas. And that goes for you too, Peter. Not a word.'

They both promise me they won't say a thing.

Chapter Twenty-Five

I step into the parking lot, where pale orbs of streetlight bounce off the cars, and squirrels play in the bushes. I have to lean against a couple of cars as I make my way back to mine. My head is spinning, rather than bobbing along on the waves of a headache – the nurse gave me a shot for the pain the moment I showed up, before giving me a week's supply of non-expired painkillers. Thankfully none of the doctors or nurses chase me down for skipping out early. I sit down in my cruiser and call Hutch.

'What did the doctor say?' she asks.

'Not to get hit in the head anymore, but I've been cleared and I'm on my way back. Where are we at with Grove?'

'Search and rescue are scouring the forest. The dogs haven't picked anything up, instead they've gone in circles around the parking lot. They may as well be chasing their tails.'

'Could the smoke from the fire be putting them off?'

'The handlers don't think so. They think if there's something to find, the dogs would find it. It doesn't make sense. It's like Grove vanished into thin air. You think maybe Bigfoot got him?'

'If he did, we owe him a beer. What about the fire?'

'It's been under control for the last hour. The fire department wants to make sure the roof won't fall in on us. They got an engineer going through it now.'

I wonder if it's the same engineer who looked at my house. 'Okay. Don't go in there till I get there, okay?'

'Copy that.'

The lights in my house are on when I get home. I park up on the driveway and head in. The doors and windows are open, but there's still a smell of smoke. Cassandra steps out of Dad's bedroom and freezes when she sees me.

'What happened to you?'

'It was nothing.'

'Doesn't look like nothing,' she says, coming toward me for a closer look.

'The hospital says I'm okay, and I feel fine.'

'What happened?'

'First, how's Dad?'

'I just put him to bed. He's already forgotten the fire. He's getting worse, James.'

'I know.'

'We need to find somewhere for him.'

'I'm working on it.'

'Are you?'

I head into the kitchen, where the smell of smoke is stronger. The ceiling right above the stove is mostly intact, but it looks like it's been hosed down with charcoal. The same for the wall. The stove is black, and the benchtop has delaminated itself as it's twisted itself out of shape. The upper kitchen cabinets on either side of the stove have also been damaged. Yes, I'm thankful my family are okay, and yes, this could have been far worse, but fuck, when are things going to get better?

'You or Dad?' I ask, nodding toward the fire-extinguisher – spent – on the table. I had a couple put throughout the house when Dad arrived.

'Me,' she says. 'Your dad was back watching TV when it happened. He didn't even notice the smoke pouring into the lounge. The smoke alarm was going too. Nathan didn't hear it over his game.'

I stare at the damage, and I can't compute it. I don't know how to get this to fit in with all the other problems, so I do the next best thing, and I turn my back on it and head to the bedroom.

'Lucas said that Grove admitted to killing Freddy Holt,' I say, as Cass follows me.

Her hands go to her mouth. 'Jesus. Is he sure?'

'He seemed so. He also said that Grove was filming everything, and that his confession will be on camera.'

'Those poor boys,' she says. 'And Freddy ... I can't imagine what his family must be going through. Have you spoken to them?'

'Not yet,' I say, getting a fresh T-shirt from the wardrobe. 'Outside of Lucas and Peter, and now you, nobody knows.'

'I'll keep it to myself. Do you want Nathan to stay with me this week? I'm guessing nobody is going to want to rest until they have this monster in custody.'

'Would that be okay?'

'Of course.'

I strip out of my bloody T-shirt. There's a red line running across the bottom of my chest, a few inches thick going from one side to the other, so straight and horizontal that I could be used to level a pool table. It's tender and puffy and I expect by tomorrow morning it will be both of those things and more, and the red will have gone to purple.

'Oh my God,' Cass says.

'It's fine,' I tell her, pulling on the fresh T-shirt. 'I'll call Deborah and see if she can come here tonight, that way you can take Nathan home soon.'

'I don't mind staying tonight and we can leave in the morning.'

'I know, but it's a lot to ask of you, and if I'm being honest I'm pissed off at Nathan for not keeping an eye on Dad like I asked.'

'This wasn't Nathan's fault, James.'

'I didn't say it was.'

'And insurance will cover any damage.'

'No, it won't.'

'What?'

'It became unaffordable after the insurance company learned Dad was moving in.'

'You're kidding.'

'I wish I was.'

'Why didn't you tell me?' she asks, and she sounds angry. 'I could have helped.'

'You could have helped by staying,' I say, and immediately I regret the words, especially since I didn't mean them. 'Jesus, Cass, I'm sorry.'

'It's fine,' she says, but it's clear it's not.

'I didn't mean it.'

'It's fine.'

'Cass...'

'I said it's fine. Just be careful when you go back out there tonight, okay? You don't look good.'

I reach up and touch the side of my head where I took the blow.

'I don't just mean that, James. You look out of it.'

'I'm just tired, that's all. I need to talk to Nathan.'

'It wasn't his fault, James.'

'I know, but I want to check in on him. Does he know anything about what's been happening this afternoon?'

'He knows you're looking for somebody, but he doesn't know who, or why.'

I head to Nathan's room and knock on the door. I don't wait for an answer, because I know I wouldn't get one, so just head in.

'Scary day,' I say. 'You okay?'

'Okay apart from Grandpa trying to kill us? Sure.' He looks up from the computer. 'What happened to you?'

'It's a work thing. Let me ask you something,' I say, stepping further into his room. 'You know Lucas Connor? He's a student at your school.'

He freezes for a moment, then he looks back down at his computer. He keeps looking at it as we speak, like life beyond the monitor doesn't matter, and for Nathan maybe it doesn't.

'Nathan?'

'I don't know.'

'You don't know?'

'I mean, sure, I know who he is, but I don't really know him.'

'You ever talk to him?'

He fiddles with the keyboard and mouse, shooting bad guys taking over the world. Or maybe he's shooting the good guys. I'm not sure what he'd enjoy more.

'Nathan?'

'What?'

'Do you ever talk to Lucas Connor?'

There is gunfire and people yelling and sirens in the background, and Nathan keeps tapping at the keys. I have the urge to pull the power cord out, and perhaps that's what a better parent would do.

'Nathan?'

'No, I don't talk to him. Why would I? He's weird.'

'In what way?'

'I don't know,' Nathan says. He sighs heavily and slides the keyboard away. 'You happy now? You got me killed.'

'Tell me what you mean about Lucas being weird.'

He rolls his eyes and sighs heavily again in case I had missed it the first time. 'He's weird, you know, the way some people are. Everybody thinks so. It's why he has no friends. Is it really that important?'

'Lucas was almost killed today.' He stares at me. I finally have his attention. I carry on before I lose it. 'Somebody put him into a locker at school and left him there. He was found by the janitor, but we now know the janitor at your school is a sexual predator who has likely killed other children.'

The colour drains out of him. His eyes go big and his mouth hangs open. The death and violence he likes to surround himself within his video games have just taken a step into the real world.

'The janitor drugged Lucas and took him out to the old sawmill.'

Nathan doesn't look like he could talk even if he wanted to. He looks like a kid who got caught with a box of matches out front of a burning building.

'You wouldn't know anything about who put him in the locker?'

He slowly shakes his head. He goes to say something, still can't, swallows loudly, then gives it another go. 'Is ... is he okay?'

'Just.'

'He ... Did he get raped, or anything?' Nathan asks, and there's something in his voice, something that sounds like fear.

'No. He saved himself by putting up one hell of a fight. If I'd gotten there thirty seconds later he'd be dead.'

Nathan stares blankly at me.

'What started as a shitty prank almost got him killed, and if that had happened, we'd be looking at charging whoever put him into that locker. In fact, we still may look at charging that person anyway.'

I watch him closely as he lets that sink in. I don't say anything, knowing with everything he's just heard he will want to fill in the silence.

Sure enough, he does. 'Does that mean you don't know who it was?'

'We're looking into it.'

I study my son's body language. His shaking hands. The way he can't look at me. All the little tics and movements of a teenager freaking out on the inside. The tics and movements of a teenager lying. I think right now he has his own heavy ball of guilt in his stomach, his own short-circuiting brain. I can understand why, if Nathan was responsible for this, Lucas didn't want to tell me. He figured I might not do anything about it, or it would only make things worse. But I've seen the changes in my son, this nastiness that has taken hold of him. It's gotten worse since my dad moved in. It's been a constant subject for both Cass and myself. We've discussed getting counselling for him, but he's dead set against it. We'd push the point with him and enforce it if we could afford to pay for the sessions. I've seen the way other kids take wide berths around him, the way they look at him. When we were interviewing kids at school about Freddy Holt, we learned that Freddy wasn't the only kid known to shove others around. Nathan had a reputation of his own too. But I still believe he hasn't reached the tipping point yet, that he can still be a good kid.

'Why are you looking at me like that?' he asks.

'Like what?'

'Like I had something to do with it. I didn't put him in the locker.'

'I'm not saying you did. But do you know who might have?'

He shakes his head.

'Thing is, whoever put Lucas in there must have known there was a chance nobody would find him. Is that what they wanted? For

Lucas Connor to be in there all night as a laugh? Who at school would do that?'

'I didn't do it, Dad.'

'I'm not saying you did, but my advice would be that whoever put him into that locker would be better off avoiding him from now on.'

He throws his arms up. 'How many times do I have to tell you it wasn't me?'

'You'd tell me if you knew who did?'

'Probably not,' Nathan says, which is likely the only honest thing he's said this entire conversation.

'I'm heading back out. There's a manhunt on. Pack a bag because you're going to your mom's for the next few days.'

'Fine. Whatever. I don't want to be here anyway.'

'Call me if you need anything,' I add, and Nathan grunts an acknowledgment, his eyes already back on the computer. I want to unplug it and toss it through the window. Instead I close the door and leave him be.

Chapter Twenty-Six

Lucas is finally starting to drift off to sleep – his dad having left ten minutes ago – when his phone goes, bringing him back into the world of itchy hands and serial killers. He doesn't recognise the number. It could be a reporter – his dad said earlier not to be surprised if they reached out, though how they'd get his number he doesn't know. He's tempted not to answer it, but what if it's Sheriff Cohen, telling him they've caught the janitor? Or more importantly, ringing to warn him the janitor has been spotted in the foyer of the hospital?

'Hello?' The word feels thick in his mouth, and takes longer to come out than it should.

Nobody answers, but he can sense somebody there. It could be a wrong number, or a crank caller – maybe the janitor himself, an *I'm coming for you* call – but what the point of that would be he doesn't know.

He gives it another go. 'Hello?'

'You tell my dad it was me?'

They've never spoken on the phone, but he recognises Nathan's voice.

'I didn't tell him anything,' Lucas says, wanting to hang up, wanting this over, wanting the janitor to have snatched Nathan this afternoon instead of himself, but the world doesn't work like that, does it.

'You better not,' Nathan says, keeping his voice low and menacing. 'Not unless you want me to shove a broken baseball bat up your arse. I swear I'll do it too if you don't keep your mouth shut.'

Lucas doesn't say anything. This is just what he needs – Nathan threatening him at the end of what has been the worst day of his life.

'You hear me?'

Maybe he should have rolled the dice and told Sheriff Cohen. He still could. Or ... or he can acknowledge that this morning's Lucas has evolved. This morning's Lucas would take the insults, the mocking, the shoves and the pushes and the slaps and the punches, but this afternoon's Lucas won't. This afternoon's Lucas fought off a killer and survived, and that means he can survive Nathan too. He gets off the bed and walks over to the window. At first all he can see is his reflection looking back, a tired Lucas with eyes half closed. He can see the lights from the hospital room glowing around him, but as he gets closer to the window the angle changes and he can see down into the parking lot. His dad is down there in his car, drinking a beer. So much for going straight home. Lucas is disappointed. Not with his dad, but in himself for thinking it would be any different.

'You there?' Nathan asks.

'I'm here.'

'You think I'm tough on you now? You have no idea. You say one word and I will shit down your throat. I mean it. I will end you.'

'Are you done?' Lucas asks.

Silence for a few seconds as Nathan's rage builds. 'What did you just say to me?'

'You've made your point, and I've told you I'm not going to say anything, and I won't. But I'm tired, and we're done here.'

Nathan seems unsure of what to say. He's gotten everything he wants, so what else is there? Other than to keep insulting Lucas? 'You really are a loser. You know that, right?'

For years he might have been. But not now. 'Goodbye, Nathan.'

'You—' Nathan says, but Lucas doesn't hear the rest, because he hangs up.

He stays at the window. Nathan wouldn't really try any of what he threatened. Words like that – they're just words.

His dad crushes the empty can and tries to lob it into a garbage bin ten yards away, and manages to miss by five. He drives out of the parking lot, clipping the kerb of the garden on the way. He'll make it home fine. He always does.

Lucas switches off his phone and heads back to bed.

Chapter Twenty-Seven

The lights of Acacia fade behind me, and ahead my headlights cut arcs through the darkness of the highway, creating a tunnel of light that touches the edges of the forest. I reach the roadblock short of the sawmill and pull over. I get lit up, then waved through. I reach the sawmill. It's a hive of activity. A command post has been set up, maps are no longer spread across the hoods of cars but across truss tables in a large, open tent. Laptops are displaying aerial views of the surroundings, dots slowly moving across them representing the folks out there searching, each of them carrying GPS units, all of them in teams. There are remote-control drones parked up along one edge of the tent, too dark to be used now, but they would have been in operation earlier. The two fire trucks are still out here, but they're no longer pumping water into the building. Mostly the firefighters are walking the scene, checking to make sure the flames aren't secretly brewing anywhere. I can smell smoke even though I can't see any. Flashlights flicker through the trees as officers look for evidence as to which way Grove fled, flattening the earth and busting fronds in all directions. The air is full of conversation, no longer as urgent as it was before I left. Hutch looks tired. Everybody does. Earlier in the evening everybody was amped. Adrenaline levels were redlining. Now they're the walking dead.

'You look awful,' Hutch says, when I get out of my car.

'Thanks. Where are we at?'

'Employment records from the school show Grove took a week off work the same week Eric Delany was murdered.'

'Jesus.'

'He's taken other vacations too, so we need to look at other missing or murdered children from across the country.'

'How many?'

'Every year since he started working at the school, and we need to look at his other jobs too, before he started working at the school, and when he took time off from those.'

'Christ. I almost don't know what to say to any of this.'

'Harry Waltz, the boy who went missing ten years ago, disappeared days before Grove moved – or fled – to Acacia Pines. Given Grove had planned a vacation next week...'

'I get it.'

'I know you do, but everything that happened today has saved whoever that next child was going to be. It's ironic.'

'What is?'

'I mean, I say this on the basis that Lucas is going to be okay, and of course nobody should ever have to go through what he went through, but whoever stuffed Lucas into that locker saved that future boy.'

She's right. Nathan, in his meanness, has done the world a favour. 'I hadn't thought of it like that.'

'As far as having any idea which way he went,' she says, 'there's no sign of him. The dogs are out there chasing their tails. Best guess is he hit the highway after he knocked you out, and I missed him. It was a narrow window, but doable. He could have hitched a ride in one direction while I was driving in the other.'

'Makes sense.'

'You switched cars,' she says, looking at mine.

'I figured Grove might be willing to try and carjack somebody, and he wouldn't try that with a police vehicle.'

'Good thinking,' she says. 'But risky without a gun.'

I pat my hip where there ought to be a holster and a gun. 'Jesus, I didn't even think of that,' I say.

'You should be in hospital,' she says.

'If Grove has managed—'

'Seriously, Sheriff, speaking as your friend, you really shouldn't be here. Coming back like that, using yourself as bait and without a gun, that's ... well, there's no easy way of putting it, but that was a dumb thing to do. Last thing we need is you making poor decisions.'

I pinch the bridge of my nose and close my eyes for a few seconds. The headache waves aren't back, but I can feel the tide rising.

'You're right, but I'm staying. As I was saying, if Grove managed to get a ride, we need to figure who with, and which way he went. For all we know he might have gone into town, and not away from it.'

She frowns. She bites her bottom lip. 'I didn't see anybody go toward town after I first got here.'

'Maybe he got past the roadblock on foot.'

'Come on, surely he's putting as much distance between us and him as he can.'

'You're talking about a guy who doesn't see the world the same way we see it. For all we know he's gone back into town to hole up somewhere, and recover and plan his revenge. He could have found an empty house, or worse, could have control over one with people still in it. He might be waiting for things to die down so he can drive out of here in a week or two.'

Even under the floodlights I can see Hutch pale at the thought.

'Shit,' she says. 'You're right. Guess it's a good thing you're here.'

I carry on. 'We need folks letting us know if there are people not showing up for work, not showing up for school or brunches or outings. People need to keep an eye out for any suspicious activity. Report any houses where curtains are closed during the day or letters are piling up in the mailbox. That kind of thing. Make it clear we don't want people approaching those houses, but to let us know. We want neighbours calling neighbours to check in on them.'

'Grove would force whoever answers the phone to say everything is okay,' she says.

'Yeah, but we still have to do it.'

'Do you really think he's gone back into town?' Her face tightens as if the very question is causing her pain.

I look up at the sky, as if I can gauge an answer from up there. Small towns have big skies, and big cities have small ones. It's the light pollution that hides the beauty of it all, but out here the sky is all diamonds and darkness. I remember early dates with Cassandra when we'd have picnics in the evening, and we'd lie on blankets and stare up at the night sky and tell each other about our dreams. Life was great back then, and despite everything that's gone on, I still hold on to the hope we can get back there.

'We can't afford to think he hasn't.'

A firefighter comes over. He's a thin guy who would break in half if hit by a blast from the hose. He tells us the engineer is satisfied the building isn't going to collapse on us, and that if we want to take a look around we can. Lights have been set up inside. Dust and ash swirl through the air. We wear facemasks to avoid breathing it in. The burnt-out car looks like it dragged itself from a tar pit and shook itself dry. There's no way to tell what colour it used to be. Blackened paint hangs from it like scales. The tires have melted, so it's sitting on its rims. The windows have broken and the interior has burned down to the nuts and bolts and springs. We check out the office where Lucas was held. The mattress snagged over the windowsill earlier is now lying on the floor. Everything – the mattress, the furniture still in the office – the walls and the car and the floor, is soaking with water. Grove's overalls and shoes are burned up on the ground, along with the rest of what he was wearing.

'He's definitely still naked,' Hutch says, noticing them at the same time.

I scan the floor and spot the camera, but at the same time Hutch spots it too. It's blackened and twisted and melted some, but still recognisable. She snaps on a pair of latex gloves, picks it up and doesn't try to turn it on because the power button has fused.

'It belongs to Grove,' I tell her.

'How can you know that for sure?'

'Lucas told me. He said Grove was filming him, and you're right – he also said that Grove confessed to killing Freddy Holt.' I nod toward the camera. 'It will all be on there.'

'You're only telling me this now?'

'Sorry.'

She looks at me as though she's about to revert back to her earlier statement that I shouldn't be here. The tide keeps rising, and to make things worse, the Adderall seems to be wearing off. I've already promised myself not to take any more today, and I intend to keep it.

'Look, it was pretty much up next on my list of things to say.'

'Uh huh. You sure you're up for this?'

'I'm sure. I'll take it down to the station and get Rick to take a look at it. Maybe he can get something from it.'

She turns it upside down and pops open the bottom. The memory card inside looks like it just came out of the packet. She drops it into a small plastic bag. 'There's no reason we can't watch it now. It's the same card our cameras take.'

'I think it's best we take it in for Rick. I don't want to risk corrupting the card.'

'But if it was filming, it might have caught something that can help us figure out where Grove went. I think it's worth the risk.'

'We can't risk losing any of that data.'

'The card is undamaged, and this guy is out there, Sheriff. We need to look. Time isn't on our side here.'

We head out to her car. She keeps a camera in her glove compartment. We all do, for when we need to snap a photo of an accident or an incident. The cameras are not a lot bigger than a deck of cards, but take a much higher-quality photo than our cellphones. She switches out the memory card with the one we just found.

The tide breaks, and the waves roll in, gentle for the moment, but that will change.

'You don't look so good,' she says.

'Yeah, you said that already, but it's not that. If Grove was using the camera to keep Lucas quiet, then he may have done the same with the others. His other vacations might be on there.'

She nods, but doesn't say anything.

'These things can't be unseen, Hutch.'

'I know.'

I pull on a pair of gloves. 'Here,' I say, and I put my hand out for the camera.

'I can...'

'No. Let me check it first.'

No argument from Hutch. She hands me the camera. I get into my car and close the door. Hutch paces the ground a few feet ahead of me. I go into the play settings, and can see that there's only one file, which is a relief. I press play. The office comes into view. The window isn't broken yet and the mattress is on the floor.

There's the sound of shuffling footsteps, and then Lucas is shoved onto the mattress. Grove rolls Lucas over and puts a knee in his back and cuts away his jeans.

'Don't be embarrassed that you wet yourself. My dad, well, he'd have

laughed at you for it, but not me. It's one of the reasons I hated him so much.'

Grove goes on to tell him that he killed his own father. Lucas tells Grove he's grateful to have been let out of the locker, and that he won't tell anybody what happened since. Grove agrees, but not until after Lucas has helped him.

'Help you how?'

'I share it with you, and it softens some, and I share it again, and it softens some more. You see, the pieces keep getting smaller.'

'I don't understand.'

Nor do I. Grove tells Lucas he's going to let him go. Then adds,

'The camera makes it different this time. I didn't have it for your friend. What was his name again? Wasn't it Freddy? It was different for him, but I have it for you. It's how we can trust each other. See, you'll never say anything to anybody about what happens out here, because if you do everything I record goes out over the Internet. You wouldn't want that, would you? But your friend – I didn't own a camera back then, so I wasn't able to give him that option. It's a pity really, but it is why I couldn't let him go.'

Jesus, he really did do it.

'Please, you don't need to do this,' Lucas says.

'That's where you're wrong. This will soften the pain.'

'I still don't understand.'

'You will. After.'

Lucas throws up over himself, and the janitor leaves the room.

Lucas rolls under the desk, where he stays out of view for a minute before rolling back. This is where he gets the screw and handle he uses as a weapon. After Grove returns and pours water over him, Lucas lashes out, stabbing Grove in the eye. Grove staggers away and the camera hits the floor. There's nothing to see for a few more moments, then the footage becomes wild as Lucas throws the camera at the window. There's nothing again for a few minutes, though I can hear the car starting and stopping, then driving and hitting the wall and stalling. Lucas comes running back into the room and makes his escape, but Grove doesn't follow, finding another way out of the building instead – most likely the door I found open.

The view disappears as smoke fills the room, and soon all that can be seen is a thick black haze until the camera dies. I get out of the car.

'It's the only file on there,' I say, handing the camera to Hutch, 'and it's safe.'

She watches the footage, and I watch it again with her.

'What do you think he means about softening the pain?' she asks when it's finished.

'I have no idea. There could be other videos hidden on his computer,' I say. 'Or other memory cards hidden somewhere around his house.'

'If it's true about the camera being new, this could be the first time it was used.' She hesitates for a few moments, then adds, 'Somebody is going to have to look through the videos you already found on his computer.'

'I know,' I say, just as I know it will end up being me. How can I ask Hutch, or anybody else in the department, to do this? 'I'll do it tomorrow.'

'So now what?'

'Now we keep the search going. Let's give it till midnight. Hopefully we'll have found Grove. Hopefully he can tell us everything we need to know and then nobody will ever have to look at those videos again.'

Chapter Twenty-Eight

We don't give it to midnight like I suggested. Instead we pull the pin at eleven o'clock. By then teams are coming in from the forest anyway, all of them dejected, all of them thinking that if there was anything to find, the dogs would have found it. We all agree that

Grove found a way out of here that wasn't by foot, but that doesn't mean there won't be another search out here tomorrow. They pack up. The firefighters stay to make sure nothing is going to flare up. They say if Grove comes by, he'd be a fool to tangle with them. I don't doubt it, but I have a couple of deputies stay with them anyway, partly to protect them, and partly to guard the tent where all the equipment for the search is being kept overnight. Even small towns have big problems with theft.

The dog handlers are the first to leave. Then search and rescue. The media, of which there has been a growing presence, leave right after, now that it's apparent there's no more story out here tonight. I drive back into town, Hutch in the patrol car behind. Sometimes the headlights will catch rabbits or deer or opossums looking back from among the trees, but most of the time the headlights get soaked up by the forest, making it feel like we've driven off the edge of the world. The farms get smaller and the farmhouses get closer to the road as we near town.

We reach the truss bridge on the outskirts, long metal beams and big rivets all freshly painted red. The bridge is a short drive over a long river that comes out of the trees, sweeps across the front of Acacia Pines, then sweeps back in. On the other side of the bridge all signs of life have been put away for the night. There are stores with dim lights in the windows, cold neons outside bars, streetlights with moths swarming them, nobody walking the streets, just the occasional car taking somebody home.

We drive to the home of Mr and Mrs Holt – Freddy's parents. The street is quiet, dark windows everywhere – except for the Holt house, which is all lit up like a plane is coming in to land, a ranch-style house with a big double garage jutting out from the side. I've been here a few times over the last couple of months when their house has been vandalised – *Killer* spraypainted on the walls, their lawns and gardens poisoned off, windows smashed. Whether it was one neighbour involved or all of them we never could figure out.

We've barely stepped onto their property when the front door swings open. Allan Holt steps out onto the porch. He's a solid guy, wearing a shirt with the sleeves rolled up and his tie askew, like he rushed home from work. Julie, his wife, is right on his heels, streaks of mascara around her eyes from wiped-away tears. For two months they have wondered where their son has gone, and today's news might have given them an idea, and seeing us here is no doubt confirming it for them. Allan storms down the path toward me, surrounded by waves of anger. I know what he's about to do, and decide to let him, figuring it will help us move forward quicker, and of course there's a part of me that thinks I have this coming. He swings his fist and I step into it to stop it from reaching full speed, and I turn my head away so he doesn't get me where the rebar did, but rather in the side of the jaw. The effect is immediate. The small waves become big waves, which immediately turn into a tsunami. I stumble back and it takes all my strength not to fall over. Hutch puts her hands on Allan's chest and pushes him back.

'You let everybody think our son bullied that boy into dying,' he yells, pointing at me while letting himself be pushed back by Hutch. 'You let everybody think that, and this whole time – this whole time – he was out there somewhere and you weren't even looking for him.'

'That's not the way it was at all,' Hutch says.

'It's why you're here, isn't it? The janitor from Freddy's school, he did something to him, didn't he?'

'We believe so,' Hutch says, while I can't say a damn thing. I can also barely hear them because of the ringing in my ears. The only way I know Allan is yelling is because he looks like he is. The veins in his neck are tight, and there's one throbbing in his forehead. Coming here is the last thing I wanted to do, but there was no putting it off.

Allan looks ready to launch himself at Hutch, but when Julie puts a hand on his shoulder, the anger drains out of him quickly, and it must be the only thing holding him up because he clutches at her and ends up pulling her down with him, their arms around each other as they sit on the pathway to the house.

'Is our son dead?' Julie asks.

'We believe so,' Hutch replies, then she tells them what Simon Grove said to Lucas, and that there was a camera that confirms it. Julie turns her face into Allan's chest and sobs. Allan holds her, trying to look strong. I avoid the temptation to put my hands on my head to see if it's swelling from the pressure, because it sure feels that way.

'All this time he was dead, and you let everybody think our son was the reason Taylor Reed jumped,' Julie says, her words easier to hear as the ringing starts to fade.

'We can't help what other people think,' Hutch says, and I wish she wouldn't try to defend us.

'No, but you sure as hell didn't put them straight,' Allan says. 'If you had, we wouldn't have had people throwing rocks through our windows. You think Freddy is out there, don't you, buried among the trees?'

'We're going to send teams out there tomorrow to look.'

They ask who could have done something like this. They ask what kind of man could take a boy's life. What kind of monster films himself killing kids. They ask what kind of world we're living in, and Hutch has no answers for them, only assurances that we're going to find Simon Grove, that we're going to find out what he did with Freddy.

'And you,' Allan asks, looking at me. 'You have anything to say, other than you're sorry, and other than you'll get this guy?'

'I know that there's nothing I can say that will make this any better,' I tell them.

'Well at least you got something fucking right,' Allan says. 'I'll tell you what, since you got everything else so badly wrong, then here's something you can do right. When you get the guy who did this, I need you to give me some alone time with him.'

'I can't do that.'

'Five minutes. That's all I'm asking.'

'You know I can't let you do that.'

'You owe us. You goddamn owe us.'

They have to help each other back into the house. Neither of them look human anymore; instead they look like something life chewed up and spat out, nothing left to them but pain and sorrow and anger, and nothing in the future to change any of that.

At the doorway, Allan turns to look at us. 'This is on both of you,' he says. 'On all your department. You'll be hearing from our lawyers.'

*

It's well after midnight when we get to the station. The station doesn't have a lot of shape to it, the kind of building a small kid could draw with a crayon and have their parents recognise. It's rectangular, with a flat roof, brownstone walls, floor-to-ceiling windows lining the front, and big gold letters across those windows spelling out *Acacia Pines Sheriff Office*. The windows are cleaned every week because they become hazy with small-town life, exhaust fumes, and a mixture of saw and quarry dust blown in from the south. At the moment the station is almost abandoned, with only one patrol car parked out front.

We head inside. Sharon is still at her desk. She should have gone home hours ago. She doesn't look tired, or shocked. She's so battle-hardened the station could fall into a sinkhole and she wouldn't blink. She has red-framed glasses hanging from a chain around her neck, and her grey hair is pushed back behind her ears. When she frowns, the wrinkles in her forehead are deep enough to hide a penny.

The confrontation with the Holts has drained me, but I resist the temptation to go into my office and slump behind my desk for a spell. 'You should go home,' I tell Sharon, as I unlock the gun vault.

'Getting ready to. Deputy Wagner is in the bathroom, and has been for the last hour, having eaten something that's disagreed with him, and when that disagreeing ends, he'll take over. How's the jaw?'

'I've had worse.'

I get myself a new handgun. I go into my office and sit on the desk and load it. Hutch follows me. 'I don't know if that was brave or stupid of you letting Holt hit you like that.'

'I don't know either.'

'I feel like going home right now is the wrong thing to do.'

'Go home,' I say. 'You need sleep. We both do. Let's have a press conference in the morning. A lot of people have a lot of questions. We can't keep putting everybody off. You want to handle it?'

'You don't want to do it?'

'Not looking like this,' I say, pointing to my forehead. 'Plus I want to go and see Lucas in the morning.'

'I've never done one before,' she says.

'You'll be great.'

She looks me up and down, and comes to a stop on the gun that I've just holstered. She frowns at me. 'You look like you're heading back out there. You're not going to trawl the highway in the hope he's going to flag you down, are you?'

'Grove isn't out there. He's holed up somewhere, and driving the streets isn't going to find him. We'll get him tomorrow.'

'You think so?'

'Yeah. I think so.'

I watch her walk out the door. I watch through the windows as she drives away.

I double-check my gun is loaded, then I head back out there.

Chapter Twenty-Nine

Slipping in and out of consciousness with his eye hurting beyond anything he has ever experienced, Simon has been thinking about his parents – and how the blame for all of it lies on all of them. From the abuse he's received, to the abuse given, to his punctured eye and hiding out in a freezer that's barely big enough to contain him. His original mom was okay, but his dad was a monster. There were days he'd come home from work and give Simon a toy, and there were days he'd come home and give him the back of his hand. He can plot his years of misfortune and misery back to many turning points, but this was the first and, therefore, the most foundational.

Back then he had a little brother, Jack, who he loved wholeheartedly. Jack, who had a small stutter, who slept with a stuffed rabbit named Charlie, and who was prone to getting colds. His nose was a snot factory, and his arm was part of the production line that transferred that snot to his sleeve, unless it was on strike, which it sometimes was, and on those days Jack's face would crust over with it. Sometimes they would both find that funny, not that their dad ever did. He remembers his dad once slapping Jack's face so hard that their pet dog yelped and took off at such speed it ran head first into the coffee table and knocked over a vase, breaking it, which angered their dad so much they got rid of the dog. Together he and Jack lived in fear of their dad's moods, and he didn't recognise it as a child, but he's sure their mom lived the same way. If she'd been stronger, maybe things would have gone different, not that any of the blame was hers.

The day he and his family died started with waffles at a roadside diner. They were Jack's favourites, and they were Simon's favourites too, and maybe it wasn't an accident that this was where their dad took them. He doesn't remember how the argument started, or even what it was about, but he does remember being dragged to the car and belted into the backseat along with Jack. He remembers his dad driving away erratically and clipping a parked car on the way out of the lot, and he remembers his mom screaming as they steered off the highway a minute later, down the bank toward the water. The splash was loud, the water cold, and the screaming came to a stop as their lungs flooded. It was a stranger who saved him. A man dove in and shattered the back window with a rock and got both him and Jack out – so he was told. He has no memory of it. His parents died at the bottom of the lake. Jack couldn't be saved, but Simon was. He was resuscitated – why the man chose to revive him over Jack he will never know. He was in a coma for a week, and after he came out of it the doctors said they were concerned about potential brain damage. It seemed likely – it just came down to the extent, for which he would be tested. But that testing never took place, not in a system where hospital bills were expensive and there was nobody to pay, a system where kids without parents were routinely dumped into foster care. One day Simon had a family, and the next day he did not.

He was eight years old when he met his second parents, Harold and Irene Lassiter. They were a nice couple who had fostered children for thirty years, who lived on a small farm with two dogs and a handful of sheep and a bigger handful of cows. Four years in, and Harold dropped dead on the kitchen floor from a heart attack, and Irene couldn't raise Simon alone. So he went to live with a new family, Ron and Gloria Gardner, a couple who returned him the same way you would return a TV or a dishwasher that didn't live up to expectations. Simon was difficult, they said, and hell, who wouldn't be after the shit he'd gone through. At the age of twelve, he was fostered to Patrick and Fleur Conningway. The abuse was subtle, at first. Teachers thought he was being kept home from school because he was sick, or he was having issues due to the brain damage from the car accident, but it was none of that. Patrick and Fleur routinely beat the shit out of him, something others discovered after Patrick hit Simon's left hand so badly with an iron that two fingers were shattered and had to be removed. Of course that was when the doctors found the cigarette burns on his arms and chest too.

It only makes sense that the world would continue to beat him down. It's how it balances itself. People think that karma is where good and bad things are balanced out for a person – but that's bullshit. The world balances by having only good things happen to some people, and only bad things to others. For every rock star, there's some kid getting raped in a basement. At thirteen he knew this for an absolute certainty, because he wasn't the rock star. His final parents, Stan and Leigh Clayton, made sure of that.

And here he is again with the universe giving him another big fuck-you. He's in the dark, no sense of time, no sense of place, his eye hurting like a motherfucker and when the surgeons remove it, karma will make sure the procedure doesn't go to plan, or they're out of glass eyeballs at the eyeball store, and he'll be left with a big gaping hole that will stop him from ever getting within a hundred feet of another kid...

The thought grinds to a halt as he hears footsteps coming his way. He holds his breath and tries to focus. All he can hear is his heartbeat. Maybe he made a mistake and didn't hear steps at all. Maybe—

No, there they are again. Footsteps, getting closer, louder. The freezer lid is propped open an inch, held in place so he doesn't suffocate. He shifts his weight and puts his good eye to the thin gap – but can't see anything.

A moment later something loud is being removed from above him, and a moment after that the lid is ripped open. Having spent hours in the dark, his hands tied behind him, his ankles locked to his wrists, he's immediately blinded by the flashlight. He looks up and, having been able to work the duct tape around from his mouth, he asks Sheriff Cohen the big question...

'Why?'

Day Two

Chapter Thirty

By seven a.m., I'm heading to Saint John's with my dad, a church that once used to be in the centre of town, until town started being pushed and pulled in different directions as it expanded. The church can fit a few hundred people, but I can't imagine it ever filling all those seats in one go again unless Jesus himself showed up to run the meat raffle. The weatherboards have been freshly painted and the gardens freshly watered, the whole thing looking picture perfect. I used to come here as a child, dragged along by parents who tried to instil a sense of religion in me, but it didn't take. They kept on coming, and my dad's faith never wavered, not even when Mom dropped dead of a brain aneurysm at the age of fifty-six. Nor did it waver when the doctors told us to brace ourselves because things were going to get tough.

We park in the lot out front, and walk around to the back, Dad shuffling a little. I did manage to get a couple of hours of sleep after I got back from the Kelly farm last night, but it was fitful. Right now I've got both painkillers and Adderall helping me put one foot in front of the other.

We enter the small community space where nativity plays are organised and Alcoholics Anonymous meetings take place. The mesh blinds are down to soften the sunlight, and a window has been opened, but by tonight this room will be uncomfortably hot. I wouldn't be surprised if the folks at this evening's AA meeting will end up knocking back a few beers just to stay cool. Father Barrett is putting out the chairs – more than are needed, and I don't know if that's him being optimistic or pessimistic. Barrett is big and bald, with a lumberjack's beard and an undertaker's kind smile. He was posted to Acacia Pines early last year after God didn't remove the previous priest's cancer. Dad walks over to the wall and looks at the flyers for cake sales and charity lawn-bowling matches, reading them out loud to himself.

'I really appreciate this,' I tell Barrett, which is what I said on the phone earlier when I called to ask for his help. 'Like I said, I wouldn't have asked, but...'

But I have a man locked up in my basement and can't have Dad wandering around while I question him.

'It's understandable that you have your hands full right now, and of course I'm happy to help. Your dad is always welcome here.'

Sure, until he burns the place down.

My dad has been going to Saint John's for most of his life, and had become close friends with Father Frank Davidson, the former priest. When Father Barrett arrived, he seemed eager to step into the same friendships Father Davidson had had. After Dad burned down the care home, Father Barrett reached out, offering the help and support of the church if we needed it. I didn't think we would, but over the months, as the money got tighter, and our options became fewer, we took Barrett up on his offer, with him filling in the blanks if Deborah was busy, or other family couldn't help. I try not to see him as a last-minute babysitter, but if you had to put a label on it...

'How about we get you some breakfast,' Father Barrett says to Dad, walking over and putting an arm around his shoulders. 'Then we can walk the gardens a little?'

'Fuck the gardens,' my dad says, shrugging the hand off his shoulder and going back to reading the flyers aloud.

Unperturbed, Father Barrett carries on. 'Does the same go for breakfast?'

'What breakfast?'

'Father Barrett is offering to make you breakfast, Dad.'

'Father Barrett is dead.'

'I assure you I'm very much alive,' Father Barrett says.

'Bullshit. You're not Father Barrett.'

Father Barrett smiles an *it's going to be one of those days* smiles at me, and follows it up with, 'We'll be okay if you want to get back to it.'

'I can try to find somewhere else if—'

'Don't be silly. We'll be fine here, won't we, Randolph?'

Dad doesn't answer, but he does stop reading the flyers.

'I'll be back as soon as I can,' I say.

'There's no hurry.'

I head back home, not looking forward to what is waiting there for me. Last night, before I dragged Grove out of the freezer I had stuffed him into at the Kelly farm, he had asked me the question *why*? Yesterday it was a very easy question to answer.

Why? Because my dad burned down a retirement home. Because a rightfully upset family are unrightfully chasing me for every cent I have. Because my wife moved out, and the bank is going to take my house away, leaving me homeless, and my son needs counselling.

Because Simon Grove was the only lifeline I had left.

Of course I regret everything that's happened since he swung that rebar at me. He was trying to kill me, but he messed up, probably because beating on a kid is different from beating on a grown man, especially one in law enforcement, and he wasn't used to anybody fighting back. I wrestled the rebar off him and hit him in the head with it. I was worried I had cracked his skull, but if he was dead, then so be it – it was him or me, and if one of us was going to get zippered into a black bag and driven to the morgue, shouldn't it be him?

But he wasn't dead, just unconscious, and as I stood looking down at him, it hit me that this guy was more useful on the run than in handcuffs. Even now it seems like it was a different James Cohen who dragged him and stuffed him into the back of his cruiser, a different James Cohen who put him into the chest freezer with a hose keeping the door cracked open and some old furniture on top so nobody would check it. It was a different James Cohen who returned last night to get Grove, who carried him up the basement stairs. It was a different James Cohen who was frightened he was going to fall, treating each step as a landmine, knowing if one went off he'd be found down there with a broken back and Grove either dead or long gone. It wasn't me who carried Grove through the rubble – more landmines – to his SUV. I'd gone out there last night in my own car instead of my cruiser, because I couldn't return to the sawmill and risk the dogs figuring out Grove had been in it. Even then I thought I was done for when we found the camera – but thank God the room had filled with smoke before I carried Grove past it.

All of that wasn't Yesterday Me's problem. That son of a bitch made a bad decision in the heat of the moment, without any regard for how we were going to deal with any of that today. But we must. We must follow a God-awful decision with some even worse ones – I can either turn myself in, which is a bad decision, or I can stay the course. Which is worse? Both are.

By the time I get home from the church, I'm no closer to making a decision. The kitchen doesn't look any better in the light of day, nor has it fully let go of the smoke, despite the effort Cassandra made last night to clean it up before taking Nathan back to her place. I close the curtains and put some music on, a live album that I crank up enough to fill the house with vocals and guitar and an amped-up audience, but not loud enough for the neighbours to complain – particularly Mrs Larson further down the road, whose first name I can never remember, even though she's on my doorstep every few months complaining about something. I change into my gardening clothes, examining myself in the process. The line where my chest meets my stomach is tender and puffy, the bruise having both spread and darkened. The blow to my head from Grove has swollen, and my jaw where Allan Holt hit me has the early signs of a bruise. I head down into the basement. I can hear the music from upstairs. The walls pulse in time with it. Or maybe it's the headache making that happen, because it's coming back.

Not only did I swap one basement for another with Grove, but I swapped one chest freezer for another too. I open my one up. He's on his back, all folded up and sedated, thanks to the shot I gave him earlier this morning – I palmed a few needles and vials from the hospital last night. I don't know what is a good amount or a bad amount to give him, so I've been guessing. It was either that or keep hitting him in the head. I check his pulse. It's slow, but steady.

He starts to come to as I go about pulling him from the freezer. He grunts and grumbles, but doesn't seem bothered when he spills heavily onto the floor. I check the cable ties binding his wrists and ankles. The blood coming from the side of his head has dried, but the wound looks raw.

I get him upright into a chair and tie him to it. I take the tape off his mouth then crack open a phial of smelling salts and wave it under his nose to bring him all the way around. He jerks upward. One eye opens wide open, and one stays swollen shut. The swollen one is all messed up. Lucas Connor really did a number on this guy.

He tries to talk, but can't, his mouth is too dry.

'Drink this,' I say, and I put a bottle of water to his mouth and tip it upward. He drinks it greedily, losing plenty over his chin. He coughs a little when he's done, then gets himself under control.

'Okay,' I say. 'Let's get started.'

Chapter Thirty-One

The nightmares, for the first time in years, return. Tiny bugs crawling into Lucas's ears during the night that grow in the heat and damp of his insides, growing a foot long, then two, then ten, hooking with barbed feet onto the walls of his organs, feeding with sharp little mouths as they fatten and grow and multiply. He dreams of being held down, his mouth open, long metal forceps deep down his throat clutching at the worms down there, finding them, each worm screaming and writhing as it's pulled out. He dreams these things, and every two hours he's woken by a nurse so they can check on him, before returning to sleep to dream them all over again.

When he wakes up for good, it's a little after seven. He's tired, but the headaches have gone. With nothing to do until his dad arrives to pick him up, he spends the time on his phone, reading articles about Simon Grove and about yesterday's attack. He knows he absolutely shouldn't, but absolutely can't help himself reading through the comments. Like he feared, they are bad – so bad, in fact, that they distract him from his itchy hand and thoughts of worms setting up camp inside him. The comments bounce between him being a hero, to him deserving it, to him enjoying it. Some say he made it up for the attention. Somebody suggests Lucas is so ugly that he must have paid the janitor to rape him, which leads to other people agreeing, before somebody suggests it was Lucas who killed Freddy Holt, and kidnapped the janitor to do the same thing. He stops reading the comments before somebody accuses him of faking the moon landing.

'You shouldn't read any of that,' a nurse says to him, after bringing him in some breakfast. 'It'll only lead to you feeling worse leaving here than you did coming in.'

Breakfast is bacon and eggs, which makes him think the folks here are trying to clog his arteries for repeat business. Things have been coming back to him – not just from the attack, but from way before. He can remember how he got the scars on his arm that needed stitching – it was when Wolfy, his much-loved dog, bit him, which was when it became obvious Wolfy was sick and needed putting down. The pain of that memory kills his appetite, so when his dad arrives, half of his breakfast has gone untouched.

'Morning, Champ,' his dad says, which is weird because his dad has never called him champ before. He likes the way it sounds. After all, he is a champ, isn't he? The scorecard between him and people trying to kill him is 1 – 0 in his favour. His dad is still wearing yesterday's clothes, and his hair is sticking up from where it's been crushed into a couch cushion.

'Morning,' Lucas says.

'How are you feeling?'

'Good as new. In fact, I'm going to go to school today.'

His dad looks confused. 'Did I just hear you right?'

'You did,' he says, and he's been giving that a lot of thought too. Right now he has credit. He's the kid who got taken by a serial killer and lived to tell the tale. Those who usually hassle him surely can't hassle him now. Not after this. In fact, people will gravitate toward him. They're going to want to hear his story. They will listen in awe and ask questions, and they're going to tell their friends that they know him. For the first time they're going to accept him. It won't be like the comments online. It can't be. He's always thought people who say those things in that world won't say them in this one. The sooner he can get to the school, the sooner he can be the New Lucas – the one who isn't going to get tormented anymore, the one who won't be teased and tortured. 'I'll go after lunch. At least that way I can get half a day in.'

'You don't want time off?'

'What I want is for things to get back to normal.'

'Nobody is going to blame you for taking the rest of the week.'

'I'll be fine,' he says.

The same doctor who examined him yesterday comes in and asks how he's feeling. He tells her he's feeling great, but even so she examines him, shining a small light into his eyes and asking him a series of questions to which the answers come right away. She seems satisfied with the results. Lucas is pleased. His dad, who smells like he knocked back a gallon of breath freshener on his way here, is pleased too.

Then they're even more pleased, when, a moment later, the doctor tells them Lucas can go home.

Chapter Thirty-Two

'Where is Freddy Holt?'

'I don't know what you're talking about,' Grove says.

'Where is he?'

'I ... I don't know who that is.'

I slowly nod. This is what I was expecting. I can hear a guitar solo from upstairs. I wonder if I'll ever be able to listen to this album again without thinking about this moment. I study Grove. I look at his damaged eye, his mottled skin, his scraggly beard. I hate him. Hate him for who he is, for what he does. I hate him for being my one chance to get my life back on track.

But none of that comes close to how much I'm hating myself right now.

'Whatever you think I did, I didn't do.'

'Let me tell you what we know,' I say, and I walk back and forth, like an old-time lawyer in an old-time movie – *Well, here are the facts, ladies and gentlemen, and let the jury see I had no other option but to lock this man in my basement until he told me what I needed to know*. 'Your fingerprints are linked to the deaths of Eric Delany and Harry Waltz,' I say, and even though Harry was never found, we all know he's dead. 'We found the camera you were using to film yourself with Lucas Connor. You probably thought it was burned in the fire, but it wasn't. We saw the whole thing, Simon.'

'It's all make-believe. I didn't hurt anybody.'

'You admitted to killing Freddy Holt.'

He shakes his head. 'I already told you I don't know who that is.'

'He's the boy you killed two months ago.'

He stops shaking his head and he looks up at the ceiling as if he's figuring out his dates. 'I didn't hurt anybody two months ago. You have to believe me. Have to. I've never hurt anybody at all. Ever. Please don't do this to me. I need a hospital. Please, the pain is so bad, so bad...'

I stare at him and he stares back with his one open eye. He's scared. He ought to be. He's hoping things are going to get better. They won't. He knows from experience how bad things can get when you're tied up. He knows how much pain can be inflicted on somebody. I look at his hand with the missing fingers. I think about the videos we found of him. He knows better than anybody about pain.

'Were you the one who bullied Taylor Reed online?'

He's been feigning surprise at all the names I've been throwing at him, but this time it seems genuine when he says, 'The boy who jumped? I had nothing to do with that, I swear.'

'And Lucas? The boy you took yesterday?'

'What boy?' he asks, quickly falling back into his denials.

'Like I said, we got the memory card out of your camera. We watched the video, and we know everything. We heard you confessing to killing Freddy.'

'It's a misunderstanding, that's all,' he says, looking down. 'A joke. That's all. Okay, I admit I took Lucas to the sawmill, but I was goofing around, trying to, you know, trying to scare the kid.' He looks back up at me. 'That's all it was, I swear. I wasn't really going to hurt him any. And this Freddy Holt kid, I made that up. Yes, I knew who he was. Everybody does. His name was in the news a lot, and I know he'd gone to our school, so I mentioned his name to scare Lucas some more. Please, I'm begging you, you have to take me to a hospital.'

'Listen to me very carefully, Simon. You're sitting there thinking I'm some dumb cop who's going to get sick of asking the same questions over and over, and you're prepared to make the same denials over and over in the hope it will make me doubt what I'm doing. But you're wrong to think that. In fact, what you ought to be focusing on is what I'm willing to do to get you to tell me where Freddy is.'

'And what's that?'

Before I can answer, Hutch calls out my name from upstairs.

Chapter Thirty-Three

There is paperwork to sign, and prescriptions to fill, and even though Lucas is perfectly fine to walk, protocol dictates he is wheeled out of the hospital. That protocol ends when the passenger door to his dad's car opens, and then he and his dad are on their own.

'I get it,' his dad says, as they're pulling out of the parking lot.

'Get what?'

'Why you want to go to school this afternoon. You're going to be popular today, I bet. You want to enjoy it.'

'I hadn't really thought about it.'

'Everybody will be as excited to talk to you about it tomorrow as they are today.'

A patrol car follows them home, and stays parked outside, which means Simple Simon hasn't been caught. His legs ache on the walk into the house from all the pounding and running of yesterday. His feet hurt too. He goes into his room and flops on the bed and stares at the ceiling, and his thoughts quickly go from Simple Simon to the cut on his hand. He rolls over and opens his bedside drawer and rummages around for the anxiety pills he last touched when he was a foot shorter. There are two full sheets inside a flattened box. He pops two free and swallows them. He doesn't need to take any of the painkillers he was prescribed earlier – at least that is until he touches the lump on his head. What was a two out of ten immediately becomes a nine for several moments before dropping back to a four. He swallows two of them down too, then, thanks to the dreams, he adds a worming tablet. He took one on the weekend – he takes one every month – but better to be safe than sorry.

He heads for the bathroom. He showers with his bandaged hand wrapped in a plastic bag, then freshens up. When he's done, he finds his dad watching the news in the lounge. There are four empty beer bottles on the coffee table that he assumes are from last night and not this morning. The room smells of beer.

'Any news?'

'Only that the police in this town are useless,' his dad says.

Taylor Reed and Freddy Holt dead, Simon Grove on the run – Lucas owes his life to Sheriff Cohen, but his dad might have a point. On TV, Deputy Hutchison is being interviewed, standing in front of the police station. Lucas doesn't know if it's a live feed or not. She's the one Sheriff Cohen mentioned last night, and definitely the one who drove him away from the scene. She looks like she hasn't slept. She says there's every chance Simon Grove could be hiding in town. 'Do not approach him under any circumstances,' she says, before adding that neighbours should check in on neighbours, that everybody needs to be vigilant. She says there is a combined sixty-thousand-dollar reward for Simon Grove, posted by the parents of the other boys he killed, then asks for folks not to let that cloud their judgement. There is no mention that Lucas was found naked, or of the camera. He's relieved.

'You think he's still out in the forest?' he asks his dad, even though he knows his dad can't know one way or the other. But his dad is, after all, a crime writer, which gives him just as much right as anybody to weigh in on the possibility.

'He's long gone,' his dad says. 'Probably hitched a ride out of here within minutes of getting past Cohen.'

They keep watching. Lucas waits for the headline to come up that says the janitor has been eaten by a bear. He wonders if that bear will get the sixty thousand dollars, and what it would spend it on. He wonders if the families of those two boys would come here and personally shake that bear's hand, or if they're too broken to ever leave the house.

Chapter Thirty-Four

Hutch calls out again. Grove opens his mouth to yell out, but before he can I'm putting a hand over it, while unloading the contents of another syringe into his arm. A moment later his eyes close. I'm almost at the top of the stairs when Hutch opens the door.

'There you are,' she says.

I step toward her, forcing her to take a step back. 'Hey,' I say, getting the door closed behind me. 'Everything okay?'

'I tried calling you,' she says. 'When you didn't answer, I figured I should let myself in to check on you.' Hutch has a key to the house, the same way I have a key to hers. I should have thought of that. 'I wanted to make sure Grove hadn't shown up, or perhaps you were unconscious from the blow to your head yesterday.'

'I'm fine,' I say, leading her into the kitchen. 'You want a coffee?'

'You getting ready to do some gardening?'

I look down at my clothes. 'I had to take my dad out and just grabbed the first things I could find to wear.'

'How's he doing?'

'The usual.'

She stares at me for a few moments. Then, 'I heard about the fire he started yesterday. You okay?'

'I will be. So, coffee?'

'Please.'

We go into the kitchen. 'Oh my God,' she says, as she looks at the damage. 'This looks bad.'

'It could have been worse,' I say, and how many times am I going to keep coming back to that line?

'You can stay here?'

'We can. We just can't cook with a stove.'

She doesn't seem to know what else to say, so instead she updates me on the information that came through overnight while I make us coffees. We now know that Grove had an abusive dad who killed the rest of the family, and that he spent time with a family that used his body as an ashtray before landing with the family where Grove was filmed in the basement. Grove got the raw deal of raw deals. The whole time Hutch is talking I keep thinking of him down in my basement, coming to, rocking the chair until it falls over and Hutch hearing it. What then?

'Remember how he said on camera that his dad had burned?

Turns out his foster parents were both killed in a house fire,' she says, and I look at the charred walls of my kitchen and think of the fire in the sawmill. 'Simon was working on fishing boats back then, and was away when it happened. The cause of the fire was unknown, but given what we now know, it makes me think he paid somebody to do it, or shared a favour, like that Hitchcock movie where a couple of guys who meet on a train agree to kill each other's wives. We need to look at the videos found on Grove's computer and see if there are any other victims in there.'

I'm reminded once again that I have to do something I don't want to do. I try to tell myself since the poor kid in the videos had to endure it, the least I can do is endure watching it.

'You see the news?' she asks.

'No. Why?'

'I was at the station earlier and got bailed up by a reporter. I didn't say much beyond Grove is dangerous, and if you see him, don't approach, but they want more.'

'They always do.'

Hutch finishes her coffee, and I finish mine. I walk her to the door. We agree to meet at Grove's house as soon as I've spoken to Lucas, which I promise to do as soon as I leave here. I watch her drive away.

I'm actually relieved that talking to Grove is going to have to wait.

Chapter Thirty-Five

The Connor house is a fifty-year-old ranch house made to look ten. I remember seeing it as a kid, all beaten up like a tornado came to visit every Christmas. It's had a few owners since then, folks who thought they could do something with it, only for the house to bleed them dry. The Connors bought it back when Peter's books were selling enough copies to allow them to double the size and still have plenty left over, replacing every weatherboard and rooftile and window along the way. I think the only original thing left is the dirt it sits on. I've only ever seen the inside once, back when the electrician working those renovations had to be resuscitated after zapping himself.

At the moment there's a patrol car parked out front. Deputy Schmitt is inside. Schmitt is a foot shorter than me, with Popeye arms that bulge at his shirts and Clark Kent glasses that always have smudged lenses. Usually he looks like he could break people in half, but right now he looks like he's dreaming about it. I can hear him softly snoring through the open window. He startles when I tap the roof, and goes bright red as he looks at me.

'I'm sorry, boss,' he says, rubbing at his neck. 'I must have nodded off. It won't happen again.'

There's no point in telling the guy off – he knows he's messed up. Plus he's had a long night – because of me. On top of that, sitting in a car for ten hours, first at the hospital, and now here, would make anybody fall asleep. I make a mental note to have Sharon organise shorter shifts.

'Don't let it happen again,' I say, because I have to say something.

'I won't. I promise.'

I take the path up to the front door, which opens before I reach it, as if Peter has been waiting for me all morning. It reminds me of the Holts last night, only instead of collapsing into a heap, he's going to pat me on the back and shake my hand and offer me the keys to the kingdom.

'James, it's good to see you,' he says. He's a different guy from yesterday. All smiles and happiness. If he threw up there'd only be rainbows. He reaches out and shakes my hand vigorously, but I don't get the back-pat or the keys. 'You saved him.'

'Just doing my job, Peter.'

'Yeah, I know, I know,' he says, nodding as he says it. 'But it's more than that. You saved him, and if you hadn't then today we'd be planning a funeral.'

It's a grim assessment, but an accurate one. Then he goes on to say what I thought he was going to say last night at the hospital. 'When I first called you, you didn't take me seriously. Was that also you just doing your job?'

He's right – I didn't take him seriously. Kids mess around and go where they shouldn't, they show up late, they live in their own worlds, and this generation of teenagers aren't like any other. They may look like us, but they are strangers in a strange land, full of social media and selfies and hours spent staring at screens. I don't understand them – I don't understand my own son – and I don't know if I ever could. Then there's Peter – Peter and his relationship with the bottle that makes people dismiss a lot of what he has to say. Even so, if we hadn't gotten Lucas back safe and sound, I would never have been able to forgive myself for those moments lost when he first called.

'I'm sorry,' I say, because it's all I *can* say.

'Yeah, I know. I know you are, James, and it's okay because everything worked out, but if it hadn't ... I would have hated you – hated you and blamed you, and I don't know where that hate would have led me.'

I can feel the headache coming back. There's a vein throbbing in my forehead. 'Well, that's something you're never going to have to figure out. What we need to focus on now is finding Grove.'

Inside, the freshly brewed coffee isn't enough to mask the smell of beer fermenting in the weave of the carpet. The lounge isn't a mess, but it looks the way rooms look when police have been searching them – everything moved to one side and then moved back. Still, last time I was here there were cables hanging out of the walls and no carpet. Lucas comes out of his room, walking a little stiffly. There's bruising around the side of his head that didn't require bandaging, and bandaging around his hand from the cut he took from the broken window. The wounds on the outside will heal up, but as for the rest, we'll know with time.

We sit in the lounge. Peter pours me a coffee while I compare war stories with Lucas, him telling me what hurts the most is his stitched-up hand, me telling him my worst thing is the headache.

'Truth is, it feels unreal,' he says. 'Like it was all some kind of dream. Or a movie. In a way I'm not sure how I'm meant to be feeling. I know things were bad when they were happening, but thinking on it, I never really thought I was going to die. I mean, I knew it was a possibility, but ... but it's hard to explain.' He takes a moment to figure out what he's trying to say. 'Knowing I wasn't going to die made me calmer – a bit, anyway – and I think that's why I feel okay now.'

'It's the immortality of youth. Kids your age think they're going to live forever. They think nothing can hurt them.'

Lucas slowly nods. 'Is that one of those things you don't know until you get old?'

I laugh. 'One of many. You ready to tell me who put you into that locker?'

Lucas looks at his bandaged hand. He flicks at the tape holding it in place, digging his thumbnail under the corner of it.

'Lucas?'

'It's not that I don't want to tell you, it's that I can't remember. I've been thinking about it all night, but I just can't get there.'

He's a good liar, but if he doesn't want to tell me then I'm not going to push it. If it was Nathan, then he's getting a free pass. Maybe my son can use this to make himself a better person. Or maybe it's like what Hutch said – whoever put Lucas into the locker saved a future kid from a worse fate.

'Where are you at with the investigation?' Peter asks.

I update them. The manhunt. The dogs. The search-and-rescue teams. The reality Grove could be in town, or a thousand miles away, or lost in the wilderness. Lucas isn't the only one who's a good liar. 'A police car will stay outside your house until we have Grove, or until we have evidence he's fled. If you go anywhere, it will follow.'

'Did you find the video camera?' Peter asks.

'We did.'

'And?'

'And it's like Lucas said. He confesses to killing Freddy Holt.'

They both take a moment with that.

Then Peter asks what I guess any crime writer would ask. 'Has he filmed others?'

'We're going through his computer looking for evidence of it. We're also talking to his neighbours and co-workers and anybody he knew. We're checking credit-card statements, receipts, anything and everything that will tell us who this guy really is, and where he might have gone. We're turning his life upside down and rattling everything free.'

'So there could be others,' Peter says. 'Other than Freddy and the other two boys in the news.'

'It's possible.'

'The two you know about,' Lucas says. 'Can you tell me about them?'

'About what happened to them?'

Lucas shakes his head. 'No. I mean, yes, but more than that. Who *were* they?'

I take a sip of coffee. It tastes better than what I make at home. I settle the cup back on the coffee table and pull out my notebook and lean back. I flip it open to the page where I made notes yesterday. I tell them what we've learned, and both Peter and Lucas sit there without interrupting me, taking it all on board, the sheer gravity of it weighing on them more as I talk – especially Lucas. He's becoming aware teenagers aren't immortal after all. He can see himself in the fate of the others. I tell them about Harry Waltz, who went missing ten years ago. Waltz disappeared on his way home from school. He was fifteen. They never found him, but they found his schoolbag with blood on it, and fingerprints they couldn't match back then. I tell them about Eric Delany, who went missing on his way to school four years ago. He was fourteen. He walked out the door and never got the chance to walk back in. At least they found the poor kid. Fingerprints in the stolen van where his body was left matched those from Harry Waltz's schoolbag. Fingerprints that yesterday found another match. Peter was right to question if there have been others. I don't tell them Grove was planning on a vacation next week, that he was possibly working himself up for another attack. By the time I tell them what I can, the line where the sun is hitting the wall has gotten lower as the sun has gotten higher, and the coffees have gone cold.

'Will you ever find Freddy, do you think?' Lucas asks.

'My guess is he's buried somewhere out in the pines, and when we find Grove, he can lead us to him.'

'At least you sound confident you'll get this guy,' Peter says.

'We will. If not today, then tomorrow.'

'And if not tomorrow?' Peter asks.

'Then we offer a reward. That always gets people talking.'

'There's already a reward,' Lucas says. 'That hasn't helped much so far.'

He's wrong about the reward not helping. 'Now that I've told you everything I can,' I say, focusing on Lucas, 'I need you to tell me everything about yesterday. I want to know everything he said, everything he did. Any detail, no matter how small, even if you think it's something I don't need to know, everything and anything can help. Not only could it give us an idea of what Grove might do next, but it could help us figure out what happened to Freddy.'

It also might help me get Grove to talk.

'Okay,' Lucas says.

'Good. Let's start with what happened when you were inside the locker,' I say, and that's what Lucas does – he starts with Grove finding him and opening the door.

Chapter Thirty-Six

Lucas watches through the window as Sheriff Cohen drives away. The patrol car that was out front earlier has been swapped for a different one with a different deputy. His dad goes into the kitchen and rummages through the fridge, either not finding what he wants or changing his mind in the process, because he comes back empty-handed.

'You still sure you want to go to school?'

'Yeah, I really do.'

Before Sheriff Cohen left, he went out to his car and grabbed Lucas's school bag. Lucas grabs it now and they head to the car. As they drive he is reminded of yesterday, how time kept pausing, or skipping forward in chunks. Now it drags as they get caught at every red light and intersection between here and his school.

The lunch period is ending when his dad drops him off outside the driveway, and the patrol car that followed parks in behind. His dad tells him to have a good day, which Lucas is pretty sure he's going to have – after all, he feels great. No, not just great – but amazing. Better than he ever has. Sure, his hand is throbbing, and the headache is still sitting at a two, but nothing troubling. He walks to class, other students openly staring at him. They know some of what happened, but they don't know the darkest details, nor do they need to.

He doesn't make eye contact with anybody, he just keeps walking, trying to act cool, trying to act like escaping from serial killers is how he rolls. A boy from his class comes toward him. Grant, who plays football and tennis and turns all the girls' heads when he passes them. They've never spoken to each other, even though they've shared many of the same classes. Grant slows down, and Lucas slows down too, knowing what's coming. His throat is going to get sore from telling his story over and over. Perhaps he would be better off telling it at assembly in front of the entire school, getting it over in one go.

'Janet,' Grant says, then carries on walking, and Lucas can't have heard that right. He doesn't know anybody called Janet, and when he turns around, Grant is still moving along the corridor, not walking toward anybody who could be a Janet. So what did he say?

He carries on. Damien, also from his class, also somebody he's never spoken with, pushes himself away from the lockers and bumps into him. 'Watch where you're going, Janet,' he says, and this time Lucas knows he's heard correctly, only he doesn't know what to do with the information. The bell marking the end of lunch rings, turning his headache up to a three. He still feels great. Not amazing, like he did a few minutes ago, but still great.

First class after lunch is English. Students funnel into the room. There's laughter from behind that feels directed at him, only it can't be, because he hasn't done anything that warrants it. He makes his way to his seat, and Victoria Tennent, a girl he's known most of his life because they used to live on the same street, smiles at him, and he smiles back, which gets him well on his way back to feeling amazing. He's had a crush on Victoria all these years, but hasn't spoken to her since he was ten, and maybe this is his chance.

'How's it going, Janet?' she asks, which reverses the process again, and he drops from feeling great to a feeling of *not bad*. He realises she isn't smiling at him at all, but grinning. Nathan comes into the room, swaggers over to him the way arseholes swagger, and the look on his face tells Lucas his *not bad* is going to take a further hit. Nathan grins the big nasty grin Lucas has seen before, usually when Nathan is punching somebody in the stomach or shoving them face down in the mud. Neither of those things are going to happen here – surely.

'Well, Janet decided to show up I see,' Nathan says.

'Why are you calling me Janet?'

Nathan's grin stretches even further. 'It's short for Janitor's Girlfriend. He did make you his bitch, didn't he? I heard he made you his bitch so many times that it's a miracle you can even walk.'

Others nearby laugh. Lucas searches desperately for something to say, but there's nothing. He spent all morning thinking his return to school would be a good thing. His story, because he survived, is a cool story. He got kidnapped, he fought back, and he did what others may not have been able to do. Why are these people treating him like the whole ordeal was a joke?

He takes a deep breath. He hits reset. He goes from feeling okay to feeling nothing. No, not quite nothing – he's feeling like he's done with Nathan and his bullshit.

'I'm not afraid of you anymore,' he says. He pushes himself out of his chair. This is it. This is the moment he stands up to his bully and closes one chapter and moves on to another, one where he can walk down the corridor without getting shoved or stuffed into a locker. The room has gone quiet. Everybody is watching. This is it; the moment his life changes. Others may not care about him surviving a serial killer, but they'll care about this. 'I'm not—'

Nathan pushes him hard in the chest and he falls over his chair and topples to the floor, landing on his back. Nathan looks down at him and laughs, but fewer people join in on the laughter now. Pushing reset hasn't helped. The headache is cranked up to an eight, and the room is tilting and all the sharp lines are blurring. Nathan crouches over him. He's become a big shape with fuzzy edges, but he knows it's him – after all, who else would it be? He gets his face next to Lucas's and his hand on Lucas's throat. He can smell cigarette smoke and sweat.

'You remember what I told you last night?' Nathan asks, his voice low, and he tightens his grip, not a lot, but enough to let Lucas know he could tighten it a whole lot more if he wanted.

Lucas hears him. He nods.

He slaps Lucas's face lightly. Twice. 'Good. But let's pick this back up after school just to make sure.'

Nathan gets up and everybody starts talking and people turn away. Victoria puts a hand on Nathan's shoulder and says something Lucas can't hear, but whatever it is it gets them all laughing. He gets himself back into his chair. The throbbing in his hand is being replaced by an itch. He squeezes down on the cut, the pressure dulling the itch, but not as much as he'd like. He stares ahead while listening to others around him, focusing on the white noise of conversation while trying to ignore the headache, and the itch, and the embarrassment of what just happened.

Mr Lee, their teacher, comes into the classroom. Mr Lee always looks like he just climbed out of bed, messy hair and a five-o'clock shadow no matter what time of the day. He puts his bag on his desk and pats down his shirt and pants as if looking for something, then tells everybody to quieten down. He looks surprised to see Lucas, but doesn't say anything. He's always liked Mr Lee. The room goes quiet and a minute later Mr Lee is talking about the book everybody read last week. Lucas knows he read it, but can't remember a thing about it. Mr Lee asks what some of the themes were, and as per usual, nobody puts up a hand, and for the next forty-five minutes Mr Lee explains what the themes are, right through till when the bell goes off. Over the voices and chairs sliding and scuffing of feet as students start to leave, Mr Lee says, 'Lucas, a word if you don't mind.'

Everybody in the room goes, 'Oooh,' and Mr Lee tells them to knock it off.

When they're alone, he says, 'Look, Lucas, I wanted to say how sorry I am about what you went through yesterday, and that I'm glad you're okay. If you ever need anybody to talk to I'm here for you.'

Lucas nods. This is the longest conversation they've ever had. 'Thanks.'

'You sure you're up for being back so soon?'

He thought he was, but already he's wishing he had stayed at home. 'I'm sure.'

'Okay, good. Listen, I was thinking, you might find that writing about what happened to you might be quite cathartic.'

'Cathartic?'

'Healing. It could help you understand your emotions better, and might help you come to terms with it.'

Lucas hadn't thought of that, and now that he has, he doesn't see himself trying. But maybe Mr Lee knows what he's talking about. 'You want me to write an essay about my feelings to feel better?'

Mr Lee picks up his bag. It's a leather satchel so worn it can't be long until it's transparent. He hunts through it and pulls out his car keys. 'It doesn't have to be an essay. You can fictionalise it, or write about it as if the characters are other people. You're a great writer, Lucas,' he says. 'Your dad, he's a great writer too, but I see this potential in you to be just as good, possibly one day even better. You could use this experience. The way I see it, you have two choices here. You can hide from it, or you can confront it.'

Lucas has written plenty of short stories in class because it's part of the curriculum. He's always enjoyed it, but never knew he was good at it.

When Lucas doesn't say anything, Mr Lee shrugs and carries on. 'It's just a suggestion, but do me a favour and think about it a little, okay?'

'Okay.'

They walk out into the corridor. It's empty.

'I'd be happy to help you out in any way I can,' Mr Lee says. 'I'm actually working on my first novel at the moment too, and I know how rewarding a process it can be.'

Mr Lee isn't the first English teacher to have told Lucas this over the years, to hint at the possibility of Lucas's dad taking a look and giving his thoughts. But instead of asking that, Mr Lee says, 'Once again, Lucas, I'm glad you're okay.'

Mr Lee puts his hand out, and Lucas shakes it, which is a first for him with any teacher. He watches Mr Lee walk down the corridor and disappear. He wonders if there's anything to his suggestion. He could pretend Nathan was the one abducted, but if it had gone that way, no doubt Nathan would have kicked the janitor's arse and tied him up. He would have become a national hero. The school would have taken a day off in celebration. Nathan would have gotten the reward too. People wouldn't be calling him Janet. Instead he'd be in the papers, and on TV. He'd get offered to play the role of himself in the movie. His story would be told over campfires until the sun burned itself out.

Nathan.

He hates him passionately, and maybe, just maybe, there's a way to deal with him.

Lucas goes back into the classroom. Mr Lee's leather bag is still on the desk. He goes through it. There are files inside, papers, some pens, a copy of the book the class is reading. There's also a wallet. He wonders if this is cathartic – he thinks so, because putting Mr Lee's wallet into his own bag sure makes him feel better.

Mr Lee will get it back.

First Lucas is going to use it to make life better.

Chapter Thirty-Seven

Forensics have been through Simon Grove's house, looking for traces of Freddy Holt, though my guess is Freddy was never here, that he went directly to the sawmill then directly into the ground surrounding it. If Grove doesn't tell me exactly where, then hopefully the corpse dogs will. The phone used to bully Taylor Reed isn't here, and a more thorough search of his computer hasn't come up with any evidence Grove ever contacted him online, or even knew who he was. From what we know about Grove, he seems the type to throw somebody off a roof rather than bullying them into it.

Drawers have been tossed and turned upside down. Carpet has been pulled, the ceiling has been searched, and right now somebody is squeezing their way into the crawlspace under the floor, where they'll snake their way around pipes and cables. The same corpse dogs that will enter the forest later today have already gone through the house and yard and found nothing. Other than the videos on

Grove's computer, there's nothing here to suggest he wasn't anything but a quiet neighbour who kept himself to himself, all while renovating furniture that was never that great to begin with. Phone calls to the new sawmill have confirmed Grove was given a key and permission to take anything that wasn't bolted down in the old one. A chat with Grove's landlord tells us Grove was respectful and paid his rent on time, and never asked for anything. He says Grove was good with his hands and made the house look better than it ever had.

I head out with Hutch to the old sawmill. We go in the same car, with Hutch driving. My headache has gone, but there is a tiredness growing. I haven't taken any Adderall today, and was hoping not to, but it's only a matter of time. We discuss what we know and we guess about what we don't – mostly covering the same ground we've already covered. Investigating something I know the outcome to is like renovating a house before tearing it down.

We reach the sawmill. It has become a base of operations for the search for Grove, and therefore a location that has a gravity to it. The fire trucks have escaped that gravity and disappeared back into town, but armed search-and-rescue teams are still here. There are drones flying through the air, and corpse dogs are sniffing their way through the woods. Heat ebbs out of the ground, and the air over the roof of the mill is shimmering. The door pulled from the side of the building yesterday is still where it landed, and will probably stay there for the next two hundred years. I follow Hutch inside and we look at everything we looked at last night, only now in daylight. With the sun beating on the building, the temperature has risen enough in here to dry out most of the water. When the sawmill was active, all the roller doors would be open, letting the breeze flow through. Now it's a sauna. The walls near the office are blackened and charred, the floor covered in ash, broken up by footprints, and the stairs the car drove into are lying in pieces on the floor. But mostly the mill looks okay, the steel beams still solid and straight, and the roof where it ought to be. The mattress has been taken away to be checked for evidence of not only Lucas and Freddy, but others too, other children Grove potentially filmed and threatened who were too scared to say anything – or potentially children he's brought in from out of state. Forensics have been through Grove's burnt-out car and didn't turn up any melted flash drives or laptops or cellphones.

We swap updates with those out here before leaving. On the way back into town we take the turnoff for the hiking tracks. There are two deputies posted here to both warn hikers and keep an eye on the parked cars, since they'd be attractive targets for Grove. There are no signs Grove tried to break into any of them, and no puddles of glass to suggest he was successful. We go to the new sawmill, large saws spinning loudly, logging trucks coming and going, machines stripping the branches even from the biggest of trees in seconds. We talk to the foreman. He looks exactly the way I figured he was going to look – a burly guy with a big beard and a high-visibility vest over a flannel shirt. He's sweating in the heat but doesn't seem bothered by it. He says there have been no signs of forced entry. No missing vehicles. Nothing out of place. He gives us hardhats and tells us he's happy for us to look around, and stays with us to make sure we don't get cut in half. We look everywhere worth looking and don't find anything worth finding.

'Did anybody check the Kelly farm again today?' Hutch asks. We're at Earl's Garage now, the abandoned service station only a few minutes from the sawmill. We have keys to the place, and have gone through it, checking the storefront and the garage off to the side, finding nothing but mice and squirrels. We're resting against the side of the cruiser, each of us with a bottle of water in our hands, each of us staring out at the highway at what looks like water rippling on the surface in the far distance as the sun bakes it. If today is anything to go by, none of us will survive the summer.

Hutch's mention of the Kelly farm wakes up my headache.

'You okay?' she asks.

'I'm fine,' I say, rubbing at my head.

'I think we ought to at least check it out.'

We head there, parking in the same spot I parked in last night. We lean against the cruiser and look at the charred rubble that a year ago was a farmhouse. I can see the path I took through the ruins to the basement, but Hutch can't see it because she doesn't know to look for it. She pushes herself off from the cruiser and kicks through the rubble along the front edge.

'There's nothing here,' I say, still leaning against the cruiser. 'Nowhere to hide.'

'I'm going to do a perimeter.'

So we do a perimeter. She goes left and I go right, and we pass each other at the back of the house where the wall is still standing and offering shade from the sun, then we meet back up at the front. We check out the open barn next to the house. There's an old tractor, with perished tires and weeds growing out of the seat, parked next to a car that doesn't look any better.

'Isn't there a basement here?'

'There is.'

Hutch grabs a flashlight from the cruiser and we go back into the rubble. She kicks her way through it and straight to the hole in the ground. Hutch switches on her flashlight and pulls out her gun and I pull out my gun too, and we descend into the ground.

'This place hardly got touched by the fire,' she says.

'Crazy.'

'I'm going to check out the freezer,' she says.

She opens it and spends half a second looking inside, and then we spend another minute looking around the basement until Hutch is satisfied Grove was never here. We head up the stairs and the light is blinding for a few seconds.

'I don't know what else to suggest,' Hutch says when we're back to leaning against the cruiser. I've never heard her so despondent. She turns toward me. 'I'm afraid somebody is out there lying in a ditch because Grove got away.'

'Let's make a list of anybody who isn't in town. We figure out who might have pulled over for him. We check records of those who went hiking in case it was one of them. We've already put out a nationwide all-points, so maybe something will show up anyway. We already have neighbours checking on neighbours.'

'And if that doesn't get anything?' she asks. 'Then what?'

It's the question I've been waiting all day for her to ask.

'Then we offer a reward.'

Chapter Thirty-Eight

Math has always been one of his favourite subjects, and Lucas has always been good with numbers. He can see patterns in the equations. He can often see what x is going to be before having to do the hard work to get there. It's the same with movies and books – he knows who's doing what early on. When he reads his dad's books, and his dad asks what he thought, he always says he never saw the twist coming, even though he did. He knows his dad has the same gift – or used to, back when people were calling him a great writer. He's always wondered if that ability is genetic.

Fifteen minutes into the math lesson there's an announcement over the PA system. Mr Lee's wallet has been stolen, and if anybody has any information would they come to the principal's office. People in class laugh – Nathan the loudest. Lucas wonders if there's a word for somebody who revels in others' misfortune. Psychopath? Sociopath? Arsehole? If the announcement had been that Mr Lee and his family had just been killed in a traffic accident, he is sure fewer people would laugh, but those who did would probably laugh louder.

He feels bad about taking Mr Lee's wallet, and just as bad for pinching Harriet White's cellphone from her bag on the way out of math class later. By the time the final class of the day starts – phys-ed – a rumour is quickly spreading through the school that Principal

Chambers is resigning, no doubt in part because the school hired a child-molesting janitor on his watch.

Lucas can't participate in phys-ed, which makes it easy to lift Stephen Chalk's watch from the locker room. He hides the wallet and the phone and the watch in the bottom of a rubbish bin, which is a good thing, because when school ends, Nathan and two of his friends push Lucas into the locker room and rub wet toilet paper through his hair, which is bad, but would have been worse if he hadn't hidden his new acquisitions, since his bag is opened and his belongings scattered across the floor.

He texts his dad and tells him he's running ten minutes late rather than risk sending him into another panic. He scoops everything up and combs the toilet paper out of his hair with his fingers, then, when he's alone, he retrieves the stolen items. He makes his way out to the front of the school with the expectation a teacher is going to put a hand on Lucas's shoulder and ask to search him, but it doesn't happen, and, wouldn't you know it, when he gets to the car he finds his dad is completely sober.

'How was it?' his dad asks, as they're pulling away. The police car that followed them to school earlier follows them again now, which is helpful when they're keeping an eye out for serial killers, but not for high-school bullies.

'It was fine.'

'I bet you had to tell your story a million times.'

'Something like that.'

'And all the girls were impressed?'

'Mr Lee thinks I should write about what happened to me.'

'The English teacher?'

'Yeah. He thinks I should turn it into a story.'

His dad doesn't say anything. He stares ahead, his jaw tight as he grinds his teeth. Lucas wonders if his dad has spent the afternoon working on the same thing. After all, he's heard writers say you're meant to write what you know.

'You going to do it?' his dad asks.

He's been giving it some serious thought. It could be ... what was the word? Cathartic? It could be cathartic, like Mr Lee said, and who knows, maybe he'll be good at writing, like his dad. He never has landed on any single idea as to what he would like to do when he leaves school. He doesn't even know if he's going to go to college and if he does, where that might be. Perhaps he could be a writer.

He scratches at his hand. 'I was thinking that maybe you could do it.'

'Sorry?'

If his dad is working on something he's passionate about, then he'd drink less. The house would be tidier. He'd be easier to be around. 'I mean, maybe it's something you could base a book on?'

'It would make a good story,' his dad says, all too quickly, making Lucas think his dad has had the same thought. Hell, maybe he's already started.

'I think so too, and plus writing is your thing, not mine.'

'You could still write it for Mr Lee, like a short story, if you like, while I work on something larger.'

'Would be cool.'

They are halfway home when he remembers that his bike is still at the school from yesterday. He tells his dad he'll need it for tomorrow morning, that he's eager to bike to school.

'You sure? I'm happy to drive you for the next few days.'

'I just want things to get back to normal,' he says, automatically now, despite him not knowing what normal is these days. He scratches at the bandaging on his hand and wonders what's going on in there. 'And I'll be safe. There'll be a police officer following me.'

'I don't know, Lucas. Honestly, I wish you'd just stay at home. Look, let's get your bike, and we can discuss it again this evening, okay?'

That works for Lucas. He doesn't care one way or the other if he goes to school tomorrow. But his bike – he's going to need that tonight.

The wallet. The watch. The cellphone. He's going to put them to use.

Chapter Thirty-Nine

I spend the afternoon in my office scanning through the videos on Grove's computer. I have to make frequent trips to the bathroom either to be sick, or, as the afternoon rolls on and my stomach empties out, to try to be sick. After a few hours, my bathroom trips are merely to splash cold water on my face. It gets to the point where I fish out the bottle of whiskey one of my predecessors – Sheriff Haggerty – left in the bottom drawer. He used to say there would be days when whoever sat in this chair would need it. He said the trick was to work hard to make sure those days didn't come often.

I take a mouthful and let it burn. I carry on watching the videos, glancing at the screen every five or ten seconds for only a moment at a time. Thankfully I can watch them at a higher speed and with the sound turned off, only needing to see if there was anybody else involved. I pace back and forth, one video ending and another beginning, the same thing over and over but subtly different as if Stan Clayton was figuring out the best angles. At one point I unmute it to hear something Clayton says as he looks over his shoulder. *How's that look, baby?* And it is Stan Clayton – that gets confirmed when Hutch receives a photo of the guy and slides it under my door. She doesn't want to come into the office. Doesn't want to be infected by what I'm watching. I can't be sure, but I think the person Stan talks to might be his wife.

There are no other children, and no other abusers, and when I'm done I spend twenty minutes on the floor in the bathroom staring at the plumbing while making my way deeper into the bottle of whiskey. I can't blame Grove for killing his parents.

Hutch comes in to check on me, and doesn't seem annoyed that I'm half in the bag. 'How about I drive you home?'

I figure it's a good idea.

'We tracked down the camera,' she says, once we're backing out of the parking lot in her car. There's no wind, and the flags hanging from the front of the sheriff's office are completely limp and look like they could catch fire. 'It was purchased two weeks ago at Rudy's Cameras,' she says, Rudy's being a small store on Main Street that's been there for fifty years, their motto being they 'know everything about cameras unless it's something not worth knowing'. I could go there and tell them a few things about cameras they've never seen before, like how some men in this world like to use them.

We get out onto the main road.

'They barely remember him,' she says. 'The salesman can remember selling the camera, but nothing about Grove. Can't remember if he was excited, or nervous, or anything. Grove could have held his breath the entire time in the store and gone purple and the salesman wouldn't have noticed. But it does tell us Grove didn't film Freddy – at least not on that camera – and that he bought it in anticipation of his trip next week.'

'He was going to go hunting.'

'No doubt about it. But none of this is helping figure out where he is now.'

No, but it helps me get my head around what I need to do later.

'How much reward money should we put up?' she asks.

'It's already sixty,' I say, which is enough to buy me some time, but I'm still going to need more. 'What do you suggest?'

'You put money on the table, and people take notice. The current rewards have been around for years, but we add to it and it gets publicity not just here but around the country too, and maybe this time somebody comes along to claim it. Hell, these days a decent chunk of the population will probably treat it like reality TV. They'll try to find the guy just to take a selfie with him. We don't have the budget to get it up to a hundred, but I was thinking we could at least add another twenty.'

I'm going to need every dollar I can get my hands on.

'Do it.'

Chapter Forty

When they get home his dad turns on the TV and then heads into the kitchen. The news is on – the middle of an interview with Freddy Holt's parents. Freddy's dad is saying the police messed up, that they didn't look hard enough for their son, that they let people think Freddy had bullied Taylor Reed, that they're going to take the police department to court. Lucas isn't sure what to think.

His dad returns with a beer, then seems torn between sitting on the couch or heading into his office. 'You know, I'm actually itching to start on these ideas we were talking about. You're okay hanging by yourself?'

'I'm fine.'

His dad puts the beer back into the fridge then heads into his office, making Lucas feel good about his decision to suggest his dad write his story. In the same way yesterday made Lucas a new person, perhaps it's made his dad a new person too. He'll write more and drink less, and if his dad can keep that balance, they won't run out of money.

He goes to his room and shuts the door and sits on his bed. He takes out Mr Lee's wallet. There's a mixture of bills that add up to a hundred and twenty dollars. There are two credit cards, a library card, a coffee card one stamp short of a free latte, and a driver's licence with a really bad photo. There's also a family photo – Mr Lee with his arm around a woman holding a baby. Lucas pictures that woman looking under their sofa for this very wallet. He pictures Mr Lee rummaging through the car. Pictures Mrs Lee asking Mr Lee where he last left it, and Mr Lee saying if he knew that he wouldn't be needing to look for it. He pictures them coming to the conclusion it was stolen.

He hides the wallet under the mattress, along with the phone and the watch, then stares at his bed, wondering if the small lump is in his imagination, or if others would be able to see it too. He goes about doing his homework, only to find he can't focus. He switches on his computer, and a moment later he's trawling through articles about Simon Grove, about Grove's connection to Freddy Holt and the two other boys. He reads articles that turn them from statistics into people. Harry Waltz, the boy they never found, who rode his mountain bike every weekend and hated swimming and wanted to be a musician. Eric Delany, the boy they did find, who was a straight-A student and suffered from asthma and spent hours and hours practising card tricks. Harry and Eric, with lives that would have bumped into and intersected with others, alternate timelines that can't come into play now, children who won't exist in the future because Harry and Eric were stripped from this timeline, or children who do exist because the women they might have met, met other men instead. Entire family trees wiped out and created. It gives him a headache thinking about it.

Chapter Forty-One

I stand in my ruined kitchen and face the window, where the sun is coming through. I've moved on from drinking the whiskey directly out of the bottle, and am now using a glass. It makes me feel more civilised even though I'm being the most uncivilised I've ever been in my life. The sun is warming me on the outside and the whiskey warming me on the inside, yet I still feel cold. I've got an hour before Father Barrett drops my dad off. I messaged him earlier to take him up on his offer to bring my dad home, since I'm in no condition to drive. The whiskey has made the decision to take more painkillers and Adderall an easier one, and right now I don't know which of those I'm feeling the most. I wish ... I just wish there was a way to walk back the last twenty-four hours.

I finish my drink and lock the doors, and this time I wedge chairs under the handles in case anybody shows up. I don't bother with the stereo. When I go down to the basement, I leave the door open so I can hear if anybody arrives. I open the freezer. Grove is awake, and maybe he's been that way for five minutes or five hours, I don't know. I drag him out and prop him up on the seat and tie him into place, both of us getting used to the routine. He reminds me of somebody I saw a long time ago: Mrs Cargill, a keen church-going woman who in her later years ended up looking as old as religion itself. She got Alzheimer's and didn't tell anybody – maybe she didn't want to be a burden, maybe she didn't know how, or maybe she just plain forgot. She starved to death alone in her house with a pantry full of food. Our best guess is she forgot it was there, or forgot how to prepare it, or forgot to care. In death she looked the way Simon Grove looks now, cheeks sunken in, collarbones jutting out like tennis-racquet handles, skin loose, and shiny, and grey.

Only Grove looks worse. There's a rash on the side of his face and down his neck that makes him look like he fell asleep on grapes spoiling in the sun. His badly infected eye looks ready to burst, and the skin around his good eye is so loose his eye looks like it could drop out. His hair is thinner, and patchy. The skin around his fingernails has tightened, making the nails look long, and the veins in his forearms are bulging and blue. He smells of sweat and piss. The cigarette burns on his body are shiny. In less than one day I've turned him into a zombie.

I leave the tape across his mouth. I have my bottle of whiskey and the folder. The contents of this folder were emailed to the department earlier today. Though I haven't looked at what's inside, I know what is in there is going to make all the difference moving forward.

I sit on the bottom basement step. I knock back more whiskey, and I open the folder, and both of these are forms of fuel. Grove groans against the gag while I go through the photographs in the folder. The first is a series from the crime scene where Eric Delany was murdered. Blood inside the van. Eric, his eyes open, skin grey, neck and limbs at unnatural angles. Photos of him from different sides. Photos of him on a slab in the morgue. Each photo I toss onto the floor face up so Grove can see them. I have forty minutes before Dad arrives. Father Barrett promised he will text when they are on their way. With each picture my stomach tightens further and my heart quickens. I should have brought a bucket down here with me. My brain is on fire. This poor young boy with so much to live for brutally taken out of the world. I cycle through the photographs and read the autopsy report, my jaw tightening, my hands shaking, imagining how it played out. Eric Delany, hands around his throat, wishing that it would stop, wanting his mom and dad as the world darkens from the edges, leaving only his killer to focus on. I think about his parents. I picture them collapsing into heaps in their doorway, a future shaped in an impossible way, a mom and dad unable to carry on in a world turned impossible.

Grove watches me. He can't say anything because his mouth is still taped up. I don't say anything to him either. I carry on with the second set of photos – these ones for Harry Waltz. There aren't as many, because Harry was never found. But there are photos of his school bag with blood on it. There are pictures of Harry taken days before he disappeared. Pictures of his grieving parents snapped on the day of the funeral they eventually held for their son, as if the police back then were watching the parents through the lens of suspicion. I toss them onto the floor the same way as I did the others. I have twenty minutes left.

I scoop everything back up. I tap it all level and return the lot into the folder, square the pictures up with the spine and lay it down next to me. I stand up and the walls aren't pulsing anymore. I need him to know that I mean business. He watches me with a panicked look as I pull on a latex glove. That panic increases when I put my thumb over his bad eye and push – not much, but it doesn't take much. He flinches and screams into the duct tape.

'Shush, shush,' I say, keeping my thumb in place. Maybe those who hurt him in the past said the same thing as they inflicted their wants and needs on him.

He doesn't shush. Instead he yelps into the duct tape. His body jerks as if he's being electrocuted. He tries shaking his head, but my thumb stays with him. I feel sick, of course I feel sick, and I hate myself, of course I hate myself, but this is a bad man who deserves bad things to happen to him, and I am a good man who deserves not to lose everything, and don't people say God helps those who help themselves?

I let go of his eye.

'I'm going to hurt you,' I tell him, struggling to get out the words, because, even though I knew this was going to be bad, it's worse than I had suspected. 'This eye first, then the next one. I'll keep going until you tell me what I need to know. So why don't you save yourself some pain?'

Grove is squirming and crying, and his good eye is open wide. I pull the tape off his mouth.

'Please don't do this,' he says. Tears have streaked down one side of his face, blood down the other. I can feel my own tears coming.

I have ten minutes left.

'Tell me where Freddy Holt is.'

'Please, please don't.'

I ball the duct tape up and cram it into his mouth. I put my thumb back onto his eye, harder this time. Something crunches. He screams, and keeps screaming for a good thirty seconds, through all of which I tell myself over and over that this guy would have killed Lucas yesterday, and me too, if things had gone his way. I remind myself the boys he killed would have been crying too. That's what I focus on. Not on the fact that I'm torturing a man in my basement. Not on the fact that my earlier thought about being a good man is complete bullshit, because a good man never would have done what I'm doing. But surely I'm not a bad man either. Am I?

His scream runs out of steam.

I remove the duct tape from inside his mouth.

'Tell me what happened.'

He sniffs. He slowly nods. He looks at the ground with his one good eye. 'It was an accident, I swear, that's all it was,' he says.

'Who was an accident?'

'Harry Waltz. I didn't mean to kill him. I'll tell you everything. Just don't hurt me anymore.'

'Tell me.'

And he does.

Chapter Forty-Two

Grove is different from other people, and between the waves of pain coming from his eye, he tells the sheriff exactly that. Different ever since he had his lights switched off at the bottom of the lake, then switched back on as an orphan on the stony bank.

'Being without oxygen, having to be resuscitated, it changed my brain chemistry somehow. Things that people can figure out in five seconds take me ten. I get there in the end, most of the time, if *given* enough time.'

It's true too. If it weren't, he wouldn't have left the school on Monday with Lucas in the trunk of his car and a trail of breadcrumbs pointing the police his way. He thinks the ability to think things through more would make him less likely to give into biology – well, if not less likely, then perhaps he could hold out longer. As a kid, he struggled in school – struggled to grasp some of the fundamentals. His only gift was his ability to fix things. Not modern-day things with all their modern-day components, but old things, and he was equally as good at upcycling old furniture and turning it into things that were new. But there are days, for sure, when he thinks if he hadn't taken that trip to the bottom of the lake, that he could have been a scientist, or a pilot or a lawyer.

He doesn't tell the sheriff any of that, because he knows the guy would only think he was using it as an excuse. So he gets straight to the point, because the quicker he gets there the sooner he can get medical attention. It's been a day of hell, and his eye feels infected, and it sure as fuck doesn't help when somebody keeps putting their thumb into it.

'I was twenty years old when my world intersected with Harry Waltz's world. This was after I'd moved out of home – though technically I escaped. I floated around a bit, taking on odd jobs, until I ended up working on fishing boats; three weeks on and one week off, a job I grew to hate with so much passion that on my weeks off I drank to forget how bad things were. Can I have some more water?'

Cohen glances at his watch, then at his phone, then offers him a drink. He takes some, then carries on. 'A job was a job, and there weren't a lot of options – I mean, what else is there for a guy like me?'

Cohen stares at him. He's not expecting an answer, and doesn't get one.

'I was living in a shitty apartment that had four walls and a roof and not a lot else, no TV, no stereo, no computer, a microwave that worked fifty percent of the time and taps that vibrated when you turned them on.'

'What does any of this have to do with Harry?'

'Everything. Nothing. I don't know. I mean, if life had been different for me, maybe it'd have been different for all those around me. Anyway, one morning I'm driving home from a night of drinking, and this kid comes flying off the sidewalk right in front of me on a mountain bike, and the rest ... well, the rest was physics. He went right under, and I didn't know what to do.'

Cohen glances at his phone again, and maybe the guy has somewhere better to be. The air in the basement is stuffy. It's clinging to him. He can smell himself, his sweat, the blood, his eye.

'So what did you do?'

'I jumped out of the car, expecting to see tire tread lines over him like you see in cartoons, maybe flat in those places too. Maybe if I were sober I wouldn't have thought that, but ... but I wasn't sober. I had to drink lots back then because my mind filled up with bad stuff.

Still does. I can't help it. The doctors, after my old man tried to drown me, they thought my brain wouldn't fill up at all, that it'd be empty, but they were wrong. It's always full, it's always busy thinking about the bad stuff that's happened to me, always trying to figure out what I did to deserve any of it. You went through my house?'

'I did.'

'You found my computer?'

'Yes.'

'So you know what my foster parents did to me.'

'I do.'

'Those things are always with me, but out on the water there ain't no time for thinking about such bad stuff. It was the only good thing about working the boats, and why I did it, I guess. Out there a distraction can cost you your life, but off the water the only way to quiet the thoughts is to drink. I know I said I drank because I hated my job, and there's a truth to that, but there's a bigger truth too: I drank to dull the pain of my childhood, a daddy that tried to kill me, another that beat me, and one that fucked me.'

Cohen looks like he doesn't know what to say to that.

'You ever drink too much when you know you shouldn't?' Simon asks.

'Most people have.'

'Thing is, you start off knowing you should limit yourself, but the more you drink, the less you care about it. It's why people drink and drive. You go to the bar with best intentions, but those intentions dissolve once you're a couple in. Decisions you'd normally make become all kinds of different. That's what happened to me with that kid. Sober me ... sober me would have called for an ambulance. Only it wasn't sober me who ran that kid over by accident, it was drunk me, and drunk me sees things even slower than the way I usually see them. So I got out of the car, and the kid was already dead, this kid who wasn't a hell of a lot younger than me, his limbs were at weird angles and his head was twisted, and all I could think was that I was going to go to jail because he didn't have the common sense to look before gliding out into the street, and I couldn't go to jail, because jail is full of the kind of people that would do to me what my daddies used to do to me. And ... and what had happened, that wasn't my fault. If I'd been sober the accident would have played out the same way. There was nobody else around. Nobody had seen it. So I scooped him up and tossed him into the trunk and drove him out to the docks. I was shipping out the next day. A few minutes down from that boat was this old bar that had been shut down six months earlier. I hid him in there, and the next day I snuck him on board in a suitcase, and the day after that he sank to the bottom of the ocean.'

Cohen nods, then looks at the file he's hanging on to, then nods some more. He's not so sure the sheriff believes any of it.

'Eric Delany didn't bleed out,' Cohen says. 'He didn't die of shock. He was raped and strangled. For all I know the same is true of Harry Waltz. You grabbed him off his bike, and—'

'He came out in front of me and I hit him, I swear.' And it's the truth. Well, at least that part is the truth.

'Here's what I think,' Cohen says. 'I think he was alive. You went about doing the same things to him you would later do to Eric.'

'He was dead.'

'Tell me the truth, or I put you back in the freezer and we do this again tomorrow.'

'I am telling you the truth,' he says, but he's not. The truth might get Cohen poking his thumbs into both of his eyes. 'But you don't want to hear it because whatever you're planning on doing to me will be easier if you think I killed him on purpose.'

Cohen doesn't have a response to that, and it tells Simon everything he needs to know. There is no medical attention after this. No help. The only thing waiting for him is a hole in the ground, probably back out in the forest.

Cohen's phone beeps. He reads the message, then gets up.

'To be continued,' he says, and he puts duct tape over Simon's mouth and makes his way upstairs.

Chapter Forty-Three

I meet Father Barrett and my dad on the front step. I thank Father Barrett for his help, and he says Dad was no bother, which makes me think priests aren't as honest as they're meant to be. Still, if we're keeping score, I figure he's being more honest about his day than I am about mine.

'You okay?' he asks.

'Just tired, that's all.'

'I can stay and help a little if you like.'

'I'm fine, really, but I appreciate the offer.'

'Let me know if you change your mind,' he says, then heads back to his car.

'So, Dad,' I say, when we're alone and in the lounge, 'what would you like for dinner?'

'Fuck off,' he says, then quickly follows that with, 'Who the hell are you to say I can't cook?'

'I'll order something for—'

'No, I mean who the hell are you?'

'It's me, Dad. James.'

Dad shakes his head. 'You're not James.'

'Dad...'

'I don't know who the hell you are, but I spent the day with my boy.'

'That wasn't me.'

Before I can offer to prove this to him by showing him my driver's licence, he says, 'I want a drink.'

He heads toward the front door, and I steer him to the couch. I figure giving him a drink can only help the situation, so I pour him some whiskey and mix in a couple of sleeping pills. I'm getting pretty good at drugging people. He goes into his bedroom and sits on his bed and drinks it while staring at me, and soon his eyes glaze over.

'James?'

'Yeah, Dad.'

'I'm sorry.'

'I know.'

'Indian would be good.'

'I'll order some.'

'I'll rest a bit.'

'Good idea.'

I order some Indian food, and breathe a sigh of relief when my credit card works. By the time it's delivered, Dad is asleep. I eat mine and put his in the fridge. I figure between the sleeping pills and the long day, he'll sleep right through. Even so, when I go into the basement, I jam a wooden wedge into the doorframe so the door can't be pushed open from the outside. I head downstairs. If Grove has made any attempt to escape, it's not evident. He's sitting still, watching me.

'Eat this,' I say, and I rip the tape off his mouth and put a muesli bar into it. He chews it greedily, and swallows it down. He gets through the bar and then I feed him a second one.

'Thank you,' he says, when he's done, and after I've given him some water. 'Everything I said is how it happened, only ... only you're right. I jumped out of the car, and I was sure he was going to be dead ... but he wasn't. He needed help right away, but I knew an ambulance wouldn't make it in time. I swear I was going to take him to the hospital, and I was halfway there, but ... well, you need to understand something first ... I was scared of going to jail. And this kid, he was going to die anyway. That's what I thought. So before I knew it, I'm driving him to that empty bar, and you're right, he was still alive when I got him there. I knew then it wasn't going to be that easy. The thing about me is nothing has ever come to me easy. Life ain't meant to be anything but hard. My last foster daddy used to say that. It ain't meant to be anything but hard, and if it's not, then you're doing it wrong. It was bad luck what happened, the boy's bad luck, my bad luck, but there was nothing I could do but wait it out, and when the waiting got too painful for us both, I did what I had to do.' He looks up at me. 'I took no pleasure strangling him, you have to believe me about that. I tried to think of it like I was doing him a favour because he was so messed up that even if he had lived, he was never going to be the same anyway.'

'You took his bike.'

'What?'

I don't know if that's true or not, only that Henry's bike was never found. For all anybody knows, somebody else came along and took it.

'You run him over, it's all an accident, and you're thinking you need to get him to the hospital – why go to the effort of putting his bike in the car?'

He stares at me.

'Every second counts, right? And yet—'

'I don't know. Like I've been saying, I'd been drinking, and I wasn't thinking straight. I just figured I ought to take the bike too. After all, it was the kid's bike. And I also thought maybe the police would need it for evidence or something.'

Rather than pull his answer apart, I move on.

'What did you mean when you said to Lucas you were trying to soften the pain?'

'What?'

'Remember I told you we saw everything on the camera. You said you were going to share it with Lucas, whatever "it" is, and it would soften some, and what you had left was going to keep getting smaller. You said your dad taught you that.'

He looks back down.

'I think I'm getting it now. I think you had Harry Waltz beaten and broken, and you were sobering up, and you were remembering what it was like to be beaten and broken, and you figured you could put some of that onto him.'

He slowly nods, and he says nothing, and I wait him out.

Chapter Forty-Four

'It's like a pie,' he says, after Cohen has been staring silently at him for the last minute. It's hard to explain, but he gives it a go. 'I didn't know it back then, but I did after. A pie that gets sliced up, and each piece is loaded with what all my daddies did to me, and my entire life I've had to carry those slices alone. Then along came an opportunity to unload one of them on that boy, which was one less I had to carry, and suddenly hurting somebody else made my hurt hurt less.'

'And the others since then?' Cohen asks. 'You figure the more slices you offload, the better you'll feel.'

'They're only small slices,' he says. 'Enough for them to carry, and even then I would have shown them how to offload slices of their own. The more we share, the smaller those slices get. It's simple,' he says. 'Really simple.'

'Except it's not simple, because those you choose don't want any of it, and even then you kill them anyway, so you sitting there and saying you would have shown them how to offload slices of their own is bullshit.'

'No,' he says. But sure, Cohen is right. Well, he's right about those other boys, but wrong about yesterday. 'If Lucas had just listened to me yesterday, it could have gone different. I would have helped him after, I promise. See, it always feels better after you share the pain.'

'For you, but not for them. How many others have there been?'

'What?'

'How many?'

There have been six. Seven, if you count Lucas. Something like that you get a taste for. But he's not going to tell Cohen any of that. 'Just Lucas, and those two in the file.'

'I don't believe you.'

'It's the truth.'

'Killing your parents, was that like offloading a slice of pie?'

'I didn't kill them.'

'But you had somebody do it.'

He thinks about lying, but if he lies about that, then Cohen won't believe him about anything else, and despite knowing where this is going – a hole in the ground – he still has hope it may not. 'I needed an alibi.'

'Who did you use?'

'A guy I met on the boats. I can't remember his name,' he says, and it's true. 'He did it for five hundred dollars. I thought that seemed cheap.'

'And next week?'

'What?'

'The trip planned for next week. What was all that about?'

That arsehole principal must have told him about it. 'I just … wanted to get away for a bit. That's all.'

'You were watching the videos of what happened to you when you were young. I need you to tell me why.'

'You wouldn't understand.'

'Try me.'

He watches them because he tries to understand them. He wants to re-enact them. He figures the closer he is to doing to others what was done to him, the better it can make him feel. And it works that way. It really does. But there's no way he can explain that to Cohen – or anybody for that matter – and have them understand it.

'Where is this going? Are you going to help me or are you going to kill me?'

'Where is Freddy Holt?'

'I don't know.'

'You killed him.'

'I didn't.'

'You confessed to it.'

'I was lying. I was just trying to scare Lucas into doing what I wanted him to.'

'And Eric Delany. Did you accidentally run him over too?'

The change in direction throws him. Eric Delany. No, he hadn't run him over. It took him a couple of years after watching Harry Waltz sink beneath the waves to understand his own pain could be shared, and that if he could share it in the same way he had received it, then he could unburden himself of some of what his foster parents had done to him. It was too dangerous to try anything in Acacia – the idea about the camera only came to him recently – so he took a road trip. Hundreds of miles from here he snatched Eric off the side of the road one morning. He'd been driving a van he'd stolen the night before, and he was cruising for any stragglers on their way to school. He saw Eric and pulled over a hundred yards up the road. When the kid came by, he slid open the side door and wrenched him in, skateboard and all. He drove twenty minutes and parked beneath an overhead bridge and spent two minutes explaining to Eric how things were going to work, then another twenty showing him what he meant.

He lays all of that out for Cohen, staring at the floor through his one good eye as he talks, his face burning with the shame of it all. How the hell did his life turn out this way?

'I didn't hurt him more than I needed to,' he adds. 'And that's it. Now you know everything.'

'Not everything. Tell me about Taylor Reed.'

'I don't know anything about him.'

'You bullied him online.'

'I don't even know how to use social media,' he says, which is true, and sure, he saw Taylor Reed around the school like he saw other students, but he never spoke to him, never bullied him, never did anything to him. Didn't know his name until his head hit the ground like a watermelon. 'I know email, and auctions, and that's it.'

'You know videos too.'

He doesn't answer.

'You going to tell me you know nothing about Freddy Holt either?'

He shakes his head. 'Nothing. I swear. I was making that stuff up, just trying to scare the boy yesterday.'

'Did Freddy Holt give you the idea for the camera? You realised he wouldn't stay quiet without some kind of threat over him, so you killed him?'

He slowly shakes his head. 'I told you about the others, I have no reason to lie now. I never knew him, and I'm not an idiot. I know where this is going. I know you're not letting me out of here alive. I just ask you don't hurt me anymore. I've had enough hurt to last plenty of lifetimes, Sheriff. I know I have no right to ask that, considering what I've done, but I didn't do nothing to that Freddy boy, nor the one who jumped, and whether I did or didn't ain't going to change whatever it is you have planned for me. You're too far down a path to be able to take me into the station and put me behind bars, and I've known that from the moment I woke up in your basement.'

He can see his words have rubbed Cohen the wrong way. Good. The bastard needs a good dose of reality, and maybe he can shock the guy into doing the right thing.

'You might think you can kill me in cold blood and sleep at night because of what I've done, but it will haunt you. I've told you everything. So now what?'

'You haven't told me everything.'

'I don't know what happened to Freddy.'

'I don't believe you.'

'Are you going to kill me?'

'No.'

'Now I'm the one who doesn't believe you,' he says.

Cohen puts fresh tape back over his mouth. 'Truth is, I'm still deciding.'

Chapter Forty-Five

They have dinner – pizza, which is par for the course. Ever since it's just been the two of them, dinner has consisted mostly of takeout, with his dad on occasion still cooking – but when his dad does cook, it's hotdogs, or hamburgers, or grilled cheese sandwiches. Lucas has no idea why they don't weigh a ton, combined. Perhaps the alcohol keeps the weight away in his dad's case, and in his case it's simply a matter of time – that one day soon it will all catch up with him.

There's another explanation too for why he hasn't put on weight – the worms. Thinking about it makes him scratch at his hand. He'd tear the bandage away and scratch deep at the cut if the nurse hadn't put the fear of an infection into him. An infection is a breeding ground for the kind of parasites that can survive nuclear bombs.

They watch the news while they eat, but it offers nothing more than he already knows – Simon Grove is somewhere out in the wild, or maybe he's in town, or possibly neither of those two things, which can be summed up by saying that maybe the police will catch him, maybe they won't.

'I can't believe they still don't have him,' his dad says, finishing his second beer since they started dinner.

Lucas can believe it. The world is a crazy place.

'I'm gonna grab a water,' Lucas says. 'Want me to get you another beer?'

He dad weighs it up for a few seconds, which seems unlike him these days, but he course-corrects and says, 'That'd be good.'

While his dad works away at the beer, Lucas returns to his room. He sits on the bed staring out the window. Twenty minutes later he hears his dad going to the fridge for his fourth beer. He stays on the bed and watches the sun melt into the horizon, and after a while the clicking keyboard from his dad's office goes quiet. A few years ago his dad put a couch in there. This was before the drinking, when his parents were still playing happy families. The couch was so his dad could relax with a book while taking a break from writing, but over time has become a place for him to relax with a drink while *not* writing. He thinks it's a pretty safe bet his dad is on that couch now, asleep.

The bedroom window is open and Lucas can hear Mr and Mrs Courtney's dog barking, a puppy they got to replace the one they said ran away. Sometimes the puppy will poke its nose through the gate when he's passing on the way home from school, and Lucas will give it a pat or a scratch, the dog smiling and acting like the world is made up of two different types of days – great days, and even greater days. Mrs Courtney calls out to it now, and then it goes quiet, probably put inside for the night.

The sun disappears, and soon he can no longer see anything beyond the window. Even so he waits. Seconds feel like minutes. Minutes feel like hours. Ten o'clock comes and goes. He stays on the bed, figuring things in his head over and over, playing out how it's going to go. Ten-thirty comes. Ten-thirty goes. It's not going to get any darker. Even so, he waits until eleven, and then he goes to his dad's office. As he suspected, he's asleep on the couch, empty beer bottles lined up on the desk. Maybe his dad will wake up and drag himself into bed, or maybe he'll spend the night on the couch – either way, he won't notice if Lucas has gone.

He returns to his bedroom and closes the door. He grabs a jacket and stuffs the stolen items into his pockets. He climbs out the window. His bike is in the backyard, where he left it earlier. He can't go out the front because of the patrol car, but what he can do is lift his bike over the back fence. It's a struggle – he stands on the beam running along the middle and reaches down and lifts his bike, and has to fight with it some, but he gets it over the top, the pedals gouging at the fence as it goes over, then he leans over and lowers it as far as he can before letting it drop the rest of the way. He follows it, dropping softly in the backyard of Mr Collins' house – Mr Collins who is always in bed by eight o'clock and is so deaf he could sleep through his house being hit by lightning; Mr Collins who calls Lucas 'Tim' because he thinks that's Lucas's name. He wheels his bike down the side of the house to the road where there are no patrol cars.

He bikes in the dark. First time he sees a car, he stops on the sidewalk and waits for it to pass, his phone in his hand ready to call the police in case the janitor pulls over and steps out. Only the car doesn't pull over, nor does the next one, or any of them for that matter – not that there are many. It's a ten-minute ride out of his neighbourhood and into the next one. He's puffing, but still comfortable by the time he gets to Sheriff Cohen's street. The house on the corner of the block has rows of lavender lining the front yard. The lights inside, like in most of the houses, are off. He hides his bike on the other side of the lavender and steps back to the sidewalk. He walks the half-block to the sheriff's house. He watches it from across the road, hiding behind an oak tree while a black cat headbutts his ankles. Unlike the other houses, the lights in there are on.

The house is single storey, with a dark roof and almost as dark weatherboards. The yard is a mess. The garden is full of weeds and overgrown shrubs, and the lawn is ankle-deep. It's nothing a quick fire wouldn't fix. The garage is a separate building out to the right, wide enough to fit one car and so flat rain must have a hard time figuring which way to drain.

Nathan is somewhere in that house, but his parents are in there too.

He's going to have to be careful.

Lucas crosses the road.

Chapter Forty-Six

The curtains are closed, the lights are on, and the stereo is off. I've been lying on my couch for the last few hours sobering up while trying to use the peace and quiet to think, but that peace is broken by the buzzing. It started after talking to Grove. A mosquito has tunnelled deep into my brain where painkillers can't reach it. I've taken four of them and they're not doing a damn thing. They haven't helped with the nerves either. I'm trying to calm nerves that don't want to be calmed.

I stare at the ceiling. I count the dead moths and flies stuck in the glass dome beneath the light bulb – six of them; always six no matter what order I count them in. It seems like a good place for a spider to set up shop, but instead the spiders are hanging in the shadows, out of sight. I'm trying to think of a way forward that doesn't see me putting Grove in the ground all while keeping me out of jail. This is what happens when you don't make a plan, when everything comes from a moment of spontaneity, where you go down a path impossible to come back from. Only I'm still searching, and that searching is making the buzzing louder – possibly because there is no solution other than the one Grove pointed out earlier.

Despite the time creeping up toward midnight, my phone beeps with a message. It's Hutch. I've been expecting the text. She says news of the reward has been picked up by several news outlets across the country. She says hopefully by this time tomorrow we'll have gotten some calls.

Grove is worth more money tonight than he was yesterday.

I head down to the basement. I left Grove tied to the chair earlier, and sedated him again too. He doesn't wake when I shake him. I cut him free and keep his arms cable-tied behind him. Getting him down to the basement when he was unconscious was one thing, but getting him back up those stairs is another. He's heavy. Too heavy to carry. Last night I was amped when I carried him up the basement stairs at the Kelly farm. I could have carried two of him. But that strength has long gone. I use the smelling salts to wake him. It's not like earlier when he jerked awake. This is waking up with a flat battery. His eye opens slowly and won't focus. He can't say anything because I have tape over his mouth.

'Come on,' I say. I get my arm around him and my ribs flare up as I help him to his feet, but it's no good – all his time in the freezer and all the sedatives in his system have turned Grove into a guy walking like his legs are busted.

'Come on, we're almost there.'

He mumbles something that I suspect would be inaudible even if I didn't have duct tape over his mouth. I shake him a little. His eye opens again and focuses on me for a few seconds before looking past me.

'I'm taking you to a hospital. We have to go.'

I can't imagine he believes that, but he wants to. He groans something, and he makes an effort to get to his feet, and I help him. We get to the base of the stairs.

'It's going to be okay,' I tell him.

Slowly, one step at a time, we make our way up to the door.

Chapter Forty-Seven

Lucas makes his way down the narrow path between the garage and the fence until he pops out into the backyard. From here he can see it's just the lounge light that is on, and maybe one from the hallway, but this end of the house is dark. He has no way of knowing which bedroom is which, but what he does know is that he can't take the chance of trying to open a window to find out. He watches the house for a minute, trying to figure out which angle to come at it from, before deciding that the house isn't the way to go. Even if the front door were unlocked and everybody were asleep, he couldn't go in there for fear of stepping on a creaking floorboard, and he can't be sure the Cohens don't own a dog.

He turns back to the garage. It's not ideal, but it's still pretty good. He returns down the side path and tries the windows. They are all painted shut. So he continues around it, finding the same for each of them. Damn it. Unless the side door is unlocked? It doesn't seem likely, but when he tries it the handle turns freely, and better yet, when he pushes forward it swings open. He heads inside and closes the door behind him.

He uses the light from his cellphone to look around, keeping the light low and cupping his hand over it. He doesn't think Sheriff Cohen is a 'shoot first and ask questions later' kind of guy, but that doesn't make him feel any less nervous being here. Filling the centre of the garage is a dark SUV with dirt along the sides. It faces a workbench with tools hanging on the walls and shelving units full of plastic boxes. There are coils of rope and garden hose hanging from beams in the ceiling. All around the garage he sees potential hiding space after hiding space. A thousand nooks and crannies. He picks up a rag from the bench. He stays low and points the flashlight of his phone into the gaps on the shelves. He doesn't have to be picky.

He pulls the watch and the wallet out of his pockets, and gives each a thorough wipe down before dropping them one at a time behind a row of paint cans on the bottom shelf of a storage rack. Then he turns on Harriet White's cellphone. The screen takes a few seconds to light up, and then it asks for a PIN, which he doesn't know, and doesn't need. He puts the phone on mute and wipes it down and tucks it behind the same paint tins. Hopefully Harriet has tracking software on her phone, and when she wakes tomorrow she'll be able to see where it is. If she doesn't, then hopefully she makes a report to the police, and they can track its location via cell towers. Then Sheriff Cohen or one of the other cops will come here and look around and find everything, and they're going to point the finger at Nathan. Even if he's not expelled, and Lucas is sure he will be, everybody at the school is going to think that he's a thief. Sure, they're okay for him to beat the shit out of people, but the idea he might steal their stuff is a bridge they won't be willing to cross.

He brushes his hands in the manner of a job well done, and is back at the garage door when he hears footsteps approaching from the other side. He turns off his cellphone light and quickly glances through the window. There are two people out there, their arms around each other, coming toward him. In the darkness he can't tell who. Getting out is no longer an option. He turns and looks at all the nooks and crannies that were perfect for the cellphone and the wallet and watch, but all of them useless for him. Hiding also isn't an option.

He's trapped.

Chapter Forty-Eight

I keep expecting Grove to make some kind of break for it, albeit a feeble one, as I help him across the yard. Part of me even wants him to try, as if it would provide me with an excuse to put him down. But he doesn't, and maybe he really does think I'm taking him to the hospital, or maybe he thinks this day was both always coming and very much deserved.

I get the side door to the garage open. I help him down the side of the SUV, and we're almost at the tailgate when it must sink in that we're not going to the hospital after all. He elbows me in the stomach and breaks away. The impact is nowhere near as hard as the rebar was, but he gets me where those ribs are sore, making it feel the same. I fold in half and drop to my knees. Grove is no longer walking like a man with broken legs as he quickly makes his way to the end of the garage. He makes it in six steps, goes to grab the nearest thing from the wall – in this case a shovel – ends up wobbling to the side, bounces off the car, and, empty-handed, falls down. I get to my feet and am cautious when I approach him, but it turns out there's no need to be – he's passed out.

I get the tailgate popped open, then wrestle Grove off the floor and into the back, almost losing him a couple of times in the process. When he's in, I get the syringe out of my pocket and pop off the cap. I'm afraid one more shot might be one shot too many, but I'm even more afraid of him waking up on the drive. I aim the needle up with one of the existing holes in his arm and—

'What are you doing in my garage?'

My dad's voice makes me jump and I drop the syringe. I scoop it back up and try to intercept him as he makes his way towards me. I have no idea what he's seen.

'Dad, this—'

'I saw somebody.'

'It was only me.'

He shakes his head. 'No, there was somebody else. I saw him sneaking around outside. You must have seen him too.' He peers over my shoulder. 'What's going on back there?'

'Nothing, Dad, and I didn't see anybody else. It's just me out here.'

'Stop lying to me. He came here to steal from me, and...' He trails off and stares hard at me before carrying on. 'Are you stealing from me too?'

'Nobody is stealing anything, Dad,' I say, trying to sound calm, when in actuality my heart is thumping. Can Dad hear it? 'I promise you.'

'I saw somebody.'

'You saw me, that's all.'

He shakes his head. 'My son is a policeman. I'm going to call him.'

'Dad, it's me. James. I'm your son.'

'The hell you are.' He turns for the door. 'He's going to come here and arrest you and...'

His words fade out as I inject him with the dose I had for Grove. I don't need to tell myself I'm the worst person because it's apparent as I carry him back the way he came, then across the yard to the house. I get him lying down on the lounger on the deck. There's a box on the deck for cushions and blankets, and I go about making my dad comfortable while reminding myself I'm doing all of this for him as well as myself.

Chapter Forty-Nine

I wrap cable ties around Grove's feet and his wrists, and join those together, locking him into a foetal position. He's not going anywhere. I search the garage for a picnic blanket, then toss that over him. I close up the SUV and get behind the wheel and hit the remote for the garage door. It rumbles open, briefly drowning out the buzzing in my head.

I reverse out, sit in the driveway, hit the remote again and watch the door rumble closed, and then the buzzing returns. I back out where the streets are empty and the night is calm and the back of the SUV is heavy. We drive through town. The bars have closed and the only lights other than streetlights are my own. Over the last few days Acacia Pines has become a ghost of its former self. Monday night had people at bars and restaurants because folks had such a sense of disbelief that anything bad could happen to them that they rallied against it. Then Tuesday came, and that sense disappeared. The news gave them more details. Told them to be afraid. Reminded them about Freddy Holt and educated them about the boys from Grove's past and warned them Grove might still be around. Stores still opened and people went about their business as usual, all while everybody made sure they knew who was walking near them. Kids played in parks under supervision and people walked dogs and pushed strollers, but there was a sense of change in town, a sickness had gotten hold of the community. Not only were people on the lookout for Simon Grove, but they were on the lookout for the *next* Simon Grove. What other quiet men in quiet streets were hiding such dark twisted fantasies? Was Simon Grove a culmination of all of Acacia Pines' bad deeds, manifested as the bogeyman? Or was he a symptom of something even darker that made people rotten on the inside? This morning I saw more traffic on the road than I have on any other weekday morning. School traffic. Kids who normally biked or walked were driven by parents. Mothers threw suspicious glances at men they've always known. Simon Grove and the idea of another Simon Grove was a disease that was spreading.

We reach the bridge. The car changes sound as it goes over it. So far there hasn't been another car on the road, and that doesn't change between the bridge and the Kelly farm, or between the Kelly farm and the hiking tracks. We pass Earl's Garage, boarded-up windows and eye-shine from opossums on the forecourt. The long, empty highway snakes through it all, through asphalt and trees and wildlife, all the way out to the abandoned sawmill.

Chapter Fifty

Another metal coffin.

Almost.

In a garage where there were no hiding places, and where the windows wouldn't open, climbing over Grove and into the SUV was his only choice. And now Lucas is hidden in the footwell behind the driver's seat, beneath a winter jacket he found balled up on the floor. He has no idea what's going on, but he does know the window for putting his hand up and confessing to Sheriff Cohen is well and truly shut. Grove, dead or unconscious, is in the back of the SUV, not where you put somebody if you're arresting them. It seems clear to him Sheriff Cohen has known where Grove has been all this time. Whatever is happening here, if Sheriff Cohen catches him, does it mean his fate will be the same as that of the man tied up behind him?

He's turned his phone off. He can't risk a call or a text from his dad vibrating it. He can hear the road noise beneath the car. He heard them go over the bridge leading out of town earlier, and from there there's only one direction, and that's south out to farmland and forest and middle-of-nowhere places. He can hear the engine.

He can hear moaning from the back of the car as Simon Grove slowly comes round. He can hear the stereo coming from the front. He can hear his own heart beating.

There can only be one reason for coming out of town like this. One reason for having Grove tied up in the back. Every corner they take he has to tighten his muscles to restrict any movement, and now those muscles are fatiguing and on their way to cramping. He has to move soon – and movement means there's a chance of being heard. The inside of the jacket is damp from his breath. Where are they driving? New Zealand? Already they've driven so far it's going to take him hours to walk back.

Assuming he gets the chance.

The car makes a turn, then asphalt turns to gravel. It slows down. It comes to a stop. These are the same sounds from Monday. The engine dies and the door opens. The springs lift as Sheriff Cohen climbs out. Lucas holds his breath and waits for the rattling chains, but there aren't any. The small hydraulics hiss as the tailgate is opened. There's a small click, and then another, and then grunting as Sheriff Cohen wrestles with the janitor. He's swearing too. Then footsteps as he walks away, the back of the SUV left wide open.

Lucas moves the jacket. Slowly he sits up. He looks between the seats and out the windscreen. The headlights are pointing at the abandoned sawmill, lighting it up. There is a section of trees that are lit up too, and it's to those that Sheriff Cohen is walking with the janitor.

Hiding out in the back of the SUV was one hell of a risk that he's not prepared to take again. He watches as the two men walk toward the forest, and then he scrambles over the backseat and jumps out into the parking lot.

Chapter Fifty-One

The buzzing gets louder the moment we enter the trees. I've cut the cable ties from Grove's feet but have kept the ones on his wrists. He's steadier than he was earlier, but I don't anticipate him trying anything. There's a breeze picking up. It's warm and steady, fresh and revitalising. I have a three-foot chain hanging over my shoulder, a roll of duct tape in my pocket and a flashlight on my forehead. 'We're almost there. Keep going.'

He groans something but I can't tell what because of the duct tape. A moment later he collapses. I get him into a fireman's lift, and he feels light again, as if he's already decomposing. Or the Adderall I popped in the car is helping. I carry him deeper into the trees. It's hot work. I take high footsteps to avoid thick tree roots and broken branches. We're a good twenty yards in when the trees filter the headlights behind us out of existence. I carry Grove another ten, then set him up against a tree and loop the chain around him and the trunk. I lock it closed, then handcuff him to the chain. Unless the guy can pull a hundred-foot pine out of the ground, he's not going anywhere.

'Okay,' I say, crouching in front of him. His eyes are open and he's taking in his surroundings, but I can't tell if he fully understands where he is. The ground can't be comfortable to sit on, especially when you're naked. I take the duct tape off his mouth.

'I'm sorry,' Grove says, and he's crying again, and something dark is leaking out of his bad eye. 'I'm so sorry. Please don't kill me. I'm begging you, please don't kill me.'

'Tell me the truth about Freddy Holt.'

'I have.'

'Bullshit.'

He shakes his head. Harder now. 'I can prove it.'

'Yeah? How are you going to do that?'

'By telling you something even worse. By telling you something

I don't need to tell you. But you can't kill me. I know you're wanting to, and I thought I had made peace with that, but I don't want to die. Promise you won't kill me and I'll tell you what that worse thing is. See, if I'd killed that kid, I'd tell you, right?'

I move away from him and lean against a tree, facing it, my forehead resting on the backs of my hands. I already know he's done horrible things, and I don't know if I can listen to him telling me he's done worse.

Grove carries on without me looking at him. 'Because it'd be easier than what I have to say. You get it, right? Why confess to something worse? Just promise ... promise me you won't kill me. I don't ... I don't want to die.'

If anything, hearing what he has to say will make all of this easier on me. I turn away from the tree but stay where I am, Grove able to see me clearer than I can see him, and that's fine. 'I promise I won't hurt you,' I say, because I don't owe him the truth.

'I lied about Lucas,' he says. 'I ... I knew he would fight back. I knew he would be like the others. I lied to him about the camera. I figured if he thought I was going to let him go, things would go easier for him. I was always going to kill him because I knew it was the only real way to keep him quiet. That's my burden, don't you see? Sharing the pain means I have to kill these kids, and I don't want to because I was them once, but ... but it's the only way I can feel better.

'The can of gas I had in the back of my car? That was for him. When I was done with him I was going to set him on fire. I was going to drag him into the woods and dig a hole and burn him and bury him. I was going to hurt him bad. Really bad. Then nobody would ever know what had happened to him. Nobody would ever know it was me.'

I don't know what to say, so say nothing.

'There are others.'

'Ho—,' I start to say, then the words get caught in my mouth. I should have brought water out here with me. There's some in the car, but rather than go back I work up some saliva and swallow it down, then give it another go. 'How many?'

'Four more. Six in total. And you're right about next week. The camera wasn't to control them, it was for me, to watch over and over, because I figured that way I could put more time in between needing to hurt anybody. The last boy I killed was two years ago. His name was Ryan Ashcroft. And the one before that was eight years ago, and his name was Carl Nichols. The two others between were Neil Webster and Aaron McGee. I'm sorry,' he says. 'I'm so sorry, but now you know I didn't kill Freddy, right? I'd tell you if I did. I've told you everything else. And I didn't hurt that other boy either, the one who jumped.'

I run my fingers down the bark of the tree I'm leaning against, feeling how sharp it is. 'You killed six children,' I say.

'You don't have to do this,' he says.

I dig the side of my thumbnail into the bark, snapping a tiny segment away, then pushing on it deeper with my finger. It hurts, but I like it.

'Please, you don't have to do this. I could tell them I was out here the whole time. Could tell them you found me out here. All you have to do is say the same. Nobody would know what you did to me. I mean, even if I said anything it'd be your word against mine, and they'd believe you. They're your people. Tell them you found me out here and I'll say the same. Please. Please, it'll work that way.'

I dig the sliver of bark out from under my nail then turn back toward him. I honestly don't know what to think. All I know is I can't be here anymore. I wrap a loop of duct tape over his mouth and around the back of his head and over his mouth again. He mumbles something, probably a *you promised*. Then I head back the way I came, twigs and small broken branches snapping beneath my feet, each one making the same crunch his eye made when I buried my thumb into it earlier, each crunch making the doubts and the guilt swirl while turning the volume of the buzzing to high.

Chapter Fifty-Two

From inside the torn-open doorway of the mill, Lucas watches Sheriff Cohen walk out from the trees, his head down, his shoulders slumped. He looks like a man who just lost a fight. He reaches the SUV and closes the tailgate. He stares out at the forest for a moment, then slowly gets in behind the wheel. Dirt puffs out from the gravel and becomes a red mist in the taillights as he drives out to the road. When he's gone, Lucas steps into the parking lot and checks his phone. He had no signal inside the building, and outside is no different. His battery is in the red too. He'd have charged it earlier, but he didn't think he'd need to – there was plenty of power to search through Sheriff Cohen's garage, but not to go hiking through the woods.

The moon is half full and the sky is clear, and it only takes a few moments for his eyes to adjust to the dark. He steps around the door that has been pulled off, crime-scene tape caught beneath it, and heads to the trees. A glance back shows the sawmill as a pitch-black cave ready to swallow anybody who makes the mistake of going near it.

He points his phone into the trees. The light makes enough of a dent in the darkness to see broken branches and twigs that might be a path, but it could be one of many paths made when people came out here looking for Grove. He looks up at the moon. It's directly behind him. He steps in. How far should he go? Sheriff Cohen and the janitor took a straight line. As long as he sticks with the moon behind him, and then ahead when he turns around, he should be fine. He looks at the broken twigs on the side of the trees. Some breaks are dry and some are fresh. He follows the fresh ones.

A minute in and he finds the janitor. He's been secured to a tree with a length of chain. He stares at Lucas with his one good eye. The other eye is swollen and raw, crusted over with blood and goop, and Lucas doesn't feel bad about that even in the slightest. Grove mumbles something, but Lucas can't hear what because there's duct tape across his mouth. He looks like a photocopy of his original self, one where the colour has been washed out, and about as thin too. Lucas crouches next to him, then picks at an edge of the tape across his mouth, hooking up a corner until there's enough to pull. He unwinds it from around the janitor's mouth and head, not caring about the skin or hair that gets pulled with it.

The janitor exhales loudly. 'Thank God. Thank God. You have to help me. Please, you have to help me. Your sheriff is crazy.'

Lucas says nothing. He hates the idea of agreeing with the guy, but he does seem to be making a pretty valid point.

'Please, please, please help me.'

'You recognise me?' Lucas asks, pointing the light at himself.

The janitor shakes his head. 'I was walking home from work and he jumped me. Threw me into his car and brought me out here to kill. He'll kill you too if he comes back. We need to hurry.'

'Tell me you recognise me.'

'I need a hospital. My eye, it hurts so bad. I need you to help me. I'll do anything. Please just help me.'

Something moves in the tree above them. They both look up to the sound, the torch catching the eyes of an opossum looking back down. It looks from Lucas to the janitor, then back to Lucas, content to stay where it is and keep watching.

'Look at me,' Lucas says, and he gets closer so the janitor can get a better look. The janitor tilts his head to the side, his bloody eye closed up, his good eye scanning Lucas up and down.

'I ... I don't...' he says, and Lucas watches his face change as the recognition hits him.

Chapter Fifty-Three

It's the boy. The goddamn boy he tried to kill is now going to be his saviour. 'I wasn't going to hurt you, I swear, I really wasn't,' Simon says, and even though there's no chance Lucas is going to believe him, he has to try. 'I was kidding around. I was going to scare you a bit then let you go, that's all.'

'That's all?'

'I know it's a sickness, and I can't help it, but I swear you were going to be okay. I just ... I like to scare people.'

'You tried to kill me.'

'No, never. I mean ... sure, after you stabbed me I lost control a bit, but who wouldn't? You really hurt me. But I promise, I was going to let you go. I always was. You know that's true because of the camera, and even then I wasn't going to touch you. I just wanted to scare you.'

'Same way you scared the others?'

Okay, so there's no convincing Lucas anything different, but that also doesn't matter. What matters is getting help, and the kid doesn't recognise it, but he needs to help himself too. 'We have to go. If the sheriff comes back he'll kill both of us. Not just me, but you, because you're here and you shouldn't be, and this isn't normal, right? You know that, right? Or do you want to end up dead?'

Lucas shakes his head. The opossum rummaging around in the tree a few moments ago is still watching them. Once when Simon was on a picnic with his second parents, the good ones, an opossum fell out of a tree and hit his mom on the way down before scuttling off. His mom vowed never to go hiking again. That was just a few weeks before his dad had the heart attack that switched his lights off. He moves to the side so if the same thing happens now it'll miss him. He doesn't want to think about what else is out there in the darkness.

'The moment I untie you, you'll try to kill me,' Lucas says.

'You can't untie me, I'm handcuffed, but you can probably find something in the mill to pick the locks. It's easy,' he says, but he doesn't know that for a fact. Picking handcuff locks sure *looks* easy on TV. 'But I swear, I won't hurt you. Look at me. I need your help to get out of here.'

Lucas is shaking his head, looking unsure.

'Or you can call somebody for help.'

Lucas looks at his phone, then shakes his head. 'There's no signal.'

'Then walk till you find one. If you don't help me, I'll die here,' he says, then he thinks of another angle he can take. 'Otherwise you're killing me. Is that what you want? To be a killer?'

'Like you are? With the other boys you killed?'

'That was all a misunderstanding,' he says. 'I never killed anybody.'

'Uh huh. I think I should just leave you here. If Sheriff Cohen wanted you dead, he'd have killed you already. Whatever his plan is, it's not that, so maybe we just wait.'

'Come on, you're not an idiot – you know he's going to kill me.'

'Killing you would be crazy.'

'Yeah? And what about this isn't?' Lucas is nodding, and Simon can see he's scored a point. He presses on. 'He's been torturing me. He wanted to know about another boy, but I didn't touch that boy, I swear.'

'Freddy Holt.'

'That's him, but I didn't do nothing to him, I promise. I was lying when I told you I'd hurt him. I wanted to scare you some, and I figured if you thought I had killed him, you wouldn't struggle any. Between that and the camera I figured you'd do what I wanted. You have to help me.'

'I don't know. You were going to kill me, and—'

'You have to believe me about Freddy Holt. I swear I had noth—'

'I do believe you,' Lucas says.

'You do?'

'About Freddy, sure, but not about the rest of it.'

'What?'

'I knew you were lying about Freddy from the start.'

'You did?'

'Yeah. I knew it for an absolute fact.'

'You did? How ... how did...' Simon says. He trails off. No. Surely not. Surely fucking not.

'You're almost there,' Lucas says.

Simon keeps shaking his head as he keeps banging up against the answer. No, no, no. It can't be. Only ... only what else can it be?

'You? You killed him?'

Lucas reaches into his pocket and pulls out a length of crime-scene tape that likely came from the parking lot. He untangles it.

'Like Freddy, you're too far gone to be saved,' Lucas says.

'What the fuck does that—'

'It's the worm. You've got one, like he did. They bury into your brain and they pull levers in directions they've never been pulled before. It also explains what's happening here. One day Sheriff Cohen was Sheriff Cohen, and now he's something different.'

'Listen, listen, Lucas, you—'

He doesn't get to finish. Lucas loops the crime-scene tape around his neck and tightens it. There's nowhere to go, nothing to fight against, and he's scared of dying, scared of what might be waiting for him. He rallies against it, but all he can do is stomp his feet into the ground as he runs out of air...

He's back in his parents' car, his brother next to him, his parents in the front as the water floods in. The car bobs and floats at first, before the weight of the engine tips it forward, pulling it down. He's scared, so scared. It's like falling into the deepest hole in the world.

Chapter Fifty-Four

Things didn't start with Freddy. They started with Wolfy, the German Shepherd his dad brought home for Christmas when Lucas was thirteen. He fell in love with that dog. He went everywhere with Wolfy. They'd walk for miles. They'd go to the park and play catch with a tennis ball, or a Frisbee, or a stick. Wolfy looked like he was smiling all the time. Didn't matter what he was doing – chasing that Frisbee, eating, sleeping, curling up around Lucas's feet

– he wore that smile day in and day out. He even wore it right after he bit Lucas. By then Wolfy was six months old, and the week prior to the bite, worms that looked like live spaghetti had shown up in his poop, bringing back memories of the documentary Lucas watched all those years earlier, the documentaries that led to the nightmares, and the anxiety, and the Ekbom Syndrome diagnosis.

Wolfy went onto medication when the worms were found, and the vet promised it wouldn't take long to clear up. But the vet was wrong, because then came the bite, Wolfy chewing on a tennis ball one moment, then chewing on Lucas's arm the next. While Lucas's mom took him to the hospital to have his arm fixed up, his dad took Wolfy to the vet.

His dad brought Wolfy home from the vet in a box. What Wolfy had done to Lucas was very serious, and there had been no option but to have him put down. Lucas knew it was the worms that had caused this. Wolfy had been infected with the type from the documentary. A monster worm had gotten to his brain, and the thing inside Wolfy that made Wolfy Wolfy was forever altered. He also knew despite Wolfy having been put to sleep forever, the worm that had changed him was still alive.

Wolfy had been punished for something that wasn't his fault.

And the worm: what was to stop it from digging its way out of Wolfy and into something – or somebody – else? Worms, by their very nature, lived in the dirt – and this one would live there too until it found another victim.

That gave Lucas two reasons to find the worm. One – to punish it. Two – to prevent it from hurting others. His dad came out into the backyard when Lucas was elbow deep inside the dog that, up until the vet had slipped the needle in, had loved him so much, and even then Wolfy still had that smile on his face, even if the eyes were so lifeless they couldn't back that smile up. His dad had buried the dog late in the afternoon, and Lucas had unburied him in the evening. His dad found him before Lucas got the chance to hunt out the very worm the vet would have found if he had known to look for it. They never told Lucas's mom what he had done – she had been out when the digging had happened, and there was no good reason to sully her with such details. The worm escaped, but a year later he knew where to – it showed up inside the electrician his parents had hired during the renovations of the house.

The electrician, like Wolfy, would only hurt more people unless stopped. Lucas knew the electrician had a worm inside him, because he was friendly when he spoke to them, but the opposite when he didn't. He had overheard him on the phone referring to Lucas's mom as a right bitch, one he wanted to drag down into the basement and put in her place, like they had done with that waitress from the Big Bar in town, who he, along with whoever he was talking to, had followed home that night. Lucas didn't like his mom being spoken about like that, and he didn't like the idea of this man hurting waitresses. Not at all. This thing that was controlling the electrician needed to be stopped. So when the electrician switched the power off to the house, Lucas switched it back on. Electricians were used to getting jolted. He would be fine. But he expected the worm wouldn't survive.

He was expecting there to be sound when it happened. Buzzing, maybe, like those scenes in countless Frankenstein movies where the monster is given life with large power-producing generators.

There was no sound.

There wasn't much of anything at all.

At least it looked like nothing.

It was as if somebody pushed pause – the electrician stopped moving, his hands on wires he couldn't let go of, his face tightening as if he were focused intently on a problem. Maybe the fire and the melting would have come if it had been allowed to continue, but another tradesman understood the situation and killed the power. The electrician, it turned out, had heart issues, and he went into cardiac arrest. The ambulance came, and so did Sheriff Cohen – only he wasn't sheriff back then. The electrician was saved. What had happened to him was an accident – that was the conclusion. The electrician had made a mistake, and one he would learn from.

That night Lucas's dad came into his room and asked if Lucas had switched the power back on. He didn't like lying to his dad, but knew his dad would like the truth even less, so he said no. His dad nodded, said nothing, and walked back out, leaving Lucas to wonder why he had asked in the first place.

When the renovations were complete, his parents began working on the yard. His mom was planting rose bushes when she found the dog he had killed earlier that year. That was the dog who had bitten Victoria Tennent, the girl he had a crush on but hadn't spoken to since he was ten. She had come into school, her leg bandaged. She had been bitten by her neighbour's dog. He heard others say how shocked they were that the dog wasn't being put down. Of course he couldn't know for sure it was the same worm. He suspected it was – worms grew, and they multiplied. They were like a virus. So it was possible it was a different one, but still a part of the same family tree. Either way, it needed to be ended. He lured the dog away, and he got it open, and there was no worm in there. He searched thoroughly too. He had been wrong, and it was a mistake that still haunts him.

Sometimes a bad dog is nothing more than a bad dog.

No amount of apologising or justifying could convince his mom to stay after she found that dog – especially when his dad admitted he'd known what Lucas had done to Wolfy, then admitted he had known about the second dog too, a fact Lucas was surprised to hear. He didn't know if his mom was madder over what Lucas was doing or at his dad for covering it up. She packed her bags, and there was nothing either of them could say to convince her to stay.

Then there was Freddy.

A year ago Freddy hit a growth spurt, and it turned out he had something growing inside him too – a meanness that Lucas became an outlet for. Freddy started picking on him. He'd call him names and bang into him in the corridor. It was no getting stuffed into a locker and left to rot – but the fact they had once told each other ghost stories at night in sleeping bags in the backyard under big open skies made that meanness feel like a betrayal. Was Freddy's change a physical thing? A kind of parasite, a sentient tapeworm? Was it this thing that made him act out? Lucas knew the answer to all of those was a big yes.

Then Taylor Reed jumped to his death, and Lucas had liked Taylor. They weren't friends, but they were friendly. The news came out real quick that he had been bullied online mercilessly. It never occurred to Lucas that Freddy was the one behind that, not until he saw that meanness the day after Taylor died, a meanness in the form of Freddy beating on his girlfriend.

That beating had happened during the small hours of Sunday. He heard them before he saw them, Freddy and Alexandra, so he hid in a neighbour's yard and waited for them to go by. Alexandra lived a few streets over, and he was near her house – nothing to do with her, but everything to do with Mr and Mrs Courtney's dog, the one he had just completed burying, the one they would go on to believe had run away. The dog was getting old and had gone from letting Lucas pat it in the mornings to trying to nip his fingers and growling at strangers, and he knew – of course he knew – the dog was no longer making its own decisions. He had learned two things after his mom's discovery in the garden that day. The first was that he needed to bury things deeper. The second was the burying didn't have to happen in his own yard if there was an empty one a few streets away.

Alexandra's dress was torn. She was covered in grass stains and her hair was messed and she'd cried her makeup into long dirty streaks. She was walking under the streetlights like there was broken glass inside her. Freddy was a few steps behind, following her. When he put a hand on her shoulder, she turned and slapped him so hard Lucas thought everybody in the street would wake. Freddy pushed her over and kicked her in the stomach. He said something to her in a low voice Lucas couldn't hear, before spitting on her, turning, and walking away.

After a short time, Alexandra got to her feet and cried some and brushed herself down and carried on walking. Lucas was curious whether she would report what had happened, or hide it, and knew it could go either way. He was holding on to his squirrel knife – aptly named because he found it two years earlier in a park where somebody had used it to pin a dead squirrel to a tree. He was also holding the army shovel he had finished using moments earlier to pat down the last of the earth covering the Courtneys' dog. When Alexandra was gone, he followed Freddy with the shovel, now folded up in his bag. A shovel of that size made digging slow, but carrying a full-size shovel was suspicious.

Later that night he made it so Freddy could never hurt anybody else again, and even though he opened Freddy up and searched inside, he wasn't able to find the worm in him either. Once again it was possible he had made a mistake, and that sometimes a bad Freddy is nothing more than a bad Freddy. But he didn't think so. Most likely in the time between killing Freddy and cutting him open the worm had found an escape. They were quicker than he gave them credit for.

Hopefully he'll have more luck with the janitor.

Lucas shines his flashlight at him. His face is limp, and purple, and swollen. His eyes are closed. He has nothing to cut him open with, but perhaps he can find something back in the sawmill.

He turns, and only manages to take one step before his cellphone battery gives up, plunging him into the dark.

Chapter Fifty-Five

The elastic band that connected me to Grove on Monday is back, stretching the further I drive, painfully so. I reach Earl's Garage and pull over on the forecourt where the pumps used to be. Earl was a real fixture out here, a guy who looked seventy when he was twenty, and who would have looked seventy when he was a hundred if he'd made it that far. He was always pleasant, and happy to give old-man advice about cars, about life, about the world. I wish he were here right now so I could confess my sins and get his old-man take on all of this. Earl, and old-timers like Earl, have a way of seeing the world. Probably he'd clip me round the ear and call me an idiot.

I swallow a couple of painkillers and I play my conversation with Grove over and over. He's lied about most things, but his confession about the four other boys rings true – and, if that is the case, why not admit what he did to Freddy Holt, or Taylor Reed?

He would. It's that simple. Which means he didn't kill Freddy, and he didn't bully Taylor.

So where does that leave me?

And where is Freddy now?

When Freddy's parents reported him missing, the first person I spoke to was Alexandra Brannon, his girlfriend. She confirmed they had each snuck out of their houses the night before, and had met up, and that Freddy had been drinking heavily. She said he often stole money from his parents, and he had a friend who he'd pay to buy him beer, with a commission added in. We found that friend, and he confirmed he had bought alcohol for Freddy earlier that day, but we had no reason to suspect he was involved with, or knew anything about, Freddy's disappearance. My feeling while interviewing Alexandra was that she was holding something back. I asked her if it were possible that Freddy had been the one bullying Taylor Reed. She said nothing for a few moments, then nodded slowly, then cried a little and said yes, she thought it was more than likely. She said she had come to learn that Freddy wasn't the person she thought he was, that there was something inside him that frightened her, that the night he disappeared she had ended things with him. There was more, I was sure of it, only she wouldn't say. My sense was Freddy had hurt her, and not just emotionally, but in one of the worst ways a man can hurt a woman. I wasn't going to push her to tell me.

Alexandra's thought was that he had run away, and she was glad of it. But if that were true, he would have taken things with him. He would have packed clothes into a bag. There were a couple of hundred dollars in his bank that he could have drawn out but didn't

– and even now his ATM card hasn't been used. Nor has his phone. Which is why the running-away theory is one we could never fully adopt. But there was a similar theory. Freddy had walked off into the wilderness after being dumped by his girlfriend, possibly after assaulting her, after bullying Taylor Reed to his death, and he had gone out there to drink himself stupid. And maybe he drank himself to death – on purpose, or by accident.

'What do you think, Earl? What do I do with Grove?'

If Earl is around, his spirit stays quiet.

The elastic band is still tight, and the only way to ease the tension is to go back. I turn the car around. I don't know what I'm going to do, but I'm going to do something. Anything. Either put Grove out of his misery, or take him into the station.

I head back to the sawmill.

Chapter Fifty-Six

So now Lucas has two problems. First, he has no tool to open up the janitor and search for the simple that makes him Simple Simon – surely a worm so angry and full couldn't hide as well as the one in Freddy had hidden. And second, even if he did, he has no light in which to examine him, meaning he'd just be making a mess of entrails and fluids where he couldn't tell what was what. He looks up for the moon, only to find it hidden by the canopy of trees. This time of the year it's like being under a blanket. In winter all the branches would be skeletons. He'd freeze to death, sure, but at least he'd be able to see the sky. This brings him a third problem, and one that trumps the other two. He's lost.

Frustrated, he balls up the crime-scene tape and drops it into his pocket, along with his phone and the duct tape he took off the janitor's mouth. He stands with the dead man behind him, which, to his way of thinking, makes the parking lot straight ahead. He only has twenty yards to cover in the dark, maybe thirty. It shouldn't be a problem. So he puts one foot in front of the other, and his hands out to touch the trees as he walks. It's not pitch-black, which is something, and pretty soon he thinks he's near the parking lot, which is proven correct when headlights flicker into the trees. Is Sheriff Cohen here to finish off what he started? Or worse, did he figure out Lucas was hiding in the car earlier?

He turns and runs, the headlights fading quickly as he moves, then disappearing completely when his foot snags against a tree root and he topples over. He turns his body as he falls, and ends up hitting the part of his head that took the blow yesterday. The entire forest lights up then, every tree, every shadow, even the sky, it all lights up bright white like the inside of an atomic blast, before very quickly going dark. For a moment things return to the way they were when he was in the ambulance yesterday, back when time was shifting. He passes out – or thinks he does, just a couple of seconds maybe. A minute at the most. When he comes to, the headlights are gone. He stays where he is, listening for the sound of a running engine, or for footsteps coming through the trees. He doesn't know how far he's run. Thirty yards maybe. Could even be forty. His hand is itching like crazy.

He gets to his feet and feels his way between the trees back toward the parking lot, walking slowly so he doesn't bang into anything, and once he's walked thirty yards there's still no parking lot. Which means it must be forty that he ran. He walks the extra ten.

Still no end to the trees. He digs his thumb into the bandage, and there is relief, but it's short-lived. He closes his eyes and pictures the forest from above. Pictures the sawmill, the parking lot, Simple Simon, and his own position in all of that, and then walks another ten yards but still nothing. The mental map he's drawn is heavily out of whack. He might not even be facing the right direction.

The moon. Finding it is still the best way out of here. He climbs the next tree, awkward because of his bandaged hand. This is a bad idea. He can't see a thing as he climbs – all he has to do is reach for a branch that isn't there, or misplace a foot, or have his bad hand slip, and he's going to fall. He could break an arm or a leg or a neck. Rule of thumb if you're lost in the woods: you stay where you are until somebody can come and find you. That, of course, is dependent on letting somebody know you've gone into the woods. It's also dependent on not having just killed somebody. He can't hang about waiting to be found. He also can't keep wandering around in the dark.

Or can he?

It's worth a shot. Just pick a direction and walk for a few minutes and see where it gets him. North, south, west, or east. One of those will come back out into the parking lot. That gives him a one in four chance. Unless he needs to split the difference and go southeast. Or northwest, northeast, or southwest. So he has a one in eight chance. Better than curling up against the base of a tree and waiting.

He walks two minutes in what he soon starts to think isn't a straight line. His eyes continue to adjust to the dark, but he still can't see much. Just long vertical bodies with thin horizontal arms. He has a one in eight chance of picking the right direction, but a seven in eight chance of being lost forever.

And that's how it's looking.

His best bet is to wait till daylight, then he can scale a tree and look for the sawmill. If he can't see it, he'll at least hear cars out on the highway. To try and find a way out in the dark is only to risk going deeper into the forest, where even daylight won't help him.

He doesn't like it, but it's all he's got.

He sits down, leans against a tree, crosses one leg over the other and waits.

Chapter Fifty-Seven

I sit in the car with the headlights shining into the trees for a few minutes, then sit in the car with the lights off for a few minutes more. I keep fooling myself by thinking I will solve this, that there will be a way forward in which I can keep my humanity. Grove is a bad guy who deserves bad things, but he doesn't deserve what is being done to him. Or maybe he does. If I was the one reading about this in the newspaper, that somebody else had abducted Grove and treated him this way, I would sit there and go, 'He got what he deserved.' But it's a struggle to keep that mindset when I'm the somebody else.

I start the car and pull out of the parking lot, deciding on inaction – if that is indeed a decision. I'm so damn tired I can barely think straight. Maybe things will look differently in the morning. Or maybe Grove will die during the night from the cold, or from starvation, or from an infection, or maybe Bigfoot will get him, any of those things taking the decision out of my hands.

The elastic band tightens again as I drive away, making the headache worsen to the point that I have to pull over and pop a couple of painkillers. Even then it doesn't disappear, and I have to drive a little slower so as to not bump into any bridges or trees. I stumble for the first few steps when I get home, but things balance out when I see that the house hasn't been burned down and that my dad is still asleep on the deck, though I guess there's an argument to say he's actually unconscious. He doesn't wake up when I grab his shoulder, and I'm not really in the mood for lifting him, so I tie a couple of tin cans to his feet so I'll hear him when he wakes and gets up, then go into the kitchen and fire up the laptop.

I spend the next hour reading about Ryan Ashcroft and Carl Nichols, Neil Webster and Aaron McGee. Their stories are similar to Harry Waltz and Eric Delany. Four teenage boys, one found bloody and naked off the side of the road in a ditch, dumped there from a vehicle, another found bloody and naked in a dumpster behind a pizza restaurant closed down for health violations the week before. One found down a railroad embankment, and the other behind a closed-down restaurant in an abandoned strip mall. I read about their stories, about who they were, about families left devastated in the wake of Simon Grove, four unsolved murders hundreds of miles apart. There are rewards raised by each of those families, over a hundred thousand in total. I did this for the reward money, but I don't want theirs. It feels contaminated, like a bonus brought about from suffering. Reading about their stories, all the pain and misery, ought to make me feel better at where I'm at with Grove, but it doesn't. In the end I go into the bathroom and throw up. Whatever happens now, there is still what I'm now thinking of as the Freddy Holt paradox. If I'd cuffed Grove on Monday and taken him to the station, we could have questioned him. He could have made his denials about Holt, and the rest of us could have debated it, and ultimately we all would have believed him. If I shoot Grove, that effectively closes Freddy's case. I can't exactly float the idea that I think Grove was innocent of Freddy's fate. Which means if Freddy didn't wander off or get lost, then somebody killed him, and that somebody gets a free pass.

Trying to think of the solution means I need more painkillers. I'm about to take a couple when the banging of tin cans tells me my dad is awake. I head outside and find him standing on the edge of the deck, pissing into the garden. I wait for him to finish. He leaves his dick out of his pajamas and makes his way back to the lounger.

'Let's get you back to bed,' I tell him.

'I have to get ready for work,' he says. 'I got a new client first thing in the morning.'

'There's still time to get a few hours' sleep.'

'That's a loser's work ethic,' he says. 'Didn't your father teach you any better?'

'He did.'

'And what the fuck are these tin cans doing attached to me?'

I cut them free.

'I need a shower,' he says, and he heads inside, to his bedroom. He climbs into bed and immediately falls asleep.

I shut the door and rest a tin can on the handle so it will fall and wake me up if Dad tries to head out, and I figure I will hear that tin better if I sleep on the couch. I take the painkillers I had grabbed earlier, chase them down with a shot of whiskey and try to get some sleep.

Day Three

Chapter Fifty-Eight

I call Deborah first thing in the morning, and she says she's happy to come spend the day with my dad. I feel like yesterday's hangover has come back, and loading up on coffee and eggs doesn't help. In the days to come, the months and the years, I'll remember the morning I became a murderer started with sunny side up. I follow the eggs with orange juice that tastes like ash, wondering if this is how everything will taste from now on, or if it will pass. I load up the dishwasher and switch it on, strange noises coming from it that have been getting stranger by the day, the dishwasher on its final legs. If I come home to a flooded kitchen it would only be par for the course. Dad eats his breakfast in the lounge, staring at the TV, even though the TV is off.

Hutch comes and picks me up after Deborah arrives. It's still only seven a.m. Soon the sun will be out, and the forecast is for it to blaze bright and blaze hot. With every passing summer the sun feels more like it's going to set fire to the world. We drive along mostly empty streets as neighbourhoods slowly wake. I still feel tired. Sleep last night was fitful. I figure I got two hours on and off, if that – it was one of those sleeps where you really never know for sure if you slept. The Adderall I took earlier hasn't kicked in, but the painkillers have.

'I've found two unsolved cases from out of state that match Grove's M.O. and line up with his vacation times,' Hutch says. 'One's a thirteen-year-old boy by the name of Glen Kerr, the other a fourteen-year-old boy by the name of Neil Webster. I've sent everything we know to those departments, and maybe something will line up.'

They will in one of those cases, because Neil Webster is one of the names Grove gave me.

'Okay. Keep looking,' I say, and I'll look too later, because this is my way of publicly linking to Grove the other boys he told me about, and a way to bring those families at least some amount of closure.

We get to the station. The night crew is lingering, a couple of deputies who mostly sit around talking, killing the last hour of their shift. Sharon is here too, at her desk, tapping at her keyboard. Wade will arrive soon, then the day crew, and the night crew will leave. I make coffee, not that I have the appetite for it, but because it's what I always do. It's important I carry on being about as normal as I can, and not like a guy who's hiding a pretty big secret.

Sharon follows me into my office. She sits opposite. I've been lying to her pretty good lately and I figure there's still some of that left to do. She looks tired. Everybody does these days. If things go the way I think they're going to go, then tonight they can all finally get some decent sleep.

'Phone lines been heating up with reward seekers?' I ask.

'We had a few calls,' she says, and I know she's going to save the best till last, because Sharon likes to build up the drama, the excitement, and I've always thought she'd make a pretty good lawyer. 'A lot came in late last night. We've checked them out – mostly they're people who live near empty houses, offering the locations up as a possibility, but as of yet no sighting.'

I pick up my coffee. Sip it. Don't like it. Sip it some more. 'What about our resident psychic?'

'She called as soon as the new reward hit the news.'

'I bet she did,' I say. Mrs Rita Packard has had visions and messages from the dead ever since she was thrown from a horse as a teenager. Now in her sixties, Rita offers her expertise with everything from petty theft to missing pets to helping people who have hidden something in their house for safekeeping but can't figure out where. It's a statistics game for her, in the same way that even a broken clock is right twice a day – but so far she's a broken clock that's right once a month at most. She does make the best shortbread any of us have ever tasted, and when she comes to the station she always brings some with her, which is why we love hearing her theories – especially late in the afternoon when we're all getting peckish.

'She senses Simon Grove is out in the forest somewhere.'

Everything in my body tightens. What are the chances that today is the day that broken clock is right? 'How'd she come to that conclusion?'

'She said his spirit visits her.'

'She thinks he's dead? He say anything?'

'That he got lost in the woods. He doesn't know where, exactly. Says he died last night – that's why he's only just visited her in a dream. She said she's happy to take either cash or a cheque once he's found out there.'

'Tell her if his spirit visits her tonight with some GPS coordinates, then I'll take the cheque around to her first thing tomorrow.'

'There was one more caller,' Sharon says, 'and I think you're going to like this one.'

I think I will too. After all, I'm the one who made it, using a burner phone along with an app to disguise my voice.

'Call came in early this morning. Was a man who said he didn't want to be identified, but he knew where Simon Grove was.'

'Another psychic?'

'I don't think so. He asked to talk to you. He said he'll call back later this morning, but that I should run some things by you.'

I lean forward and look interested. 'What kind of things?'

'He wants the reward money, no questions asked, in cash.'

'I'm not sure we can agree to that,' I say, knowing we will.

'There's more. He said he knows Grove is still alive, and can pinpoint his location down to a square foot, and that it's a "no harm no foul" scenario. If he's wrong, then all he's done is wasted half an hour of your time, but if he's right, then he's landed us a killer.'

'You believe him?'

'He sounded believable, and he does make a good point. It's not like we're paying out the reward upfront.'

'He leave a number?'

'It was blocked. Like I said, he said he'd call back. But he's not going to like that we can't pay out the reward anonymously. There are procedures in place for such a thing.'

This was always going to be a problem. 'You're right, but the reward money being offered is from the families of the children, not from police departments, which means they set the rules. Look into it,' I say, because I did yesterday. 'Maybe there's something in there that would let the families be happy with this.'

'But not the reward we're offering,' she says. 'You know we can't pay that out to anybody anonymous. We just can't. And in cash? No chance.'

'Let's bat this around later. If Grove is out there somewhere, and this guy knows where, then maybe we just bite the bullet and pay, and if anybody complains I'll take full responsibility.'

'I still don't like it.'

'I don't either. Like I said, we can bat it around later. When he calls back, give him my cell.'

'Sure thing.'

'Anything else?'

'There's a thief at the high school.'

'A thief?'

'Yesterday one of the teachers had his wallet stolen, and one student had his phone taken, and another their watch. Somebody is making the rounds.'

My first thought is Nathan, and my second thought is to feel ashamed about my first thought. Thing is, it's not beneath my son to do that. Probably just for the thrill of it – or not even that; probably because he thinks it's a cool thing to do, especially when his dad is the sheriff.

'Send Hutch. Get her to take Rick so he can take some

fingerprints from the scenes. It might not lead to anything, but we can at least put on a small show to make the thief think twice about doing it again.'

Sharon gets to work, and I go about catching up on emails. Five minutes in, and Sharon is back in the office telling me there's been a car accident on the other side of the bridge leading in and out of town. Hutch is getting ready to head to the school, so I go to the scene with Wade, each of us in our own cruisers. There's more traffic on the road now, a lot of people taking their kids to school, others on their way to work. We reach the bridge. There's a van with folks who have come here to go hiking in the woods. The van has popped a tire and gone off the road into a tree. There's an ambulance already out here, attending to one of the tourists, who has a head gash, but aside from some bumps and bruises everybody else is okay. They tell us they were heading out there to look for Bigfoot. They're all animated when they talk about the crash, as if it's all part of their adventure.

The front of the van is all smashed up and there's glass around the base of the tree. I return to my cruiser and grab the camera from the glove compartment. I turn it on and the lens buzzes forward and I snap off a bunch of photos. I'm taking statements when a tow truck pulls up to the scene. Don Peterson steps out and we shake hands. Don took over from Dan, his father, as the local jack-of-all-trades a few years ago. Sometimes he's a locksmith, other times a tow-truck driver, or a gravedigger, or a handyman. He spreads himself thin. He's wearing a brand-new camouflage jacket and a camouflage hat, but he ought to ask for his money back because I can still see him. We make small talk while he separates the van from the tree and hauls it onto the tow truck. Wade ferries the remaining passengers and driver back into town. The hunt for Bigfoot will have to wait a few hours. The scene dies down. Soon I'm the only one out here. All this, and it's only eight-thirty.

I use my burner to call the station, and the app to again disguise my voice. I ask Sharon if I can talk to Sheriff Cohen. She tells me

I'm out of the office, and gives me my number. I don't write it down. I thank her again and hang up. Then my radio in the car comes to life. It's Sharon. I pick up. She tells me the man with information about Simon Grove called. Says she gave him my number. I tell her that's good work. Then I use the burner to call my cellphone so there is a record of the call. I let it ring a few times before answering it. I don't bother having a conversation with myself, but I do play it out in my head.

I know where Simon Grove is.

Yeah? Where?

The abandoned sawmill. Off the beaten track, about twenty yards in.

Great. We find him there, and all that money is yours.

That sounds great.

Thanks for being a wonderful citizen.

Thanks for being a wonderful cop.

I count to sixty and hang up both phones.

I drive out to the sawmill.

Chapter Fifty-Nine

Lucas's back is sore. So is his side. The ground is lumpy without any give, and finding any comfort has been impossible. He's hungry too. Last thing he ate was pizza, and that feels like a week ago. The night cooled more than he expected, and the combination of shivering and being uncomfortable brought about a series of weird dreams where Wolfy would snatch out of the air small pieces of Freddy Holt, pieces Lucas had sliced away with his squirrel knife and tossed to him. Every time Lucas would say, 'good boy,' the way he used to say it before Wolfy was no longer a good boy.

He gets to his feet and brushes himself down. He's torn away the bandage to scratch at his hand, and for a while that scratching worked pretty good, until the cut started pulsing. He knows what the problem is. Knew it was a problem from the moment blood dripped from the infected janitor and into the open cut on his palm. The worming tablet hasn't worked, and he was an idiot for thinking it would. When he studies the wound, he glimpses the slightest movement as the worm moves away from the edge and goes deeper. He pinches at it, but it is too late. He knows what the doctors would say. That it's all in his mind. It's easy to say that when you're not the one who can feel it moving inside you. He squeezes his wrist, hoping the worm will turn and head back toward the opening of the wound, and he holds it for a minute, then two, then releases it, admitting the worm has gotten away. He needs to get home. He needs medication. He doesn't want to wake up tomorrow no longer Lucas, but an altered version of him, the type of Lucas that needs to be put down. He wonders if his dad has reported him missing, or if he just thinks he's gone to school. He'll notice Lucas's school bag is still there. Then he remembers the patrol car opposite the house. The cop in that will tell his dad he hasn't seen him. Then what?

He can't hear any traffic – it could be too early for that, or he could have wandered too far into the forest. For all he knows he's a mile deep. The trees are full of birdsong. He breathes into his hands to warm them before winding the bandage back around his injured palm. His head is throbbing, and he hopes it's from where he hit it when he tripped last night, and not from the worm. Or from a second worm. One of his knees is grazed too.

He starts climbing the tree he slept against. It's hard work, but it gets easier the higher he gets as the trunk and branches get thinner and easier to grip, but then gets harder as they become too thin. He breathes out a large sigh of relief when he finds a sightline through to the roof of the sawmill, a hundred yards away at most. He climbs down and makes his way to the parking lot. He's still not sure how he'll make it home, but right now the best he can do is solve one problem at a time. He is on the edge of the parking lot when he hears a car approaching. He steps back and hunkers behind a pine tree, sap making his fingers sticky as he peeks around the side. It's Sheriff Cohen. Cohen parks where he parked last night and sits in the car, staring out at the trees. He doesn't look good, like he hasn't slept in days. His hair is a mess, he hasn't shaved, and his eyes look sunken. He doesn't seem to be in a hurry to go anywhere as he thinks something over, which Lucas assumes has everything to do with Simple Simon. He's figuring out his next move, not knowing it's already been taken away from him. What will he do, Lucas wonders, when he finds Grove dead?

Sheriff Cohen gets to the end of his thinking process, and climbs out of the cruiser. He hitches up his gun belt, rolls his shoulders back and leans against his car, suggesting the thinking process hasn't ended at all. Or perhaps it has, and he's not happy with the answer.

Then, finally, he heads for the trees.

Chapter Sixty

I repeat the story to myself over and over as I walk through the trees. I found Grove out here, he opened fire, and I was forced to return it. Where did he hide out for the last thirty-six hours? We'll never know. So I repeat the story, and I remind myself that nobody has deserved a bullet more than Grove does, and I follow the path of broken fronds and twigs and scuffed-up dirt. I can hear birds, and further away cars on the highway. The temperature drops the deeper into the trees I get, and by the time I reach Grove, I'm shivering.

Grove is grey, naked, bleeding, broken, his head tilted down, fast asleep. I recall what the resident psychic said about him being dead. I prod him and poke him and he doesn't move. Was the psychic right?

I prod him and poke him again. 'Hey,' I say, and now I slap the guy. 'Hey, wake up.'

He doesn't wake up. If he's dead, then it's going to make it difficult to explain how he was able to shoot back. It means the story changes to me getting an anonymous call, finding him, and everybody thinking who made that call is the one who killed him. It means no reward money. 'Fuck it.'

I tilt his head back. There's a red line around his neck.

'What the hell?'

I pull my gun. I do a fast three-sixty, then a slower one. There's nobody else here. Even so, I keep the gun in my hand and use my other to open Grove's good eye. It's haemorrhaged – a classic tell for strangulation. I look back out into the trees. Nothing. Only that can't be true. There has to be someone. Grove didn't strangle himself.

The questions come fast. Who did this? How much did they see last night? Was it somebody who wandered by, or was I followed? I check Grove for a pulse and don't find one, but the guy is still warm, which doesn't make sense. Or maybe I rushed things, so I take a deep breath and I check for a pulse again, and yes, there it is, faint and erratic. Which puts the original narrative of having him shoot back into play, but makes the strangulation mark around his neck hard to explain. Then again, so are all the other wounds he's gotten since I stuffed him into the trunk two days ago.

Whoever did this, did they purposely not finish the job?

And how to justify releasing the reward money?

Then it comes to me. Grove may have been in the process of being strangled when I showed up, meaning I'm definitely not out here alone. I do another three-sixty. Then I cover a ten-yard perimeter, then fifteen, spiralling out then spiralling back in, and with every step I imagine a gun sight on me, a hidden figure ready to pull the trigger. But if whoever did this had a gun, surely they would have used it on Grove. It doesn't mean they won't suddenly step out from behind a tree with a branch or a rock. I search for a few more minutes then return to the body. I don't know what to do. My original plan to shoot him can still work if we're out here alone, and if whoever did this didn't see me here last night. But who knows if either of those things are true?

I put the gun away. I unlock his cuffs and leave the chain where it is. I look around for the duct tape that's missing from Grove's mouth, but it's gone. Whoever strangled him took it with them – probably because of the fingerprints. It means they likely had a conversation. Did my name come up? The person who killed him, do they know what happened to Freddy Holt?

Was it Freddy Holt who did this?

I pick Grove up. Both my knees pop and my ribs sing out with the effort, discs and vertebrae all threatening to shift out of place. I thread my way back through the trees with him dangling over my shoulder.

Chapter Sixty-One

And like when he was a child, he comes back out of the tunnel he was heading down – there was light at the end, along with a sense of peace. At first he doesn't know where he is, or even *who* he is. He's a man all at sea, caught on the waves, and he remembers then that he works the boats, that he's a fisherman, and that his name is Simon. It all comes back to him in one large hit – his childhood, his own appetite for hurting children, getting caught by Cohen and tied up in his basement ... then Lucas strangling him with the crime-scene tape. His head hurts, his throat hurts, and if he's not dead, then what is going on? His bad eye is shut – perhaps permanently – and the world through his good eye is blurry. Something is digging into his stomach, and he can feel his arms swinging. He can see the forest floor moving beneath him like a conveyor belt. Maybe he is dead, and this is the road to hell.

A pair of legs that aren't his come into focus along with the sounds of breathing – he's being carried somewhere. Out of the forest, or deeper in? But that's not the important question – the important question is, who is carrying him? If it's Sheriff Cohen, does he know he's still alive? As things continue to focus, he becomes more and more certain it is Cohen carrying him, and then completely sure of it when he can clearly make out Cohen's gun belt. Carefully he reaches for the gun. There's a small snap fastener. Would Cohen hear it over the sounds of the forest? Either way, he has to try. He holds his breath and flicks up the fastener, and it barely makes a sound. Nor does the gun when he removes it from the holster. He is turning it back toward Cohen when they reach the edge of the parking lot, and then Cohen is changing position, hoisting him off his shoulder.

He slumps into the ground, getting the gun beneath him and falling onto it to hide it. He keeps his eye closed and his breath held, and then he is hearing footsteps as Cohen walks away. The footsteps fade, and then he can hear a car door open.

'Sharon, it's Cohen,' Cohen says. 'I'm out at the old sawmill. Caller said this is where I'd find Grove.'

He can hear a reply, but can't hear what it is.

Then Cohen says, 'No, no need for backup. I'll take a look around and let you know.'

More of a response, and again Simon can't make it out. Nor does he need to. He rolls onto his side and looks out into the parking lot. Cohen is standing in the open door of a patrol cruiser, talking into a radio, his head down, twenty yards away.

Simon brings the gun out from beneath his body and takes aim.

Chapter Sixty-Two

'I really think it's wise you're not alone out there, Sheriff,' Sharon says.

I stare at the radio for a few seconds, then, 'I'll be okay, I'm sure he's not—'

The windscreen turns into a web of cracks before I even hear the gunshot. Stuffing erupts from the passenger seat headrest. I get down low, keeping the engine block between me and the next bullet to come my way. Whoever strangled Grove is still out here. I reach for my gun, only my gun isn't in its holster.

'Idiot,' I say, because Grove must have grabbed it when I was carrying him. The narrative I was going to make up is playing out in real life.

Another shot hits the car, but I can't tell where. It sounds like thunder. I grab my cellphone and switch it to camera mode and poke it above the dashboard. I can see Grove on the screen. He's gotten to his feet. He's zigzagging left and right as he comes forward, his arms stretched ahead with the gun pointing in my direction. I'm a sitting duck here.

He fires again. The bullet hits the car, but I can't tell where. I look over to the sawmill. The way he's wobbling about, I figure it would be a miracle if he could hit me if I ran there. I reach into the cruiser and grab the keys so he can't use it. It's time to go, and I'm about to do just that when I remember my original gun, the one I said Grove stole from me, is still under the seat, waiting for me to plant it on him. I grab it. It's unloaded, but there is ammunition in the glove compartment. I get the box open and spill the shells onto the floor then scoop them up one at a time, poking them into the clip, my hands shaking. Sharon is yelling into the radio, asking me what's going on.

I grab it. 'Shots fired, shots fired. I need immediate backup,' I say. I drop the radio. I hear Sharon sending a message across all radios that I'm under fire at the old sawmill.

I use the phone to check where Grove is. He's lying down, both hands around the gun, pointing it at the car. He takes another shot, this one hitting the front wheel. He's trying to hit me in the feet.

I lean around the side of the door and draw a bead on the guy. I try to steady my hands, and I take the shot. It gets him in the shoulder, drilling down toward his chest. I fire a second shot without hesitation, and this one snaps his head to the side. He goes limp, and the gun falls out of his hands.

Even so, I stay where I am for a few more moments, gun trained on him, before making my approach. I reach him and kick his gun – my other gun – out of range. Grove rolls onto his back. My second bullet has distended the right side of his skull. He's looking up at me, his ruined eye closed, the haemorrhaged one open, the line around his neck darker now, blood coming from the two gunshot wounds. He's circling the drain fast.

'Who strangled you?'

He looks at me, then he looks past me, up into the sky, out toward the sun, looking for a rocket ship to take him to Heaven. He's looking in the wrong direction.

'Hey,' I say. 'Simon. Who was out here last night?'

His eye rolls back and his face relaxes. He's almost done. All up, this guy is getting it easy. Way easier than his six victims got it. Way easier than Lucas Connor would have gotten it. This guy got to go down fighting.

Of course I'm getting it easy too. Looking at his dead body, I still don't know if I could have done what needed to be done, and now I'll never have to know.

'You deserved worse,' I tell him, but he doesn't hear me. His open eye has already switched off and his face has gone slack.

I need to hurry.

I go back to the car. I pick up the radio. 'Sharon, situation is under control. Simon Grove is down. I repeat, Grove is down.'

'Simon Grove is dead?'

'Affirmative.'

'Are you okay?'

'I'm good. How far out is backup?'

'Ten minutes at least, Sheriff.'

'Tell them there's no need to hurry. Let's not have anybody crash on account of Simon Grove.'

'I'll let them know.'

I walk back to Grove. I swap guns, leaving him with the one everybody thinks he stole from me. I put it into his hand and get his prints all over it. Then I kick it out of his grip. It spins and skids across the parking lot. Now it looks like he opened fire on me with my original gun, and I responded with my replacement. Ballistics would suggest a different story, but ballistics won't be followed up. There's no need.

I take the same route into the trees to where I chained Grove. There are furrows in the earth where his feet kicked back and forth as he was choked. I kick at them and cover them with twigs and pinecones. I pick up the chain and head back. I put the chain under the passenger seat of my cruiser.

I sit on the hood in the sun and stare at Grove and wait for everybody to arrive.

I look out into the forest and wonder if the person who strangled Grove is looking back. I wonder what they would make of everything they just saw me do.

Chapter Sixty-Three

Sheriff Cohen's surprise when Grove opened fire, must have been equal to Lucas's own surprise when he saw that Grove was still alive. His eyes had been on the sheriff, and he hadn't even seen the janitor stumbling and slinking across the parking lot until after that first shot. It was a mistake last night not making sure the janitor was completely dead, and if the janitor were to be taken alive, he would tell...

He would tell nobody, because in the end Sheriff Cohen put two bullets into him.

And now Sheriff Cohen is sitting on the hood of the police cruiser, sometimes staring at the janitor, other times staring at random places in the forest, probably for whoever strangled Grove, while the sound of sirens approaches. The cruiser is all shot up. The steam that was coming from beneath the hood earlier has disappeared. When the sirens get closer, Lucas moves deeper into the trees. He can't imagine any reason for the police to come in this far.

He scales one of the taller trees, stopping two-thirds of the way up when he finds an angle with a view through to the parking lot. He figures he's fifty yards away. He can see flashing sirens, though they're now on mute. He sees a couple of deputies spill into the parking lot. They stand next to Sheriff Cohen, next to his cruiser, all of them with their thumbs hitched into their gun belts, all of them staring at the dead man. Sheriff Cohen waves his hands around as he talks to them, making shapes and pointing toward the trees, using them to show distances. He points at his car, at the broken windscreen. Lucas can't hear any of it, but knows what he's saying. He's giving the 'it was him or me' speech. Everybody looks happy with the outcome.

A van pulls up, and the door opens and a woman steps out. She ties her grey hair up into a bun, tucks her shirt into her jeans, then pulls on a white nylon suit. She changes shoes before approaching the body. She spends five minutes looking at things, then returns to Sheriff Cohen and the others, who are still standing by the shot-up cruiser. Then it's more shapes being cut in the air and pointing as they engage in conversation, and Lucas guesses she's getting the 'it was him or me' speech too, and unless she has something against Sheriff Cohen, she'll also be happy with the outcome. The woman in the nylon suit shakes her head, then nods, then shakes her head again. Everybody turns toward the body and Nylon Lady nods one more time. A photographer so pale that Lucas thinks this is his first time out in sunlight starts shooting the scene. He covers all the angles, and whenever he points the camera toward the trees Lucas pulls his head back in, though from fifty yards away he'll only be a pixel on a screen. Somebody else measures distances. More people arrive. Some go into the trees and he doesn't have angles to see them.

He wonders what's happening at home. The patrol car outside his house may have gone already. The danger to Lucas is no longer a thing. Will his dad have noticed he left without his school bag?

A tow truck shows up. A news van. The deputies say something to the news crew and they move back twenty yards and keep filming, and no doubt they'll get the 'it was him or me' speech too, and Lucas figures they wouldn't have minded either way who died as long as somebody did – good for ratings that way. At least that's something his dad always says. It must be around eleven o'clock now. The sun has gotten higher and rays of light are filtering into the trees. His arms and legs are numb, and he's hungry. When a patrol car shows up with somebody ferrying sandwiches and drinks, he's tempted to go down there and confess to everything just so he can eat. There have to be berries out here somewhere, right? It is a forest. But he can't see any, not from up here, and even if he finds them he can't remember what colours are good and what are bad. He also can't see any source of water. His legs are shaking. His mouth is so dry it hurts. He remembers a trick a character in one of his dad's books did when he was dying of thirst. He put a coin under his tongue to make his mouth water. Lucas digs through his pockets and finds a quarter. He puts it under his tongue, and sure enough his mouth waters, but only a little. It makes the dryness go away, but it does nothing for the thirst. He puts the quarter back into his pocket.

People come out of the trees and go through the sawmill, some pausing on the way for a bite to eat or a drink. They must be figuring that Grove was staying out here, surviving somehow. Lucas climbs down and stretches his legs, which helps with the cramp but not with the hunger. He takes the bandage off his hand and examines the cut. Three of the stitches have been torn free, and it might be infected, but none of that matters when there's a worm inside him, running around unchecked. That worm puts him on the clock. He needs to take care of it before it takes care of him.

He sits down. He listens to the forest, but can't hear anything from the parking lot where all the action is happening. He closes his eyes and lets thirty minutes go by. He can feel movement in his stomach, and doesn't know if it's the hunger, or if the worm is spiralling around in there. It's feeding off him, which is why he's starving. He climbs back up the tree. Not a lot has changed, other than the tow truck having turned around. The driver is hitching up Sheriff Cohen's cruiser. Lucas was hoping things would be winding down, only they're not. He climbs back down. He sits against the tree and tucks his knees under his chin and he rocks back and forth slowly, trying hard to ignore his stomach, but only managing to focus on it even more. He bets if Nathan were the one out here instead of him, Nathan would catch and cook a rabbit, or a bear, eat it and wear its fur as a souvenir. Songs would be written about it. People would...

Damn it.

He gets up. He paces quickly. A new thought is coming to him. What if the janitor spoke to Sheriff Cohen when Sheriff Cohen first found him? What if he was conscious, and told the sheriff everything that happened? For all he knows the sheriff carried him out after that, and was going to take him to hospital to help him. It doesn't seem likely, but he can't know anything for sure, but right now Sheriff Cohen might know who did the strangling out here last night. There could be police already at the school looking for him.

No. The first part might be true, but not the second part. If the janitor did say anything to Sheriff Cohen, then Sheriff Cohen won't tell a soul about it. He can't. Of course not.

But what *would* he do?

He keeps pacing, mulling the question over, along with potential answers, which range from him sharing the same fate as Simple Simon, to Sheriff Cohen sitting him down and telling him they each have a secret to keep. He gives it another thirty minutes, then scales the tree. Sheriff Cohen's cruiser is hooked up, and the tow-truck driver is making final checks. The janitor is in the same spot, only now he's plumping up a body bag from the inside. The woman in the nylon suit is being helped by an officer to carry a stretcher over to it. They lay it down, then together lift the body bag onto it. It gets loaded into the back of the van, the woman in the nylon suit in there for a few minutes, probably securing it down. Then she comes out, strips out of the suit, balls it up and tosses it into the passenger seat. She speaks to some of the others for a moment before driving away. The tow truck follows. The snowman taking the photographs finishes up and leaves too. People stop measuring distances and angles and start looking at their watches. They're looking up at the sky. By Lucas's guess it must be around one o'clock.

Over the next two hours he watches the scene die down. If it weren't for the hunger he'd probably fall asleep. The shadows that faced one way are now facing the other. Eventually there are only two people left: Sheriff Cohen, and Deputy Hutchison. They're leaning against her cruiser and looking out into the trees the same way the sheriff was back when the day started. He watches them chat for a while, only this time there are no big 'him or me' gestures. There must be questions as to what the janitor was doing out here, questions about the bruises around his neck, and no answers. At least none for anybody other than Sheriff Cohen.

Finally they get into the car and drive away.

Lucas climbs down, stretches his back and arms out, and makes his way through the trees to the sawmill.

Chapter Sixty-Four

It's four o'clock when we get back to the station. I'm itching for a beer, and others are itching for the same thing. Adrenaline levels are high. Over time the story of today will be embellished. They'll have me diving, rolling in the dirt, coming up on one knee and opening fire. They'll have me down to one bullet, stepping into gunfire, no fear as Simon Grove's shots go either side of me.

'I still can't believe you went out there by yourself,' Hutch says.

I'm so lost in thought I almost don't hear her. All afternoon I kept expecting somebody to walk out of the trees and tell everybody what I had done. It had been a fast crime-scene examination. Hutch had arrived, then Wade, then the medical examiner. A couple of forensics folks had shown up, media too, more police officers. None of them questioned my story. Why would they? Grove was there – there was no evidence he'd been there the entire time, no evidence to suggest where he had been hiding, just that he was there today. That was a given. What wasn't a given was what had happened to him before I arrived. They know he was kept naked, strangled, and that there are binding marks across his wrists and ankles. The theory is he broke free of them around the same time I was arriving, that the person who tied him up is the same person who called in for the reward. That theory doesn't explain why he still had my gun.

I'm not sure anybody is going to spend a lot of time thinking about who the person is who called it in and tortured him. Grove was a bad guy who opened fire on local law enforcement and lost. He was a man who had killed children and ruined lives. I told everybody that Grove's dying words were a confession to having killed four other children, but he didn't give me any names, and that he knew nothing about Freddy Holt. I had made the same point Grove had made to me, which was, why confess to others, and not to Holt? Nobody believed it to be the truth. I don't blame them either. It's the kind of thing you need to see somebody deny in person while tied up to a tree with their eyeball looking ready to burst.

Over the last few days, we've been in the process of looking for out-of-state cases that could be linked to Grove, and before coming out to the sawmill this morning, Hutch had been sent Ryan Ashcroft's file. Ryan was thirteen years old. He disappeared on his way home from baseball practice, and was found the next morning naked and strangled in a dumpster. He's one of the four Grove mentioned. We will find the rest.

'Sheriff?'

'Huh?'

'It was dangerous,' Hutch says. It's just her and me sitting in my office. I'm sipping from a beer that doesn't taste like ash. Killing Grove in self-defence rather than cold-blooded murder makes food and drink taste better, but still not as good as it ought to. My legs are twitching under my desk. I feel like I need to go for a run, or scream into a vacuum. I'm trying to fit together what might have happened last night, but it's impossible because I don't have any of the pieces.

Hutch carries on. 'Right now you're the one who could be getting sliced and diced on the autopsy table.'

Hutch is disappointed in me. She can join the club. 'It's like I keep saying, I wasn't expecting him to be there. This guy on the phone, I thought he was full of it. I only went out there to prove what I already knew – that there was no reason for Grove to be back out there.'

'So where has he been all this time?'

I like to think that if somebody was following me last night, I would have noticed, but would I have? They could have driven out there with their headlights off and I never would have seen a thing. When I turned off for the sawmill, they could have gone straight ahead and parked fifty yards further up the road. They could have followed me in on foot and seen me walking out of the trees, then gone in after.

'Sheriff?'

But why follow me to begin with? How could anybody have known I was keeping Grove in my basement?

'Sheriff?'

'Huh?'

'I was asking if you have any thoughts as to where he's been all this time.'

'None,' I say, and it's a question she's already asked, one we've all asked, over and over.

'I don't think we should pay the guy who called you,' she says.

'What?'

'I don't think we should pay him.'

My legs stop twitching.

She carries on. 'I think our Good Samaritan had Grove the whole time. We've been looking at everything wrong. We've been thinking Grove made it out to the road on Monday and waved somebody down, then carjacked them. But I think it's the other way around. I think he waved somebody down, and that somebody knew who he was and turned the tables on him, then waited for us to offer a reward.'

'But there was already a reward.'

'They figured we would add to it, and they were right. At the very least they figured to give it a few days to see what happened. And now instead of sixty grand, they're getting eighty. People would do a far lot more for far less.'

'Then why keep him alive?'

'They were worried he'd stink the place up. He would have, right? A dead guy in your basement is going to smell rank. Plus he's dead weight. Easier to get a guy to walk through the forest than carry him. We offer the reward, the next morning they make the call after getting him out there. Maybe they thought they had killed him, or maybe they tried but didn't have the stomach for it. I think it's the former. It's the only way him having your gun makes sense.'

'How so?'

'Whoever did this knew it was your gun, and left it for you or us to find. They didn't know Grove was still alive, so didn't know it was a problem. It may not be exactly that, but it feels close, you know? Like we're onto something here. Either way, I don't think we should pay the guy who called it in.'

'We have to.'

'We can't.'

'If we don't, then we lose faith in this community. If we ever offer another reward again, nobody will believe it was real. No matter how you look at it, I was the one who killed him, not the person who phoned in his location. We don't know for sure how Grove got his wounds.'

'I don't like it.'

'Nobody does, and you're going to like the next bit even less. The guy is all about being anonymous, which means he wants us to pay cash. I told him if we found Grove from his tip then we would. I assured him we'd pay the full eighty, knowing sixty will come back to us.'

'You're right,' she says. 'I really don't like that.'

'Like I said, I didn't think we'd really find him out there.'

'So what's the plan? We put the money in a paper bag and treat it like one of those ransom demands you see in movies? We drop it off in a rubbish bin in a park somewhere and walk away?'

'If that's what he asks for, yeah.'

It's time to change the subject, so I turn it to the press conference scheduled for later today. I still haven't spoken to Peter and Lucas Connor. No doubt they already know what's happened – there were enough media at the sawmill that everybody in Acacia Pines must know. Then again, Lucas will have been in school all day, and Peter might have been working, or drinking, or sleeping. Other police departments will inform the families of the other victims. I ask Hutch to get in touch with them to get the ball rolling. Earlier we pulled the officer who was watching their house.

'You want me to contact Freddy Holt's parents?'

'We still don't know for a fact it was Grove,' I say, and the words are difficult to say because I know how they sound.

'You believed him?'

'He had no reason to lie.'

'The guy has probably never said an honest word in his life.'

'Be that as it may, it seems an odd thing to do, confess to other crimes and not Freddy Holt.'

'He confessed to it on camera when he was getting ready to rape and kill Lucas Connor.'

'I know. Look, just tell them we don't know anything for sure, that we're still investigating it.'

'He really convinced you, huh?'

'Let's just give it more time, that's all I'm saying.'

'Will do.'

Hutch leaves, and I sit alone at my desk, wondering who would be motivated enough to strangle somebody chained to a tree. Lucas Connor maybe, or more likely his father – but again, they would have needed to know I was taking Grove out there, which they couldn't have done since their house was being watched last night. Earlier I was considering Freddy Holt, but if he were living out in the woods somewhere, the dogs would have found him. Plus he had no reason to strangle Grove, because Grove never laid a finger on him. Allan Holt, Freddy's father, would have reason. I can't envision any scenario where he would have been following me, but perhaps he was out in the woods looking for where his son was buried. It's possible – though extremely unlikely – that he happened upon him during that search.

Sharon comes into the office and closes the door behind her – something I've never seen her do before – killing my train of thought. Whatever she has to tell me is important, and my mind latches on to the idea that her train of thought has taken her all the way to figuring out what I've done. She doesn't sit down. She's making me nervous. God, the person who strangled Grove, they didn't just call, did they?

'I know this isn't a great time,' she says, 'but I just had Harriet White's mother on the line.'

The name throws me. 'Harriet White?'

'She's the girl from the school who had her cellphone stolen.'

I remember now. With everything going on I had forgotten there was a thief at the high school. Hutch went out there this morning, but didn't get far before being sent to the sawmill.

'Harriet got home from school a few minutes ago. She has tracking software on her phone that she activated remotely after it was stolen. It's set up so as soon as the phone is switched on it automatically emails her the location. She's only just checked her emails now that's she gotten home from school, and she has that exact email. Somebody turned on her phone, and we know where.'

'Send Wade there. Let him take care of it. Get him to bring whoever stole it into the station and—'

'There's more. There's no easy way of telling you this, Sheriff, other than doing the telling.' She pauses, doing that thing she loves to do for dramatic effect, only I don't think that's why this time. She looks genuinely upset, and unsure of how to continue. 'The address, it's yours. The stolen cellphone is at your house.'

Chapter Sixty-Five

Lucas goes through the offices in the sawmill, the kitchen, the lunch area, the bathrooms, the lockers, every cupboard and drawer in the hope somebody has left behind a protein bar or a candy bar, but there's no such luck. Maybe there's a truth to those Bigfoot rumours, and he came through earlier and cleaned everything out. He tries the taps but the water is rusty, something he didn't notice when the janitor was splashing it over him. He moves quickly, needing to get home and to his pills before the worm takes control again. He didn't recognise it before, but he thinks the worm took the reins last night when he tried killing Simple Simon.

The mountain bike he saw the first time he was in the sawmill is still here. Back then it was a piece of junk. Now it may be his salvation. The tires are flat, but there's a pump attached to the frame. He struggles because of the bandage on his hand, but he gets the tires inflated. They're bald, but as long as he doesn't run over anything remotely sharp he should be okay. The front wheel, which is bent, goes back into some semblance of shape when he pops the quick release and takes it off and lays it on its side and bounces on it. He puts it back on, and it hits the brakes a little when he spins it, and he doesn't know how to adjust that. There was a half-empty bottle of vegetable oil in the kitchen that he now pours over the chain to lubricate it. When he climbs on the bike and rides it, the whole thing is wonky and slow, but sure beats walking. It passes its first test when he bikes toward the highway and the tires don't pop and the chain doesn't turn into Lego. He takes it onto the road. The front wheel hitting the brakes makes the bike vibrate the faster he goes and makes it harder to pedal. It sounds like a slow-moving helicopter.

He hugs the right-hand edge of the highway as cars go by him at unnerving speeds. After twenty minutes he reaches an abandoned gas station. There's an old payphone out front. He's never used a payphone before, but it can't be hard to figure out. The problem is he doesn't know the number. It's always been on his cellphone so he's never had to memorise it. Thankfully there's a phonebook hanging by a cable down by his knee. He's never used a phonebook in his life either, but understands the concept. He can't tell how old it is because the cover and spine have been bleached white from the sun. He finds his last name and sure enough, the number is listed there. Thankfully they kept the same number when they shifted house.

He picks up the phone, and there's a dial tone. He drops the quarter he had under his tongue earlier into the coin slot. A couple of the buttons stay stuck down when he pushes them, and he has to pick at them with his fingernail to get them to pop back up, but he gets the number dialled and it doesn't take long for his dad to answer.

'I missed you this morning,' his dad says.

'I left early.'

'Without your bag?'

'It was a light day. I wanted to let you know I got held up doing some stuff for school. My phone went flat, so I'm calling you from here. I'll still be a while, but I'm okay. Don't go calling the police or anything.'

'I would have at five, you know that.'

He does know. It's one of the rules they made so his dad knew he wasn't out somewhere making something bleed.

'You heard the police got him?'

'The news made it around the school,' Lucas says.

'Good riddance, I say. You must feel relief.'

'I do.'

'Six o'clock,' his dad says. 'Anything later and I call Sheriff Cohen. I mean it, Lucas.'

'I know.'

They hang up. He gets back on his bike. There's still a lot of ground to cover.

Chapter Sixty-Six

I walk calmly out to one of the cruisers and drive calmly out of the parking lot and calmly onto the street while calling Deborah. I ask calmly if she can take my dad out of the house for a walk, and she says she'll do her best. I sit calmly at intersections and accelerate calmly when the lights are green, and a little less calmly at the next intersection. By the time I get into my neighbourhood I'm white-knuckling the wheel and driving faster than I should. I'm far from calm when I pull into the driveway, and I'm far from calm when I slam the door and go bounding up the path to the house. I'm so angry that I miss getting the key into the lock on the first two attempts. Thankfully Deborah and Dad aren't here.

I storm into my son's bedroom. I don't know if I'm more angry or disappointed, and I don't know if it's with Nathan or with myself, for thinking he could change, or if I'm using this to burn off all the tension. I lift the mattress. Nothing. I open the drawers. No phone. I pull out my phone and dial the stolen phone and can't hear it ringing. Earlier the email with Harriet White's phone details was forwarded to me, and I use a tablet with tracking software on it to confirm it's still here. It is. The software shows my house and there's a blue dot in the centre of it, but it's a lot of house for one small phone. I open the wardrobe. I check the top shelf. I check around the floor. It could be under a floorboard or in the ceiling. Hell, it might not even be in Nathan's bedroom – it could be anywhere in the house. I check his jacket pockets. Nothing. Nothing. Nothing. Noth— something. In the pocket of the jacket in the far corner. I reach inside. It's the cellphone. It's gone flat.

Aside from being angry and disappointed, I'm scared too. I had no idea Nathan had come home yesterday while I was at work. Which means there's every chance he went down into the basement.

Did he follow me last night and strangle Grove? Is this a case of like father, like son? It seems unlikely. After all, how would he have gotten there?

I head into the kitchen. I fill the kitchen sink and swivel the tap to the side and dunk my head. I scream into the water. It's something Sheriff Haggerty used to do sometimes. He'd dunk his head in the basin in the bathroom at the station when the injustice of the world all got too much for him. When I'm done screaming, I dry myself down and head back into Nathan's bedroom. I feel somewhat better – enough, in fact, to try and think this through rationally. I grab Harriet's phone and wake my tablet up, and notice that the blue dot is still being displayed. I refresh the screen and it doesn't disappear. It doesn't make sense, because if the phone is flat, then...

Then this can't be Harriet's phone.

'Please no,' I say, because there's a bad thought taking hold, one I don't want to be true. I carry the phone to the kitchen. It takes the same charging cable as mine, so I plug it in. A red light comes on, and twenty seconds later the screen lights up. It asks for a PIN. I carry it to the window and angle it so the screen catches the light. I can see a zig-zag swipe mark on the screen that lines up with the numbers. I replicate the pattern and get it on the second attempt.

The screen is littered with icons, including three for different types of social media. I click into them.

'Jesus,' I say, and I make my way back to the seat, only I don't make it. My hip hits the kitchen table and I stagger and fall and sit on the floor. The headache comes back, the buzzing with it. I rest up against the kitchen cabinets. The rest of my strength drains as I go through the phone, reading the messages my son sent to Taylor Reed over the months leading up to his death. I saw these same messages two months ago when I went through Taylor Reed's social media, only this is the other side of them, messages that were grey on Taylor's phone are blue on this one.

'Don't be true,' I say, but it already is. I check the call logs and see he dialled a number on Monday night. I recognise it. I check my notebook and confirm that it belongs to Lucas Connor. No wonder Lucas has been lying to me about not remembering who put him into that locker.

There's an icon for photos and videos. I click on it. There's a single video on there. I play it. It's Taylor Reed being pinned down. He's naked. Somebody else uses a gloved hand to smear what looks like dog shit through his hair before smearing it over his face. My stomach rolls and I have to look away. I'm reminded of Simon Grove's threat to Lucas, that if he didn't keep his mouth shut he would show the world the video he was about to make. Nathan has done the same thing here because Taylor Reed never spoke of his abuse. There are three people doing this – one to hold Taylor down, one to smear dog shit over him, and a third to film it. They let Taylor go, and he scrambles into the corner and tries to cover himself with his hands. He's crying hard, and the bits of his face I can see are bright red. I check the date on the video. It was filmed the day before Taylor threw himself from the roof.

I can't remember the last time I cried, but I cry now. For Taylor, for myself, for Cassandra. I honestly don't know what to do with the phone. I wish I hadn't found it. Was it a joke for Nathan, one where he didn't think about the consequences? Or did he get the result he wanted? Has he done a similar thing to Lucas?

Did my son kill Freddy Holt?

I get to my feet. I put the phone on the table and pace the room. The floor is jelly, and the walls are the walls of a ship, swaying on the tide. The phone has become radioactive, something I need to pick up with a pair of kitchen tongs and bury in the garden. The last two days have been a nightmare, but all of it pales compared to this. My son is a monster. I thought counselling could help him, but he's beyond that. I don't know how he got to this point. There's no one thing I can look at. He's been difficult to deal with ever since he became a teenager. Before then he was the happiest and friendliest kid, at least I thought he was. The last couple of years we've hardly seen him as his obsession with games and social media took hold, living out his life online. But so do a billion other kids, and sure, they say stupid shit online, and they harass people, but not like this. They're not getting kids to jump from roofs. Was this Nathan's goal? Did he really think or want Taylor to kill himself? Or was it all just a laugh? When my dad moved in, I remember Nathan saying he wished Dad had been the one to have died in the fire. I thought it was just teenage bullshit, but now I don't think so. I think he meant it.

What is my son capable of?

The question is asked by a man who tortured a guy in his basement, and drove him out to the forest to most likely kill him. I find the bottle of whiskey I brought home yesterday. There is still a quarter of the bottle left. I could chug it back and have some release from all of this, at least for a few hours. I'm about to do just that when my cellphone goes. It's my lawyer. Calling, I assume, to tell me he needs more money.

'Hell of a thing you went through,' he says, after a brief hello.

'You have no idea.'

'Listen, things might be about to go your way.'

'Yeah? How's that?'

'You know you've been all over the news the last two days, right?'

'I know.'

'And you're all over it again today with what happened this morning.'

'Okay,' I say. I haven't seen the news, but it's no surprise.

'I heard from the Suttons' lawyer,' he says – the Suttons are the family of the woman who died in the fire my dad started. 'I didn't know it, but before they moved to Acacia Pines fifteen years ago, they lost a child. They had an eight-year-old girl who was abducted and killed.'

Of course they did. Jesus Christ. I look at the bottle of whiskey. It's not enough. I need fifty more of them, then I can fill the bathtub to drown myself in it. Who the fuck wants to hang around in a world like this one?

'You still there?'

'I'm here.'

'Well, long story short, they've been watching you in the news. They know you saved Lucas Connor, and now they know you took down the man who has been killing children. He's not the man who killed their child, that guy was arrested days after it happened, but they're grateful there are people in the world like you. An hour ago they approached their lawyer and told them to drop all of this. They said they don't want a guy like you being distracted by something like this, when he should be out there saving other children.'

I start to cry again. I can't help it.

'Jesus, James, you okay?'

'Yes,' I say, but I'm not, and never can I be.

'Listen, there are still a few legal things to sort out. It'll run you a few thousand on my end, and you need to cover the Suttons' fees too, which will be another ten or twenty, but you take care of that and this is gone. You can close this chapter and put it behind you.'

I don't say anything. I can't.

'This is great news, James.'

'Not for the eight-year-old girl.'

'Of course not, and I didn't mean it like that.'

'Listen—'

'I just wanted to let you know. I'll be in touch when I know more. Goodbye,' he says, and he hangs up without waiting for an answer, and I don't blame him.

Chapter Sixty-Seven

By the time Lucas gets to the bridge, his stomach is cramping so hard he has to get off the bike. There have been moments where he considered wandering onto one of the farms and taking a bite out of something that was either growing out of the earth or roaming about on it. The thirst isn't any better. He slides down the grassy bank to the river. It's dark and slow and cold, and he plunges his good hand into it and scoops handful after handful into his mouth.

When he's done, he sits on the bank watching the river flow by. In the summer people will swim here, kids daring each other to jump off the bridge into it, nobody ever taking the challenge because the water doesn't get much more than chest-deep. Sometimes he'll see people fishing on the banks, usually old guys; they'll unfold camping chairs and shoot the breeze with their rods hanging over the water, expecting trout, but never catching any. It would be more peaceful if it weren't for traffic coming into town over the bridge, workers coming home from the new sawmill, the quarries, maybe some coming in from the farms, *bub bib* as the car goes from asphalt to tarseal, then *bib bub* as it goes back. He heads up the bank and grabs his bike and carries on. With the newfound strength he can make it back to his own bike. He's looking forward to dumping this piece of crap.

To distract himself from the worm moving around inside him, as he bikes he thinks about the last pizza he ate. The chicken, the pepperoni, the ham, all dripping with flavour, barbecue sauce spiralled over the top, melted cheese holding the slices together. He can see it. He can feel the heat that escapes from the box when you open the lid. When he bikes past Andy's Diner, he can smell burgers, and then it's all he can think about. Burgers and fries, and the crisp burn of a Coke on his throat as he takes that first mouthful. He thinks about the donuts from Bear Claw County, a store in town that sells different types of breads and sandwiches and cream buns and pastries. He imagines breaking in there and climbing into a cabinet and stuffing his mouth full of cake.

He thinks about the worm feeding on all of that, and growing.

Finally he reaches Sheriff Cohen's neighbour's house, the one with the lavender bushes where he left his bike last night. The bike is gone.

Even with the new shot of strength he found when he drank from the water, he doesn't have enough energy to be angry. Yes, he could have hidden the bike at the park two blocks from here. But last night he had no reason to. He was supposed to be in and out of Sheriff Cohen's house within five minutes. He stares at the spot where he left it. Did somebody walk by and steal it? Is it inside the house the garden belongs to? Possession being nine-tenths of the law – is that a real thing, or just something people say on TV?

Chapter Sixty-Eight

I clean up in the bathroom having thrown up in the toilet. I pop more painkillers and more Adderall and don't really care about how many of them I've been taking lately, but for now I skip the whiskey. I retrieve the tablet I was using to track Harriet White's phone and I look at the map with the dot, the blue dot sitting over my house. But it's not over my house, not exactly – more off to the side. The phone could be out in the yard. I call the number again and head outside. I walk around but can't hear it ringing. It goes through to voice mail, so I hang up and call again. I head into the garage. Just before my call cuts to voice mail, I hear something vibrating from somewhere in here. I dial again. The vibrations come from behind a couple of paint cans. I pull on a pair of latex gloves and move the cans aside. The phone is back there. So is a wallet and a watch.

It doesn't make sense.

Why would Nathan come home, turn on Harriet's phone and hide it in the garage? I check the email forwarded on from Harriet's mom. The phone went active late last light at eleven-twenty-five. Shit. That was around the time I left here.

I drop the stolen items into an evidence bag, carry them inside and dump them on the kitchen table. I check what time Hutch sent me the text about the reward money. Eleven-twenty. So I was right. I picture somebody sneaking into my garage and planting the items. They're sneaking away when they hear me coming out with Grove. They hide somewhere and watch. They peek through the garage window and see me loading Grove into the back of the car. They move quietly out to the street where their car is parked, and they wait and follow me with their lights off all the way out to the sawmill, parking past the entrance and walking around the sawmill and seeing me coming out of the trees.

But why try to kill Grove?

Why not call the police and claim the reward?

What did they see? Anything? Everything? Were they there this morning?

These are questions I can't answer. Not for sure.

Who would steal these items and leave them here to frame my son?

Well, that one's a no-brainer.

Chapter Sixty-Nine

The bike is swaying back and forth, and Lucas's limbs are so heavy he can barely pedal by the time he makes it home. Strength comes back when he sees a police cruiser parked out front. He sits on his bike on the corner of the block with his arms hanging by his sides, mouth slightly open, full of exhaustion and disbelief. He assumes it's Sheriff Cohen inside, and that he knows what he did, and now he's here to … to what? That's the question. To ask they keep each other's secret? He could turn around and start pedalling away, but where would he go? Anyway, he can't run. He needs to get inside and to his medication. He still has time to stop the worm. He knows he does, because he's still thinking clearly. But he has to act soon. He puts the bike along the side of the house where his dad won't see it and steps inside. His dad and Sheriff Cohen are sitting in the lounge, his dad is working away at a beer, Sheriff Cohen with his hands empty. Sheriff Cohen stands up. He offers his hand and stares hard at Lucas as Lucas shakes it.

'Lucas,' Sheriff Cohen says. 'Good to see you.'

Is Sheriff Cohen looking at him differently? Yes. He seems tense too, like a man who might be thinking his world is falling apart. Which it may do soon, depending on where this conversation goes.

'We got the man who hurt you,' Sheriff Cohen says.

'I heard. The news was all around school. How did you catch him?'

'An anonymous tip came in this morning with his location,' Sheriff Cohen says, still with the staring. The guy is hardly blinking either. 'I went to go and take a look, and he was out there. He opened fire. I fired back. Grove died at the scene.'

Lucas says nothing.

Sheriff Cohen says nothing.

His dad says, 'I hope he suffered.'

'I would much rather have taken him in alive,' Sheriff Cohen says, answering his dad but still looking at Lucas.

'Sure, that's what you have to say, but I for one am glad he's dead,' his dad says. 'He got what he deserved,' he adds. Of course his dad is going to say something like that. He has to. After all, his books are based on people getting what they deserve.

'So what happens now?' Lucas asks.

'Well, now everything goes back to normal. We can all breathe a sigh of relief knowing Simon Grove isn't going to hurt anybody ever again. I wanted to tell you in person, even though I figured you already knew.' He pauses then, and keeps staring at Lucas. A few seconds go by before he adds, 'Anyway, I have to go. I have a press conference to get to.'

They walk him to the door. They step outside and Sheriff Cohen shakes their hands and he stares hard at Lucas, and Lucas smiles, and Sheriff Cohen doesn't smile back, and then Sheriff Cohen says, 'Walk me to the car, would you, Lucas?'

They walk to the car, his dad having gone back inside to finish his beer or start a new one, and Lucas knows this is where both his and Sheriff Cohen's futures will be decided.

'You heard about the thefts that happened at school yesterday?'

It's not what he was expecting. 'Thefts?'

'A phone was taken, and a wallet, and a watch.'

'I heard,' Lucas says.

'The items showed up,' Sheriff Cohen says. 'Funniest thing, they showed up at my place.'

Lucas slowly shakes his head. Puts on his *I don't understand where this is going* look.

'They were squirreled away in my garage. My guess is somebody stole them with the idea of framing my son. What that person didn't know is that Nathan isn't staying with me this week.'

Lucas doesn't say anything.

Sheriff Cohen carries on. 'Right now I'd be thinking that Nathan stole those things if it hadn't been for that.'

They're at the car now. Sheriff Cohen folds his arms and stares down at him. 'I know my son ruffles a lot of feathers at school. Honestly, I wouldn't blame the kid who did this. They're probably scared of Nathan and figured this would be a good way to get him in trouble, maybe even expelled. Question is, is that person you?'

'No.'

'I've asked around,' Sheriff Cohen says. 'I heard from students it was Nathan who put you into the locker on Monday. And I know Nathan called you on Monday night to threaten you. I understand why you didn't tell me.'

'I didn't tell you because it would only make things worse. But I didn't steal that stuff.'

'I'll have a word with him, and this will stop, I promise.' He unfolds his arms and puts one hand on Lucas's shoulder. It's heavy. He thinks maybe Sheriff Cohen is pushing down a bit. 'Are you sure you didn't steal these things, Lucas? If you did, it'll stay between us. I promise.'

Lucas shakes his head.

'If you tell me now, I can help you. I can make this thing go away. But you have to be honest with me, and you have to be honest with me right now.'

'I didn't take those things,' Lucas says.

'I mean it, Lucas. I'll clean this up for you, and nobody has to know. I give you my word.'

Lucas shakes his head. 'It wasn't me. I swear.'

Sheriff Cohen says nothing for what feels like an age, but can't be much longer than ten, maybe fifteen seconds. He keeps his hand on Lucas's shoulder, staring at him, as if he's a human lie-detector.

'What will happen to Nathan?' Lucas asks.

'I'll deal with him. Stay safe, Lucas,' Sheriff Cohen says, letting him go. He opens his car door, looks like he's about to climb in, then pauses and looks back.

'By the way, I checked with your teachers. You weren't in class today.'

'I was making my way there, but couldn't face it. I didn't want to stay at home either.'

'So where did you go?'

'I just biked around.'

'All day?'

'I went to the bridge and hung out there for a while, watching the river.'

'You told your dad you were delayed at school.'

'I didn't want to worry him, but I needed some time to myself.'

'You got past the patrol car out front.'

'I went over the back fence. I didn't want to be a bother.'

'You weren't out in the forest near the old mill?'

'That's the last place I'd ever go after what happened there.'

'You sure about that?'

'Yeah. Honestly, after today, I never want to have to think about the sawmill or Simon Grove ever again.'

Sheriff Cohen stares at him for a few more moments, then nods. 'Okay, Lucas. I'll let you know if I have any more questions.'

And with that, Sheriff Cohen climbs into his car, and Lucas watches him drive away.

Chapter Seventy

I can't blame Lucas for trying to frame my son. He felt backed into a corner. Nor could I blame him for strangling Grove, if it was indeed him. I can picture him doing it, but I can't figure how he could have gotten out there. It's not like he biked or ran at seventy miles an hour to keep up with me. That alone rules him out.

I reach the station, where the parking lot is so full of media that I have to park a block away. There's still life in the sun and plenty of warmth, and a slight breeze coming through. The conference was scheduled for six, but it's already seven. In a town of thirty-thousand people, press conferences tend to be small. But today is different. Today there are competing newspapers and TV stations that have come in from other cities. Why wouldn't they? Young boy escapes serial offender, serial offender overpowers cop and goes on the run, that same cop shoots and kills said offender a couple of days later. By now the connections we have been making with Grove's past have also been made by the media. The child abuse he endured, the fire that killed his foster parents, the possible links to other cases. I imagine in a month there'll be a documentary made about the guy, and in a year a movie.

I tell Hutch about the cellphone and the wallet and the watch, how they were planted, but I don't tell her about the cellphone I found in Nathan's room. I need time to figure out what to do there. Telling Hutch means arresting my son. He could end up in jail. I don't deny that he deserves that, but he's still my son, and jail has the potential to only make him worse. Nathan can still be saved – I tell myself that over and over, and I try to believe it. Taylor's parents deserve justice, but right now my concern is with my own family.

'We can print them,' she says.

'I'll give them to Rick, but my bet is they will have been wiped clean.'

'Sheriff...'

'I know what you're thinking, but the idea of Nathan sneaking home at eleven-thirty at night to hide the items in the garage, let alone turn on the phone, it doesn't make sense.'

'Why would somebody do that?'

'I'm not sure.'

'You think it's possible he was the one who put Lucas into the locker, and this is Lucas's way of trying to get him expelled?'

'That's exactly what I think, and if that's how things went, then we owe Lucas a pass.'

'Not only that, but it means we need to do something about Nathan.'

I call Deborah. She says she's back from her walk with my dad, and that he's doing okay, but she's wondering when I'll be back to take over. I ask her to give me another hour. I tell her there's an entire Indian meal from last night in the fridge, and ask her to heat it up in the microwave for him.

The conference begins. We stand out front so the window of the department and the logo gets framed in the shot behind us, like a big advert for The Law. I'm flanked by Hutch and Wade. Further down the street restaurants and bars are hustling and bustling, life back to normal after the man who disrupted it got himself killed. Tomorrow kids will be biking and walking to school, but parents will still look at strangers wondering if this is the one who will take their child away.

I read out a statement. It's brief, but covers the simple order of events. A tip came in. We followed up on that tip. I went to the location, where Simon Grove opened fire, and I fired back. It's a short story. And a simple one. Especially when you don't mention the strangulation marks, which we don't – nor do we mention the signs Grove was tortured. That will come later.

The questions all come at once. I point to people. I pick a woman in the front from one of the local papers. I went to school with her. I was friends with her brother.

'Any idea where Grove has been holed up since Monday?'

'We still don't know,' I say. 'We don't think it's possible he was out there the entire time because the dogs would have found him, but we're going to examine the building to see if he had access to any crawlspaces. The dogs weren't allowed in the building that evening, and it's possible the fire made it impossible for them to catch his scent the following day. It's also possible he came back. We're looking into it.'

I pick out somebody else. Somebody from out of town. A guy in a shirt with circles of sweat under his armpits. 'And the person who called in the tip? What do we know about them?'

'The call was anonymous, which means we don't know anything about them,' I say, and there's a murmur of laughter even though I'm not trying to be funny. I'm too tired for that. Too on edge.

'Is the plan to find out before issuing any reward money?'

I shake my head. The buzzing is back. 'We will honour the deal we made, and that deal was this person wanted to remain anonymous.'

'You're paying in cash? Or transferring it into an account?' somebody else asks.

'I'm not going to go into those details.'

'So you're in contact with them?'

'Again, I'm not going to go into those details.'

I can't do this any longer. I don't feel well. Not at all. I get Hutch to take over then make my way inside. I go into the bathroom and splash water on my face. I don't know how much longer I can keep my nerves under control. How do bad guys deal with the stress of being bad guys?

I go back to my office. I log into a news website on my computer and watch the rest of the conference. Hutch is still being asked a whole bunch of stuff. What was Grove living on? Was it necessary to shoot him? The person who knew where he was, how did they know that? Are they local, or somebody from out of town? I open the bottom drawer before remembering the bottle of whiskey is at home. I slam it shut. Rick comes in. He tells me there are no prints on any of the items stolen from the school.

I call Cass. I've missed a few calls from her today.

'I just saw you on the news,' she says. 'I'm worried about you.'

'I looked that bad, huh?'

'Like you haven't slept. Want to talk about it?'

'Yes, but not right away. I have some news,' I say, and I tell her about my call with the lawyer.

'Thank God it's almost over,' she says.

'You'll come home?'

'You still need care for your father. Can you afford that?'

'I'm working on it.'

'Look, let's just get through the next few days with everything that's going on, then we can talk about it.'

'It sounds like you don't want to come back.'

'That's not what I'm saying.'

'Then what are you saying?'

She takes a moment with that, then says, 'We'll talk about it soon, I promise.'

I don't push her on it. Anyway, we're going to have much bigger things to talk about.

'Let's talk again tomorrow,' she says, and then we each say goodbye and she's gone.

The conference ends, and Wade and Hutch come into my office carrying coffees, including one for me. I tell them about the prints.

'We'll head back to the school tomorrow,' Hutch says, 'and ask around. See if anybody has a grudge against Nathan. Other than Lucas, of course.'

'Okay, good. Look, it's been a long day, and I'm not feeling the best.'

I stand up. Hutch and Wade stand up too. They follow me out of the office. Sharon claps, then Hutch, then Wade, then everybody else. It's embarrassing. And undeserved. Clapping because I killed a man in self-defence who I was probably going to kill anyway.

I thank them and slink out the door.

Chapter Seventy-One

His dad says they should celebrate, but Lucas is already celebrating. He's opened a bag of chips from the pantry and eaten most of them. His fingers are coated in chip dust and the salt is stinging his lips. He's eyeing up a packet of cookies and wondering about which end to open them, and he's gone through one can of soda and is popping open a second. He can feel the worming tablets doing their job – he only needed to take one, but he took three just to be safe. His dad won't stop talking – and he talks with his hands moving all over the place, his voice louder than it needs to be, and he paces too, wearing a horseshoe pattern into the carpet, pausing only to take a drink. All of this makes Lucas think his dad wishes he'd been the one to shoot the janitor. It'd be flipping the whole write-what-you-know thing on its head.

'Let's get pizza,' his dad says, which sounds less like a celebration and more like any other night of the week.

'Sure,' Lucas says, worried if he doesn't give his dad something to do the horseshoe in the carpet will wear through to the basement.

It does seem like a weird thing to be celebrating. Monday he almost died, and today the man who tried killing him is dead.

While his dad orders dinner, Lucas takes a shower, washing off the grime from his night in the woods and the sweat from his bike ride home. He removes the bandage from his hand and inspects the cut. The skin is pale and shrivelled, and any blood that leaked from it has dried. He's definitely raked out some of the stitches by scratching at it. The wound has opened a little too. It doesn't look infected, but that may change with all the dirt he's surely gotten into it. He pours iodine into it, the wound stinging, but between that and the worming tablets he's taken care of not only the worm, but any microscopic eggs that may still be there. To be sure, he'll take more tablets over the next few days. He ought to go to the hospital to get the wound re-stitched, but instead he bandages it up nice and tight. He can go tomorrow.

He sits in his room and connects his phone to his computer. Last night he used it to film Sheriff Cohen helping Grove into the woods. It's one of the reasons his battery didn't last as long as it should have. He hasn't had the chance to watch the footage, and he does that now, worried it's going to be one blurry figure pushing another blurry figure, kind of like the Bigfoot videos people have been posting. But it's nothing like that at all, because both men are caught in the headlights of the car, all lit up and clearly identifiable. He saves a copy onto a USB drive and hides it in his wardrobe as insurance. It's his 'get out of jail free' card if Sheriff Cohen does suspect Lucas of being out there last night. He takes the crime-scene tape he used to strangle the janitor with outside, and, along with the duct tape he tore from Grove's mouth, he melts them in the barbecue. It stinks, and there's black smoke, and he steps back to avoid breathing it in. The plastic shrinks into a blob.

When he returns to the lounge, his dad has stopped pacing and is instead watching the news conference. The pizza arrives. They make a start on dinner. On TV, Sheriff Cohen is out front of the police station talking to a bunch of reporters. There's a small graphic in the top corner of the screen saying the footage was recorded half an hour ago. Sheriff Cohen doesn't look like he's having a good time. Lucas wonders if driving the janitor out to the sawmill was the first bad thing Sheriff Cohen has ever done. If he were to cut him open, would there be a worm inside making him do these things?

Of course he has no desire ever to do that. Sheriff Cohen is a good man, but possibly one under the influence of some kind of parasite. Lucas hopes not, because if that is the case, then, like Wolfy, and the electrician, and Freddy, and the janitor, it would mean Sheriff Cohen can't be saved.

It would mean putting him down.

Chapter Seventy-Two

Deborah hugs me when I get home, and tells me how relieved she is that I'm okay.

'Everything you've done over the last few days – the world owes you,' she says.

I don't tell her the news my lawyer gave me. I'm too tired for that. 'How's Dad?'

'He asked if he could see my breasts this afternoon.'

'Oh geez.'

'He reminded me of the date I had the other night. But James, you do know you can't sustain this, right? I'm happy to help, but it's getting beyond my ability.'

'I know.'

'He needs to be in a care home.'

'I know that too. Did he have dinner?'

'Most of it. The rest ended up on the lounge wall. Don't worry, I've cleaned it up.'

'Thanks, Deborah. I don't know how we'd get through this without you.'

Deborah leaves, and I sit in the lounge with my dad, and we watch TV together and don't make any conversation. I don't know if he knows I'm here. I take the moment to use my burner cellphone to call my primary one. I leave the two connected for a minute then hang up, creating a phone record in which Mr Anonymous gave me instructions for the payoff. My lawyer's call earlier doesn't pull me out of any kind of financial hole. There are still more bills, and I still need to give the bank some money, and I have to do something about Dad. Then there is Nathan, but what the hell we're going to do about him I have no idea. That's where my life is now – hoping my son won't grow up to be a serial killer.

My dad gets up and goes to the corner of the room, where he gets ready to take a piss. I guide him into the bathroom just in time, and then he goes to bed. I do the tin-can trick again with his door handle and head back into the lounge. I fight the temptation to drive to Cassandra's house and drag Nathan away from his computer and shake him over and over. The way I fight that is by taking my bottle of whiskey and sitting out on the back porch and watching the big blue sky with the sun arcing toward the edge of it. I drink from a glass for the class, but I feel anything but classy. I'll deal with Nathan tomorrow. The light fades and the bugs start up a chorus from the bushes that gets louder as the day gets quieter. The whiskey slowly disappears.

The weather is going to break tomorrow, so the news says, the dry swept away by a storm. Right now the moon is so large it's washing my backyard with pale-blue light. My mind is racing so fast, but everything is in free fall. It's panicked thinking, and none of it useful. I'm angry and scared and have no outlet for any of that. I could fill up the basin and scream into it, or I could go and arrest my son, or I could confess my crimes, but instead I finish off my whiskey and then grab a beer from the fridge. The night is so still, so warm, so heart-achingly beautiful. All the insects that went into silent mode when I first walked out here go about making all the noises insects like to make. I sip at my beer, hoping that after a while I might finally fall asleep.

A few beers later, and I do.

Day Four

Chapter Seventy-Three

Nathan is waiting for Lucas outside the school. He has his arms folded and is leaning against the low wall, staring right at him, as though his entire existence this morning has been all about looking for Lucas. Which Lucas figures it has been. He's still using the mountain bike from the sawmill. His legs are sore from all that biking, and he's tired, having not slept well last night, having spent much of it lying still, trying to recognise if something was moving beneath the surface of his skin.

Nathan pushes himself away from the wall and puts his hands on the handlebars, forcing Lucas to stop. His jaw is tight and his face narrow and his forehead crunched up. Lucas doesn't say anything. He's always figured it's easier that way. Other students walk by, none of them paying any attention. Why would they? It's nothing new.

'I bet you're sad today,' Nathan says, 'Given that my dad killed your boyfriend. I thought you'd be at home crying into your pillow about how unfair the world is, then going online to find some other janitor to molest you.'

'Why are you like this?' Lucas asks.

'What?'

'Can't you just leave me alone?'

'No,' Nathan says, and then Social Darwinism kicks in, and Nathan does what he does best – and that's shove Lucas; and Lucas does what he does best – and that's fall over. That's the thing about the Nathans of the world who behave this way – they're always going to be bigger than the person they shove.

Lucas lies on the ground with the bike on his leg, the front wheel slowly spinning, thudding gently against the brakes. He cradles his hand. It's bandaged up tight, but the knock it just took when he fell might have jarred the wound. It's already a mess in there, and it wouldn't surprise him if it's bleeding. He was going to go to the hospital after school to get it looked at, but he doesn't think he can wait that long.

Nathan leans over him. His face is red. He smells like sweat. He sniffs, then slowly lets a wad of phlegm dangle from his mouth. Lucas turns away from it, but it still gets him on the side of the face, gooey and warm like a soft-boiled oyster.

Nathan laughs, then just like that it's over, his bully walking away while Lucas wipes the side of his face, then wipes what he finds there against the ground. He gets to his feet and straightens his clothes and picks up his bike.

He shouldn't have come in today.

He shouldn't have come in this week.

The centre of his bandage has gone from white to red.

He gets on his bike and heads for the hospital.

Chapter Seventy-Four

I end up sleeping right through the night for the first time in months, but I also sleep through the tin can falling off Dad's door, because I wake up to the sounds of him trying to cook eggs on the stove. Thankfully I disconnected the power to it after the fire, otherwise I might have been waking to the sounds of the rest of my house going up in flames.

'Let me help you there, Dad.'

'Everything you've been through over the last few days, Timothy, it's the least I can do.'

I don't know who Timothy is, but I take him not swearing at me as a win.

That win disappears when, a moment later, he says, 'Why the fuck doesn't the stove work?'

'Go sit down in the lounge, Dad, and I'll take care of breakfast.'

'You? You're a fucking imbecile. You couldn't even make toast.'

I prove him wrong, because that is what I end up making him. I poach some eggs in the microwave, and pour some bowls of cereal, and we sit out on the deck to have it. For a day that's promising rain, there's sure no sign of it. I eat my breakfast and drink my coffee while thinking over the big questions from yesterday. The bad news is I have a slight hangover from last night, but the good news is today things don't seem to taste as bad.

My phone rings. It seems twice as loud as it ought to be. It's Cassandra.

'Hi,' I say, my voice a little slurred.

'Hi,' she says. 'Listen, I feel bad about how we left things yesterday. With everything that was going on, I just wasn't feeling myself.'

'I can relate.'

'Of course I want things to work between us, and with this lawsuit not hanging over our heads, I'm sure we can figure out the rest of it. Let's get together on the weekend to talk about it.'

'I'd love that.'

'But for today, is it okay if Nathan comes back to your place tonight? I have a lot of work to catch up on, and—'

'Of course,' I say. Nathan will be a big part of the weekend conversation, and the next big thing to be hanging over our heads.

When Deborah shows up to look after Dad, I freshen up and head into work. Everybody in the station looks rested, having slept well too. Hutch tells me they have more unsolved cases that were sent our way that could potentially be linked to Grove. She shows me a list of seven names. Aaron McGee and Carl Nichols are both on there. Over the next few weeks Grove's victims will be confirmed. The others on the list – I wonder if they were his victims too.

I sit in my office with the door closed reading over everything we have from Freddy Holt's disappearance. I still don't believe Grove had anything to do with it, but last night, as I sat on the deck drinking my beers, an unsettling thought took hold that I wasn't able to shake. Did Nathan have something to do with Freddy's disappearance? I know they were friends, but that doesn't mean there wasn't some kind of fight that got out of control, and then some kind of coverup. I add it to the list of things I'm going to have to confront him about.

Going through everything we have about Freddy takes me through to lunch. I go into the bullpen. Hutch and Wade are at their desks taking care of paperwork – yesterday's events created a lot of it. Sharon is on her computer typing. I ask her to go to the bank and get out forty of the eighty thousand dollars we have set aside for the reward money. Ideally I'd like to get the entire eighty, and I had originally said that's what we would be doing, but I'm worried half the police force would storm out in protest. As it is, the only thing that brought people around to my way of thinking was the promise that we would stake out the drop-off point. Sharon grabs her handbag and puts on her sunglasses and heads out the door, and I'm reminded of that scene in *Psycho*, where the secretary goes on the run with the money rather than going to the bank. I can only hope things work out better for me than they did for her.

I head back into my office, sit behind my desk and massage my headache and wait for her to come back.

A minute into that waiting I get a phone call from the medical examiner.

She tells me she needs to see me.

Chapter Seventy-Five

Lucas is peeing in the bathroom during the lunch break when Nathan comes in and pushes him in the back. He bounces off the front of the urinal and pees over the front of his shorts. Before he can balance himself, Nathan grabs him by the collar, pulls him back and topples him over, all while Lucas tries to zip himself up. Getting pushed over and bullied is one thing, but having that happen while your dick is out is another thing entirely.

He's dragged into the centre of the room, giving him a view of a false ceiling where balls of wadded up wet toilet paper have been thrown and stuck. There are fresh stitches in his hand from earlier this morning, and it's still numb from the injection. The wound did turn out to be infected, and he's been given antibiotics to take. The nurse gave him a stern lecture for scratching out the stitches, and he promised her he would do better. He figures right now that promise is getting broken.

There are three people standing over him: Nathan, a boy called Carson, and another called Jeff. They're the same three that stuffed him into the locker, something that feels like it happened a year ago. They're all the same size – big, the way bullies tend to be, reaching adult size years before they ought to. Carson, the biggest of the three, has a thin shadow above his lip from a moustache he's been unsuccessfully trying to grow, and a chin that juts out as far as his nose, giving his face a crescent-moon shape. Jeff has the face of a distant planet, red skin, pockmarked and cratered with small black-and-white volcanos, ready to erupt.

'I found out what you did,' Nathan says. His face is dark, his muscles tight, and when he talks there's spittle flying from his lips. Lucas has never seen him this angry before.

The bathroom shrinks in size as the walls close in. Nathan is standing over him, pointing down at him. Carson is to his side, and Jeff is in the process of jamming a rubber wedge under the bathroom door so it can't be opened from the outside.

'Turns out Harriet got her phone back, and that it was found at my dad's house. Somebody put it there with the other stolen shit to get me in trouble. I know it was you.'

'It wasn't me,' Lucas says, and how didn't he see this coming? Of course Nathan would figure out it was him.

'Do it,' Nathan says, looking from one of his friends to the other.

Carson straddles Lucas and pushes down on Lucas's chest with his hands. Jeff pulls Lucas's shoes off, then reaches for the bottom of his shorts and tugs those away too, his underwear going with it, giving Lucas flashbacks to the sawmill, only there the janitor was using scissors. At the same time Nathan reaches down and pulls at Lucas's T-shirt, Carson forcing his arms upward so it slips away. It happens quickly, and smoothly, like this isn't the first time these three have done such a thing. A moment later Lucas is naked except for a pair of socks. Jeff shoves Lucas's underwear into his mouth, then pulls Lucas's bandaged hand to the side to stand on it, putting all his body weight into it. He smiles as he pulls a cellphone out of his pocket and points it at him. While this is happening, Nathan puts a foot on Lucas's other hand, and Carson gets a good grip on Lucas's feet. Three boys who are more men than boys, all bigger, all heavier, and Lucas isn't going anywhere, no matter how hard he struggles. And he does struggle. He screams into his underwear and he jerks his body back and forth, but it's no use.

'Keep holding him,' Nathan says, while working at undoing the front of his pants. Is Nathan picking up from where the janitor left off? He closes his eyes and struggles harder, and a moment later something is splashing on his face, and he doesn't need to open his eyes to know Nathan is pissing on him. The stench, the revulsion, is instant, but none of that stacks up to the humiliation as urine runs through his hair and down the side of his neck and pools up in his nose and eyes. It burns. The underwear in his mouth swells as piss soaks into it, and what doesn't soak into it runs onto his tongue and to the back of his throat, making him choke. Is this what waterboarding feels like? When he turns away to try and clear his throat, more runs into his ear and down the side of his face, Nathan redirecting the stream to cover all of Lucas's chest and neck, all while laughing, laughing, the three of them having the best time, laughing themselves onto a list of people that Lucas needs to examine for parasitic tapeworms, the top of that list being Nathan. He doesn't know what he hates the sound of more – the laughing, or Nathan's piss splashing over him and the floor. He didn't enjoy cutting open Wolfy that day when he needed to examine him, or Freddy, but he will enjoy cutting these three.

'People have been thinking I'm a thief,' Nathan says, shifting the stream back to Lucas's face, and Jesus, how much is there? Has Nathan held onto it all day for this moment? 'Only now they're going to know it was you,' he says, the flow slowing down now, and then stopping, the final few drops hitting Lucas in the nose. He hears Nathan zip himself away, and a moment later they let go of him. He pulls the underwear from his mouth while scrambling back toward the wall. He wipes at his eyes with his bandaged hand, and opens them. They sting, and he blinks away the piss and the pain until things come into focus. Nathan is watching the footage on the phone with Jeff, while Carson, who has been hit with friendly fire, cleans himself at the sink. Nathan and Jeff laugh hard as they watch the footage, and cringe, and a few times make 'aw' sounds, like they can't believe what they're seeing.

Lucas's clothes are a few feet to his right. He reaches out and snatches them up and holds them against his body like a shield, but nobody is paying him any attention now. Carson finishes cleaning up, and comes over to watch the video. Even though his underwear is wet, Lucas still pulls it on.

His three tormentors finish watching the footage, then head for the door. Carson pulls out the rubber wedge and opens it.

'Give me a moment,' Nathan says, and his friends look surprised, but don't say anything. They disappear into the corridor and Nathan comes back over to Lucas. He can't believe how much shame he feels. He really thought things would be different after what happened with Grove. He was wrong.

'What's it to be?' Nathan asks. 'You want everybody to see you naked and covered in piss? Or are you going to keep your mouth shut?'

'I'll keep my mouth shut.'

'I need you to answer something else for me,' Nathan says.

'Somebody who lets himself get molested by the janitor, who lets himself get pissed on, seriously, how do you do it? How do you live with yourself?'

Lucas doesn't say anything. He doubts Nathan is expecting him to.

'I mean, seriously, anybody with any sense of shame would have killed themselves by now. You're an embarrassment.' He holds up the phone. 'And don't even think about going to my dad about this. You do that, and I'm going to put this video online so the whole world sees your tiny dick and piss-covered body. Is that what you want?'

Lucas shakes his head. No. It's not what he wants. It's the janitor all over again. Is that what people do these days? Film the hurt, then threaten to expose the humiliation? And if it is, why do they all seem to think he's the perfect target for it?

'You understand me?'

Yes, he understands him. He also understands something else too. 'Is this what you did to Taylor Reed?'

Nathan kicks him hard in the balls then, so hard that he instantly throws up, his chest and stomach covered in vomit. He rolls onto his side, his hands in his groin as the room rocks and sways and darkens.

'Taylor Reed was a loser, just like you,' Nathan says, and even though Lucas can hear him, he can't make sense of the words. His muscles are on fire, and his bones have turned to glass. There is no way he will ever get to hunt for the worm in Nathan, because he's never going to be able to move again. Soon somebody will find him here – perhaps the new janitor if there is one already – and he'll either be scooped up and put into the back of an ambulance or the trunk of a car.

'He did us all a favour, and you know what?'

Lucas doesn't know, and right now he doesn't care. He's paralysed, and everything hurts – God it hurts. He tries to look up at Nathan, and is relieved when he can. He wiggles his fingers and sees them move.

'You ought to do us the same favour,' Nathan says. 'Everybody at the school wants you to kill yourself. We'd all be better off, including you.'

He isn't sure he's going to be able to speak, and is surprised when he clearly asks, 'What did I ever do to you?'

'You tried to get me expelled.'

'I mean from the very beginning. What did I ever do to you to make you single me out?'

Nathan shrugs. 'Nothing.'

'Then why?'

'Because I can.'

Chapter Seventy-Six

The medical examiner's office is in the basement of the hospital, just one floor separating folks with good luck from folks with bad. I step out of the lift into a cinderblock corridor, the cream paint on the walls so thick it's made them shiny and smooth. At the end is a set of double doors that swing open so dead folks with questions can be rolled in, then dead folks with answers can be rolled back out.

I head in and turn right, toward an office that could belong to an accountant – a desk, a computer, filing cabinets and paperwork and printers, nothing to suggest this is where death is catalogued. Marie, the medical examiner, is at her desk. She sees me through the window and mouths she'll only be a moment. I look around the morgue where there are all the things you wouldn't find in an accountant's office, unless your accountant is a serial killer. Fluorescent lights reflect off tools designed for cutting and snapping and shearing. There are drains to sluice away blood, scales for weighing organs, and rows of what look like small square refrigerator doors with temporary homes on the other side.

Marie joins me. Her grey hair is tied up into a bun and her glasses are dangling on a chain around her neck. She smiles when she sees me and gives me a brief hug and a kiss on the side of the cheek. Then she pulls back and keeps her hands on my arms and she says, 'I'm so glad you're okay. There's every reason this could have been you lying on my table.'

'I'm glad I'm okay too.'

She leads me over to the body. Grove has a sheet pulled over him, and now she pulls it back. He looks like an art project some kid got terribly wrong. His chest is sunken in, his ribs are on display, his cheeks are so hollow the insides must be resting on his tongue. His good eye has sunk into its socket, making his forehead look huge, and his bad eye is something from a seafood restaurant that's sat out in the sun for too long. His hair has been swept up from a barbershop floor, coated in glue, and tossed in his general direction. There are strangulation marks around his neck and bruises around his wrists and feet.

'You okay?' Marie asks. 'You look pale.'

'Headache,' I say, and it's true. Seeing Grove has brought it on very quickly.

She runs through the details. Simon Grove's cause of death was a bullet to the side of the head. She shows me the impact point. The skull is punctured and cracks have spread out like a spider web. She says Grove was severely dehydrated and malnourished, despite being fed what looked like a couple of muesli bars and water. She says he would have been in a lot of pain. She says it'll be a few days for the toxicology report, but fresh injection points on his arm lead her to believe he was sedated. She points to the bullet wound in his shoulder. It caused nerve and bone damage, and even with intense rehabilitation it would never have gotten back to being right. She points to the red ring around his neck. It's a narrow band maybe a quarter of an inch thick that has gotten darker since he's died. 'This wasn't done with hands, nor with rope – and there are no fibres. Some kind of cord.'

'There was some crime-scene tape out at the scene that was missing.'

She doesn't say anything for a few moments, then nods. 'That'd do it.'

'Anything here to point me in the next direction?'

She doesn't answer for a few moments, then asks, 'How long have we known each other, James?'

Her question gives me pause. Does she know? 'I don't know. Almost twenty years?'

'Twenty years,' she says. 'It's a long time. A guy like Simon Grove, it's easy to say he got what he deserved, but this – what was done to him – that ain't nothing any man should go through, even somebody as bad as he was.'

I don't say anything. She keeps staring at the body. I know there's more.

'I don't blame you for shooting him.'

'I had no choice.'

'Uh huh. There's something else. Something I didn't put in the report.'

'Which is?'

'You said after you shot him, you stood over him, and you watched him die.'

'That's right.'

'You said he told you there were four others, and that he didn't hurt Freddy Holt.'

'That's right.'

'You sure about that?'

I don't say anything.

'See, the bullet entered his frontal lobe and tunnelled down deep. The effect would have been immediate. Even if by some miracle he was able to speak, he would have had no idea what he was saying.'

I don't say anything.

'An abnormality like that, well, it just throws a spanner into the works, and I don't like abnormalities. I figured it best not to include it in the report. If I did, then whoever reads it might think you'd gotten those names out of him before you shot him, which wouldn't be a good look. It might make it seem like after Grove opened fire, you shot him in the shoulder, had control of the situation, got him to confess a few things, then put him down. The shoot wouldn't look so clean then.'

I have an option now. What she's suggesting is far better than the truth, and I don't want her to suspect I had anything to do with how Grove got into the condition he was in, so I slowly nod.

'Listen—'

'Let's not say anything,' she says. 'Like I said, it's not in the report because I don't like abnormalities. As for the rest...' She shakes her head. 'Simon Grove was a bad guy, no doubt about it, but whoever did this was equally as bad. This is torture. His eye,' she says, pointing at it, 'was punctured on Monday when Lucas Connor defended himself, but whoever tied Grove up doubled down on that. They've prodded and poked at it. They've starved him and tortured him. If this person thought they were doing the right thing, then this is somebody with some serious psychological issues. I can't tell you who did this; all I can say is they're the kind of person you need to find, Sheriff. People around here probably think whoever did that deserves a medal, but the truth is they're a monster who needs to be locked away forever.'

Chapter Seventy-Seven

Lucas sits in one of the stalls stinking of piss and vomit, dressed in only his underwear and socks as he waits out the rest of the lunch break. He doesn't want to be standing almost naked at one of the sinks cleaning himself down when other people come in. And as it happens, others do – they come in, they use the bathroom, some come in to smoke, and he waits them out. His groin still feels hot, but the pain has eased to a dull throb. When the bell goes, he waits another few minutes before stepping out.

He scoops water from beneath the tap and washes his hair and face before starting on his body. He continues to smell of vomit and urine, but none of it – not the pain, not the stench, not the taste – none of it comes close to hurting as much as the humiliation. Somehow he feels even worse than he did when he was lying on the mattress in the sawmill. But maybe that's because he got out of that mostly unscathed – except for the worm.

He takes off his bandage and rinses it out under the tap. Now he knows why Taylor Reed jumped, and he can't deny part of him is thinking it's a good option. He should never have tried to get Nathan expelled. He should have just stuck to the routine of getting bullied every day, and putting up with it.

He uses soap and builds up lather and goes back through his hair and over his body, but it doesn't help with the smell. There is urine on his clothes, and he rinses those out too. He wrings everything out as tight as he can, and gets dressed, and he stares at himself in the mirror, wondering how life got to this. First Wolfy turned on him, then Freddy, now it's serial-killer janitors and ... and whatever the hell it is that Nathan is. There are no answers, and, knowing he can't go to class looking and smelling like this, he heads into the corridor and for the exit, ducking beneath the windows of the doors leading into each classroom. He needs to let somebody know he's not coming back before they think he's gone missing again. When he gets to the bike stands he rings the school office from his cellphone and tells them he's not well, and heading home, and the woman he speaks to doesn't question it – why would she? After what he's been through?

He bikes home on his shitty bike, his hair drying on the way, his T-shirt still damp and his bandage still soaking by the time he gets there. His dad is in the office working. He calls out to him, but doesn't open the door – doesn't want his dad to be invaded by the stench. In the shower he goes through half a bottle of shampoo as he washes his hair over and over until the smell has gone. He carefully cleans the wound on his hand. He can't feel the worm anymore, but he knows the tablets yesterday didn't kill it. They can't have, otherwise he wouldn't be having these thoughts about what to do to Nathan. He opens the packet of pills, and hesitates, then closes it. He likes these thoughts, and the courage that comes with them. For the first time ever, the worm is his friend. He might change his mind tomorrow, but for today he needs the strength and encouragement his friend will provide.

He hunts through the drawer for the hair clippers his mom used to use on him. He can't smell the piss, but he can feel it in there. He selects the quarter-inch attachment. The cutter goes through quickly, and smoothly, and he's two strips in when he realises his mistake. Tomorrow when people question Nathan Cohen's disappearance, a change like shaving his head will draw attention – after all, that's what they say in the news, isn't it? That the person who killed such-and-such will be behaving differently? But he can't stop now. He cuts more strips, his hair tumbling into the basin. When he's done he runs his fingers through his new haircut. He can see his scalp, pale, beneath it. He doesn't like how it looks, but he likes how clean it feels. He scoops up the hair and dumps it into the small trash can under the sink. He carefully dresses the wound on his hand. He thinks about what Sheriff Cohen said yesterday about Nathan staying at his mom's this week – which means Nathan's parents have split up. If that's the case, then Lucas is going to have to figure out where Nathan's mom lives. Easiest way to do that is to go back to school and follow him from there.

He gets dressed then goes down to the basement. When the house got renovated, his dad spent a lot of money on the basement, turning it into a man cave, with the idea of putting in a big-screen TV and comfortable chairs and a beer fridge, but none of that went in there. Instead it's become storage space for old furniture and things from their past his dad clings to. There's a workbench his dad never uses, and power tools that have never been plugged in. The squirrel knife he used on Freddy Holt is beneath the floorboards.

Freddy is under there too, surrounded by kitty litter and wrapped in thick plastic to absorb the smell.

He pries the floorboard up and grabs the knife.

Chapter Seventy-Eight

Forty thousand dollars doesn't look impressive when stacked in a single pile only two inches thick. It's one of those times where facts and feelings don't line up – it fits easily into an envelope, but feels like it should take up an entire briefcase. I go through each stack like I'm thumbing down the edges of a deck of cards, a small draught against my face as the notes flip quickly through the air. It's a life-changing amount of money, and there will be more to come.

It's one-thirty, with the drop-off scheduled for two. Sharon wishes us good luck, and Hutch climbs into the back of the cruiser and lies across the backseat, which can't be that comfortable, but it's not like I can tell her there's no point. Wade pulls out of the parking lot a few minutes after us – his part in the plan is to park at Earl's Garage in an unmarked sedan and note down every car that drives by, with the hope somebody will drive past him from the left, then ten minutes later drive past him from the right.

We drive past the Kelly farm, where the owners took large amounts of sleeping pills years ago and died holding hands on their bed. We pass the hiking trails where others have gotten lost, some found, some not. We drive past Earl's Garage, the owner shot last year, dead before he hit the floor. We reach the sawmill where Grove tried to kill Lucas Connor, and was himself shot and killed a few days later. It's a stretch of highway that says all the wrong things about Acacia Pines.

Fifty yards short of the turnoff to the old sawmill, I pull over. Hutch jumps out, runs into the trees and disappears. I take the turn and follow the curve, and the sawmill comes into view. I park short of where I parked yesterday, that spot easily identifiable by the fluids that leaked when the cruiser was shot.

I take the envelope and I walk over to the building and through the doorway where the door was torn off. I take a hard left so there's no possible line of sight between me and Hutch. I stuff the envelope of cash into my pants. I told Hutch earlier the caller wanted the cash left in the trunk of the burnt-out car, so I walk over to that now, hang about for a few seconds as if I'm putting it in there, then make my way back to the cruiser.

I don't see Hutch as I leave. I pass Wade on the way back into town, his car parked around the side of Earl's Garage, where he has a good view of traffic without them having one of him.

I radio Hutch. I ask her if there's anything, and she says not yet, that she's hiding in the trees with a line of sight to the door. She can make out the burnt-out car and is reluctant to go any closer. I lower her expectations and tell her it's possible our guy picked up the cash before I even got back to my car.

'For all we know he went out one of the other doors and is long gone. He might have walked into the forest and is parked miles away along the highway.'

'It was always the flaw with the plan.'

'We had to pay it, Hutch.'

'Did we?'

I don't answer her.

'I'll give it a few hours,' she says, 'then I'll check. If the money is gone then Wade can come and get me. How's the headache?'

'It's fine.'

'You really should go and see a doctor.'

'I should,' I say, but I think it will fade soon enough.

'It's been a stressful few days,' she says. 'More for you than the rest of us. Why not take the rest of the day off?'

It's a good suggestion.

'You're right,' I say. There's nothing I can do at work today except stress some more about who tried to kill Simon Grove, and I can do all that stressing from home.

Chapter Seventy-Nine

I pass Lucas Connor on my way home. I almost don't recognise him because he's cut his hair short. He's biking toward school, possibly trying to make the last class of the day. He's so focused on the road I don't think he sees me. I don't blame him for lying to me. I don't blame him for trying to frame Nathan. I just wish I could know for sure he didn't see me dragging Grove out to my car.

I get home. Dad and Deborah are out. I sit at the table in the peace and quiet and stare at the money. Because I've kept to myself how close I am to losing the house, it means nobody is going to ask any questions as to how I've managed to hang on to it. Only the bank manager knows how bad things are, and I can easily tell him I got a cash loan from somewhere, or perhaps that I sold the story rights of my last few days to a newspaper or magazine.

I hear a key slide into the front door. I scoop the cash up and jam it into my pocket. A moment later Deborah and my dad come in. Deborah smiles at me, but my dad looks at me like I'm a stranger.

'How's he been?' I ask.

'He's been fine,' she says, but her smile is strained, and I know from previous conversations that her definition of fine has changed multiple times since looking after him. 'I was going to make us some tea. Would you like one?'

'Sure, but I'll make them.'

I make three cups, and to my surprise Dad drinks his. We sit at the table and make small talk, and even though my dad doesn't participate, I start to think about the way he used to be, back when he worked at his restaurant, cutting vegetables at a hundred miles an hour and cooking perfect steaks. It was a good life, and he was a good father, and sometimes it's easy for the dementia not only to wipe out his memories of his past, but to wipe the memories of those of us who knew him as that man.

We finish our drinks and Deborah heads home. I stay sitting with Dad, keeping him company. When Nathan gets home, he barely acknowledges us, just hunts out food from the pantry.

'How was school?'

'It sucked, like always,' he says. Before I tell him his day is about to get worse, he says, 'I guess I should thank you.'

'What for?'

'For not accusing me of stealing that stuff.'

'You heard about that, huh?'

'Everybody did. Harriet told people that her phone got switched on at our house. If I'd been here, would you have thought it was me?'

'Of course not.'

He smiles. I can't remember the last time I saw him smile. The problem is there's no warmth in it. 'You're lying.'

'I might have thought it, but we'd have talked about it, and I would have believed you.'

'Sure, I bet that's exactly how that conversation would have gone. You know who put them there?'

'No,' I say. 'Do you?'

'No,' he says.

I say nothing.

He says nothing.

My dad says nothing as he stares into empty space.

Then I say, 'Is there anything else you want to tell me?'

'No.'

'Nothing?'

'If you've got something you want to accuse me of, then go ahead and say it.'

This is the moment I confront him about Taylor Reed and tell him I know he stuffed Lucas into that locker. And yet, when I go to say something, I clam up. This is a conversation I need to have with Cass first.

'Fine,' he says, and he disappears to his bedroom, taking the opportunity with him. However, that opportunity comes back a minute later when he returns and asks, 'Have you been in my room?'

'When?'

'While I was gone.'

Again I don't say what needs saying because it wouldn't be fair to Cass. 'No. Why?'

He doesn't have an answer. He's looking for his secret phone, but his secret phone is in my pocket. He can't ask if I know where it is.

'You sure?' he asks.

'I have no reason to go in there.'

He turns to Dad. 'How about you, Grandpa? You been in there?'

It takes Dad a moment to realise he's being spoken to, then, 'What?'

'Did you go into my room?' Nathan asks, aggressive now.

'Don't,' I say.

'Well, did you?'

'Nathan, he hasn't been into your room.'

'You don't know that,' he says. 'He goes anywhere he wants and has no idea about it. He takes shit and puts things where they're not meant to be. It's no wonder Mom moved out. When are you going to put him into another home?'

'We're going to try.'

'I fucking hate it here,' he adds, and he goes back into his room. I stay at the table, listening to him turning his room inside out looking for his phone, not knowing what I'm meant to do next.

Chapter Eighty

Instead of following Nathan to his mom's place, Lucas ends up following him to his dad's, which probably means he's staying there tonight. He had no plan on how he was going to get to Nathan tonight at his mom's house, or now at his dad's, but he's working on it.

When he gets home he can hear typing coming from the office, and the door is closed, which is his dad's way of saying he should be left alone, which Lucas is happy to comply with. He plops himself on the couch and turns on the TV, switching channels. He stops switching when he comes across a news bulletin. Until this week, the news was only ever white noise to him. People doing bad things – that's what it was. Over and over and over. You could record the news one night and play it to a room full of people a week later and nobody would know the difference. But this week he's been watching it to keep updated on the janitor. Right now there's a reporter cooking in the sun outside the police station. She's saying the police haven't confirmed any connection between Simon Grove and Freddy Holt, but that there are other cases from across the country that may have potential links. Then she says the police have confirmed that the first half of the reward payment has been paid to the anonymous source who phoned in Simon Grove's location – forty thousand dollars.

Lucas had forgotten about the reward money.

He puts the TV on mute. Is that what this has been about the entire time? Sheriff Cohen probably found Simple Simon within minutes of showing up at the sawmill on Monday. Did he abduct him, knowing a reward would be offered?

He goes online and looks up what happens with reward money. Sometimes the money can go to the entire department, but it's rare, and certainly the money never goes to individual police officers – otherwise it would be like they were working for tips. Police departments can hold back on paying rewards if they have a just reason, but it can damage the public trust.

There is no anonymous caller.

There has only been Sheriff Cohen.

He doesn't need the rest of the afternoon to figure out what he needs to do.

He goes into the basement and gets Freddy's phone out from under the floorboards.

Chapter Eighty-One

I make burgers on the barbecue while Nathan builds up an appetite searching his room. Despite burgers being his favourite food, I don't see them putting him into a better mood. Even so, I do it because I can't imagine we're going to have many more meals together after this. Once we confront him, he may never want to be in the same room with us again. After a while he gives up looking for the phone, and I can hear screaming and shouting and gunshots as he goes back to his game. How different being a teenager is these days compared to when I was young. How Nathan enjoys that stuff I have no idea. How video-game makers figured out death and violence were going to turn kids on I also have no idea – or maybe they figured it out the same way Hollywood and writers and artists all figured it out. I bet early drawings found on cave walls depicted people getting bitten by zombies.

When everything is ready I let Nathan know. He doesn't put on a big song and dance when I ask him to sit outside so the three of us can eat together. We bite into our burgers, except for my dad, who throws his out into the yard, then watches the bubbles rising in his soda. It's seven-thirty and the insects in the long grass are making a lot of noise. A neighbour starts up their lawnmower – which is always the way the moment you sit outside to relax. On the horizon clouds are forming a long chain. The rain we were promised is waiting out there in the distance.

'You want a beer?' I ask Nathan. 'I'm going to grab myself one.'

He looks up fast enough to tweak his neck. He rubs at it, and he smiles, and I remember how he used to look that way when he was younger, how he'd laugh when I tickled him, how he'd get lost in his own world playing with toys in the bath, how he'd lie down with his eyes wide open while I read him a story. Back then I used to be his hero. This boy is not that boy. He hasn't been that boy for a long time.

'Hell yeah.'

It's the first time I've ever offered him a beer, not that I have any doubt he's drunk plenty of them in the past. I grab a couple from inside and come back out. He opens his and I open mine and we clink cans. We finish our burgers and Nathan finishes his beer and asks if he can have another one. If I say no, he'll return to his moody self, and I'd like to keep him happy with me, even if it is only for a few more minutes. My dad lowers his head into his arms and falls asleep.

'One more, then that's it. And don't tell your mother,' I add, giving a conspiratorial wink.

He goes into the kitchen and grabs a beer and comes back out. He doesn't ask if I want another one. He probably never thought to ask. I don't ask him to help me tidy up because wars have started over less. If we're going to fight, it may as well be about something we need to fight about. Which we will do when Cass is here on the weekend. What our son has done will destroy her. It will destroy our family.

'Listen, Nathan, I need to talk to you about something,' I say, the words out of my mouth before I even knew I was going to say them.

'Please don't tell me you and Mom are getting back together.'

His words hurt. The clouds are getting closer. It's getting darker out there. The trees in the backyard are moving. We might be in for more than rain. My phone beeps. I ignore it.

'This has nothing to do with your mother, or with me. Are you sure there's nothing you want to tell me? You can come to me about anything. I can help you with anything.'

He stares at me. His fresh beer is open and he's taken a few sips. I'm hoping it will loosen him up a little. 'There's nothing.'

'Yesterday when I came here looking for Harriet's cellphone, I started searching the house.'

'You went into my room.'

'I did.'

'You said before you hadn't.'

'I know.'

'You lied.'

'I did.'

'You went in there because you thought I had stolen it. Jesus, Dad, why do you always have the lowest opinion of—'

'I found this.' I pull his secret cellphone out of my pocket and put it on the table.

He stares at it, and he says nothing, and I say nothing, and the storm gets closer.

Then, 'You had no right to go into my room.'

'I have every right, and this isn't about that. It's about what you did to Taylor Reed. I unlocked the phone. I saw the video, and I saw the messages you were sending him.'

He pushes himself out of his seat. 'This is bullshit.'

He walks away and I go right after him, catching him in the kitchen. I wrap my hand around his arm and hold on to him. 'You're not going anywhere. Not yet.'

'Fuck you,' he says.

He tries to wrench his arm free, but I hang on, tightening my grip. There will be bruises tomorrow. 'Did you know he was going to kill himself? Is that what you wanted, or did you think it was some kind of joke?'

'Let go of me.'

'A boy is dead, goddamn it. You answer me.'

'It's no wonder Mom left you.'

'You tormented that boy over and over and he killed himself, Nathan, and then you let us all think somebody else was responsible for it, and I think you're doing it again to Lucas Connor.'

'Let go of me.'

'Were you here the other night?'

'What?'

'Were you here? Two nights ago, were you here?'

'No, I wasn't here.'

'Do you know what happened to Freddy Holt?'

'What is wrong with you?'

'Did you kill him?'

'You're out of your mind.'

'Why'd you do it, son? Did Taylor Reed upset you? Were you just curious as to whether you could get him to do it? Jesus, Nathan, you can go to jail for this. You could be put away for years. And you ask what's wrong with me? What is wrong with me is I have a son who feels no remorse for—'

He punches me in the chest, his fist making contact with my bruised ribs. I let his arm go, and he shoves me and I hit the edge of the table and fall to the floor, coming to a stop when I bump against the fridge. He stands over me. 'Taylor was a loser just like you. This family would be better off if you'd been the one shot yesterday.'

He snatches the phone off the table and storms out of the kitchen. I stay on the floor, stunned at what just happened. I was kidding myself if I thought the conversation would go any different from this. I don't see a way forward now, other than to go into the station tomorrow and tell them what my son did. I thought I could help him. I thought if I could get our family back together, we could save him. I was wrong. The money I was going to use to save my house will all disappear on lawyers, once again.

Before all that I'm going to have to tell Cassandra. She's going to hate me for confronting him without her, and she has every right to.

I get up and go outside. Dad has woken up and has retrieved his burger from the yard and is eating it. I leave him to it. I check the message that came in on my phone earlier. It's from a number I don't recognise.

The message is a video. I try to sit down on the table and almost miss. My legs are shaking and my arms are so heavy I have to put the phone on the table to avoid dropping it. I already know what it's going to be before I press play. The gunshots and screaming start up louder than ever from Nathan's bedroom as he vents his anger into his computer.

I press play.

The video is of me pushing Grove into the trees, all lit up from the headlights of my car. His hands are cuffed behind him. It looks like he's being led to his execution. Then there's a cut, and then there's footage of me from a different angle, coming back out all alone.

'Where's the goddamn waiter?' Dad asks, stepping back onto the deck.

If I'd been followed, there would have been no time for somebody to park out on the road and still film me. Which means they would have had to have driven in, in which case I would have heard them. Which means I wasn't followed. Whoever did this was already out there. Why were they out there? And not just out there, but out there and in position to film me?

'Hey? Where's the fucking waiter?'

It could be somebody who works for me, or somebody from search and rescue. It could be somebody who was encouraged enough by the reward to go out there and take a look around. Perhaps it was a thrill-seeker who likes going to sites where crimes have been committed. A hiker, maybe, who'd gotten lost? Bigfoot, maybe, or somebody looking for him? Then why not claim the reward?

'Are you him?'

'There is no waiter, Dad.'

'Can you tell him the burger was excellent?'

My beer is still out here. I gulp it down. My hands are shaking. The clouds are closer and darker, and the wind has gotten stronger.

The storm has arrived, that's for damn sure.

'Fine, I'll tell him myself,' Dad says, and he heads inside.

The phone beeps again. And again. Multiple messages broken up into smaller ones:

> *I know what you did. I know you had Simon Grove in custody the entire time, waiting for the reward money to go up in value. I know today you got $40,000 of*

> *that reward and the rest is on the way. If you don't give it to me I'm going to send this footage to the media. You will go to jail. Drop that $40,000 at the same tree where*

> *you tied Simon Grove up at ten o'clock tonight. Otherwise the world will know you tortured and murdered him.*

The messages stop coming through. I send one back.

> *Who is this?*

Nothing. I launch the empty beer can out into the yard. I have no choice but to take the money out there, but taking it out there will only lead to further blackmail. They'll bleed me dry, and then turn the footage over to the media anyway. I call the station, then hang up halfway through dialling. I can't ask anybody there to look the number up I was messaged from. I can't involve anybody. I can't do anything, other than exactly what I've been asked to do. If I hadn't been with Nathan when that first message came through, I might have thought it was him. But it wasn't him.

The person who filmed me, this person who strangled Grove, they own me.

I go into Nathan's room without knocking.

'What the hell—'

'Shut up, Nathan, and if you—'

'Don't—'

'I said shut the fuck up.'

He does just that. He looks shocked.

'You need help, Nathan. I don't know if you really wanted Taylor to kill himself or not, and worse, I don't even think you care.'

'I—'

'And right now I have to go out, but you and me, we're going to finish this conversation when I get back home, but for now I want you here looking after your grandfather. You do anything other than that, and I swear to God I will put your arse in jail when I get home. You hear me?'

He nods.

'Do you fucking hear me?'

'I hear you.'

'And turn that shit off,' I say, nodding toward his computer. 'Make yourself useful and tidy up all the dishes from dinner.'

I leave him in his room, grab the money, and head for the door.

Chapter Eighty-Two

I almost run Mrs Larson over – the neighbour whose first name I can never remember, the neighbour who is always finding a reason to complain. She's pushing a mountain bike along the sidewalk. The only consolation I had about losing my house was knowing I'd be moving away from her. She points her finger at me and shakes her head and yells something, all while giving me the kind of look that suggests I'm the worst sheriff in the world. It's hard to argue against that. Her hair is getting blown all about and her clothes are snapping against her body. I can picture her with a news crew, standing outside her house, saying into the camera, *I always knew there was something odd about that sheriff.* I wave an apology, then I peel out of the street. I'm in my SUV, rather than using the cruiser I've been borrowing.

I radio Hutch. She's still staked out in the trees, watching the sawmill. She tells me it's getting rough out there, that the trees are struggling to stay anchored to the ground. I tell her she's waited long enough, that it's time to see if the money is gone from the car. I listen as she approaches the building. She checks out the car. She goes through the trunk.

'There's nothing here,' she says, and she sounds annoyed. 'Where exactly did you leave it?'

'Right in the centre of the trunk. You couldn't miss it.'

'Then it's definitely gone. Our guy must have taken the money before I got into position. He was probably hidden in the factory when you arrived. We'll get him when we make the next payment. I'll call Wade to come get me.'

People are walking with their shoulders hunched up and their faces down to keep the dirt and dust from blowing into their eyes. Plastic and paper bags and scraps of rubbish float through the air. The wind buffets the car. I go into the station and mumble hellos to anybody who offers them my way. I close the door to my office and stand behind my desk and punch the phone number from the text message into the computer. I'm expecting it to come up with nothing, that it'll be a pre-pay cellphone, but I still have to check.

A name comes up.

I drop into my seat. There's a shift in the air, like lightning could erupt inside the station. The phone belongs to Freddy Holt.

Is he still alive, hiding in the woods on and off, maybe a nearby farm too? Or is he dead, and the person who killed him took his phone, and that same person is now blackmailing me? If it is Freddy, he can have the forty grand and I'll even give him a ride out of Acacia Pines if that's what he asks for. Him strangling Grove – well, how can I judge him for that when I was doing worse?

I call the number.

Nobody answers.

I have to wait for Hutch and Wade to return. I can't have them see me driving out to the sawmill. I drum my fingers against the desk. Tap my feet. Stare out the window to the parking lot, wondering where in the hell they are. It's getting dark fast, and over the following few minutes the parking lot disappears, replaced by my reflection. I drum the fingers of both hands on the desk. Tap both feet. Headlights break the dark. It's Wade and Hutch. They don't come in. Instead they jump into their own cars and drive away.

I head outside. The wind is cold. And strong. It rocks the car as I head out of the parking lot. It rocks it even more as I speed over the bridge and out of town. There's a wall of rain heading at me from the south. I put my foot down and drive toward it.

Chapter Eighty-Three

From under the bridge, Lucas watches Sheriff Cohen drive away from town. It's a little after nine o'clock, which means Sheriff Cohen is getting out to the sawmill early, which Lucas figured he would. He also figures the sheriff will stay out there later too, first hiding his car, then hiding himself in the trees to see who's going to come for the money.

He carries his bike up the bank to the road. The wind is picking up. Clouds hover over the town like a dirty blanket. Earlier he swapped the sim card from Freddy's phone into his to send the messages to Sheriff Cohen, in case Freddy's phone was set up to email its location when it was turned back on, like Harriet White's phone.

He bikes through town, the rain closing in behind him. People scurry in and out of takeout stores, the smell of Chinese food and pizza and Indian from restaurants mingling, but soon the smell of the oncoming rain overpowers it, and moments later that rain arrives, hard and fast, like water balloons the size of cars are being popped directly above. He likes storms – always has. Loves the sound of thunder cracking apart the sky, the lightning gutting it, the way the air crackles with energy. There's a beauty to it, and a danger, like the world is being torn open to reveal all its secrets.

His clothes stick to his body, and he has to keep wiping water out of his eyes. At the rate he's going through bandages he ought to buy them in bulk, because this one is already ruined. After what happened at school today, he thinks of the rain as cleansing. His scalp feels cold due to the short hair. The wind picks up from the south, helping him rather than hindering. Even so, on this rusted piece of crap it takes him twice as long to bike anywhere as it should. The streets are emptying out as the gutters fill. Leaves and trash float at a faster rate than he can bike, piling up around the storm drains and then clogging them. It takes him twenty minutes to get to the park where he should have dumped his bike two nights ago. The wheels sink an inch into the lawn, and when he walks back out his shoes squelch and fill with water.

He looks at his watch. It's nine twenty-five.

He figures he has at least half an hour. Closer to an hour.

He heads to Sheriff Cohen's house.

Chapter Eighty-Four

The wind howls through the trees from all angles, whipping the rain back and forth and rocking the car. It's so loud I can't hear the engine. My window wipers struggle to keep up, the windscreen looking like layers of food wrap are stuck to it. The ditches between the highway and the forest are on their way to becoming streams. It feels like the end of the world. Endless weeks of hot days are often broken by a storm that comes and goes like this, sometimes lasting no more than twenty minutes, other times all night. Trees are bending, pulling at the roots, thick trunks at breaking point. Pine needles become blow darts. Pinecones become baseballs. Tomorrow crews with chainsaws will tidy up trees that have fallen up and down the highway. They'll clear the roads and remove broken branches and fix up twisted road signs, then rest up until the summer heat gets broken all over again.

A blast of wind tries to lift my SUV when I take the corner to the sawmill. A pinecone bounces off the centre of the windscreen and makes me jump. The elements are conspiring against me. They're warning me this is a bad idea. I park up in my usual spot. The only light out here is coming from my headlights. From the glove compartment I grab a flashlight and the camera for traffic accidents that I took from the station. The camera is fully charged and has enough memory to store two hours of recording. I stuff it into my pocket, along with a pair of cable ties.

I push my door open and the wind pushes it back. I give it another go, more strength into it this time, and get outside, the wind throwing the door closed behind me before rain can turn the SUV into a pool. I head for the trees, shielding my eyes from the water and wind whipping at me. Freddy could be hiding within a few feet of the edge and I'd have no idea.

My clothes snap back and forth, and then they become too wet to move, sticking to me instead. The plastic bag I have the cash in rustles as the wind pushes me along. I step into a puddle that goes up to my ankles, turning my toes numb. The sawmill looks like an abandoned slaughterhouse where people from nightmares come to play. The sky flashes white, a long spine of lightning with twisted ribs branching off to the sides, thunder immediately following, a flash so bright it burns my eyes and a sound so loud it splits open my skull. I jump so hard my shoulders reach for my ears, my heart racing, my hands tingling as the air around me fills with electricity. The bag falls from my fingers. It hits the ground. Before I can scoop it up, the wind grabs hold of it and tosses it into the air, opening it and turning it into a parachute. It gets pulled further away from me, gets caught in a crosswind, then hundred-dollar bills pour from the opening like a faulty ATM spewing money.

Forty thousand dollars scatters into the storm.

Chapter Eighty-Five

Lucas's first attempt at knocking on the door is drowned out by the thunder. For what he has planned, he could not have asked for better weather. It's dark, there's nobody about, and the rain is so loud you could scream your lungs out and not be heard. There are lights on inside, and he hopes that means Nathan is home.

He knocks again, and rings the bell, and alternates between the two until he can see a shape through the small panes of frosted glass in the door – Nathan approaching. It opens, and then Nathan is framed in the doorway, holding on to it with one hand while the other holds on to a beer, the wind battering him.

'What the fuck do you—'

Lucas throws the lump of mud he's scooped up from the garden before Nathan can finish. It hits him squarely in the face, and Lucas doesn't hang about to see what happens next. He turns and runs. Nathan will follow – of course he will. He hits the sidewalk before Nathan even gets off the porch. He was never going to need much of a head start. He slows down, letting Nathan match his pace, but keeping ten yards between them. His feet stomp into the ground and throw water up behind him. The wind has become a headwind, one he has to lean into. Nathan yells something but he doesn't hear what. He jumps off the kerb at the end of the block, crosses the street and skips over the kerb to the next block, his feet sloshing through the water in the gutters.

He keeps the ten yards between them.

There is still nobody around.

He turns into the park. His feet sink into the lawn, leaving tracks behind him. Up ahead is a playground, the swings bouncing in the wind, chains snapping tight, the merry-go-round twitching, pieces of bark tossed out from beneath it all. He runs past the slide. Past a park bench. Toward the trees where the streetlights don't reach, then falls over and slips when he's trying to get back up.

Just like he practised.

Nathan reaches him.

Lucas cowers, the same way Nathan is used to seeing people cower. Nathan stands over him, the rain washing the mud from his face.

'You prick,' Nathan yells.

Lucas shifts from his cowering position and goes into a ball. Nathan kicks him in the arms, kicks him in the back, and Lucas whimpers the way he's meant to, and he takes the kicks, willing to make the sacrifice. When the kicking is over he looks up, Nathan still standing over him. 'I'm going to post the video of you being pissed on. Everybody will see it.'

Lucas mumbles, keeping his voice low. 'It's not your fault.'

'What was that?'

He mumbles the same thing. Softer this time. Drawing Nathan in.

Nathan crouches down to hear him. 'Tell me what you said.'

Lucas slides the squirrel knife into Nathan's side.

For his part, Nathan starts out by showing all the wrong emotions. It starts with confusion. He knows something has happened, but doesn't know what. He stands, and takes a step back, and Lucas keeps hold of the knife so it slides out of him. Then Nathan smiles. And he laughs. It's as if the idea of something bad happening to him is so crazy it's funny. He shakes his head. He looks down and puts his hand on the wound, then looks at his hand, at the blood, watches the rain dilute it and wash it from his fingers. He takes another step back. He looks at Lucas, at the knife, then back to the wound. Still that smile is there, but he's frowning also, amused and confused. He's somebody whose eyes are telling him one thing, but his brain telling him another. He takes two more steps back. Then he looks down where blood is soaking his shirt and his shorts and is running down his leg. He puts his hand on the wound to try and close it and staunch the bleeding.

'What...' he says, then shakes his head, then adds, 'did you do?'

By now Lucas is on his feet. He walks over to him. Nathan takes a step back and his energy is running out of him along with all that blood. Lucas wonders where the parasite is, if it's going to climb through that hole and escape into the grass. Nathan sinks to his knees. He looks at Lucas and puts his hand up cowering, the same way Lucas has cowered in front of this guy so many times now. How easy it would be to bury the squirrel knife into his neck, his chest, his arms and legs.

'Please,' Nathan says. He's crying. 'Please don't.'

If the roles were reversed, Nathan would keep on stabbing him. That is what Nathan was destined for, wasn't it? A life of cutting, or making people want to cut themselves.

Nathan tries to get back to his feet, but only ends up falling in the process. He rolls onto his front and crawls, one hand grabbing at the ground, the other at the wound, and when he shouts out his cries are lost to the storm.

Lucas rolls him onto his back. He's so pale now. He's already a ghost. The rain beats down on his face. Lucas crouches over him.

'What I said is, it's not your fault,' Lucas says. And it isn't. It's the worm inside, so big now, so mean, that the damage it has done is irreparable.

Nathan is shivering. There are goosebumps all over his arms. His lips have turned blue. His eyes are flicking left and right, small movements that make them look like they're vibrating. Lightning forks overhead, it lights Nathan up, a microsecond of him in pain seared into Lucas's mind like a happy photograph.

He will find that worm, but not here. He needs time. And privacy. He also doesn't need the worm escaping through the wound, so he pulls the roll of duct tape from his pocket and uses it to patch the hole in Nathan, which has the added advantage of slowing down the bleeding.

He has to focus on getting Nathan out of here.

Like his dad taught him, no body means no evidence.

He's going to do the same thing he did with Freddy Holt.

He calls his dad.

Chapter Eighty-Six

The wind shunts the plastic bag back into the puddle, water snagging it for long enough for me to snatch it up. There are still some bills in there, but not many. Other bills are in the same puddle. I tuck the flashlight into the band of my pants so I can use both hands to snatch them up, relying on the light coming from the car. Most of the bills are thrown out into the trees – not floating, because floating would suggest a calmness about it – these hundred-dollar bills are being hurled around on a roller coaster of wind. Some have climbed higher than the treetops, disappearing beyond the range of the headlights and out into the forest. Others are caught in the base of the tree line. I scoop them up and stuff them into the bag. I reach the ones snagged in the lower branches and ignore the ones that are higher, figuring it would be a case of diminishing returns, especially when many would blow away again just as I was reaching for them.

I do what I can. I pick up wet and dirty bills and keep stuffing them into the bag. There's a second flash of lightning, and I hang on to the bag tight as the thunder rolls by. The air is buzzing. This is insane. I'm running around in a thunderstorm begging to be hit by a bolt of lightning – and the way my luck is going, why wouldn't I?

I can't see any more bills in easy-to-get locations, so go back to the car. I'm soaking wet. I open the bag and count out what's left.

Seven thousand, six hundred dollars. I won't be buying back the footage of me with Grove for that amount.

I get out of the car and take the bag with me, my grip on it tight. I reach the trees and drop some stones into my pockets. I use the flashlight to make my way to the tree where I chained Grove, picking up another six hundred dollars along the way. The wind and the rain eases off the further in I get. I use the stones to weigh down the bag at the base of the tree. I grab the camera out of my pocket and smear dirt on it to camouflage it, then cable-tie it to a branch a couple of trees away, pointing it at the cash. I switch it on and press the record button. Whoever comes out here will be carrying a flashlight – my hope is there'll be enough light to see who it is.

I make my way back to the car.

If whoever texted me is already out here, then they've seen what happened with the money. If they're still on their way, then they're in for some disappointment. My guess is they're parked somewhere between, waiting till I drive by.

I can't even text Freddy's phone – there's no signal out here.

I turn the car around and follow the thunder and lightning into town.

Chapter Eighty-Seven

Two months ago, Lucas caught up with Freddy a few streets over from where he'd pushed Alexandra over. There was a house on that street for sale. It belonged to a used car salesman who went hunting in the pines the previous year with friends. Some say they got drunk and wandered off the track. Others say Bigfoot got them. The lawns of the now empty house were long and the garden overgrown, and the for-sale sign out front had faded some over the months. Lucas timed his approach to arrive at the same time Freddy was about to pass it. Freddy heard him coming, and turned to face him.

'What do you want?'

'I found something,' Lucas said.

'Found what?'

'Something you're going to want to see.'

He didn't wait for a reply. He stepped past the for-sale sign staked into the ground and walked along the side of the house, unzipping his bag as he did so. Freddy waited on the sidewalk for a few seconds before curiosity got the better of him.

Once they rounded the corner, Lucas had the shovel out of his bag and was all over Freddy in a heartbeat – which was something Freddy stopped having a few seconds later. As the blood pooled into the dirt, Lucas had a decision to make. He couldn't cut into Freddy and leave him here because somebody would notice. He could bury Freddy in the garden, but it would require a much bigger hole than he was used to digging, and even then there was every chance the next owners would find it.

He called his father.

His dad had his own parasitic worm growing inside of him, one Lucas saw in action the day he helped his dad bury his mom under the same floorboards in the basement where Freddy is now buried – where Nathan will go too when all is said and done. His mom's death had been an accident. Lucas's dad had tried to convince her to stay that day she went to walk out. He'd tried to explain the dead animals, that all Lucas needed was help, tried so hard that he ended up pushing her down the basement stairs when all he was trying to do was reason with her. The problem is people still went to jail for accidents – and Lucas's dad had, after all, pushed her. They buried her suitcases in the basement with her, then told everybody the story about how she'd met a man online she thought could give her a better life. His dad put into practice all the things he'd learned from being a crime writer. If his dad had been a dentist or an accountant, he'd have been arrested for murder.

His dad showed up to help with Freddy like Lucas knew he would. What choice did he have? They each now had a secret that put them on the path of mutually reassured destruction. Dad was angry, and he voiced this as they rolled Freddy into clear polythene, blood smearing the insides of it, making him look like he was wrapped inside red fog, but what could he do about it, other than help?

They put him into the trunk of the car, and Lucas shovelled the earth where blood had fallen, hiding it, then they had driven home. Together they carried Freddy into the basement, and while Lucas went exploring for the worm he wouldn't find, his dad went exploring the liquor cabinet for something he would.

The following morning they spoke about it. His dad was still drunk at ten a.m. He'd been drinking a lot since Lucas's mom died – and would begin to drink even more after Freddy. That was when his dad put the curfew on him – no more sneaking out at nights, and from now on he had to be home from school by five. If he was one minute later than that, then God help him, he would call the police, mutually assured destruction be damned. His dad couldn't go through this again.

Lucas had believed him.

And to his dad's credit, he wasn't bluffing. He called the police on Monday when Lucas wasn't home on time – though he did go looking for him first.

He's aware of the irony that by taking Freddy's life he had saved his own. If he hadn't killed his former friend, there would have been no curfew. His dad wouldn't have come looking for him, wouldn't have called the police, and Sheriff Cohen wouldn't have shown up to save him. Putting Freddy in the ground is the thing that kept Lucas out of it.

And now his dad is showing up again. He was asleep when Lucas had snuck out of the house earlier, and Lucas left a note saying he was out picking up dinner, which he hoped would circumnavigate the curfew. But it was clear his dad was still asleep when he called him. His dad stops at the entrance to the park, one wheel bouncing onto the kerb. He turns the engine and lights off and walks to where Lucas is waiting. The rain has washed away all the blood, except for the stuff that's already stained Nathan's clothing. There's none on Lucas – he's checked. His dad is carrying another piece of clear polythene. They've had it lying around since the renovations were done, and he thinks environmentalists would be happy they've found a use for it, rather than seeing it end up in a landfill.

The closer his dad gets the more he can see him swaying, and when his dad reaches him he can smell the beer. The wind is flapping at his dad's clothes and his hair is plastered to his forehead. He's wearing a pair of slippers. He looks down at Nathan. Earlier Lucas thought Nathan was going to bleed out in front of him, but he's held on long enough to bleed out in front of him and his dad.

'Jesus, is that the sheriff's boy?' His dad's speech is slow and stilted, as though he has to focus on each word to say it right.

'This is the boy who bullied Taylor Reed into jumping off the roof,' Lucas says.

'Is that why we're here? Because of what he did?'

Explaining it isn't going to change what's to come. 'Let's get him into the car.'

'He's still alive.'

'Let's roll him up.'

His dad tries to lay the polythene out, but the wind keeps catching it and twisting it. It takes both of them to get it flat, hands and knees pinning the corners, water landing louder on that than on the grass. They roll Nathan onto it. He groans. They roll him up like a giant burrito. They fold over the end by his feet, and his dad duct-tapes it shut, but they leave the other end open so Nathan can breathe. Lucas wants to hear Nathan tell him that he's sorry, and beg him not to do this, before he kills him. He wants that more than he should, and he realises this is a dark thought and one that isn't his own, which means the worm living inside him is beginning to make the decisions. He needs to get this over with and get to the hospital so they can help him find it.

Lucas waits while his dad gets the car. It's going to leave big marks through the park but it's better than dragging Nathan over to it and into the light. His dad stops the car and pops open the trunk. They grab an end of Nathan each, but Lucas struggles to get any decent grip because of the bandage around his hand. It's soaking wet and slopping about, so he takes it off and stuffs it into his pocket and tries again. This time they get Nathan into the trunk and on an angle so any blood will run deeper into the polythene rather than out. It's too dark to get a good look at his hand.

'This is the last time,' his dad says. 'Promise me. Promise me it will be the last time.'

'I promise,' Lucas says, even though he still has Nathan's friends to deal with, and there might be others too if they treat him the way Nathan has been. He retrieves the mountain bike. It won't fit in the trunk with Nathan, but it will fit across the backseat – which they get it to do, after they use the quick release to remove the front wheel and fight with the angles. It's like putting a square through a round hole. If his dad notices it's a different bike, he doesn't say anything.

'What the hell did you do to your hair?' his dad asks.

'I shaved it.'

'Why?'

'Because I wanted to.'

His dad shrugs, then they get into the car and drive out of the park. His dad hangs a left but doesn't hang it hard enough. The front of the car bounces up onto the opposite kerb. He puts the car into reverse and hits the kerb they just drove off. That's when he notices the beer in the cupholder. Damn it, his father is completely drunk.

His dad straightens the car up.

But before they can go anywhere, headlights light them up. Lucas looks out the side window to see Sheriff Cohen looking back.

Chapter Eighty-Eight

Peter Connor's three-point turn is so big the road and the sidewalk can't contain him. I come to a stop but he doesn't, he's still nudging against the kerb, fighting with the wheel, a fight he must think he needs more personal fuel to win, because he chugs on a beer. My headlights are lighting him up. His son is in the car too, and I feel bad for Lucas – hasn't he already been through enough?

I'm in my SUV. I'm not on duty, and the last thing I feel like doing right now is dealing with Peter, but he's going kill somebody driving like this – either himself, or Lucas, or whoever he runs into. I figure the only reason he hasn't crashed into anybody is because there isn't anybody around. I flash my headlights. Peter notices me for the first time. His face is pale in the headlights. He has his hand near his eyes to help with the glare. What in the hell are these guys doing out here in this weather? A beer run?

Peter gets the car turning and he pulls over three feet out from the kerb. I get out of my SUV. I'm already wet, so there's no need to be shy about getting wetter. He winds his window down. I don't need my flashlight because there's enough light from the streetlamps.

'You want to tell me what it is you're doing?'

'Just,' Peter says, and then he hiccups, and covers his mouth, and adds, 'trying to get home.'

'We're all trying to get home, but the way you're driving you're not going to make it. How much have you had to drink?'

'Nothing,' Peter says, still holding the beer.

'I'm going to need you to step out of the car,' I say, annoyed he's chosen this night of all nights to pull this shit.

'Is that really necessary?'

Is it? I can smell the booze coming off him. I can see him drinking. He's slurring his words. But my life is falling apart. I texted my mystery texter about the money disappearing into the wind and haven't heard back. I need to figure out my next move – or if I even have one. Ultimately I'm still the sheriff who has a job to do.

'It is.'

He doesn't need to unclip his seatbelt because he's not wearing it. He opens the door and hands his beer to me. I put it on the roof. He gets to his feet.

'You really need to clean yourself up, Peter.'

'I just want things to be the way they used to be.'

'Don't we all. How about you walk a straight line for me?'

Peter walks the same line I take whenever I play golf – big looping lefts and rights. He has to grab the front of the car to stay balanced at the beginning, gets ten yards down the road and walks in the gutter then trips and lands on his arse on the grass.

'Sheriff Cohen?'

Lucas is leaning through the car to talk to me. There's a bike across the back seat. It's a jumbled mess of angles and curves.

'What is it, Lucas?'

'We really just want to get home. I know my dad shouldn't be drinking, but everything that's happened since Monday has taken a toll on him. He's not normally this bad. I promise I can get him to make some changes.'

'He can't be out here like this, Lucas.'

'Please don't lock him up. We need to get home is all. I hate being out in this storm.'

'I hate it too, but I'm going to have to take your dad to the station.'

'Then what would happen to me?'

It's that question that has stopped me from arresting Peter in the past. I've taken his car off him a few times, and fined him a few times, but still haven't locked him up – though it's been a fine line. Knowing Lucas would have to go into the custody of social workers has always played on my mind.

Peter gets back to his feet.

'Okay, but I'm going to hold you to your promise,' I say, which isn't fair of me – Lucas isn't responsible for what his dad does. 'But he can't drive you home. You're going to have to leave your car here and walk.'

Peter reaches us. He tries to grab his beer but I pick it up first, drain it onto the road and toss the can in through the window. He looks at me but doesn't ask why I did that. He's heard the last part of the conversation, and he says, 'You want us to walk home in this weather?'

'You're not driving.'

'Can't you at least give us a lift?'

I want to grab him by the shoulders and shake him, yell at him that I'm not a goddamn taxi service, but really it would only be me venting my frustration about everything else going on. Plus weather like this, he's apt to fall and drown in a gutter. 'Fine,' I say, not for him, but for Lucas. 'I'll drive you home.'

'We can walk,' Lucas says.

'No, we'll get a ride,' Peter says, and goes to open the back door of his car, as if he could fit in there around the bike.

'Not in your car,' I say. 'I'm not going to walk all the way back here. You can do that tomorrow. I'll drive you home in mine.'

'Seriously, it's okay – we'll walk,' Lucas says again.

'Not in this. Come on, get in while I straighten your one up.'

The kid is embarrassed and on edge. They get into the back of my SUV, and I get in behind the wheel of their car as Lucas watches me nervously. Does he think I'm going to arrest his dad after all? I straighten it against the kerb and lock it up.

'What were you guys even doing out there anyway?' I ask, getting into my SUV.

'Biking,' Lucas says.

We pull away from the kerb. 'Why the hell would you be biking in weather like this?'

'It wasn't like this when I left home,' he says. 'I figured after what happened on Monday it'd be a good thing to get into better shape, you know? In case I need to run away from somebody again. If I'd been quicker on Monday, that guy wouldn't have caught up with me. If I start biking, and jogging too, then I'd be fitter and faster, so … so if something like this ever happens again, I'd be able to outrun it.'

I wonder if he's talking about Nathan, or if he really thinks some other serial killer is going to show up.

He carries on. 'So I was out biking, and the weather got bad real fast, so I rang Dad and he came and got me.'

'I shouldn't have driven into the park,' Peter says.

'You shouldn't have driven at all,' I say. 'Look, Lucas, I think what you're doing is great, but if there's a next time don't call your dad – call me instead, okay?'

'Okay.'

We get to their house. The lights are on inside. I pull up next to the kerb without hitting it. I still have Peter's keys, so I take them out, peel off the one for his car, and hand Lucas the rest. It's probably pointless as Peter will have a spare.

'We're going to talk tomorrow,' I say to Peter, as he's climbing out of the car.

'It won't happen again, James. It really won't.'

I watch them go into the house while checking my phone to see if I've got any new texts – there are none. Could be the person blackmailing me hasn't been out there because of the storm, or they're out there now and can't get reception. Hopefully the camera I left can give me some answers. But even if it does, what next? What do I do with the person blackmailing me?

I do a U-turn and head home first. My wet clothes are bugging the hell out of me and I want to change. I can grab a rain jacket while I'm there. I pass Peter's car. The guy is getting away with it easy. Tonight wasn't the night to arrest him to prove a point. I picture how that would have gone – me booking him, then twenty minutes later the video of me taking Grove into the woods makes it public, and a few minutes after that I'm Peter Connor's cellmate.

Chapter Eighty-Nine

'Do you want us to get caught?' Lucas asks.

They're standing in the lounge, their wet footprints leading here from the front door. A branch from the nearby acacia tree taps against the window, while roof tiles all over the house rattle. His dad turns to face him. Water is dripping from his hair and down his face. 'Of course not.'

Lucas isn't so sure. He's thinking his dad would like nothing better than to have this over. Confess and be damned. Have the basement floor dug up and spend the rest of his life in jail. He'd do it too, Lucas thinks, if prison had an open bar. 'Then why would you suggest to Sheriff Cohen that he give us a lift? Now we have to walk all the way back, rather than walking a block and waiting for him to go.'

'How do you think it would have looked if I hadn't, huh? He'd have wondered why, and he'd still be wondering.'

It's a good point. He's still looking through the window where he watched Sheriff Cohen drive away. He's not coming back. If Nathan had banged feebly against the trunk when Sheriff Cohen had been moving the car, would he have heard over the storm? Would Lucas's own worm have made him squirrel-knife Sheriff Cohen and jam him into the trunk too? Thankfully they're not questions that need answering. But there is one thing he can't figure out – why wasn't Sheriff Cohen waiting out at the sawmill? If Lucas misread that situation, then what else has he misread?

'We need to go get the car,' he says.

'Were you being truthful before about what you said? That the sheriff's son is who bullied that kid into killing himself?'

'Yes.'

'I need a drink.'

'And you can have one, once I'm back.'

'We can't go out there. If Cohen catches us we're done for. We should wait. It's going to be raining all night, nobody is going to hear that kid if he wakes up, and I doubt he's going to wake up anyway. He's probably dead already. We have time. Anyway, I'm in no state to drive.'

Lucas doesn't want to wait. 'Then I'll do it.'

'The hell you will.'

'Why not? I know how to drive,' he says, and he does – at least in theory, plus his dad's car is an automatic.

'It's too risky.'

'I'm not debating this,' Lucas says, and he puts his hand out. If by some miracle Sheriff Cohen happens to pull him over, then he'll put all his cards on the table. He'll tell him what he knows, and what he can prove.

'Come on, Dad, it's not like I can call a taxi.'

His dad takes a moment with that, then sighs, then finds the spare key for the car for him.

'Anyway,' Lucas adds, 'I won't be long. Get things ready for me, would you?'

'What the hell does that mean?'

'You know exactly what it means.'

He doesn't wait for his dad to answer. He opens the door and goes back out into the storm. The wind and the rain haven't lessened any, but the last flash of lightning was back when he was in the park. He jogs. He pictures Nathan in the car, the worm trying to crawl out from under the duct tape covering the wound, coming up against the polythene and not knowing which way to turn. He jogs faster. There are no shortcuts, he has to go block by block, street by street. There are no cars on the road. Nobody on the sidewalks. Just houses lit up in the dark as people wait out the storm. He sloshes through puddles and skirts potholes in the road, taking the same route he biked two nights ago. His lungs burn and his muscles are on fire, and he keeps pushing himself. When this is all over he really will take up jogging like he told Sheriff Cohen.

It takes twenty minutes, and he's relieved to find the car just how it was left. He gets in behind the wheel and plays with the seat adjustments. He starts the engine. Like he hoped, it pretty much drives itself.

Couldn't be easier.

Chapter Ninety

I pass my dad on the street. He's walking along the sidewalk in his bathrobe, barefoot and soaking wet. I pull over and get out.

'Dad, where are you going?'

'You and Cassidy have done so much for me,' he says. It's not the first time he's gotten Cass's name wrong, and won't be the last. 'And I thought the least I could do would be to do something nice for you. So I'm heading into town to pick up supplies and tomorrow morning I'm going to cook breakfast.'

'Thanks, Dad, that sounds great,' I say, 'but how about I give you a lift instead? We don't want you getting washed away in the storm.'

He looks up, puts his hand out and looks at it. He watches the rain hitting his palm, and though he doesn't say anything, I'm pretty sure he's only now realising that it's raining. I was an idiot for thinking Nathan could keep an eye on him.

'Come on, let me give you a lift.'

'That sounds like a grand idea,' he says, then carries on walking. I grab his arm and turn him toward the car and he doesn't complain.

I get him back home and hand him a towel but he doesn't seem to know what to do with it. When I go to help him, he shrugs me off and makes his way to his bedroom, undressing along the way. I take a few steps toward Nathan's room and then think better of it – I'm in such a foul mood that I might end up dragging him to the police station tonight and putting him behind bars. Which I should. Fuck it. I don't know, but not knowing in wet clothes is worse than not knowing in dry ones, so I get changed. My mood improves a little now. Maybe it's a sign things are going to turn around. I check in on Dad. He's changed into his pajamas and is lying in bed doing a crossword puzzle – or at least looking at one.

I go through to the kitchen. The light is still on for the back porch. I go to switch it off when I notice it through the glass panel of the door – Nathan's mountain bike out on the deck. My guess is he got it out and figured he'd bike anywhere but here, but didn't want to battle the storm. I open the door and fight with the wind to stop it from slamming into the side of the house. I bring the bike inside before a gust of wind throws it through the window.

It isn't Nathan's bike. He must have a friend here. They're probably in his room drinking all the beer. I lean the bike up against the table. I go through to his bedroom. I knock on the door and when he doesn't answer I go in.

It's empty.

I step back into the hallway. 'Nathan?'

No answer. I knock on the bathroom door. 'Nathan?'

Nothing. I open the bathroom door. I go through the rest of the house. I check the kitchen for any notes. Nothing. His wallet is on the desk next to his computer, and his house key is there too, and his cellphone. Maybe he's out disposing of his burner phone. I return to the kitchen and stare at the bike. It looks familiar, and it takes a moment to realise it's the bike my neighbour was pushing earlier down the sidewalk. I can't figure out why she would have brought it here.

I check on Dad. He's asleep. So I take the bike outside. I'm soaking wet by the time I reach the sidewalk. I head to my neighbour's house. The lights are on inside. I knock on the door and ring the bell, and Mrs Larson answers. Mrs Larson is in her seventies, a retired tax agent, with her hair in curlers and ears sticking out at right angles. She's wearing an oversized bathrobe with oversized pockets and oversized buttons. I visualise her riding the bike in that outfit. I imagine it getting tangled in the chain and her flipping over the handlebars.

'You almost ran me over earlier, Sheriff,' she says. 'I have a half mind to make an official complaint.'

'Is this your bike?'

'You aren't going to apologise?'

'You're right. I'm sorry I almost ran you over,' I say, and I think I'm only apologising for the *almost* part of that.

'I'll take that into account when I make my decision tomorrow,' she says. 'I appreciate you coming by to apologise, but next time don't make it so late. Better yet, next time don't try to run me over.'

'This bike,' I say, holding it so it doesn't topple over. 'Did it come from you?'

'It did. I gave it to your son, who, by the way, was drinking. What kind of example are you setting for him?'

I go back to picturing her flying over the handlebars. 'Why did you bring this to my house?'

'Because I didn't want to bring it to the station. It's not mine, Sheriff.'

'So who does it belong to?'

'How am I meant to know that?'

'Where did you find it?'

'In my garden. Somebody dumped it behind the lavender out front there,' she says, nodding back over my shoulder. 'I don't appreciate somebody doing that,' she says, using a tone that makes it sound like I'm the one who dumped it. 'Some of my plants got damaged, and I figure if you work out who the bike belongs to, you can have a word with them about it. Maybe arrest them.'

'When did you find the bike?' I ask, knowing she's going to say it was yesterday morning.

She does just that, then adds, 'I saw it when I walked to the mailbox. I was going to bring it over to you yesterday, but I saw the way you sped into our street, like the Devil himself was chasing you. I thought to myself, well, Sheriff Cohen isn't going to care enough about my lavender today now is he, so I waited.'

Yesterday morning ... the morning after I drove Simon Grove out into the forest.

'Even now you don't seem to care. Are you listening to anything I'm saying, Sheriff?'

'To everything,' I say, still looking at the bike. It's blue and a little worn out, but well looked after. I know this bike from somewhere else too.

'Sheriff?'

'I'll take care of it,' I tell her.

'It is why we pay your salary,' Mrs Larson says.

'Thanks for your help.'

'Just being a good citizen.'

She closes the door. I crouch next to the bike and stare at it. How do I know it? Dumped two nights ago when the cellphone and the wallet and watch were planted in my garage. By Lucas Connor? No, because I saw his mountain bike in the back of their car not long ago. It's possible he has two bikes, but why would—

'Jesus.'

This was the bike I saw locked up at school on Monday.

And just like that, I know everything.

Chapter Ninety-One

It's a five-minute drive home, in which Lucas doesn't come across another car. He loves being behind the wheel. A sense of freedom and a sense of control. He wants to get his driver's licence. Wants to buy a car. Driving would unlock the country for him. Imagine the places he could go and the things he could do.

He uses the garage door opener and parks inside, the quiet of the garage a relief from the constant rain drumming on the roof of the car. His dad is waiting for him, drinking a beer. As soon as the garage door closes, Lucas pops the trunk and his dad puts the beer down and together they lift Nathan out, careful not to tip him in a direction that'll drain blood onto the floor.

All the colour has been washed out of Nathan, and his face is clammy to touch, but he's still alive. They carry him down to the basement, his dad almost losing hold of the polythene several times. They don't make any conversation, but his dad constantly shakes his head and he looks close to tears.

They hoist Nathan onto the workbench, where a fresh piece of polythene is waiting. There's polythene on the floor surrounding it too. His dad fetches his beer and comes back and sits on the bottom step. Lucas pulls on a pair of latex gloves before running a pair of scissors along the side of the plastic cocoon. Blood spills out and slaps against the polythene around his feet. Nathan's breathing is shallow, and Lucas can see the pulse in his neck.

'This is wrong,' his dad says, speaking for the first time since Lucas got back. 'I mean, come on, Lucas, you can't keep doing this. We … we can't keep doing this. We have to find you some help. We can get you to be like a normal kid.'

'Like this guy?' Lucas asks, pointing a thumb at Nathan. 'Not only did he kill Taylor Reed, he's the one who put me in the locker, and earlier today his friends held me down while he pissed on me. He told me I should kill myself. Is that who you want me to be like?'

It takes a few moments for his dad to take that on board, then slowly he shakes his head. 'Of course not. But do you want to end up like Simon Grove? Somebody who abducts children?'

'That's not what this is,' Lucas says.

'Then what is it?'

'There's something inside Nathan that has to be stopped. If I don't do this, he will hurt other people. He will kill them.'

'Jesus, is this about the worms? Is that what you still think? That they're controlling people?'

'I knew you wouldn't understand.'

'Because there's nothing to understand! You're sick, Lucas. You have been for a long time. This … this thing you do, what you did with Wolfy, and those other animals, and to Freddy – that's not something you stop being. It's something you evolve into, and this is who you are now – an evolution of something that's evil.'

'I'm not evil,' he says, and he knows that to be a fundamental truth. If he were, he'd be out there every day causing hurt. He'd be blowing up folks or stabbing old ladies. What he is, is angry. Angry at Wolfy for biting him. Angry at his mom for trying to leave. Angry at Freddy, his only friend, who no longer wanted to be his friend, angry at what he saw him to do Alexandra.

And of course he's angry at Nathan and all the other kids like him who turn into Simple Simons.

'You are, son. This thing you've become, it's not your fault. It's mine. Mine, and your mom's. We didn't raise you right, but we tried, good God how we tried. Sometimes ... well, I guess sometimes all the trying in the world can't change something that's meant to be, and it seems to me you're exactly what you're meant to be, and I can't ... I can't be a part of that anymore. I can't.'

'You really believe that?'

'When you saw what I did to your mother, it made you think that's the way things ought to be. I'm sorry I did this to you.'

He hates how his dad can sometimes get introspective when he's been drinking. There's no talking to him when he's like this. 'Why don't you go and get another drink?'

His dad slowly nods. He drags himself to his feet. 'When you're done I want you to make this room look like nothing ever happened here, okay?'

'Okay,' Lucas says.

His dad looks like he has something else to say, but whatever it is he hangs on to it. The stairs creak as he makes his way up them. A moment later he's gone.

Chapter Ninety-Two

I look at my house as a place from which Nathan was taken, not one he left voluntarily. Two nights ago Lucas Connor biked here. He figured framing Nathan was the only way to get him out of his life. He dumped his bike at the neighbour's house and walked down to scope out the place, then snuck into my garage. That much I know for sure. The rest is a best guess, but I think he was still in the garage when I went out there with Grove. I think he hid in there and thought he was done for, and then my dad showed up. What was my dad saying? That he saw somebody. I think he saw Lucas Connor break into the garage, and I think that after I drugged Dad and moved him to the deck that Lucas, low on options, hid in the back of my car. It explains how he was able to start filming me so quickly. It explains everything. He strangled Simon Grove. Only thing I don't know is, did he let him live on purpose?

Impossible to know.

I check on Dad. He's asleep, and he doesn't feel a thing when I handcuff him to the bed. It's a horrible thing to do, but I'm out of choices. I run out to the SUV, my mind still racing as it puts the pieces together. It must have taken Lucas hours to walk home from the sawmill – no. He didn't walk. In the junk that had been left in the sawmill, there was an old mountain bike, I'm sure of it. Either way, by the time he got back to my house, Mrs Larson had found his bike and taken it into her possession. Was he still out in the forest when I went back the next day and things played out between me and Grove? Maybe he filmed that too. Either way, I don't think he cares about the money. He wanted me out of the house because he wanted to get to Nathan.

I put my foot down, swerving around corners and slowing only enough to race through intersections. There's no other traffic. I reach the park. The car is gone. Nathan ... Jesus, was he in the trunk when I moved it earlier?

I don't call for backup. I'm closer to the Connor house than anybody else anyway – and this is something I can't risk anybody making a mistake over. This is my son, and I can't let anybody mess that up.

My son, who brought this on himself.

My son, who killed Taylor Reed, and would do the same to Lucas if he could.

My son, despite all that.

When I'm a block out I turn off the headlights and pull into their street. I stop twenty yards short. If they're not here, then I will call for help. But I think they are here. I think in weather like this, there aren't many places to go. Freddy Holt ... Grove wasn't lying about him. If Lucas is capable of strangling Simon Grove and abducting my son, then he was capable of hurting Freddy too.

I go the final twenty yards on foot, the wind and rain trying to push me back, like they did out at the sawmill – perhaps another warning. All the lights are on inside the house. I go down the side of the garage and point a small flashlight into the window. Peter Connor's car is in there, rain dripping off the sides. I try the garage door. It's locked.

I make my way around to the back of the house. The back door is locked too. All the windows are closed tight. There's a garden shed in the corner of the yard. There's a padlock on it, but it's open and hanging from the handle. I slide the door open. There are wet footprints inside. The shed is a six-foot square box that has a lawnmower in the middle and shelves on one side and gardening tools hanging from a rack on the other. There's a rake and a hoe and a pitchfork. There's no shovel, but a hook where a shovel would go. There's a toolbox on a shelf. There's a crowbar the length of my forearm.

I go back to the house and bury the point of the crowbar into the bottom of a window and push down. It grips and slips and bites out a chunk of the wood, making an even bigger gap for my second attempt. I take it, and this time the lock tears from the frame, and maybe somebody inside heard it over the storm, or maybe they didn't, but either way I climb inside. I'm in a bedroom. I take out my gun and approach the hallway, look left and right. Nothing. I make my way to the lounge. Peter Connor is on the couch. He's passed out with a bottle of booze propped up on his chest. He looks like he's been drinking directly from the bottle. Could be he drinks to mask the pain of having a killer for a son. Who knew we had so much in common.

I check the kitchen. I go back into the hallway. Check the bedrooms. There's another door at the end for the basement. The shovel missing from the shed is leaning against the wall next to it. Lucas is going to be down there, because basements are where bad things tend to happen. I know that better than anybody.

I grab the door handle. It's smooth and cold. Like ice.

I take a deep breath.

I open the door.

Slowly I take the steps, and everything comes into view.

Lucas is down there, and he's getting ready to open up my son.

Chapter Ninety-Three

My gun holds fifteen rounds. I could put ten into Lucas, four into Peter, and save one for myself. My son is dead. He's dead because of what I put in motion. He's dead because I saved Lucas from Simon Grove when I shouldn't have. I should have hung up on Peter Connor on Monday.

The bench and the surrounding floor are shrouded in thick plastic. To the side, boxes and old furniture have been pulled away from the wall, and the floorboards have been pried up to reveal joists spaced a foot and a half apart beneath them. Between those joists is turned over earth. If I were to dig down into that earth, I would find Freddy Holt. I'm sure of it.

Lucas hasn't seen me. He's studying Nathan's body figuring out where to slice, tracing lines across him with his finger, like a plastic surgeon figuring out what it takes to be beautiful. Instead of firing, I take another step, my legs wobbling so much I lose my footing, only saved from spilling down the rest of the stairs by a quick grab of the rail. It gets me into a better position to see Nathan's face, but it also lets Lucas know I'm here. He turns around, but I don't look at him, I keep looking at my son. His eyes are open, and he's looking at me. He's still alive! Or at least I think he is. His skin is pale and shiny. There's a wound in his side, duct tape hanging from it, blood over his stomach and hips. There is no expression on his face at all. No shock, no fear, no nothing. And then his eyes look to me.

I look back to Lucas. 'Put down the knife!'

'I'm doing this for him,' he says, and he has the same empty expression on his face as Nathan.

'Put it—'

'I think you know he's a bad apple, but what you don't know is it's not his fault. There's something inside him that's made him wrong. Something physical. I know how that sounds, but it's true, and I can prove it to you, but it's too late for Nathan.'

'Put down the knife.' I keep the gun trained on him while reaching for my cellphone. I need an ambulance. Need backup. Need Nathan to hold on and keep breathing.

'He beats me all the time. He stuffed me into the locker. Today his friends held me down while he pissed on me. He filmed it. He was going to put it online. I can prove that to you as well. I'm sure he did it to Taylor too.'

Nathan is bleeding out, and every second counts. 'I'm not going to warn you again, Lucas. Put it down or I'm going to open fire.'

'He's not your son. He was once, but not now. If you don't let me do this, then he'll go on to infect others. Don't you see?'

'The same kind of something that made you kill Freddy?' I ask, getting my phone out of my pocket.

Lucas takes a moment, and slowly nods. 'Maybe. But it was

definitely the same something that made Freddy beat up his girlfriend. He would have hurt others too, if I hadn't stopped him. Others like Eric Delany and Harry Waltz.'

I get the station loaded on the phone and hit *call*.

'The same thing is inside you,' Lucas adds.

'What?'

'You tortured the janitor, and for what? The reward money. Don't you see how contagious it is? You need to put the gun down, and the phone, otherwise I'll tell everybody what you did. I'll show them.'

'I don't care about that,' I say.

'You should,' Lucas says. 'You'll go to jail.'

'We'll both be going.'

The call goes through.

There's a creak on the stairs above. I turn toward it, but I'm too late. Peter Connor is there. My ribs must have a huge bullseye on them because that's where he hits me with the shovel. I tumble down the rest of the stairs, the gun and the phone flying out of my grip even before I smash into the basement floor.

Chapter Ninety-Four

Lucas watches the gun bounce into what will be Nathan's grave – and what is looking like Sheriff Cohen's grave too. He likes Sheriff Cohen – a lot, actually. But the guy did torture the janitor, then kill him, and really, Acacia Pines doesn't need a sheriff like that. He hates to admit it, but Sheriff Cohen is too far gone to be saved. What's the alternative? Let him hurt others? His dad picks up the cellphone and turns it off. It's unlikely the police will trace the call – there's no reason to. They'll just think the call was cut off by the storm.

When this is over, he can release the footage he took of Sheriff Cohen, and people will think he took the reward money and ran, and took Nathan with him. It means dealing with the sheriff's SUV, which is no doubt parked out front – but figuring out the mechanics of cleaning up after a crime is his father's thing.

Sheriff Cohen is trying to get to his feet, but stops moving when his own gun is pointed back at him. His dad slowly moves back to the stairs and climbs a couple of them, keeping the gun trained on Sheriff Cohen as he does.

'Don't,' his dad says. 'Don't move.'

'You're part of this, Peter?'

'I'm just trying to protect my son.'

'At the expense of other people's sons?'

'Just don't move,' he says.

'Shoot him,' Lucas says.

'What?'

'Don't,' Sheriff Cohen says.

'It's too late for him,' Lucas says, and he wishes that weren't true, but it is. 'Nobody will hear over the storm.'

'You don't need to do this, Peter,' Sheriff Cohen says.

His dad is shaking his head. 'I'm sorry, James. I ... I have to protect him. But this will be the last time, I promise you. After this ... after this he'll be good. Things will change.'

Lucas can hear Nathan moving. He turns to look. Nathan's skin has a yellow tinge to it. It looks wet. His fingers are trying to grip the polythene. They're making streaking sounds as they slip across it. Lucas wants to get Nathan open and get that worm under control and end this once and for all.

'I know what you're going through,' Sheriff Cohen says, no longer looking at Lucas, but giving all his attention to his dad. 'My son is the same. I let him get away with making Taylor Reed take his own life. You and me, Peter, we're in the same boat. Right now we can do something about that. We can help each other. But the clock is ticking. If you let Nathan die, I can't do anything for you, but if you help me, we can help each other. We're the only ones who can make sure our children get the care they need.'

Lucas can't wait any longer. He steps toward Sheriff Cohen with the squirrel knife, but before he can swing it, his dad takes the shot. Sheriff Cohen flinches, his shoulders going up around his ears so fast his feet almost leave the ground. Lucas can't see where the sheriff was hit. Shouldn't there be blood?

There's something wrong.

Lucas's stomach is hot, and the room sways, and he no longer has the strength to hold the knife up. It falls to the floor and bounces off the handle. He takes a step back and looks down at his stomach, where a spot of red is doubling in size, then doubling again. He touches it, and looks at his fingers. He looks at his dad, and his dad is looking back, the gun in his hand, pointing at Lucas.

Lucas's legs are fast losing their strength. He sits on the floor and leans against the workbench and lifts his T-shirt. There's a hole in his stomach. He squeezes it and the dark blood coming from it comes even faster. He can feel his breath slowing.

'I'm sorry, son, I'm so sorry. It's not your fault,' his dad says, and Lucas knows that. It's the worm's fault. His dad is crying, and Lucas hasn't seen his dad cry since the day his mom went under the floorboards. 'It's just … it's just the way you are.'

The heat from the wound in his stomach has gone cold. He can feel the worm twisting up inside of him, ready to escape. This worm that has ruined his life over and over. The knife is on the floor next to them.

He has to put an end to that worm, once and for all.

He picks up the knife.

Hopefully it won't hurt too much.

Chapter Ninety-Five

I can't look away as Lucas cuts into himself. He makes the wound longer, and deeper, and wider, getting down to where the blood is so dark it looks like oil. He's wearing latex gloves, but he pulls them off and tosses them to the side before stretching the wound with one hand, then slipping the tips of his other fingers into it, rotating his wrist slowly so his fingers can screw downwards. There is nothing on his face to suggest pain. Then the wrist stops and rewinds and the fingers screw back out, blood hanging from them in long streaks, like egg yolk dripping off a fork. He holds them up and stares at them, first at arm's length, then much closer, his eyes narrowing as he studies them. He smiles, but at what, I don't know, because if he's looking for the bullet, he hasn't found it. He slowly shakes his head, and he dips them back in and the wrist rotates once again while his free hand stretches the wound even wider, and when the wound won't budge he uses the knife.

I want to stop him, only I can't. I can't move. Nor can Peter. We're motionless, both of us staring at Lucas, not knowing what we're watching, but whatever it is, it has us paralysed, and sickened, and fascinated. The look of concentration on Lucas's face is frightening. He's possessed. He gets the wound open and he gets his fingers in deeper than last time, and when he removes them, he has nothing to show for it other than the same strings of blood he had before. He studies them, closer now, rubbing them between his thumb and fingers.

He curls his hand into a fist, then bangs it into the ground, once, twice, a third time, as if trying to break something. Then he smiles. It's a big goofy smile that sends a shiver down my spine, and then his eyes roll into the back of his head and his arm slaps onto the floor, the fingers of his other hand still hooked inside his stomach.

I don't know what to say. I don't know what I've just seen.

I turn toward Peter, aware he still has the gun, concerned he's gotten into his mind that we're all better off joining his son. I'm half right. He's got the gun under his chin, pointing upward.

'Don't,' I tell him.

'He always thought there was a worm living inside of him,' Peter says.

'What?'

'I wish I had never called you on Monday,' he says. 'I should have just let the janitor have him. They're his favourite, you know,' he says nodding towards the open floor. 'There are other things buried out there, but these are the only two that matter to him.'

'Two?'

'You'll figure it out,' he says, and he closes his eyes, and takes a deep breath.

'Don't do it, Peter.'

'What would you have me do?'

I don't have a good answer for him, and even if I did, he doesn't wait around to hear it.

Chapter Ninety-Six

With the gunshot still ringing in my ears, I grab my phone. I call the station and tuck the phone under my ear while I rip off my shirt to ball against Nathan's wound. He's been stabbed. The wound is raw and still bleeding.

'It's Cohen,' I say, when the call is taken. 'I need an ambulance.' And I give the address and the details. I'm promised one will be here shortly – but in this storm, shortly could be thirty minutes or more.

Nathan is staring up at me. 'It's going to be okay,' I tell him, but I'm not so sure it will be. He's lost a lot of blood.

'I ... I'm sorry,' he says.

'I know,' I say. 'You have to fight.'

He doesn't answer. He's holding my hand. His eyes slowly open and close. He begins to cry. We're a father and son sharing a basement with a dead father and dead son. I let go of his hand and, while still holding my shirt against his wound, I reach into Lucas's pockets and find his cellphone. When I tap the button, there's a home screen with a picture of a dog, but the phone is locked. I reach down and unlock it using Lucas's fingerprint, and sure enough, the messages from earlier tonight are there. He must have put Freddy's sim card into his phone to send them. I switch it off and put it into my pocket. I weigh up carrying Nathan out of here and driving him to the hospital – lots of pros and cons, but mostly cons. My phone goes. It's Hutch, telling me she's on her way, and that paramedics are only a minute out. Two minutes later I hear those paramedics coming inside. I call out. Two of them bound down the stairs, having to step over Peter Connor's body to get past. One of the paramedics takes a moment to check him over, but that's all it is – a moment, because it's obvious he's gone. His partner reaches Lucas and makes the same call, then both reach my son.

'We've got him,' the first guy says, and they take over.

I drag Peter off the stairs to make room while they work on Nathan. There are footsteps upstairs. Others are arriving, including Hutch. A third paramedic brings down a stretcher. They get Nathan onto it and take him upstairs. I follow, barely acknowledging Hutch even though she must have a hundred questions. The paramedics lift Nathan into the ambulance and I hold the doors open so they don't blow shut. When he's loaded in I climb in with him. I ride in the back to the hospital, the wind rocking us from side to side, trying to tip us, the elements working against not just me now, but Nathan too. When we get there I try to follow them all the way into the operating theatre but get stopped by the nurses. They tell me to wait. They tell me Nathan is in good hands.

I pace the room right outside, then realise that Cassandra has no idea. I call her. There's no easy way to tell her, so I just do it.

'Is he going to make it?' she asks.

'It could go either way.'

Ten minutes later she's at the hospital and we're holding on to each other.

'Why?' she asks. 'Why would Lucas Connor do this?'

It's not the right time to tell her everything Nathan has done, but it's not like I can keep it quiet either. So we sit down and I tell her everything. She shakes her head, but soon the disbelief disappears, and by the end she has her head in her hands and is crying. When she looks up I can see something in her eyes that I've felt too – maybe we're better off if Nathan doesn't make it. But it's only a blip, and it passes, and every time a nurse walks by we ask for an update, and nobody has one. I figure every minute Nathan is in surgery is a good thing. It's a good thing because he was in a bad way. If a doctor had come out within a few minutes, the news couldn't be good.

The storm bashes at the walls of the hospital. Occasionally the lights flicker. An hour goes by. Nathan's blood is on my hands. I should wash it off, but I don't. If I leave the waiting room Nathan will die. I know it. I have to stay here. I can tell Cassandra feels the same way. I go back to pacing the room. Cassandra stays seated.

'What about your dad?' she asks.

'I handcuffed him to his bed.'

She goes to say something, but then shrugs it off, and says, 'Good idea.'

I keep expecting her to say this is my fault, and I can't figure out if it is. If I had arrested Grove on Monday rather than abducting him, it would have created a different timeline – would it have still led to this?

A second hour goes by.

Then a third.

The storm is easing up.

Six and a half hours into the surgery, the doctor comes out. She's nodding. My heart freezes in my chest, and Cassandra crushes my hand as we're given the news.

Chapter Ninety-Seven

The following morning the streets are littered with branches and upturned shrubs and torn flowers. It'll take a few days to clean up, then it'll be like it never happened. After seeing Nathan last night when he came out of surgery, and being told he was going to be okay, I went home and slept a few hours on the couch. I didn't have to worry about Dad, because Dad was gone, and in his place was a note that said, *We're looking after him.* Hutch had signed it. It also meant she had gone through the house as part of her investigation into what happened to Nathan.

Now it's like everything was a bad dream. Forensics are still searching the Connor House. They found Freddy Holt and Vivian Connor, Peter's wife, in the ground in the basement. They've also found two dogs buried in the yard, cut open, as if somebody was searching inside of them for a lost set of keys.

I drive out to the sawmill, passing a few crews who are parked off the side of the road dealing with downed trees. It's almost lunchtime, and the heat of the day has made the smaller puddles in the parking lot evaporate away, and the larger ones are getting smaller. The wind has picked up the door that was torn from the building and tossed it to the edge of the parking lot. I walk into the trees and the bag of cash I left here last night is still here now. I find another forty-two hundred dollars on the way. I remove the camera then keep searching. I'm like Hansel and Gretel following a trail of cash. I keep a compass in my hand so I can find my way back. If there is cash on branches low enough, I shake them so it'll fall. I climb a couple of trees that aren't too big. Soon the trail dries up. Out of the forty thousand I came out here with, I have a little under half of it back. It'll cover the remaining legal bills, and I'll save my house for a bit, but the ticking clock won't be going away anytime soon.

I make my way back to the parking lot, snagging another three hundred dollars on the way. My car isn't the only one out here now. Hutch is parked there. She's leaning against the hood, her arms folded, staring at me from behind a pair of aviators. I keep walking. I can only imagine how I look.

'Sheriff,' she says.

'Deputy.'

'How's Nathan doing?'

'He's doing fine,' I tell her. 'Thanks for asking.'

'Damnedest thing,' she says. 'Lucas, years ago, he was diagnosed with Ekbom Syndrome. You heard of it?'

'No.'

'People believe they have worms living inside them. Like tapeworms, and other parasites.'

I'm reminded about what Peter said last night, how Lucas thought there was a worm living inside him. I suspect that's what he was looking for in the end, and not the bullet. 'And?'

'And the autopsy this morning showed he had one. Marie put it at forty feet long.'

'Jesus, is that even possible?'

'It's less than half of what they can grow to. Still, she said it was something. She said they can live up to thirty years, and that Lucas probably had his for at least ten. Is that creepy or what?'

'It is.'

'She also said they can change people the way brain tumours can. It's one of those things I wish I never knew. You always handcuff your dad before you go out?'

'I know how it looks, but it was the safest option.'

She stares at me, and I know it's coming.

'Were you going to tell us?'

'About?'

'We searched Nathan's room. You know about the phone?'

'Yes, but I only found it the day before. I thought I could deal with it myself.'

'Well now you don't need to. Your son is not a good person, Sheriff. Yesterday his friends held Lucas down while he urinated over and assaulted him, all while filming it. We found that on his other cellphone. We're going to charge him for what he did to Taylor Reed.'

'I know.'

She nods. She stares at me. Then she reaches into her pocket and pulls out a flash drive. 'I found this in Lucas's wardrobe. I don't know if he made other copies, and I hope for your sake he didn't.'

I don't say anything.

'You're not going to ask me what's on it?'

'No,' I say, because I know what's on it. The footage of me and Grove.

'We didn't find Lucas's phone.'

I don't say anything, but Lucas's phone is long gone.

She looks at the bag in my hand. 'That's the reward money?'

'I was losing my house, Lisa. Dad burning down that care home ... the bills are endless. I was just trying to survive.'

'Lucas blackmailed you, didn't he.'

'He wanted me to bring it out here last night, but it was only a distraction to get me out here, so he could get to Nathan.'

'Was it worth it?' she asks.

I slowly shake my head. 'I didn't know it was going to lead to any of this.'

'The road to hell is paved with good intentions, and all that. Is that what you're going with?'

'No.'

'A moment ago I said Lucas didn't make any copies, but *I* did. It's in a safe place, I promise you. The money you have there, you can go ahead and keep it. Hell, I would even argue you earned it. But the rest goes to the department.'

I don't say anything. I can feel myself turning red with shame.

'I always thought you were a good man.'

'I'm sorry,' I say.

'I know you are. I think ... I think you think you're still a good man, and maybe that's true. Grove was a bad guy, but what you did...' She runs out of words. I wait her out as she looks for them. 'Maybe you are still good – part of you at least – but either way you're a shitty sheriff, and as of today, you're not even that, because you're going to resign.'

I don't argue.

She gets into her car. She doesn't glance back as she drives away. I stay standing where I am long after she's gone, and then I go back into the forest looking for more cash.

I'm going to need it.

Acknowledgements

I've been wanting to return to Acacia Pines ever since writing *Whatever it Takes* a few years back. Some stories don't work in Christchurch for various reasons, and that novel, and this, are prime examples of that fact, but I love being able to escape my home city every now and then to explore new places and characters.

2023 has been a crazy-busy year for me – perhaps the busiest of my life. I was handed the opportunity to write a TV show, based on my first book, *The Cleaner*. After googling 'how to write a screenplay' (I kid ... but there is some truth to this), I spent summer hibernating in my office, writing the entire season; and while they were filming it months later, I was hibernating and writing *His Favourite Graves*. So yes – the busiest I've ever been, but I've also had more fun this year than I ever have. I love being a writer, and getting the chance to work this much has been a real pleasure.

Of course, it's always a pleasure working with Karen Sullivan at Orenda Books. Being with Orenda is like being with a family, except one that you like, and it's always a buzz to send Karen a new book and have her help me make it better. Of course she isn't alone – there is West Camel, my editor, who's keen eye for detail keeps me on track. And there's Cole Sullivan, Danielle Price and Mark Swan for marketing and social media and the cover design, Anne Cater for blog tours and the rest of the team for everything else.

Then there is the team in New Zealand at Upstart Press. Thanks to Kevin Chapman, my friend and publisher, who knows all things books and all things gin, and who always has my back. And thanks to Gemma Finlay and Craig Violich, and the rest of the folks there, who have given my books in NZ a home.

As always, there are friends who read various drafts along the way. Thanks to Jabyn Butler for your typo hunting – and where would we be without Jabyn Fridays? Thanks to Ceren Kumova, for your feedback across multiple versions. Thanks to Kaela Fowler with your eagle eyes. Thanks to Steve Brownie and Melanie Roberts, who both had what was essentially an audiobook version of this as I talked their ears off.

There's one more person I want to give a shout-out to: a few years back I dedicated *Whatever It Takes* to Katrina Cox. Katrina was battling cancer back then, and was one of the bravest and nicest people I've ever known. I'm sure the past tense here tells you she lost that battle. Katrina was my cousin, but she saw me as her big brother and I saw her as my sister. She was thirty-six. I miss you, Katrina. And say hi to Mogue for me.

Finally, like always, let me thank you, the reader, for letting me do what I love doing the most – and that's making bad things happen...

Paul Cleave
Christchurch
September 2023